THE WILD HEIR

KARINA HALLE

METAL BLONDE BOOKS

For the Halles of Todalen – uff da!

WARNING

Although fun and fluffy, this book is not recommended for sensitive readers.

It contains the Lord's name in vain, ample amounts of swearing in English (and in Norwegian!), and some foul-mouthed sexually graphic situations.

If you are a reader who has problems with the things I mentioned above, pleeeeeease take heed.

Thank you!

A NOTE FROM THE AUTHOR

I'll try and make this quick so you can get on reading about sexy royal scandals and arranged marriages.

As you have probably guessed from the title, this is a ROYAL ROMANCE about Magnus, the Crown Prince of Norway.

As such, I must put this teeny tiny disclaimer here:

This is a work of fiction.

The actual Norwegian Royal Family is amazing.

(I am actually Norwegian myself...and Finnish and Canadian but I digress).

But this book is not based on them.

Same goes for the Liechtenstein royal family.

I know this is all without saying but people getting funny about their royals. Once again - this is totally a work of fiction and not based on any royal family.

However, I will tell you that the real Prince of Norway met his Princess when she was a single mother at an EDM festival, so when royal romance books might seem unrealistic, let's not forget the truth is stranger than fiction!

Which means, hey, your chances of meeting a prince and stealing his heart aren't that bad.

I also want to quickly point out to all my Norwegian family members - I know most of the characters have the same names as you but rest assured I did not name them after you! But of course, I was thinking about you and my beloved Norway while writing this book.

And yes, I suppose the Queen is named after my aunt Else :D

PS if you've snatched up The Wild Heir and you're wondering if you need to read another book beforehand, rest easy - you don't have to! Yes The Wild Heir is a spinoff of The Swedish Prince (where Magnus made a brief appearance) but you don't need to read The Swedish Prince before you read The Wild Heir. The Wild Heir is a complete STANDALONE!

If you do plan to read The Swedish Prince though, it's right here and FREE in KU!

HAPPY READING!

ONE

MAGNUS

"You fucked up!" Ottar says yet again.

Not exactly the thing you want to hear mere seconds before you're about to fling yourself off a 3,200-foot cliff and free fall to the fjord below.

But in this case, as Ottar has spent the last five minutes drilling into my head what an idiot I am and how badly I've fucked up my life, hurling yourself off a cliff seems like the right thing to do. Maybe the only thing to do in this situation.

As I run toward the edge of Kjerag Mountain, I keep my eyes focused straight ahead at the fjord cutting through the valley like a blue knife, and let all thoughts, all worries, all self-awareness, melt away.

I jump.

Those first few seconds of free fall are what I imagine being born is like. A terrifying rush as you're propelled from the solid and steady world you know into the cold abyss. There's nothing like it, leaving safety and life for what should be certain death.

Then you're flying, arms out, weightless, a bird in the sky, an angel's descent, a step beyond being human.

Then you're falling.

Wind rushing against your face, pulling your skin back into a smile, rattling your helmet. There's nothing to anything anymore, nothing but you and the wind and the greatest adrenaline rush you'll ever know. Better than sex, even.

Maybe.

The timer goes off, interrupting the rush before my brain has started to blur together. I quickly reach into the chute to deploy it and I'm jerked back, the blast of the free fall reversing for a second as the parachute spreads and the easy descent begins.

Usually this part of the jump is where your heart starts to slow, where you realize where you are, what you're doing —that you made it. You're safe. As you float down to earth, you carry nothing inside you but awe, knowing that you're just a tiny bright-colored parachute soaring toward a cerulean-blue fjord, eagles at eye level.

But there is no peace and tranquility today.

There is none of that sharp focus and clarity that always comes during a jump, where my scattered world seems to pause, just for one wonderful minute as I fall from the sky.

All I can focus on are Ottar's words slicing through my head. *I fucked up.* And it's not just his words either. It's my sisters, it's my parents, it's the press. It's the damn prime minister.

When you're royalty and you do something stupid, everyone in the whole world, let alone the whole country, gets to weigh in on it.

And I'm the Crown Prince of Norway, heir to the

throne, and my latest scandal just set the public image of our country back another hundred years.

No wonder it was easier to jump today than most days.

A scream pierces my thoughts and I look up, even though I can see nothing above me but the electric yellow of the chute. That was Ottar's scream. This is only the second time the guy has BASE jumped, and for him, it's one too many. Hell, no sane person would attempt this sport, but I have the nickname "Magnus the Mad" for a few good reasons.

The screaming seems to stop after a bit, which means Ottar probably pulled his chute, and now I have the ground to worry about.

Focus, fuckface, I tell myself, willing my brain to stop racing around and work before it's too late. Everything is throwing me off. I grab the pulleys in front of me and steer myself toward the people standing on the small peninsula below me, hoping Ottar follows suit. His last landing was about as graceful as a cow being flung from a catapult.

There's only a small patch of grass to land on—overshoot that and you're going to smash into rock or the ice-cold waters of the fjord. Maybe it's because my mind has been so liquid, but the grass is rushing up fast and I know that this is going to hurt like a mother.

My feet strike the ground and my legs immediately crumple, sending pain up my shins. I duck into a roll across the grass and then spring up just before my shoulder hits a slab of rock.

Helvete.

All the bystanders standing around are gawking at me and my not so graceful arrival.

I push my helmet on straighter, adjust my goggles, and

give them all a quick bow. "Not a bad landing when the alternative is death," I say with a big smile.

A few of them clap. These people just seem to be tourists, their speedboats pulled up along the shore, cameras around their necks to capture the crazy fuckers like me who do this famous jump.

And Ottar.

He's screaming again, his legs kicking out as he rapidly descends toward us, his arms jerking on the handles, completely out of control. If he doesn't slow down and steer he's going to smash right into a few people, and then the rocks behind them.

This is going to get ugly.

Everyone is scattering, unsure of what to do, and I know this is all out of Ottar's hands now. Even with his goggles covering up his eyes, I can tell they're open wide, his mouth agape as he seems to freeze from terror.

I don't even think. I start running toward him and leap up, crashing into him in the air while trying to wrap my arms around his thighs.

Somehow I manage to pull him down, like I'm plucking a big, fat, hairy bird out of the air, and then he's crashing on top of me, squeezing the air out of my lungs as I smash into the ground.

"Oh my god, Your Highness!" he yells at me, and even though my mouth is full of grass, I'm already mumbling for him to shut up.

He rolls off me, and then I lie back, trying to catch my breath and hoping no one else heard his address.

"I am so sorry!" he goes on, patting my arms and thighs. "Are you alive?"

Poor Ottar. He never wanted to do any of this shit with me. In the past, he was the guy waiting in the car, hovering on the sidelines. Then, with my father having some health issues this year, Ottar started actually going with me on my activities. If I wasn't going to quit doing them, then at least Ottar would be there closer than ever, keeping an eye on me, making sure I was, well, alive.

But now it's not just him making sure I'll survive to be king, it's to make sure I don't run off into the woods and do something stupid. Or more stupid than jumping off a cliff. I have a bad reputation with my family as being slightly impulsive. Ever since I was a little kid, I've been blowing off the bodyguards and royal guards and escaping every chance I could get.

"I'm fine," I tell him, sitting up and looking around. The people are crowded together, watching us from a distance as if Ottar was a bomb dropped from the sky.

"You saved my life, sir," Ottar says, placing his meaty palm on my shoulder. "I don't know how to repay you."

I eye his hand and then shrug it off me. "Well, you can start by dialing back your Samwise Gamgee."

"Of course, sir," he says, looking a little embarrassed. I think it's more from nearly dying and me having to save him, rather than the *Lord of the Rings* nickname, because I swear he's always two seconds away from calling me Mr. Frodo. "But again, I'm so sorry."

"Not your fault," I tell him. Not my fault either. "You could help me up though."

"Yes, sir," he says, grabbing my hands and hauling me to my feet. I can feel the crowd inspecting us even more now—probably because of the way Ottar is addressing me, like I'm *someone*—and I'm tempted to do yet another bow to play off two bad landings in a row.

But someone has their camera out, aiming it in our direction, and I can't tell if it's because they want to take a picture of the two fools who just landed or if they think I'm someone of importance.

I give the camera a tight smile and look down at Ottar, who is a good half a foot shorter than me. "We should probably get this stuff off and head to the boat."

Down along the shore is a sleek, white speedboat with teak trim, the name *Elskling* written with flourish on the side. The man waiting patiently behind the wheel is Einar, one of my bodyguards and my getaway driver. Like Ottar, he's always nearby, usually trailing me, because I'm trying to lose him. He used to be in the military though, so he's a hard man to lose.

I hear the faint click of a few more cameras coming from the crowd but this time I don't indulge them with a second glance. I quickly get my gear off and then as Ottar is still fumbling with the straps across his chest, help him too.

There's a collective "*oooh*" from the bystanders and I crane my head back to the sky where the next jumpers are descending, three of them in a row. From this distance they look like brightly colored stars that have burned through the atmosphere.

Another *click* steals my attention.

Everyone is watching the jumpers except for two men.

Men with cameras aimed right at Ottar and I.

Men I should have recognized before but with all the commotion, my mind wasn't able to focus.

You're an idiot, Magnus.

"Hey, isn't that—?" Ottar asks, but he trails off as the two men turn around and start running toward one of the waiting boats.

"Shit," I swear, wondering how many photos they got.

It's not that I was doing anything inappropriate, per se, but I had promised my family I would stay out of the paparazzi's eye for the day, and well, those two fuckers are the bane of my princely existence. The whole reason I came out here was to avoid having my photo taken since usually the paparazzi don't follow me all the way out to Kjerag.

But these guys aren't the normal paparazzi. First of all, they're Russian twins who look an awful lot like the T-1000 from *The Terminator*. Second of all, they act like the T-1000 too. They're fucking unstoppable. No matter where I go, those douchebags are there, taking photos and selling them to the highest paying gossip mag or trashy tabloid. I'm not saying that I cry myself to sleep at night over being known as the "hot and sexy single prince," but it sure makes you a media darling.

"We need to go," I tell Ottar. "Now."

Normally I would just let this go, but since these assholes will without a doubt be selling the first photos of me of what will be known as "The Aftermath" followed with the headlines "Suicidal Prince Jumps Off Cliff (His Personal Secretary Tries to Save Him)" and "Not Fit to Rule," I feel like it's my duty to care as much as it's their duty to treat me like I'm an animal in a zoo.

We start jogging across the grass to the boat and throw our stuff on board, then wade into the ice-cold water up to our knees before climbing in. Einar is at the wheel, frowning beneath his aviator glasses that glint violet and blue like they've been polarized a million times over.

I step beside him, shouldering the brute out of the way and taking over the controls.

"If you don't mind, I think I'll drive," I tell him, glancing over my shoulder at their speedboat which is zooming off, before shoving the gear into reverse and gunning it away backward from the shore.

Ottar nearly falls overboard, holding on to the rail for dear life as Einar grabs the console to steady himself.

"I'm pretty sure your mother would file this under reckless driving!" Ottar yells, trying to straighten back up, only for me to whip the boat forward and take off after the Russian's boat.

"Pretty sure my mother wouldn't want me to be paparazzi fodder either," I tell him with a wink.

"Just let it go," Ottar says with a sigh that's squeezed out of his lungs as he falls into the railing again.

But even though I'm pretty fucking good at escaping from my problems, the fact that they've followed me here says I've got to face them. Head on. Mad Magnus style.

"Let it go?" I repeat. "You're the one who told me I fucked up just moments before I jumped. I fucked up, so now I have to fix it."

"Sir," Einar says, clearing his throat. Even if his psychedelic sunglasses weren't covering his eyes, I wouldn't be able to read them. Sometimes I think Einar is built in the same robot factory as the Russians, but his maker decided to give him extra muscle.

"I've got it, Einar," I tell him. "Why don't you make sure Ottar doesn't fall overboard?"

Einar doesn't move, and from the way his mouth is pressed into a firm line, I don't think he likes it when I tell him what to do. I know he doesn't. I can order Ottar around, but Einar is just a bodyguard, there to protect me, not anyone else.

I don't need his protection, but that doesn't stop him from going everywhere I go. Even when I go on a date with a lady, he's somewhere lurking in the background. The only privacy I get is when I'm fucking them and I have to hope he's not spying through a window. Don't get me wrong, the idea of being watched while having sex excites me to no end, but seeing Einar's grave, pockmarked face would totally kill the vibe.

That said, in some ways I wish he had been watching the other week when I'd gone into Heidi's house.

When I'd gone into Heidi's room.

Not necessarily when I proceeded to screw her senseless that first time.

But the second time, when she propped up her phone and said she wanted to record us having sex as a keepsake, a memento.

I'd agreed to it, because, well why the fuck wouldn't I want to be filmed sticking my dick in her? Usually I don't even bring it up with the ladies because their adventurous sides only involve doggy-style and maybe some light choking or spanking. Filming us having sex? Forget it.

And I was feeling bad since earlier that evening I broke it off with her. Not that Heidi and I were anything serious, but we'd been on a few dates we somehow managed to hide from the public—and her father—and I could tell she wanted a lot more from me. As in, she wanted to become the next princess of Norway.

Naturally, I had to nip that in the bud, even though apparently when I break up with someone I still think it's cool to film a sex tape afterward. Just another example of my impulsiveness getting me in trouble.

God, did I ever fuck up.

But that's all out of my control and who knows what's going to happen to me now. Since the news broke yesterday, I've yet to speak to my parents about it, though I could feel their anger simmering all the way from their palace in downtown Oslo.

I'm feeling that same anger simmer through me right now with only one place for it to go.

I increase the throttle on the boat, and now we're steadily catching up to the paparazzi speedboat. Soon we'll overtake them.

"I hope you know what you're doing," Einar says quietly, his eyes focused on the boat as it gets closer and closer.

"Do I ever know what I'm doing?" I repeat, biting back a smile.

And even if this doesn't work, who cares? They deserve it and more.

"Hey!" I yell at the photographers as we pull up alongside their boat. "Get any good pics?"

My voice is carried by the wind but they both look over and in unison raise their cameras.

I proceed to give them the finger and a big fucking smile.

Then I swiftly grab the wheel and yank our boat to the side, creating a giant wake and ensuring a wave of water flows over the side of their boat, soaking them from head to toe.

I burst out laughing and then gun our boat in the opposite direction toward our boat launch at the end of the fjord, leaving the two fuckfaces yelling at us in Russian, sopping wet and shaking out their cameras which are no doubt ruined.

Serves them right.

"Nice maneuver, sir," Einar says after a moment, and I glance at him to see the hint of what could be called a smile pulling at his mouth.

"Thank you, my good man."

"You know they're going to try and sue you for that,"

Ottar pipes up, slowly staggering up the side of the deck, never letting go of the railing.

"You're a killjoy, Ottar," I tell him. "Let me have my fun."

I know it's the only fun I'm going to have for a while.

~

EVEN THOUGH I'VE ALWAYS HAD MY PICK OF WHERE I wanted to live, including various royal palaces throughout Norway, I'm rather fond of my tiny apartment. Okay, maybe it's not tiny by normal standards. It does take up the entire top floor of a corner building in Majorstuen, one of the city's "hip" neighborhoods, and I have more room than I know what to do with, but it makes me feel a lot more normal to live this way rather than in a palace.

Ignoring the fact that the floor below me is where Einar and Ottar and various rotating guards live, the floor below that is an H&M. On the street, trams trundle on by, a sound I find soothing, and people hurry to and fro, shopping and hitting up the bars.

The paparazzi know I live in the neighborhood but aren't exactly sure where. The windows that face the street are tinted, obscuring me from people and when I need sun, I head up to the roof where I have a whole private deck free from prying eyes. And there are more than a few entrances into the building, including a tunnel that pops up a block away in a small gated courtyard.

That's how my mother will be getting here tonight. I feel bad having her go through the tunnel since it was built in the 1800s and it can get pretty dank in there, but she was insistent that she come visit me as soon as possible.

It's all bad news. The fact that she wants to discuss

something with me here instead of at the palace where my father and youngest sister, Mari, are says a lot. Like there are less witnesses in case she wants to murder me.

I'm looking around the apartment, wondering if I should hide my knives, or, at the very least, the large Viking axe I have on display on the wall, when there's a knock.

I stride over to the door, running my hand through my hair to make sure it's all in order (my hair is usually messy and longer than she thinks is appropriate), take in a deep breath, and open it.

My mother and her bodyguard, Per, are standing in the hall. I catch a glimpse of Einar in the background, heading down the stairs.

"Magnus," my mother says to me in a curt voice, which is her default voice at any given moment.

"Mother," I say right back. I flash her a smile which used to charm her but doesn't seem to have that effect anymore. I meet Per's eyes, but just like Einar, they give me nothing. More robots in fine suits.

I clear my throat and gesture to the apartment. "Well. Come in, then."

She nods and glances at her bodyguards with an internal message for them to stay where they are. Then she steps inside and I close the door after her.

"You cleaned up," she says, stopping in the middle of the living room and looking around. It's an open plan apartment which means you can see most of it from any location, and normally it's a mess. Even though I have a housecleaner who comes in here every other day, it doesn't take long for the place to look like a tornado ripped through it. Let's just add Messy Magnus to my list of nicknames.

"I tried to make it fit for a queen," I tell her.

"Bullshit," she swears, shaking her head and eyeing me sharply.

That's my mother for you. She might be the Queen, but she can be as crude and blunt as I can be. While my father is easygoing and gregarious, if not a little loopy, my mother says what she wants, when she wants. She's fearless.

At least she normally is. As sharp as her gaze is tonight as it cuts into me, I can see the sparks of fear behind her eyes, which in turn brings out the fear in me.

My heart starts to speed up and she nods at the two armchairs by the fireplace, an heirloom bearskin rug between them. "Sit down. I have something I need to talk to you about, and for once, I need you to listen."

I swallow hard. "You don't want coffee or?" I glance at the kitchen as if making her an espresso will buy me some time.

"Magnus," she says sternly. "Sit."

So I sit, and she sits across from me. She's a petite woman, only about five feet, two inches tall, but even in a casual silk pantsuit that borders on pajamas, she's formidable.

She doesn't say anything for a moment which ratchets up the tension in the room to an unbearable amount. I finally have to say, "Look, I am so sorry about what happened—"

"Stop," she says, raising her palm. "Just stop. You don't need to apologize. Though I do wonder if you are ever truly sorry about anything."

That was a cheap shot.

"What happened, happened," she goes on. "There's no stopping it. All we can do is damage control, if we can even do that."

"I'm sure the prime minister understands that—"

"The prime minister," she roars, her dark eyes blazing, "does not understand! For crying out loud, Magnus, you filmed a sex tape with his daughter!"

"I was breaking up with her," I say feebly, covering my face with my hands because fuck I don't want to talk about a sex tape with my mother, even though it's all over the fucking news.

"That's how you break up with people?" She's incredulous. I peer up at her to see her shaking her head in disgust. "First of all, what the hell were you doing with Heidi Lundström to begin with?"

"She's a fan," I try to explain. "I mean, she wanted to go out with me. We've met so many times over the years, you know it was kind of inevitable. She'd just broken up with her boyfriend and we were at that fancy charity event for frogs and wetlands or something and..."

"Did you not think for one second that perhaps she was off-limits?"

I shrug. "Well, no."

"Of course not. Because you never take one second to think about anything. Always jumping into everything like you're out of control. You are out of control, Magnus. Always have been. I—*we*—have tried everything to rein you in over your twenty-eight years and nothing has worked."

"Hey," I say, hating that she throws this shit in my face. "I did think. In fact, I thought maybe for once it would be a good match since she has a similar lifestyle to mine and knows what it's like to grow up in a family of power, but she's a lot, uh, more unstable than I realized."

"Well, since you're unstable too, I can see why you bonded," she says, pretending not to notice me wince at the *unstable* remark. "But honestly, a *sex tape?*" She says the words like they're in a foreign language. "You didn't once think about the repercussions of that?"

"Why would I?"

"Because that sort of...*thing*, it always gets loose. Haven't you learned anything over the years with celebrity scandals?"

"That's Hollywood."

"And the same dynamics apply here. Obviously you've learned nothing about being a prince. Instead, you try and shun it every chance you get. Is that what you want? You want to abdicate? Is that why you're self-sabotaging?"

"I'm not self-sabotaging! And I don't want to abdicate."

But my voice trails off at the end of that sentence as it always does when abdication is brought up, when I'm reminded of what a poor choice I am for a king, how terrible I will be.

"Look," I continue, leaning forward with my elbows on my thighs, my fingers laced together as if in prayer. "I made a mistake with Heidi. I obviously didn't want to humiliate her or the prime minister, even though I think he's always hated me to begin with. Can't we do damage control here? Can't we tell the press that it's a fake? Surely someone did hack into Heidi's phone like she says. Can't we say that person made the whole thing up with, like, Photoshop or something like that?"

She exhales through her nose and gives me a steady look. "Not when Heidi has already admitted to the press what happened. Rather proudly, I might add. I think that girl has some, how do you say, daddy issues."

"You don't know the half of it," I mutter under my breath, having a flashback to some rather questionable words Heidi muttered during sex. "So what do I do?"

"I'll tell you what you're going to do, Magnus. And you're not going to like any of it."

I take in a deep breath, wondering what kind of royal terrors await me. "Okay," I say slowly. "What is it?"

She rubs her lips together, taking her time. I know she does this because I'm terribly impatient and hate having to wait. I also know she loves to see me squirm.

"First of all, you're going to have to apologize to the prime minister and Heidi. In person. And then later on camera during a press conference."

"What!?" I exclaim. "On camera? But...the world will eat that up with a fucking spoon. That will make us look weak."

She gives me a sour smile. "We already look weak, thanks to you. The entire monarchy has now been razed to sub-standard levels. We are the laughing stock of the country, of Europe, of the entire world. Magnus, the damage you've done with this is just the straw that broke the damn camel's back. All respect that this royal family has earned is gone and in a world where monarchies are no longer in vogue nor in real power, this will have lasting effects."

Well, fuck.

"Okay," I tell her, gathering my courage. "I'll do it."

"Yes. You will do it. And you'll do the next thing as well."

"What next thing? It can't be worse than that," I say softly, but from the look in her eyes I can tell it is. I brace for impact.

"The next thing..." she starts and then seems to wince at what she's about to say. "Magnus. You're going to have to get married."

TWO

MAGNUS

THE WORDS HANG IN THE AIR, REFUSING TO SINK INTO my brain. It's like I can stare at them, observing, not really understanding why they're here.

"What?" I eventually say.

My mother's eyes narrow. "You heard me. You're going to have to get married."

Still, they don't sink in. I tilt my head, not sure I heard her right either time. "I'm sorry. Married?"

"Married."

"To who?"

"To whom," she corrects me. "And I've compiled a list. I don't have it on me because I figured you would need time to warm up to the idea, but I assure you it will be someone European and of noble blood, someone this country can be proud of."

My mouth opens. Closes. My heart pounds in my head, louder and louder as I realize what she's saying.

Dear God.

What *is* she saying?

"How is...what is..." I pause. "*You want me to get married*?"

She rolls her eyes and lets out a short sigh. "I know you're not stupid, Magnus, so instead of repeating it back to me, how about you start believing it?"

"But...why? How is this your solution to a leaked sex tape?" I take in a shaking breath. "Fucking hell, you don't expect me to marry Heidi, do you?"

"Oh, calm down. We both know the girl is batty. So is the prime minister. You will get married to someone beautiful, nice, proper, and prestigious. As soon as possible. It's the only way we can save face."

"How does this save face?!" I exclaim, throwing my arms out as I jump to my feet.

"Sit down."

"Sit down? *Sit down*?" I can feel my face growing hot, my pulse beating wildly out of control. I know I should try and contain myself, especially when I get this way. "You're telling me I have to marry some stranger for no reason at all except you think it will somehow make the country and the prime minister happy?"

"Yes," she says simply, folding her hands in her lap.

I stare at her, breathing hard, daring her to mess up, to flinch, to show me that there's a part of her that feels ridiculous for suggesting such a thing.

But she only stares back at me with flames in her eyes. Those small, smoldering flames that only hint at the dragons she has caged back there.

Yeesh.

Still, I don't sit down. To sit down is to give in.

"Listen, I know this isn't something you want to do," she begins.

I scoff loudly. "You don't say."

"But honestly, what the country needs is to know a good and responsible man is representing them."

"That's what father is. Everyone loves him."

She looks away, her gaze going to the windows and the lights of the city. "Your father is very ill."

Over the course of the summer, I've heard my father been described as ill, sick, under the weather, of poor health, ever since he was diagnosed with pancreatitis. Over the last month he's had his own sick room in the palace where the doctor comes to visit and conduct tests. From all that I've heard, pancreatitis is something he'll recover from. This is the first time my mother has used the words *very ill* to describe him, the first time that I've grasped a hint of sorrow from her.

"He's getting better," I tell her, as if my words make it all true. "I saw him just two weeks ago and he looked great. Well, good. Better, anyway."

She lets out a low breath and wrings her hands together for a moment, another telltale sign that this is a lot bigger than she's letting on.

Everything inside me sinks to a depth I rarely venture.

"He's got acute pancreatitis," she says.

"I know. But you said eighty percent of people pull through."

"That's what the doctors said. He's seen a lot at this point. But even doctors can be wrong."

I don't want to ask the next words. My father just turned seventy-five. Sure he drank a lot when the world wasn't looking, but we all do in our family.

"Is he...he's going to be okay, right?"

"He's in a lot of pain, Magnus. He's got surgery coming up, and even that is risky. And even if it goes fine, he might be in a lot of pain for the rest of his life. He won't be fit to rule."

For some reason I imagined my father would live forever. Until he got sick, I didn't really think about his age. He didn't marry my mother for a long time, and it was even longer after that before she was finally pregnant with me. There's a fifteen-year age difference between them and he's always been so outgoing and spry.

Because of that, I've always thought of my role as heir to the throne as something that would never happen. Or something that would happen to someone else, even if subconsciously the idea has caused me to panic.

She looks at me and her eyes are watering.

Shit.

"If you don't wish to abdicate, then you will be king. Sooner than you think, sooner than we all hoped. With all you've put this family through over the years with your partying and your women and your damn adrenaline sports, you need to step up and be the man we want you to be. We need you to do the right thing and marry someone and start a family and do all the things that a king should be doing."

This is too much to take. My stomach is starting to twist. I sit back down, my foot tapping rapidly against the floor.

"Have you talked to father about this?" I ask quietly.

"I did," she says. "He agrees."

"This is like an arranged marriage."

"It isn't when you have a pick of who you marry," she says stiffly.

"It's an arranged marriage," I repeat, looking at her hard. "A marriage of convenience. Or inconvenience since you very well know marriage has never been on my agenda."

"You're twenty-eight. It had to be eventually."

"Why? Because that's what society says?"

"Phhffft," she says with a dismissive wave of her hand. "You've spent your whole life bucking what society says. Maybe this is about something else. Maybe you need someone, Magnus. You need someone in your life instead of all these, these *things*."

"I can guarantee you're not going to be telling any of my sisters this spiel. You've always encouraged them to do what they wanted, to date whomever they wanted, girl power and all that."

"You're different, Magnus, and you know it. I encourage them to do what they want because society is always there to try and hold them back. You have no one holding you back. I think it's time that maybe you did."

"Right. You're really selling marriage right now."

"Do you want to die alone?"

I get up again. "Okay, Mother, no offense, but I think this conversation took a turn for the worse seven minor heart attacks ago."

She closes her eyes, seeming to compose herself, then gets to her feet. I offer my hand, but as usual, she ignores it. "This went about as well as I thought it would."

She walks past me, heading to the door.

"That's it?" I ask. "You're not going to yell at me? Threaten me?"

She puts her hand on the knob, takes a moment, her shoulders seeming to grow heavier before my eyes, then glances at me. "Come over for dinner tomorrow. It's been so long since we've had the whole family in one place."

Then she opens the door, steps out into the hall, and the door shuts behind her with a resounding *click* that seems to echo inside my head.

〜

At six-thirty the next evening, Einar and Ottar practically shove me into one of the royal cars parked around the corner from my apartment and take me to the palace in the city center, which is really only a short drive away. Too short, in my opinion. I told them I could have walked but I think they both imagined me running off into the sunset. My friend Viktor, the Prince of Sweden, got to do that, to run away and pretend to be someone else, and I don't think I've ever been so envious than I am at this moment.

We go through the large palace gates and Einar parks at the back entrance, a lush park surrounding us on both sides. With it being September now, the leaves are slowly turning from green to gold and the nights are getting chilly.

Tor, my mother's butler, greets us formally and then leads me to the dining room. It's funny, even though I grew up in this house, I still feel like a commoner in it. The moment I turned seventeen I moved out, and ever since then I'd felt like this place belonged to strangers.

Or maybe it's because I turned into a stranger to everyone else. This couldn't be more apparent than when I enter the dining room and see three of my sisters' blonde heads swivel toward me in eerie synchronicity. I suppress a shudder, remembering that *Village of the Damned* movie I saw when I was young.

There's Cristina, who is only one year younger than me, though I know she couldn't be more relieved that I'm next in line and not her. All Cristina wants to do is live with her long-term Italian boyfriend on a Greek island somewhere, living off the land.

Then there's Britt, in her mid-twenties, a real party animal with mile-a-minute tendencies and grandiose plans for herself which seem to change every minute. At the moment, Britt is planning her move to America where she wants to get an internship in New York, though I can't say what for since she's always changing her mind.

There's also Irene, who is the spitting image of our mother and also finishing up at university for political sciences or something like that. Irene is about as reliable as you get. Some might say boring (I might say boring), but she's smart and efficient and honestly would make a much better queen than I would a king. There doesn't seem to be a scheming bone in her tiny little body, but if there were, I bet she'd wish I'd just abdicate already and give the throne to her.

Mari, the youngest, isn't at the table. She's seventeen, just finishing up school and still living with our parents here at the palace. Because she's the last to leave and was a complete "miracle baby," she's probably the closest to our parents right now. She's sweet, compassionate, and always willing to go above and beyond for anyone. But there's no mistaking her for a pushover either.

I'm not sure how long I seem to stand here at the head of the table, maybe no time at all, but Britt clears her throat and says, "Well, well, well, look who it is. Mr. Sex Tape."

I pinch my eyes closed, pretending she didn't just say that.

"Oh my god," Irene mutters. "Can we not talk about that?"

"It's the elephant in the room," Britt argues.

"It's not proper dining room etiquette," Irene argues back.

Cristina snorts. "What is etiquette anymore than just an antiquated set of rules set to control our society? It's a prison of manners, that's what it is."

"Hello to all of you too," I tell them, taking a seat beside

Cristina. "Now that it's out of the way, the elephant has been revealed and shit on all the rules of etiquette or whatever, let's just go on and pretend it never happened. Okay?"

All three blonde heads nod. Creepy. Do they know they do it in unison?

Suddenly Mari appears at the doorway, giving us all an anxious smile.

"Hi, Magnus," she says quietly, then addresses everyone else. "Father is coming. He's, uh, feeling pretty good because of the drugs the doctor gave him, but they don't give him much of an appetite and they tire him out. He'll only be here for the soup and then I'll take him back to his room."

Shit.

Here is beautiful young Mari helping my father, the fucking *King*, like she's his nurse. Not only is she way too young to be doing this, but it's reminding me that I've been a fucking moron, living my life without a single thought to others, oblivious to the lives straining around me. This is my family, in pain, and I've absolutely let everyone down, including myself. Maybe my mother is right. I really should get married. I spent all last night and all today stewing over what a horrible idea this whole thing is and how terribly unfair, and how I wouldn't agree to it no matter what...

And now I'm thinking maybe this is the kind of punishment I deserve.

As Wayne Campbell says, marriage is punishment for shoplifting in some countries.

So I sit here, tongue-tied and feeling like garbage while Mari disappears around the corner, presumably to get my father.

I glance over at my sisters, and all their brows are furrowed, lips being bitten and gnawed on in fear and sympathy. How much do they know? More than me? Am I the odd one out, the prodigal son with his head in the clouds?

I'm about to open my mouth to ask them how he really is when their attention is diverted to the doorway and my father appears, with Mari and my mother on either side of him, arms hooked around his elbows as he slowly shuffles forward.

My first thought is that it isn't my father. That they've hired some actor to portray him as "sickly" and they're doing an overdramatic version of it. The way he's hunched over, the ashen pallor of his skin, his hairline that seems to be reduced to wispy tufts. He's changed a staggering amount since I last saw him and that honestly was only a few weeks ago. Has he always looked like this only now I'm actually seeing it for what it is?

"Father," I say, the words escaping me in a hush and I'm ready to get up and help him, embrace him, tell him I'm sorry for bringing all this fucking trouble and shame to us when he's barely hanging on.

"Sit," he says with a smile. "You just stay put there, Magnus." And with those words, his warmth flows through him. He is my father after all, buried beneath an exterior that seems to shrink from pain.

I hang on to that because I can't let myself fall to worry. If I do, it will be the end of me. I'll obsess over it, as I often do. I'll let myself luxuriate in darkness, in pity, in the travesty of it all. I know myself enough to keep out of those low spots when I can.

"I hope dinner is klipfisk," he says, looking at my mother as she holds on to him. "The Lord knows I have to be nearly dying for you to let Gette indulge that delicacy."

The word nearly springs some hope into my heart, and of course, we all laugh in relief that there's something to be

25

laughed about. My mother was raised in a fishing town on the coast where *klipfisk* is a specialty. It's salted cod, which makes for a tasty stew or even pizza. No one else in Norway really eats it that much, but when my father was dating my mother, he tried to impress her every chance he had by making it.

Turns out my mother detests the stuff, all while he was growing a real appreciation for it.

Mari pulls out a chair for him at the head of the table while my mother eases him into his seat. I'm surprised they're helping him and not a private nurse. After all, he is the King and I know he has the best medical care.

But maybe that's exactly why. As easygoing as my father is, he has an insurmountable amount of pride and probably doesn't think he warrants the help of a nurse in front of us. He's been the same in the few public appearances he's made—so far, the public only thinks he's had a bout of mild pneumonia.

As it is, the starter for dinner is his beloved klipfisk soup, brought out by the head cook Gette, who looks rather proud of the meal, waiting for a few moments before my father takes a hearty sip and gives her his approval.

My father doesn't talk much, just takes time sipping tea (no more brandy for him) and slurping the soup, asking everyone questions when the conversation lulls.

I've noticed that the questions never quite come my way and I'm both grateful and disappointed. Usually my father and I are discussing Formula One, rally driving, or moto racing or he has me filling him in on all that I've been up to. But this time there's nothing.

I know why. That whole sex tape elephant in the room. He's not ignoring me either because from time to time he'll look at me and give me a reassuring smile, though I'm not sure if he's reassuring me or himself that everything is going to be okay.

He makes it through the first salad before he clears his throat and announces to us that he doesn't want to risk passing out on top of Gette's famous roast grouse. I wonder if I should arrange to speak with him privately because I know we have a lot to talk about, but as Mari helps him out of his seat, my mother comes over and lays a hand on my shoulder and whispers into my ear, "When we're done with dinner, he'd like to speak with you."

After that, dinner seems to drag on, no matter how engrossing Cristina's tale about her trip to the Amazon rain-forest the other month or how delicious the roasted grouse is.

When it's finally over and I've pushed back a half-eaten slice of cake and slammed back the rest of my red wine, my mother gives me a nod and it's time to go.

I follow her out of the dining room and into the opulent halls of the palace, heading to the elevator at the end that will take us to the north wing on the third floor.

My mother pauses outside the large doors to his room and I almost ask if they've always slept in separate bedrooms and if I've only just noticed now or if this started since he became ill.

I don't ask and she doesn't say a word to me, except with her eyes which always say the hardest words for her. Now she wants me to be here, be grave, be present.

I nod back at her and step inside.

I don't know what I was expecting, but I'm relieved to see that things look as grand and formal as ever in this room with the high ceilings and long velvet curtains, dark wood floors, and a smattering of paintings.

My father isn't in his double poster bed at all but

instead is in a chaise lounge by the crackling fireplace, a heavy wool blanket drawn up to his chin. The only things out of place are the IV drip connected to one of his arms, the bag hanging from a wheeled stand beside him, and an unblinking female nurse who seems to appear from the shadows.

"There you are," my father says to me with a big smile before nodding at the nurse. "This is Ingrid, my nurse. She's on her way out. Just wanted to make sure I got my vitamins before bedtime."

Ingrid hurries past me without making eye contact, then she's gone out the door. I think I hear my mother's voice talking to her out in the hall.

"Does that hurt?" I ask my father, sitting down in the chair across from him as I nod at the IV. I'd been in the hospital plenty of times as a child for carelessly caused broken bones and sprains but I don't remember getting an IV.

He rolls his eyes. "Hurt? My boy. A needle to the arm feels as sweet as a kiss when it takes away the real pain."

My throat feels dry, scratchy. I swallow but it doesn't seem to do any good.

"Don't look so worried," he says to me, his eyes squinting briefly as he takes me in. "It doesn't suit you."

"I would have come to see you sooner. I had no idea you were..."

"I'm fine," he says, then winces as he adjusts himself. "I promise. I've been better, of course, and things have taken a little turn for the worse this last week, but I'll pull out of it. I'm in good shape otherwise, you know. The doctors say I should be grateful for all those years running and skiing. I have to say that's all because of you, Magnus."

"Me?" It was rare that I felt anyone was better off because of me.

"You were as much of a handful then as you are now. All those sports you were always active in, I had to keep up with you somehow. Honestly, the only downside to all of this is that I can't drink anymore. God, I wish for a snifter of something but dying is a pretty big trade off. Cristina has me drinking this awful new stuff called Kombucha. Have you heard of it? She says it's healthy for me."

"I've heard of it," I tell him softly. I've missed talking with him on this level. Not that we ever discuss business either, but sometimes it gets hard trying to separate my father from the king, or my mother from the queen.

He lets out a soft sigh, his eyes closing briefly. When he opens them, they're sharper than they were before—he's getting down to business.

"Magnus, I'm not going to bore you with the details of what has happened. I'm not going to tell you about the fallout behind closed doors that you have no idea about, I'm not going to try and make you feel bad or guilty about what you've done because it's all a moot point. It doesn't change anything to just talk about something that's happened. There has to be a mental and physical change."

"I know. Father, I am so sorry," I tell him, hating how much I've disappointed him, hating that I hear it in his words and on his face even though he's trying hard not to say as much. But I know. "What happened...it was stupid and I wasn't thinking and—"

"It's *done*," he says emphatically with a heavy gaze that goes right into my soul. "It's in the past."

"But it's affecting things right now."

"It is, but you can't change what was done. I forget sometimes that you're my heir, you know? It's my fault as much as yours. You wanted freedom so we gave you freedom. We wanted you to have the life you chose for yourself, not a life that was imposed upon you. My childhood was stifled because of my duties and we didn't want that for you at all. But somewhere along the way you stopped being an heir entirely. It's gone on for too long. You're turning thirty soon, and you haven't spent a single day at my side, learning what this role takes. Now, I'm afraid you either have to step up and learn and show you're serious about this business or...you won't be the king at all."

I rub my lips together anxiously. I hadn't expected an ultimatum but I don't know why I'm surprised. Of course this is where this had to go—it's the only way for my parents to find out where I stand. The only way I can change is if I'm forced to.

"I don't mean to sound harsh," my father says with a tired sigh, "but it's the truth. You've long said you don't want to abdicate, and if that's the truth, now is the time to become the person you're meant to be."

I nod. "And I can do that. Start including me in your weekly council meetings. Start bringing me to the parliament or on official dinners or..."

"I will," he says. "I just wish I had started sooner, before my condition started to deteriorate. But you know that's only solving one half of the problem."

For some reason I had hoped my father wasn't going to bring up the marriage thing. That it would stay this crazy idea of my mother's. But that doesn't seem to be the case.

He reaches down to the low table on the other side of him and lifts up a clipboard with paper. There's a few grainy black and white pictures of a girl, which must make this the list that my mother has compiled.

Shit is about to get weird.

"Is that the list?"

"It's the list," he says, flipping through a few pages. "I know this is the last thing you expected, but I have to say I think your mother is on the right track with this."

"Do you really?" I hate having to question him in this state but I don't think either one of them realize what a big fucking step this is.

"It's not conventional," he admits, glancing at me quickly. "But what about our lives is conventional?"

"So you're just going to give me this list and expect me to pick out a girl and then we'll get married and that will be the end of it?"

"Something like that."

My heart is starting to race again at the idea, my lungs feeling choked. "You do realize this isn't how the world works."

"It's how our world works, right now, at this moment."

"Marriage won't change me."

He chuckles. "Oh, it will. And for the better. More than that, it will change you in the eye of the public and that's all we really care about right now."

"More than my own feelings, my own freedom."

That brings a sharp look out of him. "Magnus. Sometimes there is something bigger than your thoughts and feelings. This is one of those times."

"You loved my mother."

He narrows his eyes. "I still do."

"Sorry. What I meant was that you married her for love. Didn't you? I mean, she was a commoner. You had to plead your case to your own father and he basically made you choose her or the throne."

He gives me a barely perceptible nod, his eyes not leaving mine. "If there had been another potential heir, I

31

wouldn't be here. I was his only hope. He had no choice but to let me marry her."

"So that's love. That's real love. You fought for her for years and years before you were finally allowed to marry her. What you're prescribing me is the opposite of that."

"And since when do you care about love, Magnus? Have you ever been in love? Do you want to be in love? Is that what you're doing every night with all these different women, are you bedding them because you're searching for love?"

I blink at him for a moment, my thoughts becoming heavy, clouded. "No. I don't know what I'm looking for."

"And I know you don't love any of them either. So what's the difference?"

I give him a poignant look. I really don't want to explain, but he's leaving me no choice. "I like sex. Okay?"

My father rolls his eyes and snorts. "Dear boy. That is more than apparent. I know this is the last thing you want to hear, but just because you're getting married doesn't mean you stop having sex."

I throw my hands up. "It doesn't matter. I don't want to marry someone I don't know, let alone someone I do know. I don't want to have sex with the same woman for the rest of my life."

He cocks a brow. "Not even if it's good sex?"

I don't want to talk about this anymore. It's still beyond mind-boggling that we're even having this conversation to begin with.

"I don't know what else to say," I tell him, "other than I don't want to do this and you have to understand why. It's 2018. This sort of shit shouldn't happen."

"You'd be surprised how many marriages out there— genuinely happy ones—started out just this way. Royals, celebrities, we're all very good at pulling the wool over the public's eyes. And that's precisely what we're going to do with you. You will marry someone, Magnus, or you won't be king. You will marry someone and your relationship will look believable to the world, and I promise you, in time, if you let it happen, you will learn to believe it too."

He hands me the clipboard and I'm surprised to find my hands are shaking as I hold it, my eyes glancing absently at the girl on the first page, some pretty, dark-haired brunette princess from Spain. Who isn't too far from the women I date but marriage is a whole other ballgame.

"Your mother is looking for prestige. And looks," my father says to me with a wink. "So she can have grandchildren the world will fawn over. But, Son, don't go for that. Go for the nicest, smartest one. The one with the biggest heart and the boldest mouth. Being kept on your toes is more attractive than anything, believe me. Have a smart woman in your marriage and you'll never be bored a day in your life. Be with someone you can have a conversation with, who will challenge you, no matter what she looks like."

So far in life, my ideal woman has been someone who keeps me on my toes until I'm ready to move on to someone else who keeps me on my toes. I don't think any type of personality—or looks—will change the fact that after a week or so, I'm already moving on and looking for someone else. I'm not even doing that to be a non-committal asshole, I honestly have never met anyone who captures the attention of my heart, soul, and dick for long enough.

When I look up from the clipboard, my father's eyes are closed and his head is back against the chair.

"Father?" I ask softly, and his eyes open briefly.

"Sorry," he mumbles. "I'm afraid I've gotten to the

useless part of the night." He yawns and then closes his eyes again. "Remember, we're not only doing this for all of us. We're doing it for you, too. You just can't see it yet, but one day you will. You'll see that..." He trails off and starts to snore.

I stare at him for a few moments, wishing I could talk to him more, selfishly, of course, just to argue and try and get out of this. But there is no getting out of this.

After I leave his room, the nurse comes back in to help him to bed and I wander the halls aimlessly, not sure what to do with myself and how to handle the ticking time bomb I'm holding in my hands. My mother and sisters all seem to have disappeared, so I hunt down Einar and he takes me back to my place.

With my father's words ringing through my head, I turn on a lamp, sit down in my armchair with a beer, and start flipping through the pages of princesses.

THREE
ELLA
ST. ANDREWS, SCOTLAND

I'm having that dream again.

The one where I'm standing on the pebbled shoreline of some northern island, maybe the Outer Hebrides of Scotland, maybe the Faroe Islands. The clouds are low, dark, and broken, stretching from the gray horizon of the sea across to the barren lands behind me. The wind is strong and sharp, the kind that would drive you insane over time.

As usual, I am alone on the beach. Alone, except for the dozens of beached pilot whales that stretch out in the surf, their shiny black bodies floundering for air, struggling to breathe. The waves pound over them but it's not enough to carry them back into the sea.

They are dying and I am powerless to stop them. I can only stand there and stare. My mouth is mute.

Then the black oil bubbles up from their blowholes, a sticky ebony glaze that coats them, the waves, the shore, until it's swirling around my ankles, then my knees. I will drown with them here.

But this time the dream changes. Off in the distance,

from around the bend of the clay cliffs, I see the figure of a tall man, sloshing through the oil toward me.

He's come to save me.

For the first time, this dream brings a ray of hope along with it.

But before he gets any closer, the oil rises, and I am covered from head to toe, unable to breathe, unable to speak.

Unable to scream.

I wake up as I usually do, sweating and out of breath and it takes me a few moments to realize where I am.

In my room.

In the evening.

The last vestiges of twilight coming in through the window.

What on earth just happened?

I blink and fumble for my phone, finding it underneath my arm. It's seven forty-five in the evening. The wine and cheese party started fifteen minutes ago.

"Shit," I swear, jumping out of bed. Thank god I'm fully clothed and still wearing makeup so I can just join the fun. I didn't mean to fall asleep, but I guess that's what happens when you have too many late nights of studying in a row.

I double-check myself in the mirror to make sure I don't look horrendous and then head out the door into the lounge and kitchen area that I share with my three other roommates, ready to apologize for falling asleep and being late.

Except that there's no one here. The flat is empty.

Odd.

"Audrey!" I call out, not wanting to go around banging on their doors. "Catherine?"

I look at my phone again. It's Thursday night and it's wine and cheese night here in our dorm. Or at least it's supposed to be. That was what Audrey had said before I closed the door to my room and proceeded to pass out.

Actually, that was what I had said to her. "I got the best gouda I could find for tonight," I'd told her, overly proud, like the big dork that I am. Only I don't think she ever responded to me, just gave me a tight smile and kept walking past.

Shit. What if wine and cheese night isn't tonight?

I take in a deep breath and try to think. I've only been living in this dorm for a month now and the girls had said they wanted to do a wine and cheese night on the first Thursday night of the month. And it's the first Thursday of October, so...

Maybe they went out and they're late coming back, I think to myself, trying to stay positive. I go over to the fridge and take out the gouda and sopressa plate I had made earlier, surprised to see all their cheese plates are gone. They were there this morning.

I don't know the girls that well. I've been trying to for the last month but making friends doesn't come easy to me, especially when they discover who I really am and that ship sailed the moment they found out that Jane was living down the hall.

I lean against the kitchen counter and peel back the plastic wrap I'd put over the cheese, sneaking a slice and munching on it with a defeated sigh. I'd really been looking forward to tonight. I'd been studying so much lately and just throwing myself into all my classes, and my social life has come at a cost. Now I'm trying to catch up, as is what seems to happen every school year. I just thought maybe this year, my third year, would be different.

I gather my courage and text Audrey since she's the one who is usually the nicest to me: **Hey Audrey it's your**

flatmate Ella! Just wondering where you are. I thought the wine and cheese party was tonight and I fell asleep so I think I missed you.

Thankfully she doesn't take too long to get back to me. I'm in the middle of a second piece of gouda when I get her text: **Party is already happening. It's over at Zelda's at Hawthorne Hall. Didn't want to wake you.**

I swallow hard as I stare at the text. Ouch. The party was moved. I wasn't told. They didn't want to wake me up. I don't know who Zelda is and I think I've been told to bugger off.

With shaking hands, I text back: **Okay, thanks! I'll see you when you get home.** And then add a bunch of wine and cheese emojis.

Shit. I know I shouldn't feel upset by all of this, but I'm always the one tagging along, never feeling welcome. There's a reason I've been a loner for most of my life.

Most of it has to do with the fact that as hard as I try to be average, I'm not your average girl. My father is the Prince of Liechtenstein, which makes me a princess. Princess Isabella, to be more precise.

It's more in title than anything else. There are no kings and queens in my country and it's not a monarchy. Prince is just another word for leader and my father is the head of state, having full power along with the government. Nonetheless, I grew up as the sole daughter of the leader of a tiny European country, which means I was raised in a world that was exclusively for the powerful and wealthy.

I wasn't alone in it, not at the beginning anyway. I have three older brothers who are mirror images of my father. Our mother died when I was just three years old. Cancer.

Apparently it took a long time for her to succumb to the disease, barely hanging on while the world's best doctors couldn't do a thing for her. They say my father was a different person after she died, which makes me wish I knew him before.

If my brothers take after him, I take after my mother. That's probably why, when I turned thirteen, my father sent me as far away as possible and hasn't had much to do with me ever since. I look too much like her.

Not that I haven't tried to forge a relationship with him, or my brothers. When I was all alone in boarding school in the south of England, I called and wrote all the time, telling him how well I was doing in my classes, practically begging for him to be proud of me, to acknowledge what I was doing. Here I was, a teenager with only her lady-in-waiting, Jane, as her guardian, adapting to life on her own and getting nothing from him in return except a birthday card and the annual trip back home at Christmas time.

I look at my phone, my heart feeling heavier than normal, and wish there was someone else I could call. But there isn't. There's only Jane.

I text her: **Do you want to come over? I have wine and cheese.**

Jane has been my lady-in-waiting for nine years now, and the two of us are pretty close. Well, she's the closest person to me but that's to be expected. I know it's ridiculous to even have a lady-in-waiting since I'm not really a princess and the term sounds like it's been ripped straight from medieval times, but it's the rules and I guess it's more for security purposes than anything else.

Jane texts back: **What kind of wine?**

Any wine you want, I text her, knowing I went

above and beyond for this stupid wine and cheese night and got both red and white.

Two minutes later there's a knock at the door.

"It's open," I call out to her.

The door opens and there's Jane in her fluffy leopard-print bathrobe, her dark hair pulled tight off her face except for her blunt bangs which nearly hang in her eyes. Jane is nearly sixty years old, with a round face, a big smile, and an outgoing attitude which usually makes her the life of the party in most places. With this being my third year of schooling, I know that she's the happiest here in this hall of residence than she's ever been, and I think she's living out the college days she missed out on, if only just in her head.

"You're lucky. I was moments away from putting my hair up in curlers," she says to me, shutting the door behind her. She claps her hands together and grins maniacally as soon as she spots the cheese. "Oh, what have we here?"

She shuffles on over to the kitchen counter and I step out of the way to give her full access to the cheese.

"It's just gouda," I tell her.

"Just gouda?" she repeats, looking me dead in the eye, as if I've insulted her cheese sensibilities, a slice dangling from her fingers.

"Listen," I say dryly. "You know me. It was the best damn gouda I could find. It's more than gouda-nough."

She pinches her lips together and gives me a mock glare. "You know I didn't come over here for your cheese puns." A wave of sympathy flashes through her dark eyes, the kind of sympathy that makes me wince internally, like something in my heart just bunched up. Pity. "What happened to your wine and cheese gathering?"

I shrug. "Who is to say I didn't want just you over?"

She tilts her head, examining me. "As much as I know

you love my good looks and outstanding personality, I also know you were looking forward to tonight and getting to know your roommates. So what happened?"

"I don't know," I say, trying to sound breezy but failing. I turn my attention to the bottle of grenache and unscrew the cap. "I fell asleep and I guess they didn't want to wake me up, and the party ended up moving somewhere else."

"So why don't you go to where it moved to?"

I grab the glasses and pour each of us some wine. "I don't think I'm wanted."

Jane doesn't say anything, so I glance up at her. Her lips are pursed together and under her bangs I know she's raising a brow.

"What?" I ask, that look meaning something.

"You're always wanted, Ella," she says. "I know making friends is hard for you, but it just means you have to be a little more persistent and braver than normal."

"If they wanted me there, wouldn't they have told me? Texted me? Tried to wake me up anyway?"

"Maybe they don't know you enough or feel comfortable with you to do that. You are a princess, after all, and they know that. You know that people aren't sure how to handle it, how to behave. Maybe they think waking up Princess Isabella from a nap gets you bloody hanged in Liechtenstein, I don't know."

I manage a smile. "That's definitely why the guys stay away from me."

"It is what it is, dear." She takes the glass and swirls the red wine around. "And it isn't going to change. It doesn't matter where you are or what school you go to because you are what you are. Even if you changed your name and pretended to be some dumb redneck named Mindy from

Arkansas, you'd still struggle. You have to be bold, my friend. Be bold and brilliant in all things."

"So what do you suggest I do?"

She takes a long sip of her wine, briefly closing her eyes and sighing happily. "Speaking of bold and brilliant, this wine is something else."

"Jane..."

She looks at me in surprise. "What do I suggest you do? Just take this cheese and that other wine, leaving this one here with me, and go find out where the party moved to and show up there."

I shake my head, feeling panic swirl through me. "That's pushy. I'll get on their nerves."

"You won't and so what?"

"I hate feeling like a tag-a-long."

"But maybe that's just a feeling. They might not see you that way. They might just say, oh hey, it's Ella, she came after all. Glad she's here, now it's a party."

I shake my head, knowing full well that won't happen. I take my glass of wine and head over to the couch, plopping down. The thought of doing that brings me nothing but anxiety. I don't want to be a pain in the ass, so it's just easier if I stay here and pretend the whole thing never happened.

I avoid Jane's eyes as she watches me, trying to figure out what she can say next to convince me, but then, as usual, she concedes. With a heavy sigh she brings her glass and the bottle and the gouda, balancing all with ease, and comes to sit beside me on the couch.

"Are there any new episodes of that *Making of a Murderer* show on Netflix?" she asks, getting herself comfortable before reaching for a slice of cheese.

I grab the remote and turn the TV on. "Let's find out."

∼

THE NEXT MORNING IS DREARY AND DRIZZLY. I SPEND too much time looking for an umbrella, which already puts me a few minutes behind my schedule, and when I give up and head out onto the campus, the skies decide to open, drenching me in seconds before I reach shelter under an elm tree.

Not the best start to the day. I drank a little too much wine with Jane last night, and despite passing out on the couch early and then dragging myself to bed before my flatmates got home, I still woke up feeling like crap.

Now my head is still muddled and there's a chance I might be late to one of my favorite classes, Marine Ecosystems. I'm always punctual, early even, and the professor doesn't look too kindly toward students who come in late.

I cringe at the thought of having everyone in the class stare at me, probably making comments at what a "princess" I am who thinks she needs special treatment or something like that. I crane my neck to look at the sky but it seems to have grown even darker.

Suddenly "Don't Let the Sun Go Down on Me" bellows out from my book bag, making me jump, and it takes me a moment to recognize what it is. My ringtone. It has been so long since someone actually called it—usually I talk to Jane or my family through text or email—that I didn't remember what I'd set my ringtone to.

I quickly fish the phone out of my bag then nearly drop it when I see the words on the screen. The call is from Liechtenstein, though the number is blocked and private.

Oh, please no, did something happen to my father or brothers?

I press the talk button and hold it to my ear, taking in a deep breath.

"Hello?"

"Is this Princess Isabella?" a familiar male voice says in German.

"Yes," I answer back, switching languages easily. "Who is calling?"

"This is Schnell, your father's butler," he says. I didn't recognize his nasally voice at first, but Schnell has been working alongside my father as his right-hand man for decades now. I'm used to seeing Schnell as much as my father, maybe even more so.

"Hi, Schnell. Sorry I didn't recognize your voice," I tell him, my heart gripped by panic as I realize why he could be calling. "Is my father all right? Are my brothers?"

"Yes, yes, they are all fine. I'm calling on behalf of your father, actually. He has a meeting today and couldn't call you himself but it's a matter of importance."

"Okay," I tell him, relieved that everyone is fine. It's not unusual for Schnell to do most of my father's phone calls, even when it comes to state matters. "What is it? Is there a problem?"

"Not a problem," he says. "But you have been invited to dinner tomorrow night at the Royal Palace in Oslo."

What?

"Uh, can you repeat that, Schnell?"

"Yes, madam. The Norwegian royal family has invited you for dinner tomorrow night and your father thinks it's very important that you attend."

"But...why? Why me?"

I mean, this is most unusual. I'm never invited anywhere, let alone any place royal. My princess status has been nothing but a hindrance ever since I left my own country. I don't think the world even knows I exist.

"I am not sure," he says. "Your father didn't say much except to say it was mutually beneficial." He pauses and I swear I hear some murmuring in the background. "Perhaps you can use this opportunity to speak to them about one of your issues."

I think by issues he means environmental issues. As socially progressive as Norway is, the country has done a lot of harm to the environment with fishing practices and whaling and it's something I care deeply about. Maybe too deeply. I'm not sure how well a dinner will go if I get all passionate and heated and start yelling at the King and Queen about their policies. I may be shy and quiet ninety-nine percent of the time but when there's something that gets under my skin, I'm hard to shut up.

Schnell clears his throat and goes on. "We've already booked a flight for you and Lady Jane tomorrow afternoon from Edinburgh to Oslo. You will be picked up at the airport by one of their men and taken straight to the palace. You are to wear something demure and appropriate for the occasion. Buy something today if you have to but do make sure you look your best. You're representing Liechtenstein after all."

"Okay," I tell him, though it's kind of weird to have old Schnell give me advice on how to dress. Though maybe I need it. I glance down at my fluffy black cardigan and ripped jeans. Not exactly the regal look.

"Your father will call you directly after the dinner," he says. "Take care now, madam, and do reach out to me if you have any questions."

"How do I reach out if your number is private?" I quickly ask, but it's too late. He's already hung up.

I stare at the phone in disbelief for a few moments, trying to wrap my head around what just happened.

Why on earth would I be invited to dinner at the Norwegian palace? It doesn't make any sense at all. I'm... nobody. Honestly. And though sometimes I wish I had a bigger voice about the issues I care about—hence why I'm going to university—I kind of like the fact that beyond this campus, no one knows who I am. I shouldn't be on any monarchy's radar whatsoever.

Unless I'm being used as some sort of chess piece in some inter-country power play. Since I was sent away from my own family and country at an early enough age, I was never fully immersed in the politics and goings on that surround my father and the thirty-seven thousand people that he represents. Could it be there's something that either my father wants from Norway or vice versa?

Paranoia doesn't suit me, but I can't help thinking that's more than likely the reason for all this. Still, that doesn't change the fact that I'm going, and now I'm more curious than ever. Perhaps I'll be an unwitting spy.

First things first though—I need a dress, and there isn't much time to get one. I've never skipped class before, and I feel guilty for doing so, but these kinds of opportunities never come up for me, and it's not like I can say no to my father when he never asks me to do anything.

Instead of texting Jane, I turn around and run back through the rain all the way to my dorm. I shuffle down the hall, the wet soles of my shoes squeaking across the floor, and then knock on Jane's door.

It takes her a moment to open, and when she does, she's peering at me suspiciously.

"It's me," I tell her. "I need to talk to you."

"I know it's you, I'm not blind," she says, opening her door wider so I can come in. "Why aren't you in class?"

"I have news," I tell her as I step into her closet-sized room.

"Why are you so wet?"

I run my hand over the top of my head, wincing at how soaked it is. "I forgot my umbrella. And I'm not going to class today. Instead, you and I are going to Edinburgh."

"Edinburgh?" she exclaims loudly. I knew she'd get all excitable about this. She never keeps things very subtle.

"Yes. Now promise you won't get all, you know, *loud* about this," I warn her, putting out my palms as a way of calming her before she can start.

"I'm not loud," she says extra quietly.

I give her a steady look. "Anyway," I go on, "Schnell called me. Just now on the way to class."

"Oh my god, is everything all right!?" she cries out, hand to her chest.

"Jane," I warn her. "This is you. Being loud. This is what loud is. And yes, everything is fine, don't worry. It's just that he called with an unusual request on behalf of my father."

"Why didn't your father call?"

"You know why."

She narrows her eyes. Even though my father is the one who pays her salary, I know Jane doesn't like him. Her personality with his is like oil and water.

"What does he want?" she asks.

"Well," I say, taking in a deep breath, "it seems I've been invited to dinner tomorrow night at the royal palace in Norway."

She stares at me for a few moments before she goes, "Say what? You're not pulling my leg, are you?"

47

"Someone might be pulling mine, but I'm still going. Both of us are. Tomorrow we fly out of Edinburgh for Oslo. I need something to wear—I assume you do too, unless you've got some fancy dress in your closet here"—I pause to glance at the closet by her bed which looks like it holds maybe three hangers—"so I thought we would just head to Edinburgh right now and get some shopping in."

She's still staring at me with the same blank expression as before. I stare right back at her, brows raised, waiting for some sort of explosion. "Why?" she asks.

"I don't know. Maybe it's some horrible joke my brothers are playing on me. Maybe I'll go there and no one will be there to pick me up. Though my brothers would first have to know I exist before that could happen..."

"Bloody hell," Jane exclaims breathlessly, her eyes growing wider by the second. "You're serious."

"When am I not?"

"We're going to an actual royal palace!"

"You act like you're not the lady-in-waiting to an actual princess," I remind her stiffly. "You've seen the palace I grew up in."

"And you know that it's not the same," she says, clapping her hands together. "Your family's palace is a castle fit for Count Dracula. That's what happens when you have only men ruling your country. Oh, if only my mum could see me now. She was so bloody obsessed with all royal families, the type to collect every single mug and collector plate she could get her hands on. Ooooh," she goes on, "maybe the Prince will be there!"

I roll my eyes and shudder. "Ew. I hope not."

Jane recoils at that and gawks at me like I have two heads. "Prince Magnus? What's your problem with him?"

Ugh. Don't get me started. Maybe it's because I've only

been mercilessly teased by those types back in boarding school (princesses are an easy target), I have no patience for men who act like boys or think with their dicks, and it seems like Prince Magnus of Norway is nothing more than a glorified playboy with a fancy title. All I ever see when I flip through the blogs and news is him racing motorcycles or hooking up with a new socialite.

Now there's a sex video floating around of him and the prime minister of Norway's daughter, which seems like bad news all around, though I shouldn't be surprised at the lengths that people go to for more and more fame. "He just seems like an idiot. That stupid smug smile I always see, like everyone wants him or wants to be him. And flaunting all those women around. I mean, hello, who the hell makes sex tapes anymore unless it's for attention? Yeah right, it was accidently leaked."

She chuckles. "Believe me, I don't think he did that for attention. He has enough of it already." She pauses, a strange gleam in her eyes. "Have you watched it?"

I scrunch up my nose. "God, no. Why would I?"

She shrugs and looks away.

"Jane," I say slowly. "Have you?"

Her head tilts and she's unable to hide her smile. "Maybe."

"Ugh, you're supposed to be refined, Jane."

"I am refined!" she yells, her round cheeks going pink. "I just have a healthy dose of curiosity." She pauses. "It's going to be hard having dinner with him after I know what he looks like naked. How he moves...the man has skills, Ella. Skills you need to see."

I raise my palm. "Please, *please* stop talking. I don't share my...sex life with you."

"This isn't my sex life," she says with a snort. "It's *his*

49

sex tape and it's all over the news. And need I remind you that you can't share your sex life with me if you don't have one."

I turn around. "This is getting wildly inappropriate."

"Sometimes you need to get inappropriate," she calls after me as I head over to the door, my shoes sloshing as I walk. "It would do you some good!"

I open the door and look over my shoulder. "With any luck he won't even be there so I don't have to be embarrassed over my *lady-in-waiting* drooling over the Crown Prince and picturing him naked. I'm going to pack and I'll come back here in an hour. Just promise me when I do you keep your head out of the gutter."

She gives me a grave nod, standing up straighter, and I know there will be no promises. Sometimes it feels like I'm the one keeping Jane in line and not the other way around. This time though, I know the both of us have no idea what to expect.

For once I'm going to have to put on my princess face and act like I belong.

FOUR
MAGNUS

When I was younger, I was the world's shittiest student. It explained why going to university after high school was never even on my radar. What was the point when everything to do with studying bored me to tears? Besides, even if there was something I was interested in, the testing system was always designed to make me fail. Every time I sat down to take a test, it didn't matter how well I knew the subject, I totally froze. I couldn't decide on the right answer for the life of me. Everything I knew went out the window and my mind went a million other places instead. As a result, I flunked.

So you can see why I'm having second, third, and fourth thoughts about my choice of princesses from the fact sheet.

Let's just push aside the truth for a moment, that what I'm doing is extremely unrealistic, and, well, silly. Let's forget that I'm actually selecting a human being to be my motherfucking wife and get down to the gritty facts and logistics. Those being that even though I spent a good week pouring over my options and Google and Facebook and Instagram stalking these blue-blooded, noble ladies to the extreme, I'm still having doubts that I've picked the right one.

But how can I even know that at this point? How can I pick the right one if I haven't even met them face-to-face? There's so much more than just what my father said about intelligence and wit and it's got nothing to do with looks. It has to do with sexual chemistry. I've been with my fair share of women and not all of them are stellar supermodels. Okay, some literally are. Sometimes I'm after the same pack of women as Leonardo DiCaprio. Hell, sometimes I see Leo at the same party and we do this head nod as if to say, what up brother, keep doing you.

Where am I even going with this? Right. So sometimes I've been with women who aren't conventionally beautiful for one reason or another, but I connected with them on another level. If you want to get into that deep shit, you could say that it's our souls that forged with one another. If you want to stay real, it's more that your bodies want to forge. You want to fuck and you're both very good at it, so you do it and go your separate ways. That's that.

Anyway, I've had to scour page after page of these women and try and settle on one of them, and even though I was never fully confident about my pick—because how can I be—I'm doubting myself now.

As I pace back and forth in the main hall of the royal palace.

Hands behind my back.

Waiting for her arrival.

I don't know what was said or what was promised, but the moment I went to my parents and told them I'd settled on Princess Isabella of Liechtenstein, calls were made, and then I was told she'd be here tonight for dinner so I could meet her in person.

I'm not sure if this is just a trial dinner, you know, like speed dating, princess-style, or something more. I'm pretty sure if I don't like her, if she turns out to be a total bore, if we have zero spark or chemistry, I can move on to my second and third choice picks, though honestly, I can't remember who they are right now which tells you a lot.

The reason I picked Isabella was because she looked the most normal. Apparently she was in a boarding school in England during her high school years and now is studying at St. Andrews University in Scotland. Other than a barely updated Facebook page, there isn't a lot of information on her, which I took as a good sign. The tabloids don't follow her, she doesn't do anything that makes the news, and for the most part, it looks as if she lives a life of total anonymity.

And, yes, of course, she's pretty as hell. Striking, even. Tall, blonde, sparkling eyes, and a big smile. She exudes charm and warmth through her photographs, more than any of the others did. There was no formality in them, no forced cheer. She just seemed real.

Lord knows if she'll match my expectations.

"Nervous?"

I stop my pacing and turn around to see Mari standing in the doorway to the sitting room. Her blonde hair is braided down both sides, and her black and red dress almost looks like the traditional Norwegian dress. It strikes me that Mari is closer to Princess Isabella's age than I am.

"Me, nervous?" I ask her with a smile.

"Of course not," she says, slowly walking over. "Prince Magnus worries about nothing."

My smile falters slightly. I wish that perception of me were true.

"Do you think I made the right choice?" I ask her as she

walks over to the window and peers down at the courtyard at the back of the palace.

"For your wife to-be?" she asks, her eyes growing wide.

"I wish I could say." She takes in a deep breath. "Magnus..."

I nod and come over to the window beside her. "I know."

"This is so ridiculous."

I give her a hopeful look. "I'm glad you agree. Now perhaps you can talk mother and father out of it?"

"I wish," she says with a shake of her head. "I've never seen them so adamant before. More than that, I've never seen them so...I don't know. Excited."

"Excited?"

She gives a slight shrug and starts playing with one of her braids. "You're the first one of us to get married. They thought it would never happen for you."

"With good reason," I mutter, trying to keep the anger out of my voice. All this unfairness has been simmering inside me for the last twenty-four hours but my youngest sister doesn't deserve to hear it.

"And now, it's something new to do. They get to ensure that their legacy will live on. Mother gets to plan a wedding. Father gets to see you settle down. The world's focus on us will be in a positive way again."

"All while I'm throwing the rest of my life away."

She glances at me thoughtfully, gnawing briefly on her bottom lip. Mari always has this rather unnerving way of seeing straight through you that at the same time makes you see straight through her. Sometimes I think I see an old soul trapped in a teenager's body. "I know this is a bitter pill to swallow," she says softly. "Never in a million years did I think this would be a solution to anything. But now that it is their solution to a big, big problem, I don't think it's the end of the world necessarily. Your friend, the Crown Prince of Sweden, is getting married."

"Viktor is getting married to a woman he's fallen madly in love with. So mad that it's not just her he's bringing into his royal family but all her sisters and brothers as well. If anyone deserves to get married it's those two. Not me. Not to someone I don't know."

"Yeah," she says after a moment, looking back out the window. "I'm just trying to see the positive in the situation here."

"There is no positive, not for me," I tell her.

"Well, in that case, maybe you can at least go into this knowing this is making our parents—and it will make our country—very happy."

I don't care much about the latter but that's probably something I need to work on, and fast. I do care about my parents though. But enough to actually go through with this? That remains to be seen.

"Also, you should remember that you have a choice," she says to me. "You don't have to do this if you don't want to. You can abdicate."

"And let Cristina sit on the throne? She'd kill me."

"You know that Irene would do it in a heartbeat."

I swallow hard, feeling that same wave of anxiety wash over me. "He wants me to be king. I won't abdicate. Not now. I won't let him down."

"He also wants you to be happy," she says. "And I know if you said that you didn't want the crown, he'd understand."

He would understand. He'd probably expect it. Everyone probably does. Everyone knows as well as I do that I'm just not cut out for it. But, fuck, that fact makes me want to prove people wrong sometimes.

Is that why I'm doing this? Willing to marry a stranger just to prove everyone wrong, including myself?

"I think this is them," Mari says as headlights come down the drive and one of our security officers at his post talks to the driver of the car. The gates open and the car glides in, parking alongside the other official vehicles.

Holy shit. This is happening.

"Now are you nervous?" Mari asks me.

It almost feels like I'm about to leap off a cliff.

Without a chute.

I watch as Tor strides out of the palace toward the car and opens the back door. Though it's twilight and the sky is a hazy, pale gray, the car is directly under the lights and I can see Isabella in fine detail. Her hair somehow seems blonder, pulled back high off her face with a few pieces hanging loose. She's wearing a black fuzzy looking coat and flat shoes. I'm both relieved that she's just as pretty as her pictures, almost more ethereal and graceful, yet she's looking at Tor and around at the palace like she's completely out of her element.

"She's got great eyebrows," Mari comments, and I have to do a double take. Her eyebrows are pretty nice, I guess. They're dark compared to her hair.

"You know I don't give a fuck about eyebrows, don't you?"

Mari sticks her tongue out at me. "Every YouTube tutorial is about getting brows as thick and shapely as those."

"The only thing I want thick and shapely are her thighs and ass," I tell her, peering back out the window. "And with that coat, I can't see either."

"Well, she's pretty, anyway," Mari says approvingly. "Even more so in person. Taller, too. Wait, who is that?"

Another woman comes shuffling rather comically out of

the back seat, dressed in a bright yellow raincoat. She's, well, the polite term would be to describe her as pleasantly plump and she's already laughing as she struggles to get out of the car, holding on to Tor's arm who is taking it all in stride.

"Maybe that's her mother," I say, though her face is round, her hair black, her skin tanned, looking very different from the Galadriel-like paleness of Isabella.

"Princess Isabella's mother died when she was a child," Mari says, not taking her eyes off of them.

"Oh," I say, feeling sympathy for her. Even though my mother and I don't always see eye-to-eye, I can't imagine growing up without her.

"She's probably her private secretary," Mari says. My sister has one of her own though I don't see them together very often. "Though she seems rather, uh..."

She trails off just as the woman starts laughing again, so loudly that we can hear it through the thick-paned windows. I can tell already I'm going to like her. I especially like how embarrassed Isabella looks, gesturing with her hands for the woman to keep it down.

I exchange a look with Mari. This is going to get interesting.

"She's here," my mother says from behind us, her voice urgent and hushed.

We turn around to see my mother dressed in a dark silvery dress that catches the light, something that she would normally wear for an official event. From the anxiety sparking in her eyes, I know this is a big deal for her. She's meeting her potential daughter-in-law and wants to put on her best face possible.

Fucking hell.

The thought hits me again for the millionth time that day.

Just what the fuck am I doing?

My mother looks us both up and down quickly. "You look fine, Mari. Magnus, you could have shaved. And an orange tie? Really?"

I glance down at my tie. I'm in a navy Tom Ford suit that fits me like a fucking glove thanks to the family tailor and I always try to inject a little bit of personality into my clothes via color. "What's wrong with orange?"

My mother shakes her head and then hurries off.

I look over at Mari. "Seriously, what's wrong with it?"

"Nothing," she says reassuringly, taking my arm and pulling me toward the door. "Let's go."

We head down the stairs and stop outside "The Bird Room," the formal antechamber for visitors and guests, where the walls are painted with scenes of Norway and adorned with different birds. My mother is waiting outside the doors beside my father's butler, Sven, and I'm surprised to see father already there, discussing something with the nurse before she nods and walks away.

My father is dressed in a tuxedo that must be new since he's lost a bit of weight from being ill and this fits him better than his other clothes. He flashes me a warm smile, his cheeks ruddy which has to be a good sign, as my mother quickly reaches over and adjusts his bowtie.

Shit. Was I supposed to wear a tux too? Is that what my mother had issues with? Next to my father I look out of place. Then again, he is the King. Maybe that's the point.

"I think you made a great choice," my father says to me.

I point at the tie. "The Queen doesn't seem to think so."

"I mean with Princess Isabella," he says patiently. He

glances at his wife. "And in this case, I think the Queen agrees."

"She's certainly beautiful and seems to have brains," my mother says quickly. "Let's see what else she has to offer us."

Suddenly I feel sorry for Isabella and what she's about to be subjected to, like a prized cow being paraded in front of discerning judges, sizing her up on the sheen of her coat, the way she handles, how big her udders are. Okay, maybe it's only me who is interested in that last part.

Kidding. I'm kidding.

There's a certain order in the way that we enter rooms when we're together—by rank. So with Sven opening the door and announcing us, my father is the first to step in, followed by my mother, then me, then Mari.

Isabella and her assistant are already standing and giving the standard curtsey to my father and lightly bowing before him as he offers his hand to shake.

"Thank you so much for coming tonight, Princess Isabella," my father says to her in English, and I remind myself that Isabella won't understand a lick of Norwegian. Luckily we all speak English fluently, as do most Norwegians these days.

"It was a great honor to accept," Isabella says, her voice soft and airy, her accent unusual, like mild German with a British tone and refinement. Though I can see clear over my mother's head in front of me, I have to crane my neck to get a good look at her around my father's back.

My father moves on to the other woman, who, in a very loud and twangy British accent, addresses herself as Lady Jane, and the moment she says it, Mari kicks the back of my calf lightly because she just knows I'm about to laugh. I've met a lot of "ladies" in my day and I don't think Lady Jane is one of them, which of course makes me like her even more.

I bite back my smile at that and my eyes shift over to Isabella. Her eyes are trained on my mother who is now coming forward with her hand extended. Not once have we made eye contact, but at least now I can get a good look at her while she's preoccupied.

In person and up close, Isabella is pretty. That's the first word that comes to mind. Not necessarily hot, not in her demure, long, floaty blue gown with cape-like sleeves that only shows off her pale collarbones. Not necessarily sexual with her prim mannerisms, her hair up, and her makeup light and casual, with just a dusting of pink on her cheeks and her lips like bruised cherries, like she's been kissing for a long time.

Fuck. Maybe she *is* hot and sexual. I could definitely look at those lips all day, bring that same flush to her cheeks my own way.

Then she smiles at my mother as she greets her, and hot and sexual and pretty don't seem to cover it anymore. She's absolutely *gorgeous*, her smile so wide and real that it stuns me, making me momentarily forget that this is supposed to be a horrible and unjust experience.

Until my mother moves on to Lady Jane and I'm up next.

Isabella meets my eyes rather reluctantly.

Just for a second before she curtsies.

And that second is all it takes to get her message across.

She does not like me.

Whatever radiant light was shining out of her a moment ago when she was greeting my parents has now dimmed like an oncoming storm and I swear I feel a wave of pure animosity rolling toward me.

I really wouldn't have thought she would have come at all if that's the way she felt.

Then again, maybe it meant nothing at all, just that the light was in her eyes. Maybe she's nervous. Maybe my thoughts are starting to do that thing again where they ramble along at a mile a minute.

I take in a deep breath, reminding myself to speak slowly and clearly. Sometimes when I get like this and my thoughts seem all over the place and I feel like I'm driving in a car in the rain and the windshield wipers aren't working, I tend to blurt out the first thing I'm thinking.

In this case, it wouldn't help at all. It would be "what the hell is your problem with me?"

Instead, I manage to rein it in and extend my hand to her and flash her a smile that makes normal girls weak in the knees.

It's hard to tell if it works since she's curtseying anyway.

"Very nice to meet you," I tell her. My words sound stiff and absolutely rehearsed even though I never gave any thought to this. I probably should have so I didn't sound like such an idiot.

She gives me a tight smile, seems to think twice about what she's going to say, and then says, "Very nice to meet you as well." She shakes my hand and I'm surprised at how firm it is. I expected a limp noodle but it's like she wants to break my hand in two. I guess it matches the venom in her dark eyes.

Then her attention immediately goes to Mari behind me and her hand drops out of mine like I was never even there to begin with.

Well, fuck. This is going to be a hell of an interesting dinner with my potential bride. Which, after this, I'm pretty sure I'll have to hit that list again because there's no way in hell I'm hitting that, whether in marriage, in bed, even on a fucking date.

Especially as I watch her greet Mari like she's her long-lost relative or something, back to being all smiley and beautiful and warm.

The clearing of my father's throat brings my focus back to him.

Back to Lady Jane who is waiting in front of me.

At least she looks happy to see me. I think her smile might just break her face in two and her dancing eyes are along for the ride.

"Lady Jane," I say warmly, and it's impossible not to smile back at her. "So thrilled that you could join us tonight."

"Oh, the pleasure is all mine, Your Highness," Lady Jane says. "But, please, if you can, call me Jane. I'm definitely not a lady."

I burst out laughing and shake her hand even harder. Even though up close she seems to be middle-aged, maybe in her mid-fifties, there's seems to be youthful exuberance escaping every pore. This is a woman who hasn't lost her lust for life. Perhaps she could teach the princess a thing or two.

"I'll keep that in mind," I tell her and then lean in to whisper in her ear. "Between you and me, there aren't that many ladies in this house to begin with."

Now it's my mother clearing her throat. I pull away from Lady Jane and avoid my mother's eyes. The Queen's hearing is second to none. She can hear a bubble-wrapped pin drop on a floor of cotton balls a mile away.

We then leave The Bird Room and proceed down the hall to the formal banquet room, my mother and father walking beside each other, heads held high. The last time I was in here was a few months ago when the Duke and Duchess of Cambridge came to visit, but it looks kind of silly now when it's dinner for just the six of us in this large, ornate room.

There is a round table in the center of the room lavishly decorated with gleaming place settings and hydrangea flowers in heirloom vases, and I hear Lady Jane suck in her breath appreciatively.

"How darling," she coos. "Oh, Ella, would you look at all this."

I glance at her over my shoulder. Not Isabella but Ella, huh? She didn't even address her as madam or Your Highness.

And Ella doesn't seem to notice that until she catches me looking at her. Then her cheeks go even pinker than before and she elbows Jane in the side who doesn't even pay attention to the jab.

We all sit down, with Ella and Jane's places right across from me and Mari, my father and mother between us on either side. Two of our waiters come out with various bottles of wine and sparkling water, a nice little distraction before things settle into being awkward as fuck.

Because how can it not be? This is like a blind date, only I'm on it with my entire family. If I let myself think about it too much, I might just get up and leave. I have a hard time sitting through dinners as it is.

But then I look at my father and he looks like a completely different person from the one I saw hooked up to the IV last week. There's a spark in his eyes that wasn't there before and the way he keeps glancing at my mother as they exchange secret thoughts makes my chest feel like it's way too tight. For reasons I don't understand, this really is bringing them joy, and as Mari said, at least there's that.

I take in a deep breath and decide to approach this with all I've got. This is happening whether I like it or not, so I may as well take what control I have over the situation.

"Your Highness," I address Ella as I pick up my glass of red wine, and her eyes go to mine, startled. "May I propose a toast to you and your country of Liechtenstein. Thank you so much for coming to stay with us this evening. I know myself and my family have been very excited to meet you."

She raises her brows, as if this whole thing is catching her off guard. Perhaps she didn't expect me to talk. Well she's going to have to get used to it. If things go well here, she'll have to get used to it for the rest of her life.

And yet the way she's looking at me, as if I'm from another planet entirely, maybe of some low life form, like an amoeba or something, makes me wonder if she even wants to be here with me at all.

"Here, here," my father says, raising his glass of sparkling water.

We all say cheers and then the appetizers are spread out and the small talk begins.

"So, Princess," the Queen says, "I've heard that you left Liechtenstein at a rather young age. Has Lady Jane been with you that whole time?"

"Since she was thirteen, Your Majesty," Lady Jane says and then quickly covers her mouth with her napkin as Ella gives her a look for talking out of turn.

My mother takes it in stride. "Thirteen. So young. And you went to boarding school in England...I do hope you were able to go home to see your family during the holidays and the summer."

Ella manages a small smile. "Yes," she says carefully. "I went home often enough. But I didn't find boarding school to be a lonely experience. It taught me a lot. It especially taught me to put all my focus into my studies."

"And you are at St. Andrews University, correct?" my father asks as she nods. "What are you taking?"

She gives him another tight smile and seems to pause, momentarily staring down at her plate and seeming to take in a deep breath before she speaks. "Environmental studies."

"That's very interesting," my mother says before spearing a piece of salad with her fork.

"What kind?" Mari speaks up. "I mean, what are you learning about?"

Again, the princess seems to take a moment. "It's a lot to do with climate change, with global protection acts, with protecting resources."

"So you're an environmentalist in the making," my father says with a nod. "A female Leonardo DiCaprio. You know Magnus here knows him."

"That's nice," she says, giving me a quick, curt smile.

Her tone basically says "good for fucking you" and damn does it ever get under my skin. So I say to her, "Well, Norway recently vetoed potential seismic drilling around Lofoten in order to protect the orcas up there."

A flicker of surprise, like she's impressed, runs through her dark eyes but it's quickly buried. "The only reason Norway did that was because of public pressure. There was a lot of campaigning on behalf of activists such as Sea Legacy and journalists from all around the globe, campaigning that went directly to the Norwegian people to let them have a say in what their government was planning to do. It was only then that the prime minister and your government, and maybe even yourselves, decided to prevent the oil and gas exploration up in the Arctic. The change came from outside."

There's so much heat in her voice, a fire in her eyes, that she suddenly doesn't seem so quiet and demure anymore.

I glance at my father, waiting for his response. I mean, she pretty much just took any credit away from us, from what little we had to do with the end result.

But he chuckles softly. "You certainly know your stuff. And you are very correct. I'm afraid if it wasn't for activists and environmental crusaders, nothing would have changed and the drilling would have been allowed. Rest assured, that area is now protected."

"But that's just one area," she says quickly. "When will the government stop whaling? When will sustainable practices be used for commercial fishing?"

"We have pledged to become climate-neutral by 2030," Mari speaks up.

"And yet you're one of the world's largest exporters of oil and gas."

"Among students, though, we're really pushing for change with the country," Mari tells her with almost as much passion. "Renewable energy is a lot of our focus, even in high school. We're challenging the government, challenging the companies."

My father clears his throat loudly. "Seems the two of you are both the voices of the future. You must understand, Your Highness, that this nation is trying to become as green as it can be."

"But so far you are more of an environmental hypocrite rather than a hero."

"Ella," Jane chides her, glancing around furtively. "I don't think insulting the country is appropriate when you're currently its guest."

Ella's face falls at that, her skin seeming to grow even paler.

"Oh, don't worry," my father says good-naturedly. "It's very rare that we have guests over that speak their mind the way that you do, and I can tell that these issues are very important to you. There's nothing wrong with that and I can whole-heartedly agree that as a country we have a long way to go. It will take time but it's people like you who are pressing for the change. I think it's rather charming that you feel so strongly. Don't ever be afraid to argue with me." He glances at me. "In fact, you remind me a bit of Magnus. He's also never afraid to argue, even when he knows he'll lose."

I cock my brow. "When have I ever lost?"

But the knowing gleam in his eyes reminds me that I'm currently losing at this very moment.

With Princess Planet finishing her spiel about Norway and the environment, the conversation turns to safer topics such as favorite travel spots or the latest programs on TV. When my mother asks Lady Jane about herself, she takes the questions and runs with it for most of the meal.

Which is more than fine with me. It gives me time to watch Ella closely, to really take her in. Normally I have a hard time focusing on people, like I'm able to look at them but not really *see* them. But with her, I have tunnel vision. I can't look away even if I wanted to.

And I want to. Despite the craziness of this arrangement, despite the fact that I rarely care about what people think, I don't want to be known as this crazy creeper who won't stop staring at her.

But it's probably too late for that. When she meets my eyes from time to time, it's only for a second and then she quickly looks away. I've heard from women that my gaze can be intimidating and intense but all those times I was only faking it, faking my interest. Now that I'm really absorbing all her little details, I might just look certifiably insane. Magnus the Mad, indeed.

Since I've seen how outspoken she can be, she's become a little less ethereal in my eyes. Still fairy-like and dainty, but there's a fiery realness to her. Her eyes are this rich dark brown and narrow, like she's permanently squinting, which is also kind of hot since she looks like she's thinking of what sexual things she could do to you. Her mouth is wide, her lips soft but not outrageously plumped as it seems to be in style these days. Half the time I'm with a woman I can't tell if those are her actual lips sucking me off or the plastic surgeon's filler.

I think the most endearing thing about her are her teeth, which she doesn't show much unless she's smiling or laughing. The front ones are large and there's the slightest gap between them. It's both adorable and extremely sexy.

I just wish she'd show them off more often. Or, to put it another way, I wish I was the one making her smile. Usually the women around me can't stop smiling at me. At first anyway. The scowling comes later (and there's a fuckload of that).

Once dessert is finished, we all stand up and move into the parlor for drinks and digestifs in the world's smallest cocktail party.

Before Ella gets settled though, she anxiously turns to my mother and asks where the washrooms are, then politely excuses herself and Jane as they head over to them.

I watch Ella carefully as she disappears from sight, still unable to tell if she's nervous because of me, my family, the whole marriage thing, or everything combined.

I turn to my mother. "I don't remember. There's no window she can escape from in the washroom, is there?"

She laughs. "I think it's all going fine, don't you? She's lovely."

"And feisty," my father says. "Oh, I look forward to arguing with her. She seems so quiet but I can see there's a spitfire underneath."

"She's okay," I concede, still unsure exactly how I feel about her. I'm definitely attracted to her, intrigued even, but whether we have any chemistry remains to be seen. I'm trying to not even think about marriage.

But I should probably start. I exchange a look with Mari and then say to my mother, "Don't you get the feeling that she doesn't know why she's here?"

"Nonsense," my mother says. She looks at my father, brows raised. "You did tell the Prince of Liechtenstein why Princess Isabella was invited, didn't you?"

"Of course I did," he says, looking rebuked. "I was completely honest and upfront about the whole thing. You know me. I told him that you were looking for a bride and that Isabella captured your interest and you wanted to meet."

"Wait, wait, wait," I say, waving my hands as I shake my head. "You told him I was looking for a bride? You didn't tell him that I had no choice in the matter, that we're doing this because of a scandal?"

He frowns. "Goodness, no. That would be most insulting, not to mention presumptuous. That would reflect very badly on us."

I stare at him, open-mouthed. She honestly thinks she's here because I want to potentially marry her, not because I'm being forced into the matter? She thinks this is...genuine?

If she even thinks it at all.

"You know this is all going to blow up in our face," I tell him. "There's no way around it."

"Calm down, Son," he says, his eyes wistfully going to a glass of champagne that my mother is plucking from one of the trays the waiter is carrying. "I'm not saying that we won't tell her the truth. We will. She has to know what she's getting into. But I couldn't very well tell her father that on the phone."

"So when do we tell her the truth?" Mari asks, taking a champagne for herself.

My father looks at me.

Fuck it. I need another glass of something. I finish the one in my hand and plunk it down on the waiter's tray before grabbing another one. I meet the waiter's eyes for a second, and even though they've got this blankness that so many of our servants seem to have, the look that tells you they aren't listening, that they aren't even here, I can see that this guy thinks the whole thing is crazy. I bet when he took this job he had no idea what our royal family was really like.

"You know what I think? I don't even think she knows why she's here at all, not the whole truth anyway," I tell them, my eyes darting to the washroom doors, far enough away that I know they can't hear us. "And I really think one of us ought to spell it out for her, and soon."

All six eyes land on me. Because of course I'll have to be the one to make sure she knows.

I'm just not sure how to tell her.

And if she'll even want to hear it.

FIVE

ELLA

"THERE'S SOMETHING FISHY GOING ON HERE," JANE says from inside the toilet stall.

"Jane, please, I think you've been oversharing too much lately," I tell her wryly. I continue to wash my hands, frantically pumping out the lavender scented soap from the dispenser. Who knew that excessive hand-washing was a thing I did when I was nervous because I feel like I'm going to scrub my skin raw.

She sighs, exasperated, and I hear the toilet flush. "I don't mean with me," she cries out in annoyance as she barges out of the stall. "I mean here. In this place." She flings her hands around.

"Try not to do that until after you've washed your hands," I comment, lifting a small soft hand towel from the ornate holder on the granite countertop. With four stalls and three sinks, this bathroom seems more like the type you'd see in a fancy restaurant but I guess they have enough visitors and guests to warrant it. Growing up in our palace, it felt like barely anyone was over when I was younger, though it could be because my mother had been the one to love entertaining.

"Honestly," she says, shaking her head as she comes over to the sink and washes up. "I mean, why are you here? They haven't even said. They're just all talking and talking like you always come over here for dinner."

I shrug as I toss the towel in the wicker basket under the sink. Actually, it's more Jane that's been doing the talking and talking. "I don't know. For a moment there I thought maybe it was something to do with the environment, but I'm not sure if they took what I was saying seriously or not."

"Everyone takes you seriously when you talk about what matters to you. It's impossible not to."

I wince. "I guess I was a little blunt, wasn't I?" I hadn't meant to start blabbering on like that but I couldn't help myself.

"You're just being Ella, that's all," she says.

"Which reminds me, please try not to call me Ella. Your Highness or Madam will have to do."

Jane stares at me for a moment and then sighs. "Yes, of course, *Your Highness*. You can't blame me for getting confused since you would absolutely murder me on campus if I dared to call you that."

"I know. I just think that they're expecting someone royal and proper and refined. Everything I'm not."

"You are all those things and more," Jane says, reaching out to grab my chin and tilt my head so that I'm looking at myself in the mirror. "Look at you. You look like the princess you are."

All I see are the same two eyes that look back at me every single day. The fancy blue dress I bought and the elegant updo doesn't change any of that. My title escapes me, even on days like today.

"You know," I tell her, "I don't even think I like this royal life. Living in a palace, all these formalities."

She takes her hand away and rolls her eyes. "Bloody hell, is there anything you do like these days? Loosen up, *Princess*. Whatever reason you're here, it can't be anything sinister, so just relax and enjoy it. Maybe it really does have to do with better relations between your countries and your father thought that you were the most amiable representative. You've certainly got more brains and wit than any of your brothers."

"Are you kidding me? My brothers are younger versions of my father."

"As I was saying," she says sternly, "you have warmth and personality and sometimes that's far more important in these kind of situations than all the class and manners in the world. Your brothers are like royal robots, always saying the right things but never meaning them. And you, Ella, Your Highness, Madam, you are not a robot."

I'm not sure that not being a robot should be considered one of my selling points but it will have to do for now. Because that's what all of this comes down to, isn't it? Someone here is selling something and I just have to figure out what it is.

"Now come on, we've been in here long enough." She grabs my arm and pulls me toward the door, trying not to step on my dress. "Let's go drink and be merry." She pauses. "But not too merry. You don't want to be known as Princess Lush, either."

I bite my lip. I'm not a heavy drinker and three glasses of wine can make me crawl to bed, but Jane is the one I should really be watching out for. I swear she must have trained for the drinking Olympics at one point in her life, or maybe that's just every English person.

We step out into the hall and I try to steady my breath and calm my nerves as we walk toward the parlor room where the Norwegian royal family is speaking to each other rather passionately about something.

I have to admit, I like them. I like that they're nowhere near as stuffy as I thought they'd be, I like that when I started talking about the environment, the King didn't take offense to the fact that I was basically putting down his country's policies, I like that there seems to be a lot of love between the four of them. They feel like an actual family unit and not just a monarchy.

Except for the odd one out. Magnus. He doesn't quite fit in and it's not just the way he's dressed with that ugly orange tie and his dark longish hair constantly falling in his face, or the scruff on his masculine jaw and strong chin—the opposite of the clean-shaven, tidy, and elegant royals you usually see. It's like he's observing everyone all the time, locked in his head until he blurts something out that most would consider to be inappropriate.

I hate to admit it, but he intrigues me. I don't want him to because it's such a cliché to find the bad boy, the rich boy, the royal boy, interesting because the world is crammed full of those types of girls. But there is something about him that steals my attention, something that appeals to some very deep, basic level inside me. Like he speaks to my body, not my brain. I have to constantly remind myself that he's not my type, that I'm not his type, that he's just here and has nothing to do with the reason that I'm here.

And yet, during the meal, every time I looked over at him, he was looking at me. His eyes are dark and intense, and they have this way of holding your attention until it's almost uncomfortable. I felt like he was trying to creep into every nook and cranny inside me. I often had to look away.

"He's just a tall drink of water, isn't he?" Jane murmurs to me just before we enter the room, her eyes drifting all over Magnus. I'm tempted to jab her in the side again, but I know it doesn't do me any good.

Besides, she's right. I won't admit to her that she's right because then she'll probably try some match-making scheme and I'd hate to see how that would go (knowing her, it would probably be along the lines of her telling him I want to shag him or something equally as embarrassing), but he's a damn handsome man in his own rugged, overly confident way. He's tall, with shoulders like mountains, and I know that underneath that fitted suit he's covered in tattoos and loads of muscle, no thanks to all the paparazzi pics of him sunbathing on the royal yacht in the summer.

But even though I can appreciate how blessed he is in the looks department (and I'm not surprised, the King is handsome, and the Queen and his sister are gorgeous), that doesn't mean I'm going to turn into a bumbling fool, even if there is something about his gaze that leaves me rather unnerved and tongue-tied.

And so, right now, as we approach the party, I can feel his eyes burning on me. I don't even have to look up at him. Instead, I keep my attention on Mari, his sister, who seems only a few years younger than me and because of that is a lot more approachable.

"Champagne?" the Queen asks me as a waiter brings over a tray.

"Yes, thank you," I tell her as I take a glass off the tray and Jane does the same. I notice that the King isn't drinking anything at all and that he hadn't at dinner either. I know that the Norwegian royal family is known for partaking in good food and drink, but it would be rude of me to bring it up. Perhaps he's quitting for health reasons. I remember reading somewhere recently that he had pneumonia at the start of the summer.

"So," the King says, "how are you liking your school? I know we touched on it briefly earlier but obviously you picked St. Andrews for a reason."

My first instinct is to shrug, but I know I have to sound as concise as possible. "I had a year off between finishing up my boarding school and before starting university. I decided to travel around the UK, and I absolutely fell in love with Scotland. I'm afraid I'm there more for the country than the school, though of course it's a very well-regarded university."

"You know Oslo has a very good university as well," he points out and quickly exchanges a glance with the Queen.

Okay. That's kind of an odd thing to bring up, as if it's a competition. "I'm afraid I haven't heard much about the schools in Norway. Actually, I don't know too much about Norway in general."

"But you seem to know an awful lot about Norway's environmental policies," Magnus speaks up.

I whip my head over to him and catch a hint of a smile playing on his full lips. I'm not sure why my mind is noticing how full and lush they are considering what he just said and I urge my brain to ignore them. "Yes, well it's hard not to know those things when they stand out like a sore thumb among the world's developed countries."

"Were you a fan of Captain Planet when you were growing up?" he asks, now fully smiling. The royal bastard has a lovely smile.

"I have no idea what you're talking about," I tell him quickly and then realize that perhaps that wasn't the best way to speak to the Crown Prince of Norway. "I'm sorry, Your Highness."

"It's quite all right, *Your Highness*," he says right back. "I think it was before your time. How old are you again?"

"Magnus," his mother chides him. "Don't you know it's rude to ask a woman's age?"

"Woman?" he says, jerking his chin at me. "She's just a girl."

"I'm twenty-two," I say stiffly. "And whether I'm a girl or a woman, that's not for you to speculate."

This time, Jane jabs me in the side. That's a first.

I look over at her and she's giving me a stern look. Sheepishly, I look back at the royal family, expecting to see disapproving scowls on their faces, but instead they all look rather impressed, even Magnus.

"I must say, I *like* you, Princess Isabella," the King says emphatically, and the curious praise makes me feel warm inside. "We need more people around here to keep the Prince in his place."

"Yeah, that's just what I need," Magnus mumbles before finishing the rest of his champagne and walking across the room to plop the glass down on a side table, which makes his mother gasp at the meeting of the glass and the wood.

"Magnus," his father calls after him as Magnus yanks open what looks to be a liquor cabinet and starts rifling through it. "You know not using a coaster amounts to treason in this family."

"I'm sure the schools in Norway are very good," Jane says eagerly, trying to save face, even though the moment has passed.

"Indeed, they are," the Queen says with an appreciative nod. "Two of our girls opted to study here instead of going abroad."

I look at Mari. "And where do you plan to study when

you're done with your schooling?" I pause. "That is if you're planning on going to school."

"Of course, she is," the Queen answers for her, giving Mari a proud yet tight-lipped smile. "She's exceptionally bright."

Mari just nods though I can tell there's something holding her back. She might just need time to figure out what she wants to be.

"And after you get your degree," the King says to me, "where do you plan on living?"

Again I want to shrug. I straighten my shoulders instead. "I'm not quite sure yet. Edinburgh is lovely. London seems the right choice, but I think it's just a bit too big for me. Anywhere that I feel I can use my voice best."

"Then wouldn't you head back to Liechtenstein?"

Is this a trap? Is he trying to trick me into saying something bad about my country?

I shake my head. "While Liechtenstein will always be my home and I think it has a lot to offer, there aren't many opportunities there for what I'm interested in."

"And what is that?" the Queen asks.

I look at her in surprise. I thought that was pretty apparent. "Getting together a non-profit organization to help the environment. To do something that invokes change. That's my end goal, anyway. It's a lot harder to do than it seems."

"Your father has no interest in helping you?"

I hold back a bitter laugh. "My father has no interest in helping me at all. In fact, telling me about this dinner was the first time he acknowledged I existed since he gave me a present at Christmas."

The King raises his gray brows and exchanges a perplexed glance with his wife.

Oh shit. If this was a trap, I didn't sell my father very well.

"You see, he's a very busy man," I add quickly. "And I'm terrible at keeping in touch."

"It's true," Jane says, nodding adamantly.

"I completely understand," the King says, his voice warm and reassuring. He clears his throat. "May I ask, what exactly did your father tell you about tonight's dinner?"

At that question I notice Magnus slowly sauntering back over to us with a highball of what looks like scotch and eyeing me curiously. Actually, everyone is looking at me the same way.

"I, uh, well he didn't exactly say," I admit stupidly, feeling my cheeks grow hot. "He just said that Jane and I were invited for dinner and that was it."

"You didn't ask what it was for?" the Queen asks, frowning.

I feel even stupider. "Well, no. My father didn't tell me himself, his butler did. And he wasn't sure. I just know to take my father's word that if he tells me to go somewhere and do something, I do it."

"So obedient," the King says under his breath, almost wistfully, before he looks over at Magnus.

Magnus nods at him and then says to me, "Listen. Ella, right? I need to speak to you in private for a moment."

I blink at him, totally confused as to what's going on and then give Jane a helpless look. She only gives a slight shrug, her eyes getting that devious glint in them, the one that means she's getting inappropriate thoughts that I pray she keeps to herself.

"Sure," I tell him, and I step back away from the group as he lightly places his fingers at my elbow, guiding me toward a set of French doors. From the moment his skin makes contact with mine, I feel a subtle jolt of electricity travel through my veins, like I'm some kind of conductor, and I nearly jump back from it. I don't know if it's his smell, like a pine forest with a hint of booze, his proximity to me, or what, but it's never been more obvious that I'm sorely out of practice even just socializing with the opposite sex.

I glance over my shoulder at the others and they all seem to be holding their breath, except Jane, who is downing her glass of champagne.

Magnus opens the doors with ease and we step out onto a stone path that winds its way through a few bushes filled with night-blooming flowers and a bench, before it turns into the back courtyard and parking area we first arrived in.

"It's lovely out here," I tell him, my voice shaking a little, from both nerves and the bracing air.

"It's ridiculous is what it is," Magnus says, leading me over to the stone bench and then running his hands over it, brushing off any dirt. "Here, sit."

I hesitate a moment before I do, still so unsure of what's going on. "What's ridiculous?"

"What isn't?" he asks, and I notice he's not sitting. He stands in front of me, and from here he looks even more massive and powerful than before. He's intimidating, that's for sure. "This is what constitutes my mother's garden. It's the only place she has in private to enjoy her flowers." He gestures to the park behind the palace. "In the summer, the park and main gardens are open to the public. Hell, a lot of the palace inside is too. I don't know why they choose to live like they're fish in a bowl."

"Our palace back home is completely blocked off," I tell him. "No one can even get near, though of course it's pretty useless since no one really cares about us. No one even knows where Liechtenstein is."

"They have some great places to go abseiling," he says. "Some great women too."

I shouldn't roll my eyes at the Crown Prince of Norway, but I do.

"Hey, you could be one of them," he says.

"I'll pass," I tell him with a scoff, folding my hands in my lap. "So, may I ask what we're doing out here? What was all of that inside?"

He gnaws on his lip for a moment, that damn full bottom lip. He's almost wincing.

This isn't going to be good, is it?

SIX

ELLA

"You honestly don't know why you're here?" he asks as he stares down at me.

My heart starts to thump harder in my chest and I shift uncomfortably on the bench. "No," I say quietly, wishing now I had the courage to not agree to any of this until I had talked to my father. I have no idea what I've gotten myself into by coming here, but I have a feeling I'm about to find out.

He presses his lips together, raising his brows as if to say, *oh boy, here we go.*

"Right, well. I'm going to be straight with you. More so than I think my family would like, but since we're both involved in this, I think honesty is the only thing we've got right now."

"Okay..." Jesus, what is it?

"I'll start by telling you what my father told your father." He runs his hand through his hair and starts to shift his weight from one foot to the other.

"Why don't you sit down?" I tell him.

He shakes his head and I know I shouldn't take any

offense to the fact that he won't sit next to me, but I kind of do. Do I smell? I fight the urge to take a whiff.

"The reason you are here, Princess Isabella of Liechtenstein," he goes on, "is that my father told your father that I was very interested in meeting you."

Huh? Come again?

"You were interested in meeting me?"

He shrugs with one shoulder.

"But that's not true, is it?" I continue, still confused.

His jaw tenses as he thinks that over and for once he looks away. "It's not about...it doesn't matter. That's what he told him. And so, you were invited here for dinner like this was a set-up, a blind date of sorts."

I can only stare at him. The Prince of Norway is telling me that the reason I'm here is because of him, that he wanted to take me on a date?

"My father's butler never mentioned that," I manage to say after a beat.

"Which surprises me," he says, "or maybe it's that he wanted you to come, and if you'd known the truth, you would have said no." He pauses, giving me a furtive glance. "Would you have?"

Hell. I don't have an answer to that. I suppose if my father had told me the truth and expressed any importance to it, I still would have come here, to please him and make him happy.

I shrug. "Sure. I mean, this is just a dinner, that's all. It would have been a...new experience."

"You don't have to worry about sparing my feelings," he tells me. "I don't have that many to begin with."

"I wouldn't be proud of that."

"I'm not proud. Just honest."

"Okay, fine. Are you asking if I would have *wanted* to go

on a dinner date with you? Well, no. You're not really my type."

"And you're not my type either," he says quickly, like he's throwing what I said back in my face.

I frown, not understanding. "If I'm not your type, then why did you invite me here for dinner?"

"Because I had to. I picked you."

I blink slowly. "Picked me for what?"

"Marriage."

Am I hearing this right?

My lips move to make words but no sounds come out. Finally, I manage a breathless, *"What?"*

"I know," he says with a deep sigh, sticking his hands in his pockets and rocking back on his feet. "It's going to take you a lot of time to come to grips with it. Fuck knows I still am. I mean, this is absolutely surreal to say the least, not to mention ridiculous, unfair and, well, cruel, but it is what it is."

None of what he's saying is making any sense at all. Am I being filmed? Is this a joke? I start looking around for cameras and of course there are a million of them on the palace walls and lampposts for security reasons.

"So your father doesn't know the whole truth," he goes on. "My father left that part out. But the fact is that I need to get married and I'm trying to figure out if it should be you. You were my first pick of the lot."

"First pick of the lot?" I repeat. "Magnus, Your Highness, I'm sorry, but I have no idea what you're talking about. And to be honest, it's starting to scare me a little."

He exhales loudly and runs his hands down his face. "I can't believe these are the words that are coming out of my mouth," he mumbles. He then looks up at me, hair wild, eyes brimming with intensity. "In order for me to inherit the throne and earn back my family's good graces in the public eye, I have to get married. I have to get married soon and to someone who would be a good fit, someone of the right bloodline, someone who would make our crazy fucking family look good. This is the last thing I want, but I'm willing to do it for the sake of the throne, for my father, for the country. And the only way I can do it is if you agree to it."

I stare at him for a few moments until I burst out laughing. "You have got to be kidding me!"

"I've been wanting to make you laugh tonight but not like this," he says quietly. He clears this throat. "I'm not kidding. It's not a joke."

If it's not a joke, then this man is clearly crazy. "I know you're into those high-risk sports but I question if you hit your head one too many times. You're supposed to wear a helmet for a reason."

"Look, I know this is insane—"

"Insane?" I close my eyes, trying to compose my thoughts. "It's beyond insane. This is...ludicrous." Shaking my head, I look at him, trying desperately to see the reasoning in all of this. "You're being forced into marrying someone against your will?"

"I'm not being forced," he says sternly. "I have a choice. I'm choosing to do this."

"What about marrying for love? You don't even know me. You don't even like me."

"I never said I don't like you," he says quickly. "I do. I think you're, uh, you have great eyebrows."

"*Eyebrows!?*"

"And no, I don't know you but perhaps when it comes down to it, we'll be a good match."

I stand up, my skin feeling tight and agitated, my head

swimming as it tries to grapple with this. "Well, since I know the throne is more important to you than love, I'll let you know that when I plan to marry, I plan to do it for love."

His eyes narrow, his gaze so sharp that it makes me feel breathless. "The throne isn't more important than love is. I'm doing this because I love my family, my father." I watch his throat as he swallows hard, taking in a deep breath. "This is what my father wishes for me, and I'm the one who fucked up bigtime. I don't have to tell you what I'm trying to make up for here."

The sex tape, no doubt.

He continues, his tone becoming soft as he looks away, staring off into nothing. "Look, this is just between you and me, but my father isn't doing well, and all this extra stress I've put the family under isn't helping. I'm supposed to make a public apology to the prime minister in a few days, on camera, and that will help but it won't put him at ease. I just don't know what else to do and this seems like the only way out, and the only way I can help him. He deserves this." He pauses. "I need to do this."

I feel a pang of sympathy for him but it in no way changes anything. "I'm sorry that you've found yourself in this hole, and I'm sure you're charming and resourceful enough to climb your way out, but I'm not your answer. Marrying me isn't a rope...unless it's a rope around both our necks."

"That's fucking morbid," he says, giving me an odd look.

I stand up straighter. "I'm not getting married to you, Your Highness. Not for love, not for your debt, not for your country. I will gladly sacrifice myself for things I care about, but I don't care about you. You're a stranger to me and I'm a stranger to you, and there's no way that's going to change.

I'm sorry, but you're going to have to go back to your list and find another woman to take my place."

He nods, chewing on his lip. His hair falls across his face, obscuring his eyes. "All right. I respect that. I didn't think you were cut out for this sort of life anyway. You're too soft and dainty for the public eye."

"Excuse me?" I ask him, feeling a rush of hot blood roll through me. "Soft and dainty?"

He brushes his hair from his eyes as he takes me in. "That's what I said. You've lived a life of anonymity with no one expecting anything of you, it seems. Not even your father. Why would you trade in the life of an average student for one of prestige and power? It makes no sense at all."

Is he trying to do reverse psychology on me?

"I'm not playing this game," I tell him.

"There are no games."

"I highly doubt that with you." I cross my arms. "And please, indulge me for a moment. You would be completely okay with being married to a stranger? You'd be okay with marriage in general? You do know you have a *horrible* reputation amongst women, don't you?"

He glares at me. "I wouldn't call it horrible."

"You're a manwhore, playboy, womanizer." I tick off my fingers. "Wannabe Casanova."

"Wannabe? I think I've fully achieved Casanova status at this point."

"You're proud of it, too. So how on earth do you expect to settle down with someone and marry them? You do know what marriage vows are, don't you?"

"This might be different," he says.

"You mean you would break those vows?"

"Wouldn't you, if you had to?"

I dismiss him with a wave of my hand. "I don't even know why I'm discussing this with you. Of course you'd be okay with a lifetime full of illicit affairs as long as your public image remains pure."

"There are a lot of marriages like that, more than you'd think, and it would be naïve of you to think otherwise."

"Then maybe I am naïve and maybe I'm a bit of a romantic. And maybe I have morals and I take things like marriage seriously, which you obviously don't since you don't seem to take anything seriously. You think this world is your giant playground."

He sucks in a breath as if I've seriously insulted him. The glint in his eyes turns mean. "You don't know me. I take things that matter to me seriously and this matters to me. This is serious. And it would help if you took it seriously too."

I press my hand to my chest. "I *am* taking it seriously. I think this is seriously messed up and that I'm seriously not interested in getting involved in a sham marriage with you."

"That's it?"

"Yeah, that's it." He almost looks hurt and I realize I've been a little harsh with him. It seems like that's the only way to get through to him. "Sorry. I'm sorry you have to be put in this position, and honestly, I do wish you the best of luck and happiness. But after this dinner, I have no plans to ever see you again."

He nods, exhaling through his nose. "Man. I'm starting to feel sorry for every girl I've told that to."

I roll my eyes and start to walk away. Unbelievable.

Just then the French doors open and the Queen steps out, holding up the hem of her dress so she doesn't trod on it, a cell phone in her other hand.

"Princess Isabella," the Queen says in a hush, holding the phone out for me. "It's your father."

"Is everything all right?" I ask, taking the phone from her.

She nods, a strange look in her eyes as she looks from me to Magnus. "He's fine. He wishes to speak to you about our arrangement."

My brows raise and I look back at Magnus in surprise. Arrangement? There is no arrangement.

I put the phone to my ear, completely expecting to hear Schnell's voice. "Hello?"

"Isabella," my father says in his thick German accent. "How are you?"

Oh my god. It's actually my father.

"Father," I say, feeling both breathless and giddy, like just hearing his voice is putting everything right again in my world. "I'm so happy to hear from you." I glance at Magnus and notice him staring at me. I need to tone it down a bit. "Why are you calling?"

"I was just having a discussion with King Anders about you."

"Oh, yes," I say, my voice going higher. "What about?"

I mean, did he call the King? Did the King call my father? Have they always talked on the phone and I just didn't know about it? Who else does my father know on a *calling your cell phone* basis?

"I'm sure you know what about, Isabella," he says to me. "And I must say how thrilled I am at your decision."

Oh god. Oh no.

"What decision?" I ask cautiously.

"To marry Prince Magnus."

My mouth drops open. "I, uh...what did the King say?"

I glance wildly at the Queen hoping for some sort of

clue but she's a hard nut to crack and her face remains impassive except for the quick glances she keeps throwing at Magnus.

"Well, when he first called me yesterday he said that Prince Magnus was interested in getting to know you. I had hopes, of course, as any good father would, that this could lead to something grand and so I made sure you went to Oslo right away. But now that I've been talking to him, he said that you both hit it off and it looks like it will be a royal match. He did just propose right now, didn't he? That's what the King said. He took you out to the garden and popped the question."

I slowly look over at Magnus and I can see that he has absolutely no idea what my father could be saying and he certainly didn't so much as pop the question as to suggest it, like he was deciding what TV show we should watch tonight.

Oh, I could bloody well kill the King of Norway right now.

"Hopefully you said yes," my father says, his voice going lower in that same disapproving way he'd use when I was younger. Every time he thought poorly of me he'd use that voice. *"Oh, you only got a B on your math test? You did study, didn't you?"*

I don't like to use the F-word without warrant but...

FUCK.

Tell him you said no. Tell him there was no proposal. Tell him the King was wrongly informed. Tell him...

"I know your mother would be so proud of you," he says, "just as I am. This is everything we could have wished for you. When I sent you off to England I had hopes that you would meet someone right for you. Had hopes you would aim high and marry someone great, someone worthy in title and stature. And now you are. Now you're living out your mother's dream for you."

Oh fuck. FUCK.

"Plus, I know you benefit as well," he adds. "Now you'll have a position of power. You'll have that voice you've always wanted. You'll have the money and means to make a difference. Isn't that what you told me a few years ago, your plans for after university? I always thought it was very noble and altruistic of you, albeit a futile path. But now, now you can actually make a difference. That must feel good."

Shit. He just keeps talking. I don't think I've ever heard him talk so much, nor have I heard him sound so happy, and so damn...proud of me. Not only that, but he actually has a point. He's appealing to my sacrificial side. The side of me that could actually go through with this in order to get my lifelong dream.

It makes me sick.

Because this is all a lie.

And I have to burst his bubble.

I have to disappoint him and everyone else who is staring at me right now.

"Isabella?" my father asks. "Are you there?"

"Yes," I say softly, then clear my throat as if that will give me resolve. "Yes, I'm here. It's just a lot to process."

"I understand," he says. "Just know that you've made the right choice."

Tell him. Tell him now.

"I'm so proud of you, darling," he adds.

Aaaaaand I'm dying.

Okay. Okay, so maybe I don't have to correct him now. Maybe I'll just correct him later. Like tomorrow. Or in a few days. Let him think that we're getting married and then I'll tell him the truth. I just don't want to spoil the moment.

By pretending to go all in, it feels like the easier way out.

"Thank you," I tell him, my tongue feeling sluggish as I talk. "I should probably get back to the dinner party."

"Of course, dear. I will call you in a couple of days to check up on you."

"Okay." I pause, wondering if I should tell him I love him even though sometimes in the past it's gone unanswered.

"Take care," he says and hangs up, and that answers that.

I stare at the phone in my hand and then slowly pass it over to the Queen, reluctant to meet her probing eyes.

"Well?" she asks. "What did he have to say? Anders was talking to him for quite a bit in the other room, and I never heard what they were discussing."

I think I'm going to faint. I sway a bit on my feet and suddenly Magnus is at my side, his arm going around my waist and holding me up.

"Are you okay?" he asks, peering down at me.

I nod. "I think I had too much champagne and excitement," I manage to say. I try to straighten myself so that my body isn't pressed back against his massive chest. The man is built like a boulder.

The man? You mean your fiancé.

No. No brain, don't you even start.

He leads me back inside and through my weary gaze I see the King looking at me with a sheepish expression on his face, like he's just gotten busted for lying.

Which he has.

Bigtime.

I can't believe he did that!

But more than that, I can't believe I didn't have the

nerve to stand up to my father and tell him the truth. I just made everything a million times worse by lying because I'm eventually going to have to burst his bubble.

I'll have to make him disappointed in me once again.

It's either that or I actually get married to Magnus.

Who actually hasn't proposed, mind you.

I sigh loudly as Jane approaches me, her steps wobbly, champagne in her hand. "Do you want something to drink?" she asks and her eyes go to Magnus standing right behind me, his hand still at my lower back. Suddenly it's all I can focus on. The warmth of his large, flat palm, the strength in the way he presses against me. The fact that he's still here shows concern that I didn't peg him to have.

But as much as I need to talk to Jane and fill her in on what the hell is going on, this is about me and Magnus and he needs to know more than anyone.

"I think I've had too much champagne," I tell her and then glance up at Magnus over my shoulder. "Perhaps Magnus could show me to my room."

His eyes widen ever so slightly but he just nods. "Of course I can." He looks over at his mother. "Where is she sleeping?"

"Take her to the blue room beside Mari's," the Queen says. "Her bag is already there."

I can tell there are a million glances and silent messages being passed between everyone here, and not everyone is thinking the same thing. I'm pretty sure at this point only the King and I know what's going on.

"I am so sorry to bow out of the evening early," I tell them, trying to give them a warm and genuine smile that doesn't at all show the turmoil that's rolling inside of me.

"We are so delighted you were able to come," the Queen says.

"Very much so," the King says delicately.

Mari just nods. "We will see you in the morning."

Jane raises her glass of champagne. "Cheers, Princess."

Magnus guides me out of the parlor room and into the hall.

"Elevators are right over here," he says as we walk along the tile floor. "Your room will be on the third floor. That's pretty much the real 'house' of this whole place."

He presses the button for the elevator and I blurt out, "And if we were to be married, would we be staying here or have a palace of our own?"

He frowns. "You're rather confusing, did anyone ever tell you that?"

"And your family is bloody insane, has anyone ever told you that?"

The elevator doors ding open as if on cue. He gestures with his arm. "After you." Then he steps inside, standing beside me. "And yes, I've been told that. A lot of people blame my mother for being a commoner and introducing her wild blood and ways into the family, but to be honest with you, she's the sane one here."

"I can tell. She's the one who has no idea what's going on and I know once the truth comes out, she's going to be furious with your father."

The elevator doors open. We step out into the hall but don't move.

"What did my father do?" he asks.

I tilt my head, really examining him. Aside from being tall and burly and, well, fidgety, he seems to come by his confusion honestly.

"That's why I wanted to talk to you in private."

"So getting me to escort you to your room wasn't an invitation?"

"Are you kidding me?" I shake my head. "No. Why does everything have to do with sex when it comes to you?"

He shrugs, grins. It's charming and it shouldn't be. "I don't know, I guess I'm just used to it. Bad habits, Your Highness."

"Well, I guess you can chalk me up to being one of your bad habits," I say with a sigh as I look up and down the halls. The palace is opulent, but up here in the residential wing, things are a lot more subdued. No more marble statues, just rustic paintings instead. It's almost homey.

"What does that mean?"

"How about you show me to my room first?"

He squints at me. "I swear you're a different person from the one at the start of dinner. Maybe even two seconds ago."

I choke on a laugh. "No kidding. The person I was at the start of dinner had no bloody idea what the hell she was getting herself into. Now I do."

"Your British slang is very cute."

"Get stuffed."

"There you go again," he says but starts off walking down the hall, gesturing with a nod of his head for me to follow him.

He opens the door to one of the rooms, and I step inside as he flicks the lights on. It's smaller than I thought and maybe a bit drafty, but the bed looks warm, with loads of wool blankets piled on top. My little suitcase is sitting on an ottoman.

I turn around to look at him, feeling more indignant than nervous now.

"So, if you didn't invite me up here for nefarious purposes, what did you invite me here for?" he asks.

I take in a deep breath. I feel like this evening has just

been a series of very deep breaths. "That was my father on the phone."

"Yes, I figured that."

"Your father and he had a long chat while we were out in the garden."

He purses his lips. "Okay..."

"Your father," I continue, "told my father that you were proposing to me."

Magnus stares at me for a second, eyes wide as it very slowly sinks into his thick skull. "But...I wasn't. I mean, I was telling you the deal, the truth and all that, but...oh fucking hell. Do they think...does your father think this is actually a real official thing?"

He's starting to freak out. It makes me feel good for a nanosecond to know that this wasn't what he expected either.

"Yes. Your father said you were proposing and that's why I was invited here, and he said we were a good match. My father automatically assumed I had said yes, because for crying out loud, why would I ever say no to anyone?"

Okay, so that last outburst is more about me than it is about him, but still.

"And you didn't tell him otherwise?"

"This isn't about me, okay?"

He looks out into the hall and then shuts the door behind him so it's just the both of us in this room. "It kind of is. First you shoot me down, repeatedly, like you're playing Duck Hunt and running out of quarters—"

"You're twenty-eight! Why are you referencing things that are old? And anyway, I never shot you down because you never asked me anything."

"I told you the plan."

"Yes, in some round about half-assed way."

"Hey, I was putting my full *ass* into it," he says snidely. "You're forgetting the big picture here, and that is...why the hell didn't you tell him that my father was being premature and talking out of line?"

"You don't know my father," I tell him. "Or our relationship. To say it's strained is putting it mildly, and anyway I didn't exactly want to admit that your father, the King of Norway, is a big fat liar!"

"But now we have to get married!" he cries out.

"This was your idea!"

"This was my parents' idea," he counters, shaking his finger in my face. "And now it's real. Jesus. I'm not ready for this."

"You're insane," I mumble. "And it doesn't matter. I'll tell my father the truth in a few days. I just didn't want to tonight. He sounded so happy and, well, you told me that this was all worth it to make your father happy, right?"

He seems to think that over before he nods with a heavy sigh. "Yeah."

"And it's the same for me. Only I don't have the relationship you have. I don't have one with him at all. And I wasn't about to sever the little contact we just had because of some technicality."

He lets out a dry laugh. "You make it sound like it's wording on a legal document."

"If we're not careful, that's what it's going to be. Only the legal document will be a marriage certificate."

"I need to talk to my father," he says, turning around and opening the door.

"And tell him what?"

He pauses and looks over his shoulder at me. "I don't know. Just that he's put you in a very awkward position."

"And what about you?"

"I'm fine. It's no different than before, I had just hoped or assumed that when I told you the truth about all of this that you would decide to do it based on your own merit and not anyone else's lies. I can have my father call yours in the morning and explain that everything has been a big mistake."

Ugh. That hurts my heart. Not just in terms of my own father being disappointed, but Magnus' too. He actually cares for his father and vice versa. That might be a blow neither can handle at a time like this.

"No," I tell him. "Let me just think about it for a few days and get back to you. Let it go with your father. I just need time to process everything and figure out the right thing to do."

"But isn't the right thing to do to call it off?" he says. "I mean, in your mind."

God, I'm tired. Exhausted to every last brain cell and weary to the bone. And yet there's something blocking me from agreeing to what he's just said.

Maybe it was the promise of respect.

Of power.

Of a voice to make change in ways I'd never dreamed of.

I only nod to Magnus. "What I really need right now is sleep. Perhaps I'll see you in the morning."

His dark brows knit together. "I can't believe you might actually give this a chance."

"I wouldn't hold your breath," I tell him.

He nods. "Goodnight, Princess."

"Goodnight, Your Highness."

He shuts the door, locking me in with my thoughts.

SEVEN

MAGNUS

"Sir, I really don't think you should go out there," Ottar says, pulling back the curtains and peering out my window.

It's not just that the weather has taken a turn for the worse and it's absolutely pouring, dark and dreary, like October has decided to strangle the last breath out of summer.

It's that last night as I was walking back from the pub I was harassed by not only the paparazzi but a few party boys looking to cause trouble with Mad Magnus. It took a lot of restraint not to punch them out, because, believe me, I could have with ease, and it wouldn't have mattered how big they were. But with the paparazzi on my trail and cameras at the ready, I couldn't afford to blow it.

So I just took their insults. Apparently I'm an attention whore, I'm not fit to rule, and I'm the laughing stock of the country. You know, the usual things I've been hearing these days.

I guess it didn't help that earlier in the day a press

conference had been called at the palace. I had to stand, with my parents flanked on either side of me, before a row of photographers and journalists, including those damn Russian twins, and make a public apology to the prime minister, to his daughter, to my family, and to the Norwegian people.

I don't even know how I got through it. It was humiliating to say the very least but I guess that was the point of the whole thing. Plus, I did mean what I was saying. I am beyond sorry that all of this happened, not just because it's brought deep shame to my family, my father especially, but because it's pretty much ruined my life.

Then, after the press conference and the profuse apologies, I had to head over to the prime minister's office and apologize to him in person. Thank god his daughter wasn't there.

Prime Minister Erling Lundström has never liked me. That's been apparent from his glib comments over the years about my reputation, and the way he kind of sneers at me when we're face to face, as if I'm the chewed up gum beneath his shoe.

This meeting was no different and there were many times I wanted to wipe that smug look off his face with a cutting remark or two. But, for the sake of everything and everyone, I managed to bite my tongue and behave. I nearly had tears rolling down my face, and I hope he thought it was because of how sorry I was that I humiliated him, not because I was thinking about having to spend the rest of my life married to a stranger.

Which is another reason why I want to go outside and walk around, to let the rain soak me from head to toe as I stroll from pub to pub, hoping to wash all the bullshit off me and get belligerently drunk. It's been a few days now since Ella and I had apparently gotten engaged and I'm still waiting to hear if this is actually happening or not.

I mean, it's ridiculous, but what isn't these days? After Ella had me escort her to her room and proceeded to tell me what happened, I immediately pulled my father aside. Not to get mad at him, though believe me, I was livid. He had absolutely no right to tell her father that I was proposing to her when he knew I was just talking to her and explaining the situation.

He, of course, thought he was helping, and I didn't have the heart to tell him that he wasn't and that he'd put Ella in a very uncomfortable situation. I did tell him, though, that she still needs to think about it and will give us her answer soon.

But at the moment, it's later rather than sooner. Ella and Lady Jane went back to Edinburgh the next morning and I haven't heard from her since. Not that we exchanged phone numbers or anything, I just assumed she would have contacted my parents in one way or another. Patience isn't my strong suit, and the longer I go not knowing where my future is heading, the more agitated I get.

Hence the need to leave the confines of this apartment and get smashed on whisky and aquavit.

"I think I should go with you," Ottar says quietly, shutting the curtains.

"I'll behave," I tell him. "You know you don't have to follow me."

"I won't be following you," he says. "That's what Einar is for. I'll go *with* you. As your friend. You look like you need someone to talk to."

"Do I?" I ask wryly.

"You've been under a lot of stress lately and we both know that stress can have an adverse affect on you, particularly emotional stress. I mean, you are getting *married* and that's enough to make a normal man piss his pants, let alone you."

I narrow my eyes at him. "There's nothing emotional about any of this," I tell him. Though the fact that he's even mentioned it has made my heart rate start to pace. The smart thing for me to do would be to go for another run through the park like I did early this morning, or at least hit up the treadmill in my private gym, lift some weights until my muscles shake. Sometimes exercise is the only way I'm able to think clearly at all. It's a positive place for all this pent-up energy and frustration to go.

"Are you sure you won't stay in? You have all the booze in the world to get yourself bludgeoned. I think this is just going to cause trouble. I'm not sure if the public quite believes your apology or not."

"Well, that's on them," I tell him, throwing on my coat and a newsboy cap. "I did the best I could and if they choose not to believe me, there's nothing I can do about it."

"Just..." He trails off and sighs. "Be careful, sir."

"I always am," I tell him and step out the door. I pass Einar in the hallway and wave my arm, gesturing for him to follow me. "Come on, Einar, old friend, let's have another night on the town."

"Sir," Einar says but he doesn't follow it up with anything else. Once I get my heart set on something it's hard to talk me out of it.

I head down the tunnel and pop out of a door on a quiet back street, then I walk along until I get to one of my favorite drinking spots, Harold's.

Harold is the owner of Harold's (not just a clever name), and also the bartender and the doorman and everything else in between. He's about seventy years old with a hunchback and a glass eye and tufts of grey hair coming out of his ears that makes it look like he's smuggling a Husky inside his head.

His place is dark, with a fine layer of dust covering the top shelf bottles that he can't reach. It's also about the size of my kitchen with just two booths and five seats at the long, stained copper bar. Tiny wood-framed paintings of whales adorn the green walls, which remind me of Ella. I wonder if she'd like this place, I wonder if she likes going out to bars at all. At first glance she strikes me as too goody two-shoes for that and though she said she drank too much at dinner, she only had two glasses.

I shouldn't be thinking about her though. That's why I've come to the bar to begin with. That and it's one of the safer places for me to go. Sure, I'm not going to meet any single ladies when I'm here, but Harold won't let any paparazzi inside, there's a no camera or cell phone use rule, and I've gotten to know the regulars pretty well.

They don't give a rat's ass about me.

There's Maud, who used to be a film actress in ye olden days whose biggest claim to fame is that she stole Ingrid Bergman's husband after Ingrid dumped him for Roberto Rossellini. She's got lavender hair, always wears red lipstick, and talks about classic actors as if they were best friends and is never shy with giving you drunken thoughts about love.

There's Guillermo, who moved to Oslo from Spain who knows when, and doesn't know a lick of Norwegian. The more he drinks, the more Spanish he speaks, and from what I gather he used to be a monk. I can't tell how old he is or if he's telling the truth, but it doesn't really matter. But he never speaks above a whisper.

Then there's Erik. Tall, skinny, and pale as snow, I call him Slender Man. Doesn't help that he's always wearing the same black suit and his features are decidedly flat, his mannerisms subtle, his voice monotonous. Truth is, Slender Man got laid off a year ago and is going through a terrible divorce, so when he does speak, you can bet it will take the wind out of your sails.

"Prince," Harold greets me as I step inside, the bell ringing above my head. He doesn't call me Prince Magnus, just Prince. Like the singer. Can't say I mind.

Einar follows me in and gets a head nod from Harold. Usually he's stationed outside or he finds a space at the end of the bar where he nurses a cup of instant coffee that Harold whips up for him, pretending he doesn't know me.

Today only Maud and Guillermo are at the bar, sitting side by side.

"Where's Slender Man?" I ask as I sit down next to Maud. Einar takes a spot at a booth, trying to blend in with the wall.

She barely looks at me. "Why do you call him that?" she asks in her hoarse voice, her long, crookedly glued-on nails tapping against her glass. "Slender Man."

"Nothing you'd understand," I tell her. I raise my finger at Harold. "Scotch, please, and keep them coming."

"Won't understand because I'm too old? I'm only too old now. I used to be young."

"Just go back to your drinking, Maud," I tell her as Harold hands me my drink. "I'm afraid Slender Man is too classless for you."

She laughs and starts coughing. Though I've never seen

her smoke I always get the feeling that she started as a baby and quit only yesterday. "Sometimes I have to remind myself of who you are," she says when she recovers.

"I saw the press conference on the news," Harold says, putting on the kettle for Einar's coffee. "I can see why you need a drink."

"Like he ever needs an excuse," Maud says, and Guillermo giggles softly beside her.

"Hey, I come to this bar for your support," I protest, finishing the rest of my scotch, savoring the delicious burn in my throat.

"You come here because we hassle you," Harold says. "That's what every good ruler needs, to be hassled from time to time by the people who care about you."

"That's what my parents are for," I grumble.

"I remember when Ingrid left Petter for Roberto," Maud says, waving her hands around. "What a scandal that was. She was thrown out of Hollywood for that affair. She didn't work in the US for decades. All because she chose the love of Roberto over Petter. Now that was a scandal, but it was a scandal for love. You, Magnus, your scandal only cheapens you."

Ouch. I clear my throat and slide my empty glass toward Harold. "I'm aware of that." I take in a deep breath, knowing this is probably the right time to tell them about my news. "It doesn't matter anyway. I've met a wonderful woman and we're getting married."

They all stop and stare at me. I can even feel Einar's eyes burning into the back of my head, and I have to wonder if he knows exactly what's going on.

But even though things aren't settled with Ella yet, the fact is I'm going to have to get married to someone and I might as well start telling people now if it's going to seem believable at all.

"Married?" Harold repeats. "To the prime minister's daughter?"

"Oh hell no," I tell him, wincing. "Not her. A lovely blue-blooded woman that I think you'd all approve of."

"What's her name?" Maud asks. "Where is she from? Is she Norwegian?"

Shit. It's harder than I thought it would be to be vague about this. I can't exactly say Ella if it doesn't end up being her.

"I can't say too much," I tell her with a wink. "You understand. I shouldn't be talking about it at all with you, but I trust you guys."

"Well, then," Maud says, sounding impressed. "Harold, I think this calls for a toast. On the house, right? Our drunken prince here has fallen in love." She gives me a rarely used smile, showing off a row of fake teeth. "I am so proud of you. You need any advice on marriage and you come to me. I'm an expert."

"Because you've been married four times," Harold says derisively, but he decides to grab a bottle of champagne from the fridge. "Though I do think this is worth making a toast about. Here's our prince, overcoming his adversity by doing something completely adverse."

"Out of flames and into the frying pan," Guillermo whispers in broken English.

I laugh. If only they knew the half of it.

So Harold fixes us all a glass of celebratory champagne, plus the coffee for Einar, and we all say cheers to this sad, sorry state of affairs.

I spend a couple of hours at the bar and manage to behave myself, drinking a little less than I had planned. Just enough to calm my mind and give my brain a break from the constant flurry of thoughts.

I walk back to my apartment with Einar half a block behind me, and I'm almost at the secret entrance when someone steps out of the bushes.

Instinctively I raise my fist, ready to fight, but thankfully the alcohol has slowed my reaction time because it's not a photographer or assailant at all but Heidi Lundström, the prime minister's daughter.

"Sorry!" she cries out softly, throwing her hands out. "I didn't mean to scare you."

"Then you probably shouldn't be leaping out of people's bushes." I glance over my shoulder to see Einar trotting up to me but give him a slight shake of my head to let him know it's okay.

He backs off and I turn my attention back to Heidi. She's not wearing a coat, just jeans and a very low-cut sweater that shows off her ample cleavage. Her face is done up with more makeup than I've ever seen on her, her red hair styled in waves around her face.

She's more hot than pretty and just the right amount of inhibited and crazy in bed. But my instincts have never steered me wrong, and I have a feeling she's just as crazy outside the bedroom. Hence the fact that she seems to have been stalking me.

"What are you doing here?" I ask her, giving her a tight smile before I look around to make sure no one is coming up the street. Wouldn't that be the million-dollar picture.

"I know," she says quickly, taking a step toward me and grabbing my arm. Her breath smells like peach schnapps. "I wasn't sure how else to reach you."

"You used to text me," I remind her, not sure that I like her holding on to me.

"You haven't responded to my texts," she says, a hint of sharpness to her tone.

She's right. She has texted me a lot over the last week and I've seen them and ignored them. I'm not the best at texting people back in general, but I was making sure I wasn't touching Heidi again with a ten-foot pole.

And yet here she is, in the dark of night, hanging on to my arm outside the entrance to my apartment. I hadn't even shown her where I lived—we always went to her place to screw—but somehow she found it.

"I don't think it's wise we text each other," I tell her, taking a step back so that her hand falls away, "let alone see each other."

"But I need to talk to you," she pleads, her face crumpling.

I don't handle crying chicks very well. They're my kryptonite. But I straighten my back and resolve to stay strong, no matter what she does. It was her crying when I broke up with her that led us into this whole mess. "So talk. And make it quick."

She frowns at that. "That was kind of rude."

"Well, you did just ninja jump out of the bushes at me when I was about to go home, *aaaaaaaand* it was your idea to film a sex tape and it was your phone that somehow got hacked into, so yeah, sorry if I seem a bit rude but I've had a hell of a week."

Her eyes get all wide and twitchy. "You think this is my fault? You don't believe me? My phone was *hacked*, Magnus. It wasn't just that sex tape. There were a ton of naked photos of me on there that got shown to the public."

"You have a great body, so what do you care?" I tell her, looking over my shoulder and nodding at Einar. Not for him

108

to do anything, just for him to kind of stand-by in case she becomes a stage-five clinger.

"You really think I have a great body?"

I look back at her, frowning. "What? Yeah. Sure. Look, Heidi, what we had was fun until it really fucking wasn't. Now it's time for us to part ways and never speak again. For real."

"You're such an asshole," she sneers. "I could ruin your life, you know."

I tilt my eyes skyward. "Right. What else could you possibly do?"

"First of all," she says, shoving her finger into my chest. At that I know Einar is making his way over, because it's pretty much against the law for anyone to touch me in a threatening manner. "I didn't do anything. I was hacked. Okay? Second of all, you are an asshole. Everyone knows it. Third of all, you're going to die alone."

I tilt my head at her. "You know, telling the Prince of your country that he's going to die, whether alone or not, can be seen as a threat. If I really was an asshole, I could lock your sorry ass up right now."

"Oh really?" she says, withdrawing her finger and crossing her arms. "I'm sure that will fly when my father runs this country. You're from a monarchy that has no power. Sure, everyone loves you and you get all the prestige and attention and the validation, but my father is the one who runs this place."

Validation? That was an odd choice of words. "Are you done?"

"Yes," she says and then grabs her head, starts tugging at her hair. "No. Magnus. We had something. Don't let what happened ruin that. It's been hard but no one understands me the way you do and no one understands you the way I do." Her arms drop and she steps toward me, her eyes glistening, looking hopeful. "Being in the public eye, being judged. Feeling like people don't see the real you. I get that. I live that. You shouldn't give up so easily."

Oh boy. There's only one way out of this.

"I'm not giving up easily," I tell her, just as Einar joins my side. "I've met someone else."

She blinks at me for a moment before it hits her. I can tell she wants to explode, but Einar tenses up and her eyes go to him and she knows she has to hold it together. She hisses, "You what?"

I nod. "I've met someone else. Fallen in love. She's swept me right off my damn feet."

"You're a liar," she says. "You're a liar and an asshole."

I shrug. "You'll find out soon enough," I tell her. "When we get married and it's all over the news."

Then I step back out of the way while Einar steps between us, his hands out, ready to move her. "You have to go, ma'am," he says gruffly.

"I'm going, I'm going," she says, shuffling backward and turning away from Einar's reach. "Don't touch me. Don't you know who I am?"

Einar just stands there, arms crossed, and I'm more than grateful for his formidable silent type persona right now because it hints at how lethal the man can be. I mean, I've never seen it myself, but my father has told me stories and he certainly plays the part.

At any rate, Heidi takes heed. She turns and walks away, swaying slightly, until she disappears around the corner. I feel a twang of pity for her. I know from the few dates we went on that she's a little lost, neglected by her father, obsessed with notoriety and attention. But my pity doesn't stretch that far. I'm still not convinced it wasn't her that leaked the sex tape to the press.

Satisfied that Heidi won't be returning, Einar turns around and gives me a nod.

"Back in Tromso, we had a name for women like her," he says gravely. "A barnacle."

I laugh and slap Einar on the back. "If you say she's a barnacle, she's a barnacle."

"What would you call her?" he asks.

I think for a moment. "Psycho hose beast."

"I'm afraid I haven't heard of that one," he says. "But I must say it fits."

～

THE NEXT MORNING I'M WOKEN UP WITH A CALL FROM my mother.

"She's coming today. I need you here in thirty minutes," she says.

I rub the heel of my palm between my eyes and groan. "What are you talking about? Who? What time is it?"

"The time? It's time for you to grow up," she says sharply. "Why on earth are you sleeping until ten o'clock? Half the morning is gone already."

I sigh and roll over, trying to wake up. I don't think I slept very well. Running into Heidi right before I went to bed was bad timing.

"Who is coming?" I repeat.

"Princess Isabella of Liechtenstein."

"Okay, first of all you don't have to say her full name every time. And second of all...what?"

My mother gives an overblown sigh I can practically

feel whistle through my ear. "She's coming over. She and her lady."

"To Norway? So she said yes?"

My heart is already racing. The fear is real.

"Not exactly," she says after a pause. "She said she has a lot to discuss with us. Negotiations. It's to be expected, I suppose. I'm not sure you made the best impression on her so you better not screw it up this time. If you don't win her over, I don't think she's coming back."

My mother is right. I know I didn't leave a good impression on Ella and I don't know why I was so surprised that she didn't want anything to do with marrying me when she normally would never give me the time of day.

But winning her over sounds like a rather tall order.

Doesn't mean I won't try.

"Okay," I tell her, swinging my legs out of bed. "I'll come right over."

"Oh, and Magnus. Do shave. And do something with your hair. This isn't the medieval ages and you're not a Viking."

I grumble something and hang up. I'm not sure if this outing calls for a suit again but because I'm expected to make a better second impression, I pull out a black suit anyway, no tie (lest my mother be outraged). But I don't touch my hair. I run an electric razor over my beard and raze it down to stubble, but I refuse to be clean shaven.

That will have to do.

Soon, Einar is pulling in through the palace gates and Ottar is trying to rein in his curiosity. I told him he should come since negotiations sometime involve paperwork, and paperwork is my nemesis. I think he's just overjoyed to be involved in this thing anyway he can be.

Ella won't arrive for another hour, or so my mother says, so that gives us time to gather in the sitting room and fret.

Actually, I'm not the one fretting. My father is upstairs taking a nap, though I'm assured he'll be down later. Mari is at school, so it's just my mother, Tor, and her lawyer, Sigurd, and of course me and Ottar.

My mother is pacing back and forth, dressed to the nines in a bright fuchsia silk pantsuit, and I can see where I at least get some of my fidgeting tendencies from.

"Princess Isabella might try to play hardball with us," she says.

"I would assume so," I tell her, watching her go back and forth. "There isn't much for her to gain here."

She stops pacing and faces me, shock pulling back her face. "Are you serious, Magnus? Nothing to gain? She would become a princess and eventually a queen. The queen. She'll take my place."

"She's already a princess," I remind her.

"But she'll never be a queen of her country, even if she didn't have her brothers. That's not how it works in their country. No woman will ever inherit the throne. It's their law. Isabella will never be able to move past her title, and it's one without many privileges."

"I really don't think she has any interest in being queen."

"How would you know? You barely spoke to her."

"Well, according to father, I spoke to her long enough to propose to her. You know, I wasn't going to say this to him because he's under enough stress as it is, but he really fucked things up there."

"You watch your mouth," my mother says, shaking a finger in my face, her eyes sharp as daggers. "For heaven's sake. And by the way, you're the one who fucked up."

Sigurd inhales sharply and my mother spears him with her gaze. "What? It's my house. I'm allowed to swear. I'm the goddamn queen!"

"Look," I say slowly, trying to prevent her from having an aneurysm. "My point is, it put Ella in a tough spot. She had to lie to her father."

"That's on her," my mother says dismissively. "If she wasn't open to the idea at all, she wouldn't have lied and she wouldn't be arriving here at any moment to discuss this."

"She might be. She strikes me as a person with honor and morals, and maybe she thinks flying here and letting us down face-to-face is the right way to do things," I tell her. "And that whole moral thing is also why I think she won't go for it. Hey, I'm stuck. This is my bed and it's full of shit and I'm lying in it. But I'm pretty sure she's the type who imagined when she one day got married it would be to someone she loved."

"She could learn to love you," my mother says softly, almost embarrassed.

I'm certainly embarrassed. I wince. "I doubt that. But my point stands. She has no reason to say yes, not that I know of."

"Well, you don't know her at all. None of us do." She gestures around the room. She then sits down on the couch and has a sip of her coffee which is probably cold by now. She sits back and studies me. "And say she says no. Then what? Are you going to be disappointed?"

I lift one shoulder in a half-hearted shrug.

I hate to say it, but in a way I think I would be. Because if it's not her it will be someone else and I think I rather like Ella. At least I'm still intrigued by her, not to mention attracted to her. There's something about her demeanor, the way she looks so classy and quiet, but I've seen the fire inside her already and I'd love to see what she looks like, completely disheveled with that fire unleashed.

Who knows if I'll even have the chance.

And if I did, who knows if she would let me.

"Your Majesty." My father's butler appears at the door. "She's here."

My mother gets to her feet and looks at me.

Show time.

EIGHT

ELLA

THIS IS A HUGE MISTAKE.

I knew the moment I booked the ticket.

The moment I stepped on the plane.

The moment I arrived at the airport in Oslo and got into the hired car.

The moment that car pulled up to the palace gates.

A big, big mistake.

I've spent the last few days going over the scenario in my head, trying to understand my situation the best that I can. I've missed all my classes, calling in sick, because I can't concentrate on anything else. I've made countless pros and cons lists, I've had debates with Jane, I've even tried meditation to find the right answer, as if the universe will enlighten me with one.

And I've honestly come up with nothing.

Which is so ridiculous considering what's at stake here. I shouldn't even be entertaining this idea. The moment that Magnus told me the real reason behind everything, I should have just left. I mean, I tried to. But then my father called and he sounded so damn proud of me and happy and it's like for one wonderful moment, for one lie, I had everything I ever craved right in my hands.

His love.

His acceptance.

I caved. I should have told him the truth, but not only did I not want to disappoint him, I didn't want to erase what I had fought so long to have.

And now I'm stuck. Between a rock and a hard place known as Magnus's muscles.

But I don't want to marry Magnus.

I don't want to marry anyone right now.

I certainly don't want to move to Norway and give up my studies, everything I've thrown myself into and worked so hard for over the years.

Is the risk of disappointing my father really worth giving up my freedom, my life, my future?

I still don't know.

I should know but I don't.

What I do know is that I don't trust myself to make any permanent decisions right now and the fact that I even want to talk it over with them all is a bad idea. If I had a backbone at all I would have told them no over the phone and been done with it.

And then what would you have done? I think. *Then you'd go back to your classes, tagging along after your roommates, eating dinner with only Jane for company, struggling for the world to take you seriously, floundering after university with no support, no voice. No father to tell you he's proud of you. Just a lifetime of being stuck in a life you don't really want.*

But isn't that what marrying Magnus would be like?

I look over at Jane as the car parks beneath the palace, my nerves on fire, my heart jittery and jumping all over the place like I'd injected it with caffeine concentrate. Or maybe it was the several cups of tea I had on the plane.

"What am I doing?" I ask, my eyes wide in panic as I watch the butler approaching the car. "I can't do this."

Jane rolls her eyes with an exaggerated sigh. "Will you stop overthinking this? You've had a million times to say no and call it off and you haven't yet. Instead, you've spent the last few days thinking about it. That means you need to be here, even if just to hear what else they have to say."

"But this is ridiculous," I say frantically, my palms growing sweaty. "I should just get the driver to turn around and take us back to the airport. I shouldn't even be entertaining this. I don't—"

The car door opens and the butler says, "Your Serene Highness."

Which makes me wince. Technically that is the way you're supposed to address me but I haven't heard it since I was a young girl and even then it sounded too formal.

I stare at the butler's outstretched hand, and in that moment I know that if I grab it, if I let him help me out of the car, if I step foot in that palace, I'm committing myself even further, making it harder to back out.

But I do it. I reach out for his hand and he helps me out, Jane right behind me.

The palace looks different in the morning and I'm aware now that it's in the middle of the city. I can hear cars, people walking past outside the gates. They blocked off the area so that you can't actually see the courtyard, and from the paparazzi I spied as we drove in, I know it's for good reason.

"Your Majesty is expecting you," he says, and leads me toward the main doors. We don't have any luggage with us this time. In fact, regardless of what happens, Jane and I are booked back on a flight to Edinburgh later that evening. I don't want to make the mistake of staying over again, especially if I end up saying no. That would be rather awkward.

This time the butler takes us directly to another room instead of the Bird Room where we had to wait last time. I guess all the formalities are gone now.

The room we're led into is just as opulent as the others, with hanging chandeliers, floor-to-ceiling curtains, and teak and velvet furniture done up in shades of cream and baby blue.

Standing around the biggest coffee table I've ever seen in the middle of the room, are Queen Else, Magnus, and two other people I don't recognize: a short man with a round baby face and a bald, thin man in glasses who holds a stack of papers and folders in his hands.

I'm not sure the proper protocol to enter a room that they already occupy so I immediately bow and curtsey with Jane doing the same.

"Your Majesty," I say, artfully looking down at the pale grey carpet. "Your Royal Highness."

"Please," the Queen says. "You can call me Else. Or Madam. I'd rather things not be so formal between us." I gradually lift my gaze to meet hers. She's smiling warmly.

She's talking as if I've already told them yes. That's not a good sign. I need to take back some control without making them feel slighted. "Thank you so much for having me here on such short notice, madam," I say to her. "This is the type of thing I believe would be better discussed in person."

It hits me all at once at what I'm doing—standing before the Norwegian royal family and telling them what's going on, telling them where I stand, being the one who is dictating the situation. Never in a million years did I think I would ever have the confidence to do this. I'm still in shock.

I push that realization out of my mind. If I think about it anymore I'll be running for the hills.

"And we appreciate that," she says, exchanging a quick glance with Magnus. "Please, sit down."

I sit down on the couch, Jane beside me, and as the butler pours everyone coffee—which I decline—my eyes go to Magnus. I've been trying not to look at him in case he influences me one way or the other.

But the fact is, he is influencing me. And he should. This is the man I'm considering marrying. This is the person I may have to spend the rest of my life with. I don't know him at all, except what seems to be all his bad qualities, and based on our meeting the other night, I can't say that we get along even slightly.

His gaze is as intense as ever, those dark eyes of his seeming to hold me in my place as I sit before him. It feels like he's looking for answers from me this time, rather than the way he looked last time—like he was looking for his own answers inside me.

Do I take this man to be my lawfully married husband? It doesn't matter that he's built like a Viking, that he's gorgeous in his own rugged way and oozes alpha testosterone, or that he's a prince who will one day be the king. None of that matters when I don't know the guy. And if I don't know Magnus like I should, then I have absolutely no idea what I'm getting into and I'm not sure anything—even losing my father's acceptance—is worth that.

I had originally come here not really knowing what my answer would be, but I do have my own list of negotiations that I'd tapped out in the notes section of my phone, just in case it came down to it.

I wrote down that I wanted an easy out before the wedding, and I wanted an easy out after, if I was at all publically humiliated by Magnus in any way.

I wrote that I wanted to continue my studies in Oslo.

I wanted my own non-profit organization off the bat with built-in media interest and the brightest minds working for me.

I wanted a house or palace of my choosing.

I wanted a rich personal life away from the prying eyes of the media.

And I wanted a dog (I've always wanted a dog).

I considered adding a clause in there that roughly said that I was under no obligation to have children or to have a sexual relationship with Magnus, but I decided that would probably be something to discuss privately since no one wants their wife-to-be admitting to their family that she would never touch him with a ten-foot pole.

Hmmm. In his case, make it twenty.

But now that I'm looking at this man, this stranger, I realize that the negotiations are worthless.

There's only one reasonable, sane, and smart thing to do here.

"I want two weeks," I tell them.

Everyone stares at me in surprise and Jane nudges me questionably in the side. I ignore her.

"I'm afraid I don't understand," the Queen says. "Two weeks of what?"

"I have a list of negotiations here," I tell them, awkwardly fishing out my phone and pointing at it. "Things that must be agreed upon before I even consider this. I assume there will be a contract between us before the actual marriage? Something that will make sure that none of us talk about the truth, that this is an arranged marriage?"

The Queen looks over at the bald man who nods. "Yes, of course," he says, and I'm guessing he's the lawyer. "Everything will be airtight."

"Good," I continue, trying to hide the shakiness in my voice. It's like I'm possessed and someone else is talking for me. Maybe Ella of the future, if you want to get all metaphysical. Perhaps I've been meditating too much. I clear my throat. "Then I would like my list of demands added to the contract. But only after two weeks, if I agree to it."

"And what's happening during these two weeks?" Magnus asks.

I meet his eyes again and smile tightly. "It's a trial period. To figure out if we can stand to be around each other." I quickly give his mother an apologetic look. "You've raised a good son and I'm sure he's a good man. But I have to know this for myself. With all due respect, having good looks and blue blood isn't enough for me. We have to be compatible, even in the most basic way, before I'll consider it."

"Look, *Princess*," Magnus says, and it doesn't escape me that every time he calls me princess, he does it in a slightly mocking way. "This goes both ways. In two weeks I might decide I'd rather be chained to the Princess of Belgium instead."

"Magnus," the Queen says sharply, giving him a glare that would melt the strongest steel. "These comments are exactly the reason why she's asking for this." She sighs, closing her eyes briefly and then looks to me with an apologetic tilt of her head. "This makes sense to me and I completely understand. It took the King years to win me over and convince me to become queen. We can afford you two weeks to do the same."

"Thank you," I tell her, breathing out a sigh of relief.

"But," she goes on, exchanging a look with her lawyer, "after those two weeks are up, we will need an answer. And once you give that answer and the documents are signed, things will need to happen very, very fast. We're looking at a winter wedding, around Christmas."

Jeez, that is fast. It's the start of October. If I give my answer in the middle of the month, we'll have just a month to get everything planned. I want to ask why the urgency—surely saving face doesn't have an expiration date, especially after I saw the public apology Magnus made the other day—but I bite my tongue and save my curiosity for later.

After all, I'll have two weeks to get all the answers I need.

~

I DIDN'T HANG AROUND FOR LONG AFTER THE MEETING. We all shook hands—I swore Magnus was trying to break mine in two so I tried to match his grip, which then led to us holding hands for longer than I wanted to—and then Jane and I headed into Oslo to grab some lunch and shopping before getting on the plane back.

The Queen invited us to stay longer, saying her husband, who was noticeably absent from the meeting, would love to say hello, but I figured it was just better to get out while I could. There's a lot I have to do.

And yet here I am, standing in the middle of my dorm room, taking far too long to figure out what to pack. My room looks like it's been ransacked with clothes and bras and books.

At least I have some idea what to expect. Over the next two weeks, Magnus and I are supposed to move into one of the royal estates located in the Asker region which isn't too far outside of Oslo. It's a pastoral area and the estate has a lot of land, so it will be a completely private setting.

Also, I'm not to leave the estate at all just in case the paparazzi get wind of me, but at this point I don't mind. It's just two weeks. At the very least I can pretend to be Jane Eyre and the estate can be my Thornfield Hall.

Anyway, originally they suggested I move into Magnus's two-bedroom apartment downtown but I quickly vetoed that idea. I want to get to know him better but I still need my own space, and being confined to an apartment with him is a recipe for disaster.

And I still need Jane. I'm not doing this on my own. I'm going to be completely out of my element and need as much moral support as I can get.

"So why do you get to take two weeks off again?" a voice asks from my doorway and I look up, bras and undies in my hands, to see one of my flatmates, Michelle, staring at me with a dry expression on her face.

"I have some, um, business to attend to back home," I tell her, feeling my face grow hot from the lie. When I approached the school and told them that I needed two weeks away from my classes, I couldn't very well tell them that I was figuring out if I wanted to marry the Prince of Norway or not. But they let me take the time off, regardless, probably because of my upbringing. When I was at boarding school, it was the same kind of thing.

"Must be nice," she says with a tight smile. "Well, have a nice time, Ella. Sorry. I mean, *Princess*." She walks off down the hall to the kitchen.

I sigh. She says it the same way Magnus does, but with less warmth. Whatever progress I'd made with them before the wine and cheese night has now been erased. It's like I've gone backward, no longer someone they tolerate tagging along, but someone they don't want anything to do with. If (when) I come back from these two weeks, I know I'm going to have a very lonely year ahead of me.

In the end, I throw pretty much everything I own into a giant suitcase, check with Jane to make sure she's packed too, and then try and get some sleep. Our flight to Oslo is fairly early. When I said I needed two weeks, I didn't know that the clock would start ticking so soon.

But I barely sleep.

I toss and turn.

When I do fall asleep, I have dreams.

Those same dreams again about the whales beached on the pebbled shoreline, cold wind in my hair, oil filling up the ocean.

And just like last time there is a man walking toward me. I can't see his face—it's too hazy, too blurry—but he's in a suit.

His arm stretches out for mine.

And just before the haze around his face seems to clear, when I can grasp his features, the oil slides up over my mouth, my eyes, and everything is black again.

I am alone.

That loneliness clings to me when I wake up, my throat dry, my head feeling like it's stuffed with soggy cotton balls. It doesn't help that the weather in Scotland has taken a turn for the worse again and when I learn on the plane that it's sunny in Oslo, I feel a twinge of excitement for the first time. If anything, maybe the next two weeks will be a nice break from my normal life.

That's why I'm doing this, isn't it? A chance to be someone else, to be *someone* in general, just for a while?

"That's the spirit," Jane says beside me as the plane

descends over sown fields and raging rivers, doing a wide arc toward the runway.

"What?" I ask. As far as I know, I've been keeping everything inside my head. Where it belongs.

She studies me for a moment and then shrugs. "Oh, nothing. You just looked hopeful for one moment. Must have been the light in your eyes."

I ignore that.

It's not long before we get our bags and step into the limo that the family has sent for us. The drive to Thornfield Hall (officially known as Skaugum Palace, but it's Thornfield to me now) is about an hour, along wooded mountains and rolling countryside, the leaves in the trees now red and gold. While the sun is warm, there's a distinct chill when you're in the shade.

After we drive down a narrow road, passing fields full of horses and a large red school with children playing outside, the driver guides the limo between a pair of gates that it barely fits through. The Royal Guards nod at us from their station house and we continue on our way down a tiny, bumpy road covered by fallen leaves from the trees above.

Then the trees diminish.

I'm not sure what I was expecting at all but I don't think this was it. It's actually a lot more like the Thornfield I had imagined in my head while reading Jane Eyre, rather than an opulent palace fit for royals.

It's an L-shaped white building, two stories high, with some groomed grounds and landscaping around it, set up on a hill at the base of a bigger mountain. Simple and classy, but other than the vast view over the farmlands below, it's nothing to write home about.

"It's quaint," Jane says in a chipper voice in case the

limo driver will report her. Then she leans into me. "It's definitely no Vaduz Castle."

Vaduz is where I grew up and where my father still resides in Liechtenstein. It's a legitimate castle with turrets and the works, built into the side of a cliff in the eleventh century.

"Definitely not," I tell her. But actually, even though the idea of being in Magnus's apartment put me off, the thought of being in a big, cold palace wasn't too inviting either. This place seems right in between, the Goldilocks effect.

But there are no bears in this fairy tale. Instead, it feels like I'm about to step into the den of the very big, very bad wolf.

NINE

MAGNUS

Growing up, I spent a lot of summers at this estate. It was paradise, a respite from the restrictions of school, the forced learning, the structure. Here I was finally free, surrounded by fresh air and summer sun, and I had nothing to do all day except precisely what I wanted.

Which, when I wasn't terrorizing my sisters, included a lot of sports. If I wasn't beating Cristina's ass at tennis matches, I was playing soccer or rugby against various butlers and guards. The only thing I didn't do here was horseback riding—I left that to my sisters. I don't get along with horses.

This morning, I'm on a long run through the woods and up the mountain right behind the house. I know Ella and Jane are expected at any minute and then the two-week countdown begins, but the amount of nervous energy I have coursing through me has to go somewhere.

So I run several laps around the small lake nearby until sweat is pouring off of me and my heart feels like it might burst through my chest, and finally, finally my thoughts cease. I'm no longer worried about anything—having to live with Ella for two weeks, not knowing what's going to happen after—none of that matters. My mind is blissfully blank.

By the time I get back to the house, my damp shirt is off and bunched up in my hands, my skin slick, my hair sticking to my forehead.

I see a limo parked in the driveway.

They're here.

And so it begins.

I run up the front stairs and through the main doors and hear voices coming from the parlor room.

Ella and Jane are talking to Ottar about the crown moldings or something and I can only guess he's pretending to know what he's talking about.

"Sir, you're back," Ottar says, then frowns. "And you've lost your shirt."

I hold up the shirt. "Didn't lose it. It's right here."

Look, I know what I'm doing. I know I've worked my ass off for this body and I'm not afraid to use it. It's at least working on Lady Jane, who is staring at my abs and chest in a very unladylike way.

Ella, however, immediately averts her eyes the moment she takes one shocked look at me. But I'm not blind. Her cheeks are going pink. She likes what she sees even if she wouldn't be caught dead admitting it.

I can work with that. For the next two weeks, I can definitely work with that.

"Do you run?" Lady Jane asks, finally tearing her eyes away from my body and up to my eyes. "Like, as exercise?"

I nod. "There are a lot of trails around here. Hiking trails too, right to the top of the mountain. You should go at some point."

Jane laughs, a kind of belly laugh that shakes the whole

room. "Please. My idea of exercise is a good brisk sit. Preferably with a hydrating beverage in hand. Chardonnay is best."

"Chardonnay isn't very hydrating," Ottar comments, which I'm pretty sure causes everyone to roll their eyes. He can be quite the literal one.

"She's joking, Samwise," I tell him. "So, how was your flight?" I ask her, making small talk now. As Jane chatters away about the plane, I walk further into the room, purposely passing close to Ella as I grab an apple from the fruit bowl that the help must have laid out for us. I stand right behind Ella, staring down at her delicate neck.

Her hair is up in a messy bun, but there are a few loose strands with a bit of curl to them, which makes me wonder if her hair is naturally curly or not. The nape of her neck is pale and there's a tiny freckle just behind her ear.

I wonder what it's like to kiss her there. If I'll ever get a chance.

The thoughts are fleeting but they're there. Usually I don't have to work so hard to wear a woman down, but this is a whole new ballgame, and at this point I can't expect anything.

What I do know is that the next two weeks will become a lot more interesting if I make it my goal to get under her skin. Whether she likes it or not, I think provoking her might be my next adrenaline sport. She wants to see if we're compatible? I'll show her we're combatable.

She can tell I'm staring at her too, from the way she adjusts herself in her seat like she's uncomfortable. She's not listening to Jane at all. Her focus is entirely on me, whether she wants it to be or not.

Finally, Ella whips her head around to glance up at me

with a dirty look, and I smile and open my mouth to take a smooth chomp out of the apple.

Only to realize it's fake.

Wax.

Oh god.

I keep the smile plastered on my face, frozen mid-bite, until she turns back around. Then I spit the apple out.

I glance up to see Ottar staring at me with his brows furrowed, having seen the whole thing.

"Sir?" he asks with concern.

I ignore him. "So," I say to everyone, clearing my throat. "Now that everyone is here, I guess we should go over the rules."

"What rules?" Jane asks suspiciously.

"The rules," Ottar says.

"Ottar is a *huge* fan of rules," I point out. "I like to break them but I do think some of them have merit. The big one, of course, is that Ella, you're not allowed to leave the estate at any point. I'm still public enemy number one and on the paps radar and there are Russian twins who are crazy enough to set up camp outside the main gates. We're just lucky that word hasn't traveled yet that I'm staying here, but it will."

"It's like being trapped on the moors," she says quietly.

"If it makes you feel any better, then yes. Just pretend I'm Heathcliff."

"Like you've even read *Wuthering Heights*."

"Hey," I tell her, gesturing to my muscles. "Just because I look like this doesn't mean I'm stupid."

Ottar stifles a laugh and I give him a look to shut his face.

Ella twists in her seat to face me. "Okay. So have you read *Wuthering Heights*?"

"Well, no."

"Any books at all?" She looks so fucking smug, like she knows I'm going to admit that I don't read.

I automatically narrow my eyes at her. "I'll have you know that I'm a huge fan of audiobooks." When I can find the time and the patience to listen to them, of course. Somehow I found the time to listen to *The Lord of the Rings* numerous times but I'm not sure admitting that I love Tolkien will impress her enough. She seems like the type who would only be impressed by someone who has been dead longer than he has.

"Back to the rules," Ottar says. "Can we have a no quarrelling rule in there because it's making things awkward for the rest of us."

"Speaking of the rest of you," I tell them, "both you and Lady Jane have your own quarters in the servants' house next door. For the sake of Ella and I getting to know each other, there should be a rule that you aren't to pop by here after eleven at night."

"That's ridiculous," Ella says, getting to her feet. "You make it sound like there will be something going on here for them to interrupt."

I give her a quick smile. "Well, don't count that out."

"Sir," Ottar says to me, this time in Norwegian, "I don't say this to be a cockblocker, but I think it would be best that her lady-in-waiting be able to stay here for the princess' piece of mind."

"You're always trying to be a cockblocker, Ottar," I tell him, also in Norwegian.

"Wait a minute," Ella speaks up. "What are you both talking about?"

"Nothing," I say quickly in English.

"That should be a rule too," she says. "English only. No

Norwegian. I don't want to hear your secret language and you can bet I'm going to be Googling what *kuk* means."

"You won't be surprised," I tell her dryly. "Okay, fine. No Norwegian. We wouldn't want *you* to feel stupid."

She shakes her head slightly and sighs. "Anything else with these rules or is that it?"

"Not really. I'm sure you'll get used to see the royal guards walking about. My personal bodyguard is Einar, so you'll probably see him a lot. I don't know where he is right now. Probably hiding where no one can see him."

"I'm right here," Einar says from behind me, making me jump.

"Jesus," I yelp, seeing him sitting in an armchair in the corner of the room. "How long have you been there?"

He doesn't say anything. Also he's wearing those damn sunglasses inside.

I shake my head at him and then face Ella. "So that's Einar."

He nods at her.

"There are also a few cooks and cleaners," Ottar tells her. "But they'll mostly be staying in the other house."

I clap my hands together. "So there we have it. That's how the next two weeks are going to go. I can't promise that we'll be friends by the end of it, let alone engaged, but I can promise you that you're about to get really, really bored."

Ella and Jane exchange a look. "And where do I sleep?" Ella asks. "It's not going to be with you."

"I wasn't offering," I tell her. "And you can sleep in any of the bedrooms upstairs. Maybe avoid the ones that are haunted."

"Haunted?" she asks, eyes wide. "Which ones are haunted?"

I shrug. "I can't remember. You'll find out soon, I'm

sure. Okay, I'm off to take a shower." I walk past the fruit bowl and toss the half-bitten wax apple back into it before heading upstairs. "Don't eat the fruit. It's fake."

～

To say that my first day with Ella is awkward as fuck is an understatement. She does her best to avoid me, spending her time with Jane by her side, and even when we pass each other in the halls, she barely looks at me.

Which makes me wonder why bother going through with this two-week plan at all if she's not going to make the effort? Why didn't she just say she wasn't interested when she had the chance? No one would have held her accountable to anything, except for her father, and that's her business, not mine.

I keep thinking this as we have dinner together. I was planning on it being just us two originally, but when she was insistent that Lady Jane eat with us, I insisted that Ottar and Einar join us too. The more the merrier, the more to take the pressure off both of us.

She didn't say much during the meal, which meant most of the conversation was dominated by Jane and Ottar, who seemed to get along like long lost relatives. I know I have a tendency to float away and become locked in my head and couldn't help wondering if Ella was doing the same. She just picked at her food, lost in her thoughts.

It could be that Ella is shy for the most part. I've seen her be bold, especially with me. But this has taken her out of her element. She's no longer in university, living on campus. She's no longer a student. Instead she's here, at this isolated estate in a foreign country, where she's to remain for the next two weeks as she decides whether she wants to marry me or not.

I mean. Fuck.

I actually feel sorry for her. I certainly feel sorry for myself for being in the same stupid situation, but at least this is my home and it's my life that she's come into. She's got Jane here and that's it.

Though it makes me wonder if it's the same thing back in Scotland. Is she the life of the party? Does she have a large group of friends? Is she involved in sports teams or does she tutor other students or was she seeing someone before all of this shit blew up? Does she moonlight as an exotic dancer with the name Pantyless Princess?

I know nothing about her.

And if I don't do something about this, I'll still know nothing about her by the time she leaves.

And as much as my ego hates being taken down a notch or two, I have to man up here and provoke her a little more than I had intended.

Once dinner is over, she immediately retires to her room while I try to place a call to my friend Viktor, the Crown Prince of Sweden. I haven't told him yet about the developments in my life and I could honestly use a friend and some advice from someone outside of this royal family, and Ottar doesn't count. He's under my father's payroll, after all.

But with Viktor not answering (not that I blame him, he's been busy with his own fiancé), I start roaming the halls like a ghost. Too much restless energy than I know what to do with.

Finally, I go to her room and rap on the door. Naturally she's chosen the room at the opposite end of the hall from my bedroom, as far away as possible.

"Who is it?" I hear her ask through the door.

"Prince Fucking Charming," I tell her.

I hear a muffled laugh, probably Jane, and a few long seconds tick by before the door opens.

Ella stands there looking unimpressed, dressed as she was before in black leggings and a pale blue sweater that falls off one shoulder. Her blonde hair has been braided to one side, her face bare of any makeup. She looks astonishingly pretty.

Except for the fact that she's glaring at me. "What do you want?"

I raise my brow and stare at her expectantly.

She sighs. "What do you want...Your Highness?"

I smile. "That's better. And actually, I was hoping to steal you away from your Lady over there so I can talk to you in private."

"What about?"

I squint at her and then look over her shoulder at Jane who is sitting on an ottoman at the foot of the bed. "Is she always this grouchy in the evening? I would have thought giving her food would have helped."

"Clearly you've never owned a mogwai before, sir," Jane deadpans.

Ella looks back at her. "What did you just call me?"

"Listen, Gizmo," I tell her, pushing the door open further, "we have two weeks to get to know each other and I'm not sure if you're here just to get a free trip to Norway or what, but at any rate, we need to talk." I pause. "I have a game I'd like to play."

"What kind of game?" She looks both scared and curious.

Good.

"You'll see." I nod at Jane. "Sorry to interrupt."

"Please," Jane says with a dismissive wave. It's only then

that I notice she has curlers in her hair. "We were talking about rubbish which is what we usually do. Please take Ella and don't bring her back for a long time."

"Jane," Ella chides her, but I reach out and grab her arm.

"Come on. I won't bite," I tell her, pulling her gently toward the door.

"Unless I want you to, right?" she asks wryly but still lets me drag her out into the hall, the door shutting behind her.

"I didn't say it," I tell her. I don't let go of her arm either; instead, I slip my hand down until I'm holding hers.

"What are you doing?" she asks, trying to wrestle her hand out of mine.

"Holding your hand," I tell her. "I'm dastardly like that."

"More like bastardly," she mumbles under breath.

"That's the spirit," I goad her. "A few more back and forths like that and it'll be like we can hold an actual conversation."

She doesn't say anything after that. Still holding her hand in mine, I take her down the stairs and into the parlor, sitting her down in a giant leather wingback chair beside the fireplace.

"What are you having to drink?" I ask her, heading for the little bar cart I had Ottar help set up earlier. There may be fake fruit in the bowls but the booze is very real.

"I'm okay," she says.

"Scotch then," I tell her, filling her up a highball glass.

She sighs as I bring it over to her and reluctantly takes it from me. "Thank you," she says quietly, and I know that's just an automatic reaction from her upbringing.

"No problem." I get my own glass and sit down across

from her in another chair. The fire is roaring—courtesy of Ottar again—and everything looks downright cozy in here.

Ella sits in her chair primly, her ankles crossed, taking delicate sips of her drink. A bird would drink it faster.

She stares at the fire rather than at me, which gives me the freedom to stare at her. Her profile is rather cute, her nose turning up just slightly at the end. With the way the flames are lighting up her face and her hair, she's positively angelic.

My eyes drift to her bare shoulder where I don't catch sight of a bra strap. The skin of her palm felt soft and smooth, and I can only wonder what the skin on her shoulder feels like. Silk, probably.

I haven't seen Ella expose much skin. At dinner with my family, her gown practically covered her all up except her lower arms. When she came to negotiate, she was wearing black pants and a white turtleneck. Today's glimpse of her shoulder is probably the most I've seen of her skin.

I know women think that wearing a revealing outfit is sexy, and while I have no objections to seeing a lot of leg, a lot of tits, or a lot of ass, there's something equally as sensual as only showcasing one spot of skin.

I'm starting to fixate on it, hyper-focus.

"Did anyone ever tell you that you have quite the intense stare?" Ella says, still not looking at me.

I tear my eyes away from her shoulder and take a gulp of my drink. "I've heard it a few times. Nothing I can do about it. I feel things intensely most of the time."

I can tell she wants to roll her eyes. "So what is this game you speak of? Please tell me it's not a drinking game because I'm not interested."

I let out a chuckle. "You're in what, third year of university, living in a dorm, in Scotland of all places, the only other place I know that can match Norwegians for their drinking prowess, and you aren't interested in drinking games? Please tell me you have a fun bone in your body."

Now I have her attention. She snaps her eyes onto me and I can't help but smile at the sparks flying out of them, which probably only angers her more.

"Just because I'm not out boozing and cruising with everyone else at school doesn't mean I'm not fun. I'm fun."

"Okay, so tell me your idea of fun."

"Oh no," she says, shaking her head. "Not with you. Your idea of fun is jumping off a cliff or racing a motorbike. Or filming a sex tape. Or getting herpes. My idea of fun will always pale in comparison to yours."

"Okay, first of all, herpes?" I scoff, leaning forward in my seat. "You don't seem to play very fair."

She shrugs. "You started it. You said I wasn't fun."

"For the record, I don't have herpes," I tell her. "I'm clean as a whistle."

She snort-laughs. At any other time it would have been adorable.

"It's true," I protest. "I have the tests to prove it. And by the way, I think that's a big plus going into this marriage."

She fixes her eyes on me with a pleading look. "Oh, please. Come on, Magnus, we both know this marriage isn't happening."

I still. That catches me off-guard. "What do you mean?"

She sighs and looks down at her glass as she swirls the liquid around. "I mean...let's be reasonable here. This can't possibly happen."

"Why not? You said you'd give it two weeks."

"I'm just buying time," she says. "I mean, I meant it, but at the same time, now that I'm here...how is this even going to work? Do you really think in two weeks I'll be able to look at you and agree to spend the rest of my life with you?"

It shouldn't sting but it cuts pretty deep. Thankfully my face shows nothing.

"And you," she goes on, "how can you think the same about me? If you do, it's only because you have to. That's the only reason we're both here now. Because you have to be."

I clear my throat, feeling the wind taken out of my sails.

She's right.

Or at least she was. If suddenly my father decided to call the whole thing off, said, I didn't need to do this, if it was no longer his wish, would I part ways and never think about Ella again? Or would I pursue her relentlessly because there's something inside me that's determined to uncover who she really is? I joked that she didn't have a fun bone in her body but the truth is I think she does. I think she's just waiting for it to be exposed.

"So I have to because it's what my father wants," I tell her. "And you have to because you don't want to disappoint your own father. It doesn't mean that we can't have a little fun over the next two weeks."

She chews on her lip for a moment. "I thought you said I wasn't fun."

"Prove me wrong then, Princess."

She doesn't say anything but takes a rather large gulp of her scotch, coughing as it goes down.

"Well, that's step one," I tell her. "Step two is playing the game. And no, don't worry, it's not a drinking game. It's a getting to know you game. I call it...*question tiiiiime!*" I sing that last bit like it's part of a game show.

She cocks a brow. "Question time?"

"*Question tiiiiime!* You have to sing it."

"And how do you play?"

I'm actually making this game up on the spot and my mind wants to run with it in a million different directions with dares and stunts and pop quizzes and verbal shoot-outs, but I decide to keep it deceptively simple.

"I ask you a question. It can be any question I choose. You have to answer it honestly. There is no lying, no evading, no avoiding the question, no matter what it is. In return, you then get to ask me one question, only it can't be a question I've previously asked you."

She wiggles her mouth in thought and makes a "hmmmm" sound.

I go on. "We can play two times a day, morning, night, whenever the person wants to call it. And the most questions we can ask at a time are three. If you have more than three, you have to save it for later. But if I ask you three, you have to ask me three. If I ask you one, you have to ask me one."

"Sounds simple enough," she says carefully.

"Hey, you said you wanted to get to know me. I think by the time these two weeks are up, you'll know me pretty well. And vice versa. Providing you're not a liar."

"I'm not a liar," she says haughtily.

"Don't get all high and mighty. According to your father, we're currently engaged. What did you tell him anyway? You must have spoken to him after?"

"Does this count as a question?"

"No," I tell her. "If it's question time, you have to sing it. This is just me being curious."

She sighs long and hard and has another sip of her scotch. When I'm done with this woman she's going to be drinking like a fish. "I didn't speak to him. I spoke to Schnell. His butler. And I told Schnell to tell my father to keep things on the downlow because we are hammering out the details."

"Hammering out the details, huh? So that's what this is."

"More or less."

"Definitely less hammering than I'm used to."

She shakes her head at that and a piece of golden hair falls in front of her eyes. She blows it off her face.

She does a really good job of not looking at me most of the time. Which spurs my first question. "Okay. *Question tiiime.*"

She swallows uneasily but sits up straighter. "What?" she asks, staring at the fire.

I rub my lips together, trying to figure out the best way to get an answer. "Ella—oh, yes, that's the other thing, we have to use each other's names. Nicknames will suffice too. Okay, Ella...do I make you uncomfortable?"

She balks at that. "What?"

"You heard me. Do I make you uncomfortable?"

"No," she says. Her answer is weak.

"Ella...be truthful. Don't make me call you Princess Lying Pants." I lean forward with my elbows on my thighs, watching her try not to twitch.

She exhales sharply through her nose, taking a moment, her dark eyes seeming to wrestle with the truth. Finally she says, "Okay, a little." She glances at me and for once seems apologetic. "I'm just...you're very different from me. You're older. You're, well, a bloody prince. You're...look, I don't have a lot of experience with men like you."

"Or men in general?"

"Is that an official question?"

"No." I have to save my questions. I have a lot.

"Anyway, yeah. I guess. I guess I'm just socially

awkward or something." At that she finishes the rest of her drink and doesn't even wince.

I'm impressed.

"You didn't seem awkward at dinner with my family," I tell her honestly. "And that wasn't your average dinner with your average family either."

She shrugs and glances at me. There's a softness in her eyes that wasn't there before. It's fucking beautiful. "I don't know. I guess I just felt comfortable with them. Like they wanted me there, and no matter what I said or how weird I got about some things, they didn't seem to judge me." She pauses, looking away. "At least I hope they didn't. They might be excellent actors. I guess you would have to be to be a royal."

"That's not true," I tell her. "I'm a horrible actor."

She tilts her head and glances at me thoughtfully. "I don't know about that. I saw your public apology and I almost believed it."

"See?" I point my glass at her. "Almost."

"Well anyway, you were believable."

"I'll have you know that I was being honest in that apology."

"Right."

"It's true," I tell her, my blood getting hot over that remark. "I *am* sorry it happened. I'm sorry for the people it embarrassed, especially my family. How the fuck was I to know something I did in private would be shared with the world?"

"Is that a question?" she asks wryly.

"No." I take in a deep breath. "No. It's just...I didn't mean for that to happen. And I care what you think about me."

She laughs. "Are you serious?" Her eyes are wide and shining. "You don't seem to care about anything."

I consider that. "Maybe I should care more about certain things. But you don't know what goes on in my head. It's a fucked up place to be. I care deeply about a lot of things."

"Like what?" she asks, tucking her leg under and facing me head on, suddenly interested.

"Is that an official question?"

She shakes her head. "No. Like you were before, I'm just curious."

"I don't know." I mean, how do you explain what you care about? Where do you start? Where do you stop? "I care a lot about my family. My father. My mother. My sisters. They mean the world to me."

"That I gathered," she says. "Considering you're getting married because of them." She seems to think about that. "Can I ask you a question? Officially?"

"You have to sing it."

"Seriously?"

"It's the rules. For the first question of the bunch, you have to sing it. It's like the official announcement. Or battle cry, depending on how things go."

She's not impressed but she takes in a deep breath and goes, "*Question time.*"

"No, no, no." I raise my finger high in the air. "You have to sing it...*question tiiime.* Like in this high voice at the end, really drag it out. And you have to raise your finger in the air."

"This is ridiculous. You sound like Nic Cage."

"That's exactly who you need to emulate."

"Fine." She raises her finger in the air, brows raised expectantly. "*Question tiiime.*"

"Perfect." But inside I am laughing my ass off because she just did a pretty damn good impression of Nic Cage.

"My question, Magnus," she says, her face going serious, "do you want to be king?"

Obviously I've been asked that question a lot, always by my family. This is the first time an outsider has asked me and I'm not sure how truthful I should be. What if I do end up marrying Ella and I am the king?

As if she reads this on my face, she says, "Don't worry. I'm not going to say anything or judge you. I just want to know. Personally, I wouldn't be cut out for it and I don't think many people are."

I nod, running a hand over my jaw, the stubble feeling scratchy against my fingers. It's my own stupid game and I need to be as honest as I can be.

"Yes and no," I tell her, taking a breath before I explain. "It's complicated."

"Most jobs are. Most families are."

"Yeah. And most of this is tied to family. We are royals. A monarchy. It's all about family and the job, combined. There is deep shame in abdicating."

"So you would abdicate if you could?"

"Oh, I can," I tell her, something inside me pinching at the thought. "I'd just rather not."

"I'm not sure if you answered my question."

"The thing is...my father wants me to rule. Lord knows why when Irene is more qualified than I am."

"Irene...she's your sister. How old is she?"

"She's a couple of years older than you. Twenty-four. But she's dead serious about everything in her life and has taken an interest in the monarchy and position more than anyone else has. She would rule with an iron fist. She would be steadfast in her role. I can't think of anyone better."

"But she's twenty-four," Ella says slowly. "I would think that's too young."

"She *is* too young for it. But sometimes I think her twenty-four is a lot older than my twenty-eight. If you haven't noticed yet, I'm rather immature."

"You don't say," she deadpans.

"Yes, well, perhaps we're both too young. But the truth is, we may not have much choice. My father isn't doing well, and...everyone—including him, maybe especially him— think that at the very least he should step back from his role for health reasons. Which means someone has to step in, and so far the world is expecting it to be me. I am the heir apparent and I have no reason to abdicate."

"Except that you don't want the job."

I let out a long breath. "It's not that I don't want the job. It's just that I am not built for it. As you said, very few people are, and I...well, I shouldn't even run a McDonalds. I'm absolute shit at anything to do with organization, and after a week the company would be overrun with monkeys and knuckle deep in secret sauce."

She stares at me for a few moments, seeming to take me in. I have to say, I like it when she looks at me. I like the feeling that I'm finally registering to her. Though it might not be in the most complimentary way. What was I just talking about, secret sauce?

"I know what you're saying," she says quietly, her eyes dropping to study her empty glass. "But perhaps you'd be better at it than you think."

I shrug and get up, grabbing the bottle of scotch. "I doubt it. But I appreciate your faith in me." I go over to her and try to fill her glass but she places her hand over it.

"I've had enough for tonight," she says. "And if question time is over, I'd like to go to bed."

I take the bottle back, pretending not to be slighted, and sit back down in my chair, filling my glass to the brim.

"I have one more question," I tell her as she's about to rise from her seat.

She sighs and sits back down. "This is going to be a doozy, isn't it?"

I only grin at her. "You should know what to expect from me by now." I clear my throat. "Listen, it's only because of what we were talking about earlier. My first question. I asked if I made you uncomfortable and you said yes, because you don't have that much experience around men like me..."

I pause and can see her shoulders stiffen, anticipating where this is going.

"So," I continue, "I was just curious. Are you a virgin?"

Oh man, if looks could kill. She's trying to incinerate me on the spot and I know she's going to tell me it's rude, it's crude, it's none of my business, but the fact of the matter is, she has to answer truthfully, and honestly, I have no idea what she's going to do.

Finally she raises her chin and looks me dead in the eye. "Is this relevant to the marriage?"

"Meaning?"

"Meaning, am I supposed to be a virgin?"

"Oh god no." I laugh and then quickly compose myself. "Not that there's anything wrong with being a virgin. I mean, hey, that's always a trip. But this isn't that kind of marriage. There are no ancient royal Viking laws or anything that say the queen has to be a virgin. Vikings knew how to have fun."

She slowly raises a brow at that. She's not impressed with any of this.

"Not that it's any of your business," she says slowly,

getting to her feet, "but I am not a virgin. And to save you the trouble of bringing this up again in future questions, I can tell you that it happened at boarding school, his name was Malcolm, I was sixteen. We were together until the summer after we graduated when he went to Oxford and I took a year to find myself."

"And did you? Find yourself, I mean."

"No. Is that all?"

"So he was the only guy you slept with?"

"Is this another question or are you just curious?"

"Just curious?"

"Then you can keep wondering," she says, walking past me and plunking her empty glass down on the table. "I'll see you in the morning."

"Wait," I call after her before she heads down the hall. "You have to ask me another one. It's the rule."

She looks utterly dejected as she pauses in the doorway, leaning against it. Then she straightens up and looks at me over her shoulder.

"Do you really think this marriage is ever going to happen?"

Damn. She's caught me off-guard. I don't even know if I have an answer for this one.

"I don't know," I admit. "I guess I haven't given much thought to what happens when the two weeks are over." The truth is, sometimes it's hard for me to concentrate on anything else except the here and now.

And all I see right here, right now, is her.

But she doesn't object to my answer.

She just nods. "See you in the morning."

TEN

ELLA

I've been at Thornfield Hall for five days and I'm starting to lose my mind.

At first I thought it was poetic and romantic. I tried my best to fully immerse myself into the *Jane Eyre* atmosphere, picking up old books from the bookshelves and trying to read them by the fire until I realized I couldn't read Norwegian, talking to Jane as if she were Mrs. Fairfax, and wandering the grounds as if they were the moors and I were awaiting Mr. Rochester's lofty arrival.

Only there is no Mr. Rochester, and if there is he's a lot more insufferable than the one in the book.

Magnus is everywhere I look, all the time, except when he's not. He's either purposely trying to annoy me or he's gone, and I don't really have a clue where he goes except he gets into the chauffeured car with Ottar and Einar and they disappear for a few hours. Usually this happens at night, and when Magnus comes back he's good and drunk.

It pisses me right off. Mainly because I'm the one who is stuck in this place, and with the weather turning cold and spiteful, I feel especially imprisoned. Meanwhile Magnus is able to go out and do what he normally does. Or *who* he normally does, I would think.

It doesn't bother me, that part. The fact that when he leaves at night I'm certain he's going out in Oslo and getting laid. We don't owe each other anything at all. He's free to do what he wants, be who he is. Why should I stop any of that? If anything, this might be the last time he has to sow his wild oats, if wedding vows mean anything to him at all.

Except that the longer the days go by, the more I'm bothered by it.

Just a little.

The way he looks at me sometimes...

It does something to my stomach, turns it inside out and in knots.

I know he's conscious of it. But it doesn't stop his eyes from burning into mine, even when he doesn't say anything.

Maybe *especially* when he doesn't say anything.

That's when I feel him the most.

But we do talk, and often it's that fucking question time.

So far I haven't instigated any of the sessions—it's all been him.

And the questions for me have been all over the place.

Question: Have you ever shoplifted?

(No. But my friend did when I was seven and I didn't stop her.)

Question: Have you ever climbed a tree?

(Yes. Weirdo. I was young, and I can't remember the age but my brothers were there giving me the leg up.)

Question: What's your favorite movie?

(*The Princess Bride*. I always wanted to be Princess Buttercup instead of Princess Isabella.)

Question: Pet peeve?

(People who have false humility.)

Question: Bucket list band or artist?

(Elton John, without a doubt.)

Question: favorite drink?

(Chai tea latte.)

Question: favorite alcoholic drink?

(Red wine—I'm not too picky about the variety.)

Question: Have you ever had a threesome?

(What do *you* think?)

And in return I had to volley questions back at him. Some I put little thought into because I just wanted things to be over with, others I was genuinely curious about.

I wanted to know what his worst subject in school was (math), which sister was his favorite (he didn't hesitate, it was Mari, followed by Britt), what his favorite band was (Deftones), what his worst accident was (breaking his collarbone and arm during an ATV race), what his favorite dessert was (crème brûlée), what his favorite vacation spot was (Azores), what his favorite thing about Norway was (the people, the history, the land...he wouldn't shut up), who his first girlfriend was.

Interestingly enough, this question stumped him for a second. It's not that he couldn't remember her. It's that I get the feeling she did a number on him. Her name was Lise and he was rather young, only twelve. He didn't say anything more than that but it intrigued me that she might have gotten under his skin.

I'll have a follow-up question for him later.

But today, the clouds have cleared and the sun is beaming down full-strength.

All of us—Jane, Ottar, Einar, the help, and Magnus, have all wandered outside at some point or another to soak up the morning sun and blink bleary-eyed into this clear October day.

"Fancy a game of tennis?" Magnus asks me as we stand on the stone patio at the back of the house that overlooks the fields and the distant town of Asker. Both of us are cradling cups of coffee in our hands. I'm normally a tea drinker but this place has made me up my caffeine intake.

"Fancy a game of tennis?" I repeat with a smile, making fun of his proper phrasing.

As is usual with him, he's not wearing much. Just thin heather grey sweatpants and an old Ministry band t-shirt that he must have gotten from a thrift store. The sun may be warm but it's not *that* warm and more often than not he's barely dressed.

I know he does it to bug me.

Who knows why a half-dressed man should bug me so much but he does and he knows it.

I guess what it comes down to is the fact that I *want* to stare at him. He's like the bloody sun, and while only quick glances are allowed, you wish you could just stare unabashedly and really soak it all in. Every solar flare, every dancing flame, every burning storm.

But that's what Magnus wants so I have to constantly avert my eyes and pretend that I always see men that are built like him.

The fact is, I don't. I haven't. That's pretty obvious. The only man I've seen naked is Malcolm and while I was madly in love with him at the time, the teenager mind didn't care that he was skinny as a rake and freakishly smooth.

My twenty-two-year-old mind and untested hormones are being tortured by the fact that Magnus and his ridiculously toned body is everywhere I turn and I have to keep on pretending that I don't see him. I have to keep pretending that I don't wish for a moment that I could take my time dragging my eyes over his tattoos and his sinewy muscles. I have to pretend that he's of no interest to me.

Sometimes I think I'm trying to fool myself of that as well.

"Yeah, you afraid?" he asks, crossing his arms. The muscles in his forearms bulge. The man is fucking built like a tank, I swear.

Don't you ever let him know that, I chide myself. *Eyes up.*

I look him in the eyes. Dark, intense, always hinting at something sexual. "Afraid?" I ask. "Of tennis?"

"Yeah."

"Is this an official question?"

"No," he says, biting back a smile. "You think I'd waste that on tennis?"

I shrug. "I have no idea what your priorities are."

Ain't that the truth. Part of the reason why I spend a lot of my time trying to figure him out is because sometimes I can't. One minute he seems super focused on something, the next it's like it never even existed. The other day he seemed absolutely obsessed in getting a vintage billiards table for the place, spending hours online scrolling through ads and stores to get just the right one. The next morning, though, when I asked him about it, he shrugged it off like it was nothing and I haven't heard a peep about it since.

Which explains a lot when it comes to women. He'll be interested in one for a time and then he'll move on to another. At least that's what I speculate. I guess I should be somewhat flattered that it's been almost a week now and he's still staring at me with those wicked eyes like the day we first met.

Maybe even more so.

All in your head, I remind myself. *And that's the last thing you should want.*

Well, other than the fact that wanting this is kind of my agenda for these two weeks.

Honestly, this is quite the bloody mess when you think about it.

"Sure, I'll play," I tell him. I haven't played tennis in years but I figure any sort of exercise will work off the excess energy and nerves I have. I can't tell if it's my isolation here or Magnus's questions or what but every morning I wake up feeling like I might run down the street and never look back.

Magnus tells me he hasn't played tennis here since he was a teenager and though he said the court—which is located on the other side of the servants' house—was in good enough shape, he didn't know where the rackets were or what condition they were in. So while he looks for them, I run upstairs to my room and change into running tights, a sports bra, and a loose t-shirt, practically crashing into Jane as I leave my room.

"Sorry!" I apologize, running past her.

"Where are you going?" she calls after me.

"To play tennis with Magnus."

"Uh huuuh," she says after a beat and I don't have to turn around to see the expression on her face. She's been ogling him, stalking him, harping on about him since we moved in. You'd think she was the one who might be getting married.

I head out of the house and into the courtyard and stop dead in my tracks when I see Magnus there in front of me.

Gone are the sweatpants, which should be a relief since I have to battle with my brain to keep my eyes from staring at the ever-present outline of his dick. But now he's shirtless and the pants have been replaced with way too small green athletic shorts, the kind you'd see on tennis players in the eighties, and instead of a mere outline, it looks like he's smuggling an anaconda in there.

"Oh my god," I exclaim, stopping where I am and covering my eyes. "Where did you find those?"

"In storage with the tennis rackets," he says. "I think these were my father's when I was little. They're very kingly shorts, can't you see?"

I peer through my fingers, unable to keep from smiling. It's not just the tightness of the shorts, or the fact that they're so short and tiny that they show off his muscled thighs, the skin pale with a tan line near the top. But he's also found a red terry-cloth headband and has put it around his head. Combined with his wild hair, he looks exactly like Luke Wilson from the movie *The Royal Tenenbaums*, if he'd lost his shirt somewhere and was covered in tattoos.

I tell him this and he smiles. "I was going more for Björn Borg. He's a famous tennis player from Sweden." He holds out a racket for me. "In fact, I believe he's taught my father a few lessons."

I pause before I take the racket. If he's had famous athletes teaching his father, there's a good chance they've taught him too. "So how good at tennis are you?"

He shrugs and I can tell he's playing it down. "I'm okay."

"You haven't played since you were a teenager?"

"No, I haven't played *here* since I was a teenager," he says, his eyes trailing around the surroundings. "But squash is more my game these days."

"What isn't your game?"

"Not much," he says. "You afraid you'll lose?"

I laugh. "I know I'm going to lose."

"That's not a very good approach to life."

155

"Well, first of all," I say, taking a step back and pointing at him with my racket. "Look at what you're wearing. If this isn't a tactic of distraction, then I don't know what is."

The grin that spreads across his face is so smug I regret saying anything. "You find my body distracting?"

My eyes tilt to the sky. "As if you haven't been playing *that* game this last week. We all know why men wear sweatpants."

A wicked gleam comes over his eyes. "Oh you do, do you? Please enlighten me. I thought I wore them because they're comfortable."

"You wear them because they show off your...your..." Okay. Cheeks are going red. I really need to stop talking.

"My love muscle? My middle leg? The steamin' semen roadway?"

I burst out laughing in an extremely unladylike way, a combination of a horse snort and a hyena, and I have to turn my back to him to compose myself.

"Am I close?" he goes on. "It shows off Big Dick and the Twins?"

I thrust my palm out toward him, trying to catch my breath. "Please, stop."

"Are you sure you want me to stop? It seems like you've been wanting to talk about this for a while."

I take in a deep breath and turn back around to face him. "No more talking about your dick."

He covers his mouth mockingly, eyes wide. "Oh my god. You said *dick*. Have you ever said that word out loud before?"

"You are such an asshole."

"*Drittsekk,*" he says.

"What?"

"It's Norwegian. Means asshole. Though direct translation is shitbag, which I think is more elegant. I think it's about time you start learning the language, don't you?"

"How about we play some tennis first?"

"Oh you want to get your losing over with? Fine by me."

We head over to the courts and my eyes stay trained to his ass nearly the entire time. He's got a damn good one, round and muscled and bouncy, completely showcased in those teeny weeny shorts. It's like looking at the sun again but this time I can stare unabashedly.

He knows I'm staring too. He has eyes in the back of his head. I swear he even wiggles his butt a little.

The court is on the small size, nothing fancy, and it doesn't look like there's been a lot of upkeep with fallen leaves scattered all over it. I suppose the estate doesn't always have a bunch of full-time staffers if there's no one staying here.

Magnus goes to the opposite side of the net, pops open the canister of tennis balls and sticks all but one in his pockets. Now he looks even more ridiculous.

"Quit staring at my balls!" he yells at me.

"I can't help it," I tell him, heading over to center court and trying to adjust my grip on the racket. "You look lumpy."

He glances at the tennis balls bulging out the side of his shorts like goiters. "It's a glandular problem." He straightens his shoulders, flexes his pecs, then throws up the ball.

Before he even hits it I know I'm in big trouble.

The look of utter focus and determination on his face is something to behold, like he's playing against an Olympian and not me in my baggy shirt and tights.

The ball meets the racket with a satisfying thwack and then whizzes past me at the speed of light, landing right in the lines. I didn't even have a chance.

I look back at him. "Nice shot."

He just nods, his jaw set firmly, his brows drawn in concentration. It's odd to see him so serious.

He serves up the ball again, and again he muscles through with a powerful swing, this time the ball nearly taking me out. I have to sidestep out of the way to save my kneecaps.

"You know you're supposed to hit it back," he says to me, fishing another ball out of his pocket and bouncing it up and down with such ease it makes me think he's used to playing tennis with his eyes closed.

"You know that I'm rubbish at this game compared to you," I tell him. "Maybe don't try and murder me with each serve."

"Maybe step up and try to hit it back," he says.

I glare at him. Fine. I'll try. But I know he's just trying to humiliate me.

I take my stance, legs apart, butt out, and do my best to channel Serena Williams. I tense my thighs, tighten my grip on the racket, and wait, my heart beating loudly in my chest. I don't know how but Magnus has somehow managed to turn tennis into a high adrenaline sport.

Magnus serves up the ball and once again comes down on it with a hard swing that hits the ball perfectly. It goes right for me again and this time I both try to jump out of the way and attempt to swing at it.

It doesn't go well.

My swing comes up empty and the movement almost makes me topple over, and once again, the ball stays inside the court.

"Fuck!" I yell, tempted to ram my racket into the ground. I can see why tennis players have such anger issues.

If this continues for much longer I foresee myself launching the racket at his head.

"That's the spirit," he says, holding up a ball. "This is the last one I have. You better make it count."

"You're a royal *drittsekk*, you know that?"

He grins proudly, though I don't know whether it's because I managed to speak Norwegian or that he's actually proud of being a royal shitbag.

Either way, he's in it to win.

The ball goes up.

The racket comes down.

And all I see is this tennis ball coming straight at me, like a neon green meteor headed right for my face.

I'm too stunned to even try to move.

The ball bops me right on my fucking nose.

The world explodes into stars and I yell, "You son of a bitch!" while my eyes pinch shut and I crumple to my knees, holding my nose with one hand, the other keeping me up off the ground.

Don't cry, don't cry, I tell myself even though my eyes are starting to water. Fuck, it bloody hurts!

Meanwhile I can hear Magnus leaping over the net and running toward me, throwing his racket to the ground. "Holy fuck, I am so fucking sorry!"

His hands are at my back, on my arm, and I try to wave him away but it's hard when my whole face is on fire and I feel like I'm about to pass out.

"Let me see," he says, placing his hand at the back of my neck and crouching beside me.

I gradually lift my head up and hear him inhale sharply.

"What?" I say, my eyes flying open. I manage to look at my hand. It's completely covered in blood. "Ahhh!"

By the way, I don't do well with blood.

The world starts to spin again, getting fuzzy around the edges.

"It's okay," he says, though there is *nothing* reassuring about his voice.

"It's not okay!" I cry out. "You probably broke my nose, you asshole."

"Drittsekk," he corrects.

"Yeah, shitbag. Prince Shitbag." I grab my nose again, the blood dripping onto the ground. "Oh god, I'm going to faint."

"You're not," he says, grabbing my arms and trying to haul me up to my feet. "Come on, let's get you inside."

I'm pretty much putty at this point and when I'm up, my feet seem to disappear below me. I lean right into Magnus's chest. His very warm, very hard, very intimidating chest.

Which I'm currently getting blood all over.

I pinch my eyes closed, trying to stay conscious.

"Ugh, sorry," I whimper, trying to pull away.

But I swear his body is a magnet to mine and then his arms go around the small of my waist, holding me against him.

I'm powerless.

And bleeding all over him.

"I've got you," he says. His tone is serious, as is his grip. "Let's just take a moment. Breathe in. Breathe out." He pauses. "Not through your nose, of course."

I try and take in a deep breath. Let it out. Then another and another.

"You feel better?" he asks.

I give a slight shake of my head. Honestly, I just want to collapse against him even more.

"Okay, hold on," he says, and then before I know what's

going on, he's bending down and scooping me up into his arms.

I let out a yelp, one arm going around his shoulder to hold on, the other still holding on to my nose, as if it's stopping anything.

He carries me out of the court and into the house, and luckily I don't think any of the help see us. They'd probably freak out and place a phone call to the Queen or something. Who knew tennis could go so wrong?

"Jane!" I yell for her once we're inside, still in Magnus's arms. "Jane!"

"She went for a walk," Ottar says, coming around the corner. "What—" He stops dead when he sees us. "Oh, *helvete.* What on earth happened here?" He looks at Magnus accusingly.

"Tennis happened," Magnus says. "Can you grab the first aid kit? I'm sure it's somewhere."

"Of course, sir," he says and then scurries off.

"You can put me down now," I tell Magnus.

"I don't think so," he says. "You might hurt yourself again."

"Me hurt myself? You're the one who treated me like target practice."

The corner of his lips curve into a smile and it's only now that I'm realizing how close my face is to his. I've never noticed the streaks of green in his mahogany eyes before, how long and dark his lashes are, the low arch of his brows. Good lord, he's stunning.

But the feeling doesn't last very long.

Because blood is pouring off my nose at very close range to this stunning man.

Stunning man? It's only Magnus, I have to remind myself.

"Is it just your nose that hurts or do you think your brain was affected?" he asks after a moment.

"Huh?"

"The way you're looking at me," he says slowly, the pink of his tongue appearing between his lips.

"How am I looking at you?"

Wait, I don't want to know.

"Like you might actually like me."

I can't help but smile. But smiling brings a sharp jolt of pain to my nose.

"Uuugh," I moan, shutting my eyes to him, to everything. Jeez, I admire the guy *in my head* and his ego somehow already knows and is running with it.

"I've got the kit!" Ottar says, and I hear his footsteps against the wood floors as he runs over, out of breath. "And towels for the mess. I'll put them down on the couch."

Magnus takes me over to one of the couches and gently lowers me down on it, then gets down on his knees beside it so he's at my level.

"Ottar I need a wet warm washcloth, stat!" he barks.

"Yes, sir!" Ottar says and runs off again.

Meanwhile Magnus is smiling to himself.

"What?" I ask.

"I just enjoy ordering him around so much."

I roll my eyes. "Always have to be in charge, huh?"

"Something like that," he says, placing his hand over mine and trying to pry it away. "Let me see your nose."

Gingerly, I let him take my hand away and he leans in closer, inspecting it.

"How is it?"

"Oh it's just awful," he says and I have no idea if he's pulling my leg or not.

My eyes widen at that as Ottar sticks his hand in front

of us, a wet cloth dangling from his fingers. Magnus snatches it up and very gently proceeds to dab the cloth on my face.

"Let me know if it hurts," he says.

It does hurt. Every dab makes my eyes sting, sends lightning bolts of pain into my brain. But I don't say anything because I know it needs to be done.

And honestly, I think I like him doting on me like this. He's surprisingly gentle and I watch him as he concentrates, dark brows furrowed together, biting his lower lip. There's a strange tenderness and intimacy to this whole thing.

I think Ottar picks up on it too because he says, "Do you need anything else, sir?"

"I've got it from here, thank you."

Ottar walks off and Magnus does a final wipe down the side of my nose. I keep my attention off the cloth which I know is soaked with my blood. Then again, so are both of us.

"There," he says softly, tilting his head back and forth as he looks me over.

"Does it look broken?" I ask him. I would hate to have a broken nose. It already has a crooked bump in the middle of it as it is, though Jane is fairly insistent that it's all in my head.

"It's a bit swollen and it's going to leave a nasty bruise, maybe even two black eyes," he says. "Good thing you're not going anywhere."

"Yeah."

"Hey, I'm sorry about that," he says, reaching up and brushing a strand of hair off my face. My skin erupts with shivers from the rough feel of his fingers, the curious way he's gazing at me.

It leaves me momentarily tongue-tied and confused.

This is a side of him I haven't seen yet and I'm not sure I like how it makes me feel.

How it scares me in ways I don't want to articulate.

"Sorry about what?" I eventually say.

"That my body is so amazing," he says, straight-faced. "It really wasn't fair. How can you concentrate on tennis balls when you've got my own balls on your mind?"

"Magnus," I warn, not letting myself smile again. It will hurt way too much. "Not now. Please."

"I mean, I shouldn't have been showing off my yogurt slinger like that," he says.

"Your...*what*?"

And then it's over. I burst out laughing, crying out in pain at the same time. "Ow, ow, ow. Damn it, Magnus. You need to get your head checked."

"Which head?"

"Stop!" I'm alternating between crying and laughing. "This isn't fair. Don't make me laugh. It hurts."

He grins at me, a softness coming over his eyes. "I've been wanting to make you laugh like that. You're so fucking beautiful, Ella."

Oh.

Oh.

Did he seriously just say that? Was it a joke?

I stare at him, my smile faltering slightly.

He shrugs. "Too bad you have to deal with Prince Shitbag here." He pauses and sits back a bit. "Honestly, though, I am sorry for that. I don't know what came over me out there. I didn't mean to get all aggressive and hit it so hard, and I certainly didn't want to hurt you. I guess I get a bit too competitive."

He could say that again. The look that came over his face when he was serving is probably the same one he gets before he jumps off a cliff or gets behind the wheel of a rally car. I have no idea what goes on in his head and it seems that neither does he.

Or maybe that's not true.

"Question time," I tell him.

"You have to sing it," he says, but his words falter when he sees the fire in my eyes.

"I am not singing it in my condition," I snap at him, but the burst of anger just makes my nose hurt. I take in a deep, calming breath. "But seriously. What is your obsession with high adrenaline and risky sports? Why do you do it?"

He raises his brow but his amusement is forced. "Tennis is hardly a risky sport. Except maybe for you."

"Magnus."

He runs his hand through his hair and sits on the edge of the couch, staring out the windows that overlook the fields below the estate. "I don't know. I like it."

"Yeah, but why do you like it? You know that BASE jumping is one of the most dangerous sports in the world and by definition there must be something wrong with you if you actively seek it out."

He eyes me sharply. "There's nothing wrong with me." Now it's his turn to turn all snappish. I've hit a nerve. "I like it because I like it."

"That's the honest truth? That's why you risk your life to do it?"

"I'm not risking my life. I do things by the book. I'm not...reckless."

"Some would beg to differ," I tell him. "I'm sure your family wouldn't agree with that."

He sighs. "Yeah, well, they don't agree with a lot of things I do." He presses his lips together for a long moment. "Look. It gives me something that I don't often have. When

I jump, when I'm taking a sharp turn, when I'm flying over a ski hill...when I'm having hot, crazy sex..."

I swallow hard at the mention of hot, crazy sex, my mind briefly inundated with images of him sweaty and moving on top of me. I push that out of my head, ignore the flush of heat between my legs.

He goes on. "When I'm doing those things, the world just seems to fit me for once. I can focus. I can think. It's like the constantly changing TV channels of my brain finally come to a stop on one station and I can actually concentrate for once."

What he said actually makes a lot of sense and I have a feeling it's something he doesn't talk about often. Or ever.

He gets up to his feet, seemingly agitated. "Anyway, that's just the way I am. No point getting all deep and philosophical about it." He glances down at me. "Want me to take you to your room?"

I shake my head gently and hold the damp rag to my nose. "No. I'll be fine. I just want to lie here for a bit."

He nods. "Okay. Let Ottar know if you need anything."

Then he walks off.

Clearly my question bothered him but I have a feeling he doesn't even know why.

ELEVEN

MAGNUS

I feel like a total prick.

All I wanted to do with Ella was play a game of tennis, have some fun, enjoy the sunshine and all that jazz, and I ended up almost breaking her nose. Whether it was going into super competitive mode or just vainly trying to show off, I ruined a pretty good thing we had going on there.

Okay, well things have been slow going and maybe we aren't seeking each other out, wanting to spend time together. But for the first time since I met her, it felt less like she was arguing with me because she hated me and more like she was doing it because it was fun.

Now this has set us back. It didn't help either that one of her questions actually cut deeper than it should have. I know she was just curious and it shouldn't have been a big deal but it felt like it for some reason.

So during these last three days, things are back to being strained. When I do talk to her, she's a little short with me, maybe because the place starts to feel more like a prison, and as the days tick on by toward the end of our two weeks, I really don't see how we're going to come out of this in a positive way. I have a feeling I won't be seeing her ever again.

Which, I must admit, sucks.

I've grown to like her.

A lot.

I've become fascinated with her and I can't really put my finger on why. Maybe because the more questions I've asked her, the more she shows herself to me, reluctantly letting me peel back the layers. She gets softer and bolder at the same time.

I know she has a complicated relationship with her family and country. She's hurt and rejected and forever nursing a wound ever since her father shipped her off to boarding school. I can't imagine what that would be like, to lose your mother so young and then have your only surviving parent send you off like you're not wanted.

She hasn't talked about it at length with me but I can see the hurt in her eyes, her defensiveness in the set of her jaw, the vulnerability in her shoulders. I know that all of that has made her shy and second guess herself over everything it seems. Except for the things she's passionate about: environmental issues.

And, well, me.

Whether she likes me or not, I can't tell. But I do know she's passionate about how she feels about me. She's never afraid to tell me off or voice her opinion around me and I guess that's why I love rattling her cage so much, because I feel like the more I do it, the more she'll be set free.

To just be herself with everyone, and not just me.

Of course part of the reason why I'm quite besotted with her is because she damn near takes my breath away at any given moment. She's beautiful every which way but even more so when she's firing something at me, that wicked glint in her eyes, the way her skin glows, the smile she tries so often to hide but fails.

If I'm rattling her cage, she's rattling mine. Only I'm not sure she'd like the animal inside of it.

But tonight she's keeping to herself again and I'm growing anxious at the tension in the house, so I throw on a coat and tell Ottar and Einar that I'd like to head into town. I need a drink, I need out of the house.

I get into the car and then realize I left my phone in my room. I quickly run into the house, grab it, and then run right into Ella as I shut the door to my room.

"Where are you going?" she asks. Her nose is no longer swollen but it's bruised and she has a black eye. She's done her best to cover it with makeup but I know it's there. I wince internally.

"To the bars," I tell her, slipping my phone into my coat pocket.

"To do what?"

I frown. "Drink. Obviously."

"With who? Heidi?"

I'm taken aback by this. "Heidi? That barnacle? No. No one."

"So you go to the bars alone?"

I'm not sure why she sounds so suspicious. Maybe it's because I've been going every single night. Sometimes I wait until after she's asleep, just because I feel bad that she's not supposed to go.

"I have friends I see there," I say carefully, thinking of Hunchback Harold and the gang.

"Sure," she says. "Friends."

She turns to leave and I reach out and grab her arm.

"You think I've been leaving every night to see other women?" I ask her, and she raises her chin, not answering.

"Ella, the only woman's legs I want to be between are yours."

Her eyes go round like saucers.

I knew that would get her attention.

"You're free to do what you want. I wouldn't care at all if you were with other women," she says after a beat, trying to sound casual. But I know better.

"I think you're lying," I tell her, noting the way she'll only meet my gaze for a second.

"Why would I lie?"

"I don't know." I shrug but I don't let go of her arm. "To piss me off. You act like it's your job sometimes."

She makes a huffing noise and looks away.

"Don't worry," I tell her. "I happen to like it."

"I don't try and piss you off," she explains. "It just happens naturally."

Right. I'm not sure how I can explain to her that the more she fights with me, the more turned on I get. I've been walking around with a raging hard-on for most of the week we've been here together.

"Okay." I watch as I slip my hand down over her forearm to her delicate wrist, wrapping my fingers around it. I can feel her pulse racing against my skin and slowly look up to meet her eyes. "Just so you know, the more you get all mouthy with me, the more I think about what other things your mouth might be able to do."

She stiffens and tries to yank her wrist away but I hold on. "You're a brute."

I raise my brows and smile. "A brute? I like that. Isn't there a cologne called brute?"

She narrows her eyes at me. "You're a caveman. No class."

"Ouch," I say mockingly, rubbing my thumb along the

soft skin of her inner wrist. I take a step toward her. "You insulted my social standing. How will I ever recover? I know, perhaps I'll become king one day. That should solve the class problem."

"Having a high social standing, money, or position of power has nothing to do with class and you know it. You can still be king, but you'll be a crude one."

"Then wouldn't it make sense to have a sweet queen at my side? Life is all about balance."

"I am not sweet and you know it," she says.

I suck my bottom lip in for a moment and her eyes follow. Fucking hell, if I could just figure out whether she's attracted to me or not it would be so damn helpful.

"The thing is, Princess, you are sweet. You're spicy too. You're a lot of different flavors I haven't even had the chance to lick yet."

Her cheeks burn and she shakes her head. "Why do I even bother with you?"

"I'm not sure. Why do you?"

"You're a *hestkuk*."

I blink at her for a moment, my hand dropping away. Then I erupt into laughter, not believing she just said that.

"What? You called me a *hestkuk*?" I manage to say between laughs. "Where did you learn that? Do you even know what it means?"

"I asked Ottar to tell me a swear in case I needed it. He said it meant asshole. You know, more than drittsekk." A flash of worry comes over her eyes. "Doesn't it?"

"It's actually very close to English," I tell her. "It means horse cock. But your pronunciation is spot-on."

"Horse cock!?" she repeats indignantly. "How is that an insult?"

171

"It's not for me. But then again, I have one." Her eyes drop to my crotch for a second and I can't help but grin.

"Damn Ottar," she grumbles, quickly looking away.

"He's from up north, they're more creative with their swearing up there," I tell her. "But since we're on the subject of cocks again, I think we should stay there. You seemed a lot more into it before. Let's just add horse cock to the trouser snake, the master of ceremonies, and the pink bologna pony."

I thought my names would bring out another eye roll but instead she just snarls. Everything sweet is replaced with five alarm spice.

"Go fuck yourself," she says to me and then starts walking off down the hall.

Helvete. She's getting quite the mouth on her.

"Stay nasty, Princess," I call after her. "That's just the way I like you."

She just gives me the finger and keeps walking.

~

AFTER OUR HORSE COCK ALTERCATION IN THE hallway, I left for the bar and I'm sure Ella went to bed angry. Truth is, I felt bad about the whole thing—again—and just outside of Oslo I made Einar take me back to the estate. It didn't feel right going to the bar anymore after all that.

The next morning I refused to let things get weird between us again. I made sure I was at the breakfast table with her as she grumbled about our typical Norwegian breakfast, which is basically bread piled high with a million different things. I do mine with herring and pickled onion and ham, which disgusts her. She just drowns hers in Nutella.

"Hey," I say to her as I sit down across from her at the table. "I'm sorry about last night."

She shrugs, eyes focused on the Nutella.

Jane, who has been eyeing us like we're some theatrical play that's here for just her entertainment, asks, "What happened?"

"Nothing," Ella says.

"I think she's feeling a bit like she's under house arrest," I admit. "And I've been a little rude, crude, and thoughtless. So I've come up with an idea."

Ella slowly raises her head to look at me. "What?" she asks cautiously.

"Tonight when I go to the bar, you can come with me."

She frowns and starts picking about her bread. "You know I can't be seen in public."

"I know."

"Especially with this nose," she says, pointing at her bruises which are fading pretty quickly.

"You look so much better," Jane tells her. "Really."

"And it doesn't matter," I add. "Because there's only one bar I've been going to and no one knows about it. It's basically in a back street, it's a quarter of the size of this room, and the owner, Harold, doesn't let any cameras in. Plus I haven't seen paparazzi there for weeks."

Ella stares at me for a moment and I can see her inner demon and inner angel arguing with each other. The part of her that hates the fact that right at this very moment she's skipping school is telling her that leaving the estate is against the rules. The other part of her, the one that fears being left out of things and brushed aside, that part is telling her she needs to do this, that she deserves to have a little fun.

I decide to appeal to the latter side.

"You deserve a little break," I tell her. "I know what the rules are, but I promise this won't come back and bite you on your cute little ass."

"Sir," Ottar admonishes from across the kitchen as he pours his coffee. I didn't even notice him earlier.

I shrug it off. He's heard way worse than that.

"What time?" she asks. "What would I wear? I didn't pack anything for a bar or anything like that."

I give her a reassuring smile. "Believe me, you can wear the pajamas you're in right now. It's not that kind of bar."

"I'll think about it," she says before she takes a bite of her sandwich.

I'm tempted to pop *question tiiiime* on her but since it's supposed to be a thing between just us, I decide to wait for later.

And later slowly rolls around. It's nearly eight o'clock at night when Ella appears in the doorway of the parlor room as I'm scrolling on my phone by the fire.

"Okay. I'm in," she says simply.

I glance at her. She's dressed in skinny jeans and a low-cut black top that shows off just a hint of lacy black bra underneath.

Jesus. I'm pretty sure this is the first time I've seen her cleavage. I practically stagger to my feet, yanked toward her in some sort of sexual tractor beam until I'm just a foot away.

"You look..." I tell her, unable to keep my eyes from roaming all over her chest, down her arms. The fabric of her top is slinky and begs to be touched, then pulled off, preferably with my teeth.

"This is the fanciest thing I have," she says, chewing on her bottom lip.

I clear my throat. I'm fucking hard as concrete right now and I don't care if she knows it. "It's perfect," I manage to say, finally meeting her eyes. "You look amazing."

She averts her eyes shyly. "It's just some cheap top I got at H&M."

"You look beautiful," I tell her emphatically.

"Oh, well thank you," she says, and I notice she's put on a bit of makeup as well, not just covering up the bruises but adding some smoky eyeliner that makes her look a little bit older and definitely sexier.

Then again, I also think there's nothing sexier than Ella first thing in the morning, padding down the hall in her fluffy robe and slippers, her face bare, her eyes sleepy, her long blonde hair cascading messily around her. She always looks like she got rightly fucked in her sleep.

I'm starting to think I'd do anything to make her look that way myself.

Now that she's ready, we don't waste any time. Jane and Ottar stay behind so it's just Einar taking us to Oslo.

It almost feels like a date as we sit in the back seat of the car, and I debate with myself whether I should reach out and hold her hand or not. But I know at this point I have nothing to lose. Time is running out, and with each second, I know how these two weeks will end.

I grab her hand, and while she flinches at my contact, she doesn't quite pull away. She lets me hold it there, resting between us on the middle seat.

Even though it's a long car and Einar is in the front, I lower my voice and softly sing, "*Question tiiiiime.*"

She gives me a look that says, *really? Here?*

I go on. "Do you like this? Me, holding your hand?"

She stares at me with big eyes, her brows doing a dance while she once again wrestles with different answers. But finally she nods and says quietly, "Yes."

I want her to elaborate but I don't think I'll get much more out of her.

For now, I feel like I've just been handed a victory. The battle isn't over, but this is a huge step for us. Who the hell would have thought that one day I would equate hand-holding to fucking? But it's true. Holding Ella's hand feels like I'm holding on to sunshine.

We pull into the dark, wet streets of downtown Oslo and Einar parks the car around the corner from the bar.

"Do you miss this area?" Ella asks me. I'm still holding her hand as we walk down the nearly empty street, Einar trailing behind us.

"It's only been ten days," I tell her.

"I know. But it feels like it's been a lifetime somehow."

I know what she means. The estate has turned into a time warp of sorts. "Do you miss school?" I ask her.

She thinks that over. "Yes and no. I miss the classes, the learning. I don't miss living there. It was rather lonely."

Something about her admission breaks my heart a little. I don't want this girl to be lonely, not after what she's been through. "What about Jane? That must help? You two are close."

"We are." She gives me a small smile. "She's the closest person to me. But, you know, she's still paid for by my father. He gives her a paycheck to look after me, so as close as I am with her, I wonder what would happen if she were fired or my father decided it wasn't worth it anymore. Would she stick around? Maybe not."

"I'm sure she would."

"Would Ottar?"

I laugh softly. "Ottar would leave so fast it would be like one of those cartoons where you'd see an Ottar-shaped hole in the wall."

She giggles. "I can see that."

We stop outside of Harold's. The front window is all frosted glass so you can't see inside the bar from the outside. Harold's is written across it, the paint gold and peeling.

"By the way," I say, pulling her close to me before I open the door. "I may have told them that we're already engaged."

"Why would you do that?" she cries out softly.

"Hey, it's no worse than what you told your father," I remind her. "Let's just say I was feeling optimistic."

"Do you still feel optimistic?"

I raise her hand up so it's between our chests. "The fact that you've let me hold your hand this whole time gives me a reason to think so."

Then I open the door.

"Prince," Harold calls out merrily and then stops rubbing down the bar counter the moment he sees Ella. "Who have we here?"

"Is this her?" Slender Man asks from the booth, his voice so high and anxious I half expect him to start fluttering his hands. "Is this your fiancé?"

"This is her," I say proudly. "This is the future Princess Isabella of Norway."

Maud staggers out of her seat and comes forward for an inspection, peering over Ella at close range.

"Getting a good look there, Maud?" I ask, then realize I've been speaking Norwegian. I switch to English. "Ella, here, is from Liechtenstein," I say, putting my hand at her back and leading her over to the end of the bar furthest from the door. "So she doesn't know much Norwegian yet, except for some swear words. But don't worry. I'm working on teaching her more swear words."

I introduce her to everyone, and then once Einar is inside, I go over to the door and lock it, explaining to Harold that because our engagement is still a secret, we can't risk the public knowing about it.

"And don't worry, dear," Maud says to Ella between sips of her martini. "We won't tell a soul. All the souls we know are either dead or right here." Then she goes into a long speech about all the lovers she's had that died, all the classic film stars she knew that died, all the people who will probably die soon, and so on.

Luckily, Ella is enthralled by Maud's stories of old Hollywood, even if they've taken a morbid turn. She also goes out of her way to talk to Guillermo and tell him about herself, then even sits down across from Slender Man and asks him questions.

Believe me, Slender Man normally just talks and talks and when he does he's this big black hole that sucks the life out of you and the room until you're crushed under the weight of his horrible luck and life.

As a result, no one ever asks Slender Man what he's doing because, believe me, you don't want to know.

But maybe it's because Ella is drinking more than she normally does, or maybe she's just so damn happy that she's out of that house, but she's actually interested in what he has to say. And for once, his black hole of despair has no chance against her ethereal ray of sunshine. It's like watching Galadriel have a counselling session with Sauron and actually get through to him.

Fuck, I'm glad Ella can't see my thoughts. I'm not sure if being a closet LOTR fan would work against me or not.

Later on in the evening, Harold leans across the bar, fixes his one good eye on me and says, "I approve."

"Yeah?" I've been sitting here watching Ella actually make Slender Man laugh. Everyone in the bar jumped at that sound since we'd never heard it before. It sounded like a cat being strangled, but still, it was a laugh.

"She's smart, she's a delight, she's very pretty," he says. "I think she'll be good for you. I'm glad you finally decided to bring her by, especially after all you've talked about her."

I guess I have been waxing on about Ella during my nights here.

"You know," I say to him slowly, trying to figure out the right way to phrase this. "Even though we're to be married, sometimes I wonder if she's really in it for me. Or if she's doing it for other reasons."

I watch Harold carefully because he's old enough to forget about white lies and trying to spare someone's feelings. Old people wield their bluntness like a sword.

But I can't read anything negative on his weathered face. "Women like Ella, they don't pretend. She's honest and true, that one. I would think that if she wants to marry you, then she really wants to marry you. You can't fake love."

My smile feels stiff. This is where Harold is wrong. There is no love between us and if things progress as they're supposed to, as I hope, then we're both in for a world of pretending. Whatever he is reading off of her about me is entirely fake.

For the moment, though, I decide to take Harold's words to heart, and for the rest of the night, I do pretending of my own. I pretend that every time Ella looks across the bar at me and gives me a smile, that it means something. That I mean something to her.

I never knew that something so simple, just having another person want you and genuinely like you, could mean so much. Relationships, marriage...I'm starting to get it. I'm starting to realize that this horrible situation that I've been placed in might not be so horrible after all.

As long as it's Ella.

The thought makes something inside my chest wince.

It has to be her.

This won't work if it's anyone else.

We end up staying way past the usual closing hour, Guillermo and Slender Man having left ages ago, Maud falling asleep and snoring on the bar.

Einar checks to make sure the coast is clear and then Ella and I stumble, drunk and warm against each other despite the dreary night, all the way to the car.

"Well that was fun," Ella says. She moves over so that she's in the middle seat and her head is resting on my shoulder. "I don't think I've drank that much in a long time. Or talked that much either."

"I can't believe you got Slender Man to open up and turn it positive," I tell her, staring at the top of her head and fighting the urge to kiss it. The sight of her on my shoulder warms me in a million different ways.

"His name is Erik," she chides me, then yawns. "And that's a terrible nickname to have. Where did you learn your English from anyway?"

"College. And the Police Academy movies."

"You didn't go to college," she says after a pause.

I smile. "It's a line from *Wayne's World*."

"So you learned your English from *Wayne's World* then."

"That movie got me through some tough times," I admit with a sigh.

She tilts her head up at me, her dark eyes soft, her lids heavy. She stares at me for a moment before a slow smile spreads across her face. I wish she knew what that smile does to me. Maybe she does.

"What?" I ask quietly, unnerved by her attention.

"I've never met anyone like you," she says, sounding awed.

I cock my brow. "I assure you there are plenty of people who are still quoting *Wayne's World*."

"That's not what I meant," she says.

The space between us seems to grow smaller, my breath heavier, the air ripe with tension. With any other woman in any other situation I would have kissed her a long time ago. Now, I'm paralyzed by the thought. I don't think I've ever wanted something this bad, and it scares me. And what scares me only makes me focus more.

"What do you mean?" I whisper.

"All this time, I've never once thought of you as a prince."

I frown. "Thanks. I guess."

"It's a good thing. At least to me. I always assumed that you were just like your persona. Cocky and egotistical and arrogant."

"Those all mean the same thing. And I think I'm still all those things."

"I know," she says. "But that's not all you are. You're also smarter than you look. You're a quick thinker. You're attentive. You're curious and, dare I say, quirky. I don't know anyone who goes to a bar every other night to hang out with a bunch of old people. There are a lot more sides to you than just the playboy prince one that you show to the public. In fact, I think there are more sides to you than you even show to yourself."

Damn. We're getting into some pretty deep limo talk back here.

"Which brings me to *question tiiiime*," she sings softly, and it brings an automatic grin to my face. "Since I forgot to ask you earlier..."

"Shoot."

"In the bar, you kept looking at me when I was talking to Erik. What were you thinking?"

I let out a soft laugh. "You want the truth?"

"Yes. Obviously."

"I thought you were like Galadriel talking Sauron off a ledge."

"From *Lord of the Rings*?" she asks, grinning.

I nod. "That's another side that you don't know."

"Interesting. And what were you talking to the bartender about? You both seemed to be nodding at me."

"Is this an official question?"

"No," she says after a beat, snuggling in closer to me.

I swallow hard. I should just keep my fat mouth shut since I don't have to answer it.

But there's a part of me, the brave and bold part that chases down fear, that dances with it, that wants me to come out and say it anyway.

"I was asking him if he thought you were marrying me for love or for something else. If you were just pretending."

She stares at me. "Oh. What did he say?"

"He said you're the type of woman who could never fake it. You were honest and true, through and through."

Her eyes tilt downward. "I see."

"And I know it's not true," I admit. "But damn, for that moment, it was really nice to pretend."

"Pretend what?" Her voice has dropped even lower now.

"That we were doing all of this because we wanted to."

I feel the slight nod of her head against my shoulder.

And then there's silence.

My words seem to fall down around us like rain outside the car, while the two of us are shuttled back to the estate, back into hiding.

TWELVE

MAGNUS

A PHONE CALL WAKES ME.

What's the point in even setting an alarm clock if there's someone else out there in the world who is hell-bent on waking you up?

My first rule as king will be to make sure no phone calls can be placed to anyone before nine a.m., and if it's an emergency, then the receiver must have enough warning to ingest obscene amounts of coffee before the call.

I groan, my head feeling like it's been sawed open and a whole bag of concrete has been poured in there. I blindly grope for my phone and glance at it, expecting it to be my mother or father. There hasn't been a day here that one of them hasn't checked in on the status of Ella and me.

Honestly, I haven't known what to tell them other than that we're getting to know each other. Which isn't a lie. It's just a lot slower than I thought it would be.

That said, I'm surprised she agreed to come to the bar last night. Maybe all we needed to really get closer was some time out of the confines of this estate.

That, and a lot of booze.

Of course I won't be mentioning her incognito excursion to my parents.

It doesn't matter anyway since the phone's screen tells me it's Viktor calling from Sweden.

I breathe a sigh of relief that smells like stale beer and answer it.

"You, of all people, aren't supposed to call me before nine a.m."

"Magnus, it's almost noon."

I sit up in surprise. That was a mistake. The room spins. "What?" I ask, holding the side of my head while I peer at my phone. "How did that happen?"

"You tell me," he says. "Anyway, I saw you called the other day, and I'm sorry I didn't get back to you earlier."

"You're busy, so you're excused," I tell him, lying back down gently. I can't believe no one has woke me up yet. Usually Ottar is banging on my door, though perhaps Ella is sleeping in as well. "How is the wedding planning?" I ask.

He has yet to know anything about Ella and me, or that Ella even exists. He doesn't even know about the whole marriage thing on my end.

"Stressful," he says with a sigh. "And we're not getting married until April. I'm left out of the planning for the most part, but I think my mother has really gone crazy with it and taken Maggie along for the ride. Actually, that's why I'm calling. They've gone to Paris for a few days to do some shopping. My mother, Maggie, and her sisters. Girls trip, or whatever. I was seeing if you wanted to do the same."

"I don't know, Viktor. Paris bores me."

"Not to Paris, idiot," he says. "Let's go hike up to one of those royal cabins of yours in the mountains and make a campfire and get shitfaced drunk."

"You want to come to Norway?"

"Do you see any damn mountains in Sweden?"

I clear my throat, trying to think fast. I haven't seen Viktor since July, and it's long overdue for us to cause some mayhem.

But Ella is here.

I have no choice but to tell him.

"I think it's a great idea," I say. "When?"

"I'm about to get Freddie to buy me a ticket. Today. You're still at the apartment, right?"

"No," I tell him. "See, here's the thing. I'm totally down for all of this but it won't be quite the guys' trip that you think it'll be."

Silence. Then, "You want to bring your flavor of the month with us?"

"She's not the flavor of the month," I tell him, feeling defensive. "But she's here with me. We're at Skaugum Estate, outside of Oslo. And well, she has to come because I'm not about to leave her alone here. See, she's under house arrest. And we might be getting married. I'm not sure yet."

More silence. "What?"

I take in a deep breath and explain it all to Viktor the best I can.

When I'm done, he doesn't believe me.

I explain again.

Then he laughs.

And laughs, and laughs.

"You're being a real shitbag," I tell him. "You're supposed to be supporting me."

"Right, like you've ever supported me," he says, sighing. "My god, I'm actually crying. Oh Magnus, so happy for you to join the club."

"Whatever. So you want to do this or not?"

"Well, how are you going to get Cinderella out of there?"

"It's Ella. And I'll figure it out. Just get your ass over here ASAP, and we'll figure out our next move."

We hang up, and I manage to finally get out of bed. After I freshen up and slip on dark jeans and a white t-shirt that's probably too small for me, I head out into the hall.

Straight to Ella's room.

Just as Jane is coming out of it.

"Morning, sunshine," she says to me brightly.

"She in there?" I ask, running a hand through my hair to make sure I don't look completely crazy.

"Barely," she says. "I don't know what you did to her last night."

"Me?" I say innocently. "She's the one who drank. And talked. And I swear the world will never be the same."

Jane purses her lips. "Mmmm. Anyway, she's not used to that, so next time please take it easy on her."

I raise my hands in protest. "I will do nothing of the sort. Can I go in?"

She shrugs. "It's your house, Your Highness."

"Thank you, Lady Jane."

I open the door and step inside.

Ella has flung herself dramatically across the bed, lying on her back with her arm over her eyes. She's also wearing next to nothing, just a long t-shirt that has a picture of a whale on it, and I see a peek of yellow booty shorts.

Good god.

I take a moment and just stand there, admiring her long, smooth legs, wishing I could take hold of the hem of her shirt and pull it up over her, exposing her stomach and her breasts.

Don't get carried away.

I shut the door behind me. "Ella?"

She jolts and turns her head to look at me in surprise.

But she doesn't move otherwise or attempt to cover herself up, which is what I expected. In fact, she had to have known I was just standing there and ogling the hell out of her and she didn't do a thing about it.

Interesting.

I push that out of my head for now.

"Feeling okay?" I ask.

"You tried to murder me last night," she mutters, closing her eyes with a wince. "Murder me with alcohol so you can collect my inheritance."

"How much are you worth, by the way?" I ask as I saunter over to the bed, secretly thrilled that she's still lying there in her underwear.

"Me? I have no idea. Probably nothing," she says, blinking up at me as I stand over her. "Ugh." She covers her face with her hands.

"My handsomeness blinding you?"

"No," she mumbles through her fingers. "But the light behind you is."

"I notice that you didn't deny my handsomeness."

She sighs, and her hands drop away. She rolls on her side and gives me a weary look. "What do you want, Magnus?" It's then that she grabs the end of her t-shirt and covers her butt with it. I almost say something in protest.

"Considering I only got up twenty minutes ago, I wanted to see if you were alive."

"This is why I don't drink much," she says. "Jane says I turn into Princess Lush and then Princess Lush turns into Princess Fuck Me I'm Hungover."

"I do like the sound of Princess Fuck Me. Perhaps she can pay us a visit."

She gives me a caustic look. "Don't even start with me today."

"Baby, I'll start with you all day, every day." I grin and reach out for her hand, holding it in mine. "Remember when you let me do this last night? You were such a hussy."

She bursts out laughing and takes her hand back. "Hussy! Now that's a word I didn't think I'd hear you say."

"The Norwegian equivalents are rather crude."

"Let me guess, you're going to teach them to me?"

"Later. And maybe some Swedish, too."

She frowns. "Swedish?"

"Listen, I have a proposition for you."

"This better not be a marriage proposal."

"Very funny. No. But hey, thanks for letting me know where you stand at this point. You know our two weeks is almost up."

"I'm just joking," she says quietly, her gaze dropping to the sheets.

"Anyway," I smooth on over because I'm not about to get bogged down in anything serious. "I just got a call from my friend Viktor. He's the Prince of Sweden. Don't hold that against him. He called wanting to get away for a bit, I guess his fiancée and his mother are going to Paris on a girls' trip."

"Queens go on girls' trips?"

"Why not? Anyway, he's coming over and we're going to one of the family cabins north of here for a couple of nights. Just to get sloppy drunk, shoot guns into the air, jump in freezing lakes, fish, fall over into campfires, eat junk, that sort of thing."

"Oh," she says, and her voice is barely above a whisper. "That's nice."

"You're coming."

She glances up at me through her long lashes and frowns. "I am?"

I nod. "We snuck you out last night and we can do it again. We'll have private transportation all the way to the mountain, so we won't see a soul. And then we hike."

"For how long?"

"It's just a couple of hours at the most. It's easy. Mostly. Unless it snows. It probably won't." I pause. "You in?"

She bites her lip in thought. "What if I say no? Will you still go?"

Is she testing me? Fine. I'll pass.

"I wouldn't. I'd tell Viktor I'll see him another time. Look, Ella, we don't have much time together, and I'm not wasting a single second without you."

Her brows shoot up. Guess she wasn't expecting the truth outside of question time.

"Okay," she says, a small smile appearing on her lips. "Then I'm in. Wait, what about Jane?"

I sigh. The cabin is tiny. There's a loft and a bedroom beneath, and that's about it. I'm not sure how the hell we'll all fit but I shrug. "It's a tight squeeze for everyone, but I'm sure we can make it work."

But later when Ella goes to tell Jane about it, Jane quickly declines.

"Do you really think I'm going to go hiking up a bloody mountain and then stay overnight in a cabin that's probably surrounded by bears? Maybe the princess doesn't mind roughing it, but in a case like this, I'm very much a lady."

I didn't bother pointing out that Norway doesn't really have a lot of bears, but her point was made. It was also followed up with a salacious winky face, which made me think she was sitting this out for other reasons.

And maybe Ottar got a hint because he also declined.

Which left Einar—who never sits anything out—and Ella.

And Viktor, of course, who arrived at the estate fairly quickly. That's one good thing about being royalty—you're treated like royalty. He got on a private jet and landed in a rural airfield not too far from here.

"You made it," I tell him. Ella and I are standing on the front steps of the house as he gets out of the car I sent for him.

"I bribed the pilot to fly faster," he says with a wink. Viktor is a tall motherfucker, about six-foot-five and obnoxiously blessed with a movie-star face. When the tabloids would have their "Battle of the Sexy Single Princes," Viktor always came out on top. I blame his height. And his face. And his charm. You see, if anyone is meant to be king, it's him, even though I know before he met his fiancée, Maggie, he was second-guessing his role.

As Viktor smiles at Ella and approaches us, I lean into her and whisper, "It's proper to address him as *Svenskefaen*."

"Okay," she says with a nod and waits until Viktor extends his hand.

"It's so nice to meet you Your Serene Highness," he says.

Of course he would know the official way of addressing Ella.

Which makes what she's about to say that much funnier.

"Thank you, *Svenskefaen*," she says.

Viktor jerks his head back and stares at her a moment before erupting into laughter. "What?" he barks. He looks at me accusingly. "You taught her that, didn't you!"

"What, what?" Ella asks, bewildered. "What happened?"

"I'm sorry," Viktor says, trying to compose himself. "I'm so sorry. But you just called me a damn Swede."

Ella goes bright red and then turns to me. "You shitbag!"

I giggle and try to avoid her fists which are currently pounding into my arm. "Hey, you're an honorary Norwegian now. If you want to be like us, you have to learn how to insult the Swedes."

"It's true," Viktor says dryly. "Only Norwegians would come up with a derogatory slur toward Swedes. We, on the other hand, would never stoop to that level."

"Maybe you should," I tell him. "It's more fun down here."

After Ella is thoroughly embarrassed, we don't have much time to stand around. We've already packed, so we grab our backpacks that I found in one of the storage rooms and get in the car.

It's a three-hour drive to the ski resort town of Geilo, with the trail to the cabin located about thirty minutes past that. It's already dark by the time Einar swings the car into the parking spot at the end of a deserted road, and I know Ella is getting nervous.

"Shouldn't we stay in a hotel?" she asks as we stand outside the car, putting on our hats, gloves, and backpacks. Einar is lighting up everything with a lantern.

"We'll be seen in a hotel," I tell her and reach over to tighten the straps around her chest. A grin spreads across my face which in turn makes her laugh.

"You know I can do that myself," she says.

"I know," I tell her. "Any excuse to touch you."

"Besides, hotels aren't fun," Viktor speaks up. "They're boring. Unless you're alone with someone..." He trails off and in the white light I can tell he's thinking of Maggie.

Damn Swede.

I look at Ella. "What Viktor is trying to say is that this is what we always do. Hike up in the dark or around sunset. Makes it more exciting *and* makes it so you won't run across any hikers on the way up because, believe me, if people catch wind that we're there, the cabin will be surrounded before you know it."

Ella still doesn't look convinced, and I don't blame her. But she straightens the backpack on her shoulders, puts her chin up, and puts on a brave face.

Which, of course, only makes me admire her more.

And I wasn't lying either when I said the hike wasn't hard. The first quarter is up an old logging road with a fuckton of switchbacks, then the road peters out into a path through a bog, and then the path ends, and you have to just guess your way. The sky opens as the pine trees start to become sparse, and we're surrounded by rocks and moss and low cloudberry and blueberry bushes that will gleam golden under sunlight. At night everything is dark and haunting.

Aside from a soaking foot from stepping in the boggy ground, everyone handles the hike with relative ease, even as Ella huffs and puffs.

"I'm so not in shape," she whines as she hikes ahead of me.

"Well, you certainly look it. Do you want to take a breather? Need some water? A beer? Viktor's already drinking a beer."

"*Skal*," comes Viktor's voice in the dark.

"I'm fine," she says and keeps walking.

The last part of the climb is the steepest, and of course,

the higher we go, the colder it gets. As far as I can tell though there's been no recent snowfall. It's mid-October and anything goes at this time of year.

Luckily, we're over the bare face of rock and back into the treeline again where it's easy to grab tree trunks to keep ourselves on the path.

Then the cabin rises out of the forest like a ghost.

"This is it," I tell Ella as we all stop in front of it, catching our breath. "What do you think?"

"I like it," she says after a moment. "I guess I was expecting something more..."

"Royal? No. This is barely maintained, barely used, and barely functioning, and that's just the way we like it."

Originally the cabin was built by my mother's grandfather way back when, and it wasn't until she became queen that it came into the royal family's hands. It really is small, as is the custom for these types of places in the mountains. There's a little shelter to the side where firewood is stacked, as well as skis and snow boots.

Inside there's a fireplace, a tiny couch and chairs which have been the setting for many drinking games, a tinier kitchen, a bedroom and a loft upstairs, to which you have to take a long ladder. Family heirlooms and old knickknacks clutter up the rest of the space. The cabin is like a time warp to the 1940s.

It's cold as balls though, so we all rush about trying to get things heated up. Viktor starts bringing in the wood while Einar starts lighting all the candles.

"Where do I sleep?" Ella asks fretfully.

"Anywhere you want," I tell her.

Though, god, I'd so rather sleep with you than Viktor. Or Einar.

And those are my choices. I hope I'm conveying that with my eyes.

I must be, because she looks up the ladder. "There's a bed up there?"

"All yours if you want it."

She scrunches up her nose. "I'll have to pee in the night. That ladder will be the death of me. Where is the bathroom anyway?" She pokes her head around the corner into the kitchen as if she expects to see a toilet.

I jab my thumb to the door. "There's an outhouse."

A look of pure horror comes across her face.

"If it's fit for a prince, it's fit for a princess," I tell her.

"I'd rather go pee on a reindeer," she says.

I laugh. God, I could fucking kiss her right now. Why the hell did I agree to share my time with her with Viktor and Einar?

That sharp lance of fear that I've been trying not to feel over the last few days comes in and comes deadly.

We really don't have much time.

"Are you okay?" she asks softly, frowning as she looks me over.

I shake my head. "Yeah. Sorry. Just spaced out there."

"I'm used to that," she says and then gently touches my arm, as if to say she knows, as if to say she's here.

Helvete.

I need something to drink.

THIRTEEN

MAGNUS

ONCE THE FIRE IS ROARING IN THE CABIN AND THINGS are starting to warm up, candles flickering all over, the four of us sit down around the rough-hewn wooden coffee table that I'm pretty sure my grandfather cut from a tree around the corner. In fact, I think the whole cabin was built by trees felled just feet away.

On the center of the coffee table are bottles of aquavit, scotch, wine, beer, and a deck of cards. Even Einar is drinking, light beer, but still beer, since he doesn't really have to be on his guard up here. I think that's why he likes coming to the cabin. He can actually relax a little.

And we're all feeling pretty relaxed as the night goes on. Ella is beside me on the couch, and I'm doing the very adolescent thing where I'm taking up most of the space so she has no choice but to be pressed against me. She doesn't seem to mind though, and when she's laughing especially hard, she leans into me.

Jesus. It feels like I'm fifteen again and flirting with girls at a party, concentrating on every look, every touch. Gone is the Magnus that never had to choose because women were always throwing themselves at him. Here is the Magnus that has to work hard for every single inch.

"So, Ella," Viktor says to her. "Magnus tells me that you're into environmental issues and that sort of thing."

"That's right," she says. "Hope to have my own non-profit one day...perhaps here in Norway." This is sounding hopeful. "Something to keep governments accountable, to keep the people involved in what's going on with the resources, with the environment."

Viktor presses his lips together, impressed. "Considering how much alcohol we've had at this point, I'm impressed that you sound so articulate."

She shrugs and gives him a sloppy smile. "Perhaps the alcohol is tricking you into thinking I make sense."

But I've been watching Ella, and though it seems like she's drinking the same as the rest of us, she's been very slow to take sips and often has a glass of water in between. She's not drunk, she's acting the part.

Then, as if on cue, Einar gets up and tosses his two empty beer cans in the trash, which prompts Ella to get to her feet.

"What are you doing? Is that recycling?"

Einar gives her the funniest look, as if she's speaking some alien language, and I know his English is pretty good. "I beg your pardon?"

Ella marches over to the bin and pulls out the cans. "It'll be too gross to separate them later. Do you have a bag for them?"

"Ella," I tell her. "Just leave the cans on the counter. We'll deal with it the next time Viktor and I come up here. Come back and join the party."

She relents with a sigh and sits back down like nothing happened.

"*Princess Planet*," I start singing under my breath, leaning into her. "*She's a hero.*"

"*Gonna put pollution down to zero,*" Viktor finishes, grinning maniacally.

"Why do you keep singing that?" Ella asks me. It's true, I do hum it in the halls when I pass her.

"It's your song."

"Oh yeah? Well, you have a song, too."

"Was it on a kids' TV show in the nineties?"

"Prince shitbag," she starts singing into her beer, "oooh yeah, he's a bag of shit."

"That," I start, wanting to tell her that's not even a real song. But I say, "was pretty amazing."

"Princess Planet and Prince Shitbag," Viktor says, nodding his approval. "I'm rather liking this coupling."

"Shut up, you damn Swede," Ella tells him with a wicked grin.

"Fuck, that's the sexiest thing you've ever said," I tell her, my dick getting stiff. I have to adjust myself and hope she doesn't notice. With her angelic face, swearing has never sounded so good.

And then of course it turns into one long lesson of Norwegian swear words where I teach her the importance of the following swears:

Ronketryne = whack-off face

J'vla bonde = fucking farmer

Kuktryne = dickface

Jævla hore kuk = fucking whore dick

Jeg driter i melka di = I shit in your milk

After that last one, when everyone finally stops giggling, Einar suddenly shouts out, "*Jeg har runka bestefaren din!*"

Which causes both Viktor and I to exchange a look of shock before we burst out laughing.

"Einar!" I exclaim. "I never knew you had that in you."

"What does it mean?" Ella cries out. "Tell me!"

"No, no," Einar says quickly, and lo and behold, I think his face is going red. "It is not meant for your ears."

"Is it about me?" Her eyes are wide.

"Most definitely not," I assure her. But I can understand why Einar might feel ashamed if the Princess of Liechtenstein knew that he said, "I've jacked off your grandfather."

Einar, I hardly knew ye. Remind me to stay on his good side.

"Okay, I'm going to pee," Ella says, picking up a flashlight and heading to the door. "If I'm not back in five minutes...just wait longer."

The door shuts behind her and Viktor looks at me, brows raised.

"Did she just quote *Ace Ventura*?"

"I think so."

Little by little, Ella is unveiling herself to me, to everyone, her true self, the one she doesn't feel comfortable showing to many people, the one she buries because she tries hard to impress, to be included, to feel validated. If she feels all those things with me already, I think I'm winning.

"I think you've finally met your match, then," Viktor says. "I'm happy for you."

I give him a steady look as I take a long gulp of my scotch. "There's nothing to be happy about."

"You're going to get married to her."

I look at Einar and he looks away, not wanting to get involved, though I would love to know his opinion on the matter. He sees so much and says so little. Though apparently, when he does talk, he can be a crude motherfucker.

"That's not a guarantee," I remind Viktor. "I believe she

has two or three more days to make up her mind on whether she wants to go through with it or not."

"That's crazy," Viktor says. "Why wouldn't she?"

"Well, she doesn't love me, and I don't think she even likes me much."

"She likes you," Viktor says. "I can tell. Einar, what do you think?"

Einar clears his throat. "Well...I think you might be right, Your Highness. But whether she knows she likes him, whether she *wants* to like him, that's another thing." He then looks at me and raises his beer. "But you, Prince Magnus, you're head over heels for her. If you don't mind me saying, of course."

"I wouldn't go that far," I tell him, feeling slightly embarrassed.

"Don't worry," he says quickly. "She doesn't know, if that's what you're worried about. You remind me of me when I was younger. Like when I was a child."

"When was that, in the 1900s?" Viktor asks, snickering into his aquavit.

"Funny," Einar says humorlessly, his eyes spearing Viktor, not caring that he's giving stink eye to the Prince of Sweden. "When I was a child, if there was a girl I liked, I went out of the way to make her life miserable. I'd pull her hair. I'd put a thumbtack on her seat. I'd call her names. All because I wanted to get something out of her. Because I liked her. Sir, with all due respect, you remind me of that."

I can only shrug because what he's said is kind of true. If I didn't care about Ella at all, I wouldn't bother. I've never bothered with any woman before, never cared the way that I do.

But now that I know it, that I recognize it, I know I can't continue doing it. I have to tell her how I feel. That I like her and I want this to work. And I just wish that this whole marriage thing didn't exist, that I could just do this all in natural time, the way it happens for everyone else. I have real feelings in a very forced situation, and it's only getting more complicated by the second.

Ella comes back shortly after having survived her session with the outhouse and we get back into it, this time Viktor doling out playing cards and getting into a drinking game.

Ella drinks a little more this time, enough that her cheeks go red and her neck looks flushed, and soon she's getting up and saying it's too hot in here and she needs to get some air.

Naturally, I go outside and follow her.

The moon is almost full and bathing the cabin in cool light. It's cold, probably only five degrees above freezing, but it feels refreshing compared to the heat of the cabin.

"Are you okay?" I ask her, following her moonlit silhouette as she walks around the side of the cabin.

Then I remember that the cabin is built on the side of a rock face, and if she keeps walking, she'll take a nasty tumble.

I quickly run to her and grab her arm, pulling her back moments before she would have fallen.

"Hey!" she cries out, but I step back and pull her with me, not letting go.

"There's a drop-off right there," I tell her. "You almost went over."

"Shit," she swears, her hands now gripping my biceps. "I didn't know."

"It's kind of hard to tell in the dark." I jerk my head back. "The outhouse is back there. I hope you haven't been trying to pee off this ledge."

She lets out a weak laugh though I can tell she's still breathless. "No. Thank god. I just wanted to wander for a bit."

"So, are you okay?" I repeat.

"Yeah," she says. "I mean, better than if I had gone off the ledge." She glances up at me, her hands slowly trailing down my arms. "Thank you. For being here."

"If you haven't noticed, I've been here for the last two weeks."

She chews on her lip, seeming to consider that. "Yeah. Except for the times that you left."

"And now you know I was chilling in a bar with a bunch of old people. And I was talking about you."

"You were?" In the faint moonlight, her eyes seem to glow. I can hardly look away.

"Ella..." I start, then take in a deep breath. I grab her hands and keep her right against me. "I don't know if you've noticed, but I've always had trouble focusing on the right things. I've had a hard time trying to pay attention to things in life that most people do. I've struggled to make sense of the way I see the world. But...when I see you, you're all I see." I stare down at her lips. "I know that doesn't sound like much, but to me, it means everything. You're starting to mean everything to me."

Her lips part as she tries to process what I've said. I'm not being funny, I'm not being a jackass, I'm just being truthful. She's showing me parts of her, I'm showing her parts of me.

"Question time," I softly sing, sliding one of my hands to her lower back, my fingers pressing against her sweater.

She doesn't flinch. I take this as a win.

"Now?" she asks.

I only smile. "All we have is now."

She thinks that over for a moment, rubbing her lips together. "Isn't that a song?"

"A really fucking weird one, yes."

I smile and lean in a few inches. "So, my question is, Ella...if I kissed you, would you kiss me back?"

She moves her head just enough to look at me. Her eyes are searching mine, maybe to feel out my sincerity, maybe to see if she wants to. She swallows.

"No," she says.

A slow grin spreads across my face.

"Liar."

Her mouth opens. Then closes. Fear washes over her gaze. Because she knows she's lying, she knows I'm onto her.

And she knows I'll prove it.

"I'm not lying, Magnus. I..." she says, trailing off as she puts her hands up against my chest, ready to push me away.

But I'm tired of the push and pull.

I just want to pull her into me and into me and into me.

I want her to push everything else away, the way it happens for me when I'm around her, the way the world and the noise disappears except for her.

"You're a liar," I murmur again.

Then I lean in.

And I kiss her.

Her lips are soft, softer than I even imagined, and the tiniest bit wet. In the cold mountain air, they feel hot against mine, like two flames that have coiled together, and I'm suddenly struck by the immediacy of the moment, like for once I'm actually living all there is to live.

She tenses up under my kiss, under my hold on her, and I know she wants to prove something to me, that she doesn't want to kiss me back. But I don't know why.

I'm a damn good kisser.

But for as long as I can press my lips against hers, she won't yield.

And as much as I wish I was right, I won't make her.

I start to pull back in defeat but then her lips open against mine and her hand slips up to my cheek and her mouth and mine are flush.

I'm fucked. I'm totally fucked.

One kiss and it feels like my world is being cracked open.

Suddenly all I am is this desperate, trembling kind of hunger, the one that so often gets carried away. I'm hard as stone and pushing against her hip, and now my hands are going to her hair, disappearing into the silky strands that glow under the moonlight.

"Fuck," I murmur against her mouth, breathless as her tongue slides against the tip of mine. I feel like a fucking teenager again, about to bust a nut in my pants from just a simple kiss.

But no, this isn't a simple kiss. This is anything but simple. This is the kiss that might open the door to the most complicated relationship in history.

She moans something softly and that just about undoes me, like she's about to pull that one thread that will unravel me at the seams. Our kiss deepens, our lips finding their rhythm against each other, our kiss becoming as easy and passionate as our banter is.

I should have kissed her on day one.

All this time I could have had this sweet, warm, wet tongue writhing against mine and now, now it might be too late.

She pulls away slightly, breathing hard, and I can feel the pulse along her throat as my hand glides back to the base of her neck. It's beating a mile a minute and her skin is hot. I know her cheeks are pink. "Magnus," she whispers, swallowing hard, her gaze slowly trailing up from my lips to my eyes.

"I'm here," I whisper hoarsely. "I've been here all this time."

"I guess I'm a liar," she says, managing a smile that's both shy and wicked, like she's ashamed of what she did and yet is reveling in it.

Wanting more.

"I don't mind those kind of lies," I tell her, running my fingers through her hair. "So long as you don't mind when I seek out the truth."

I lean in again, but she puts her hand on my chest.

The push part of the push pull.

"We should probably go back inside," she says quietly, trying to seem crisp and composed. "You know, before they think we've been eaten by a bear. Or fallen in the outhouse."

"Or off a cliff. But I can promise you, they aren't thinking that." She rubs her lips together, about to protest, and I grab her hand. "Come on. I'm not letting go this time."

I lead her toward the cabin. Before we step back inside she says to me, "You don't mind if you and Viktor sleep up in the loft and I have the bed below?"

I pause and stare at her for a moment. For some reason I expected this to go differently, maybe because it always goes differently for me. Though with us, I should really learn that I don't know what to expect.

What had my father told me? Find someone that keeps you on your toes.

"Sure. Einar will be on the couch."

She squeezes my hand and stares up at me. "It's not that...it's not that I don't want you in my bed tonight. I just don't...I'm a bit drunk. That was one hell of a kiss. And I just don't trust myself around you...it wouldn't be appropriate. Especially here."

Oh.

She sure could have fooled me. She seems to have more control than anyone I know.

"Okay," I say with a nod. "That's not a problem."

Of course I'm wondering if she would say that if Viktor and Einar weren't here, and suddenly I'm cursing Einar and the damn Swede.

But it is what it is.

And with Ella I will gladly take whatever I can get.

I open the door for her and we step back inside the cabin, smiling at Einar and Viktor like my whole life hasn't changed out there.

FOURTEEN

ELLA

I HAVE THE DREAM AGAIN.

The same one as always.

The beached pilot whales.

The desolate beach.

The cold wind.

The man.

I still can't see his face, I can only get a vague idea of him, and every time I think I have a grasp on who he is, it flows out of my brain like water.

This time, though, he doesn't walk toward me.

He walks straight into the sea.

Past the whales, into the oil.

And I realize he was never meant to save me.

I was meant to save him.

When I wake up, it's to the sound of giggling.

I pry my eyes open and expect my brain to be sluggish, my head to be pounding. That was two nights in a row that I drank way more than I normally do. But to my surprise, I feel fine. I know I didn't drink as much as the night of the bar but maybe it's something to do with the crisp mountain air.

I slowly sit up in bed and climb out, having no idea what time it is. There's a window in the small room and it shows a light dusting of snow outside. The sight of the pure white coating the trees makes me smile. It will be nice to see what everything looks like in the daylight. I fell asleep in thermal leggings and layers of tops, so I just pull on a sweater and I'm warm enough.

I slowly open the bedroom door to see Magnus and Viktor fully dressed, standing over what seems to be a passed out Einar. Magnus has a Sharpie in his hand and has completed drawing half of a twirly mustache on Einar's face.

"You guys!" I hiss.

"Shhhhh!" Viktor shushes me, waving his hands. "We're almost done."

I shake my head and creep on over to them. Einar's nose is twitching, but he's not awake yet.

"You guys are so immature," I whisper. "To think you'll both be the kings of your country one day."

"If you think I won't draw mustaches on people when I'm king, you have another thing coming," Magnus says, concentrating as he finishes the rest of the mustache.

"Voila," Viktor says, grinning. "He looks like an evil villain."

He does. Like a cartoon character. I try not to laugh.

"He's going to kill you guys when he wakes up," I say, folding my arms. "And how is he still asleep? I didn't even think Einar blinked, let alone slept."

"This happens every time," Viktor explains. "He has a few beers and then he's dead to the world."

"What happens if someone tries to kidnap you guys and he's out cold?"

Viktor and Magnus look at each other in surprise and then Magnus says, "We'd pull a Kevin McCallister. You know. From *Home Alone*."

"But with guns," Viktor adds. "We have rifles. I was in the military. Don't worry, Princess, you're well protected."

I raise my brow. I don't know about that.

Now that the prank on Einar is over, Magnus proudly looks over his work, puts the cap back on the Sharpie with a triumphant click, and gives me a smile. "So, how did you sleep?"

"Good," I tell him, my eyes now glancing to the main window for the first time. "Oh my god, the view."

I walk over to the window and peer out. I can see now why I almost went over the edge last night. The cabin is built right on the lip of a rock face, leaving an unobstructed view of the valley below. You can see the snowline halfway down the slope of the adjacent mountain, like God just decided to stop painting. The mountains here are bare, with very few trees, which make them look otherworldly.

"Gorgeous," Magnus says from behind me, his voice so low and rough that it makes me think he might not be talking about the view at all. He stops right behind me, his hot breath on my skin.

I swallow hard and feel the little hairs on the back of my neck rise. Every memory of last night comes flooding back to me, but they had never left to begin with. I've just been too afraid to think about it.

But now, with the heat of Magnus's large body behind me, it's all I can think about. It demands I pay it attention.

The way he held me.

The way he looked at me.

The way he kissed me.

The things he'd said.

I both wanted and didn't want him to kiss me. It's all I've been wanting to think about ever since the night at the bar, when seeing him in his element with his quirky older friends made me realize there is so much more to this man than I've been giving him credit for. And when he held my hand, it made me realize how badly I'd been missing out on physical affection.

How much I've been subconsciously craving it from him.

But I also knew that if he kissed me, everything would change. It would make it harder for my decision to not get influenced by my hormones. It would make it harder to stay rational and logical. It would make it harder to not fall for this man.

And I was right.

He may have saved me from going over that edge, but his kiss sent me over it anyway.

Hopefully, there's still time to save myself.

I turn around and Magnus's face is right there, those full lips turned up into a sly smile, those dark, magnetic eyes that see right into my soul, right into every thought and intention I have. He knows what I'm about to do. That I'm going to push him away until I can think clearly again.

He's almost daring me to do it.

God help me if he springs a "question time" on me right now.

"I better go change into something warmer," I tell him, my gaze dropping from his as I quickly move past him to the bedroom. Behind me Viktor says he'll get the fire up and running.

I close the door to the bedroom and try to think. We

have another day up here in the cabin and I have no idea what's planned and—

The door to the room opens.

I whirl around in surprise to see Magnus step in and close the door behind him. "Don't you knock?" I cry out.

"I want to talk to you," he says, not looking the slightest bit ashamed of barging in.

"What about?"

"Last night," he says. He lowers his voice. "I kissed you. And, I'm sure against your better judgement, you kissed me back."

I stare at him as he walks toward me. The way he moves, so smoothly, so confidently, he reminds me of a predator. He's had way too much practice with this and that thought alone gets my hackles up.

"So?" I manage to say. There's no place for me to go, the wall is at my back.

He stops right in front of me, close, his shoes almost touching my toes. He peers down at me and I instinctively suck in my breath.

"So?" he repeats, his eyes trained on my lips. "You say that as if it didn't mean something to you."

"What was it supposed to mean?"

"That you're attracted to me."

I look away, my eyes going to the window, to the snow-dusted trees outside. Suddenly the cabin feels so small. "I think that's pretty obvious," I admit quietly.

He lets out a soft laugh. "Obvious? Ella…I can't get a read on you, no matter how hard I try."

I bring my gaze back to his, knowing that it'll be even harder now to look away. There's something so earnest in his eyes, and it disarms me. Then again, he's been steadily disarming me for days now.

"I don't think that's true," I tell him. "You had a pretty good read on me last night."

"That might have been dumb luck that you kissed me back. Or maybe I'm just that good of a kisser."

I can't help but smile at that. "You are a good kisser."

Not that I've had a ton of experience but it was definitely the best kiss that I've ever had. Kissing him was as easy and natural as breathing.

He studies me closely. "Then why do I get the feeling that you're going to go on pretending it never happened?"

Damn it.

"Ella?" he adds. "Don't make me ask again."

I look at him sharply. "Trying to boss me around? You might be the prince but this princess is her own ruler."

He grins. "Fuck you're hot when you tell me off."

"That was hardly telling you off."

"Then you're hot when you do anything. Tell me then," he says, his eyes skimming over my nose, my lips. "What are you so afraid of?"

I clear my throat, trying to stand taller. "I'm not afraid."

"Are you afraid that in a day or two you're going to say yes?"

"No."

Of course, that's exactly what I'm afraid of.

"Ella," he says softly, putting his hand at my cheek. His palm is so warm, so strong, my eyes automatically close and I lean into it. "If you say no..."

The thought wrenches something inside me.

Because if I say no, he'll have to find someone else.

Little by little, day by day, I've gone from wanting my freedom, my life that I left back in university, to having a hard time imagining a future without Magnus by my side in some way, shape, or form.

I mean, I don't love him. Most days I don't even like him. But no matter what mood we're in or who we are to each other, there's been one constant. He makes me feel *something*, like no one else ever has, even if it's just the fact that my body is starting to ache for his.

And this is why bringing sex and a physical aspect into this makes things that much more confusing.

"You only want me to say yes because you have to get married to someone," I say. "And I'm convenient. I'm right here. You've invested your time. It might as well be me."

He doesn't say anything to that and so I know I'm right. If the whole marriage thing was lifted and he was free to do whatever he wanted, I'd be pushed aside and forgotten, just like I normally am.

Some things don't change, at least not for me.

He sighs and lets his hand drop away from my face. My skin feels exposed now.

"Ella, if you don't want me now, I have a hard time believing you're ever going to change your mind," he says. From the way his arched brows are coming together, he actually looks hurt.

"I didn't say I don't want you. I just...this is a big thing."

Now he's back to his cocky grin, his default setting. "I know. Almost too big."

"You know what I mean." I lightly punch him in the chest, trying to bring this back to the easiness we had before. "I just need some space to figure things out."

He frowns, like he doesn't understand, then nods. "Okay. I can give you space. For what little time we have left." He steps away from me. "What did you want to do today? There's a small lake not too far behind here, and Viktor and I usually go fishing."

He sounds so casual now and looks the part, running his

hand through his lush hair, that it's hard to believe he just told me last night that I was everything to him.

It's just as hard to ignore the way that made me feel.

Wanted. Needed.

Desired.

I take in a deep breath. "Fishing sounds fine."

"Great, dress warm, put on your boots and—"

He's cut off by Einar yelling something in Norwegian.

Magnus and I both raise our brows at each other and run to the door, opening it to see Einar staring at himself in the mirror in pure horror while Viktor is keeling over laughing. Einar starts yelling at him again, angry and red-faced, only it just makes Viktor laugh harder. It's hard to take Einar seriously with that mustache.

"What is he saying?" I ask Magnus.

"Oh, he's letting loose a few of those swear words you learned. Viktor and I better sleep with one eye open tonight."

∼

"ARE YOU ALLOWED TO PLAY THAT QUESTION GAME with me?" Jane asks.

I look up from my book, a copy of *The Secret Garden*, to see Jane standing in the doorway. She looks like she's just gotten back from the stable and there are a few pieces of straw in her hair. While Magnus and I have gone off and done our things, she started taking an interest in riding, something she used to do as a child.

"You mean question time?"

She walks across the parlor room and sits down across from me. I don't bother pointing out that she left woodchips and dirt in her wake. She's gone from Lady Jane to Pigpen.

"Ella, you still haven't told me what happened at the cabin. Tomorrow is our last day here. You have to make your decision."

I sit up and look around, making sure Magnus or Ottar aren't hanging within earshot.

"Relax," she says. "Magnus went for a run. You'd hear him if he came back. That man can't be silent even if he tried."

"Where's Ottar?"

"He went running too."

"And Einar?"

"Right here," Einar says with his hand up, suddenly appearing in the corner of the room where apparently he'd been sitting for who knows how long.

"Jesus, Einar," I swear, always jumpy when I suddenly discover him somewhere. "You were easier to spot when you had that mustache."

He raises his brow at that but doesn't say anything as he exits the room. It took a great deal of soap and Jane's extra-strength makeup remover to get that stuff off.

Jane watches him until he's gone, then looks back to me. "So, what happened?"

"Who says something happened? I mean, other than Einar's mustache."

"You and Magnus went from being all starry-eyed and flirty with each other before the trip to staying away from each other like you both have the plague."

"We were never starry-eyed and flirty."

"You don't think so, but I know. Ella, this whole thing has been playing out in front of me like I'm watching a live version of *Downton Abbey*. It's been glorious."

I tuck my feet underneath my legs and settle deeper

into the couch. "Well, I'm glad that this has been pure entertainment for you."

"Something happened. You need to tell me."

I roll my eyes. "It's cold. We should get another log on the fire."

"If that's your way of telling me I need to put another log on the fire, I'm not playing. Or I will...if you tell me the truth. Did you sleep with him?"

"God no," I exclaim, but my face is going hot, only because of the amount of times I've thought about it.

"No?"

"No," I repeat. And then the words spill out, "He...we kissed."

Jane gives me a knowing smile. "I figured something would happen. That's why I wanted to stay out of it. How was it?"

I close my eyes and let my head tilt back against the couch, reliving that moment. The way his mouth moved with hunger, the feel of his erection pressing against my hip, hard as a rock. "It was good," I say softly.

"Then why the hell are you ignoring him? You should be snogging every chance you get! And then some."

I look at her with a sigh. "Because. I don't want that to cloud my judgement."

"Ella!" she exclaims. "It should cloud your judgement! And it's not bloody clouding it, it's illuminating it. Ella, if you want him, then marry him."

"I still don't love him. I would be marrying for all the wrong reasons. What if all we have is a marriage full of sex and nothing else?"

Jeez, does she ever look disgruntled. "Do you know how many women, myself included, would kill for a marriage full of sex? Good lord. You've gone batty."

"I want love," I tell her. "What if I never feel that way for him. What if..." And, I *know* this is the bigger fear, "what if I do feel that way for him and he never does for me?"

Jane tilts her head sympathetically. "No one has the answers. Even those who fall in love and marry for the right reasons. People fall out of love, grow apart. There are no guarantees, no matter how you go into it."

"But at least they're doing it for the right reasons. Starting off on the right foot."

"Are you marrying for the right reasons? No. Maybe not. But you do have your reasons, don't you? Otherwise you wouldn't be here right now, reading on the couch of what could be your potential home."

I hadn't even thought about making this place my home, but since I would write that into the list of demands, I guess it's possible.

She goes on, her voice quiet now. "If you say yes, you have your reasons and you know what they are already."

Originally, my biggest reasons have fallen to the wayside.

Having power and a voice.

Having the ability to make a huge difference in the world.

Having respect of people.

The admiration of my father.

The biggest reason for me to say yes is the simplest one: hope.

I don't know what lies ahead in my future, but I do know which future gives me the greatest shot at hope.

And that's being with Magnus.

There's a world of hope hidden in my heart for him.

My phone rings, jolting me out of my thoughts.

I quickly reach over to the coffee table and pick it up, glancing at the screen.

"Your father?" Jane asks.

My heart sinks. My father hasn't called once while I've been here.

Instead, I think this might be the Queen. A private number out of Oslo.

I shake my head and answer it. "Hello?"

"Ella, dear." Yup. Magnus's mother.

Clearing my throat, I say, "Good afternoon, Your Majesty."

"Please, you know it's Else."

"Did you want to talk to Magnus?" I ask, not knowing how she got this number and not wanting to talk to her on the phone.

"That's quite all right," she says. "I just wanted a word with *you*."

Oh god.

"I wanted to see how things were progressing."

Oh god.

"You know we'll be coming by tomorrow with the lawyers and the contracts to go over your final decision."

Oh god.

"Oh, yes. I thought for some reason we would be going to the palace," I tell her.

"It's too risky for that. Someone might see you. The press hasn't been able to locate Magnus lately and it's put them on edge."

I cringe thinking about the fact that I went to the bar and the cabin and she has no idea.

"Tell Magnus that we'll be by before noon tomorrow. If the cooks can put something together for the King and I, it would be much appreciated. We'll probably be famished after all the celebrating."

Oh. God.

"Okay," I whisper. "Goodbye."

I hang up, not caring if that's the proper way to end the phone call with the Queen or not. My god did she ever sound confident about my answer.

"That bad, huh?" Jane asks.

I give her a miserable look. "She thinks I'm going to say yes."

"And are you?"

I sigh, getting to my feet. "I'm going to go have a nap. I can't deal with this right now."

"You better learn to deal with it, then," Jane says. "Tomorrow will be here before you know it."

That's what I'm afraid of.

I head to my room, close the door, and promptly flop down on the bed. I just want a few moments of clarity. Time to breathe. I don't even want to think because my brain feels so overloaded.

And apparently, it's so overloaded that within seconds, the room goes black and I drift away into a blissful sleep.

Only to awake again when I hear "Ella" being whispered from someplace above me.

I open my eyes. The room is dark, except for the lights outside which stream in faintly through the far windows. It has to be at least dinnertime. And then I notice the figure hovering over me, the glint of the lights shining in his eyes.

I take in a sharp breath, but I'm not afraid.

"Magnus?" I say.

"I didn't mean to wake you," he murmurs. He's standing by the side of the bed, one hand resting on the edge of the mattress, inches away from my hip. "Dinner will be ready soon."

"Oh," I say, swallowing the sleep in my throat. "I slept that long."

"I guess you needed it." A long beat pauses. I can hear him breathing, hear the pulse of blood in my head. "I've been giving you space, Ella. But I'm over it now."

"Over it?" I manage to say.

He nods. "I let you do what you needed to do and think what you needed to think. But now it's time for my needs."

Am I dreaming? What is happening?

"What needs?"

Do I want to know?

"We both know what tomorrow is. We both know I gave you space and left you alone so you could make your decision. But I've been tired of waiting for you to come around, tired of waiting for you to make up your damn mind."

Is he kidding me? "Make up my damn mind?" I tell him, anger coursing through me. Suddenly I'm more awake than ever.

I sit up. "I know you're used to things being handed to you on a silver platter and doing whatever the fuck you want, but I'm not. This is a big deal, okay? For Christ's sake, I'm only twenty-two, Magnus! One day I'm trying to figure out how I can get my flatmates to like me and whether I can get an A or an A+ on a test, the next day I have to consider becoming the Princess of Norway. Marriage wasn't even on my radar before you came along! How do you expect me to—"

"I'm not going to marry you."

His words hit me like a fucking bomb, shrapnel lacing my heart.

"What?" I eke out, unable to breathe.

"I'm going to marry someone else," he says, so swiftly, so glibly, like he doesn't have a care in the world, as if he's not obliterating me right now. "You can't make up your mind and that's your answer right there. I'm going to go try my luck with the Princess of Belgium instead. You're off the hook, Princess Planet. Go back to your other life."

Then he turns and starts walking to the door.

I don't know whether to burst into tears or attack him.

I decide on the latter.

"You fucking asshole!" I yell at him, springing out of bed and running over to him, shoving him against the wall.

Well, attempting to shove him. He's built like a tree and those roots don't budge.

"You piece of shit!" I scream, banging my fists into him. "You, you..."

"Shitbag?" he offers, and I swear he's smiling.

"That doesn't even begin to explain what you are. You're scum. You're a fuckface. You're whatever swear word Einar said the other day."

"You jacked off my grandfather?"

"What? Oh my god. *That* was what he said? No."

He reaches out and grabs my wrists, holding them with an iron grip. "I told you I like it when you get nasty with me."

"Fuck you!" I yell, and I'm pretty sure I'm spitting in his face. In the dim light, it's hard to tell. "You played me! You used me! You told me lies, you made me think you wanted *me*!"

My god, he looks absolutely delighted that I'm screaming at him. Where the fuck does he get off, well, getting off on my anger?

"Ella," he says calmly. "I'm just making the decision for you."

"I need to make it myself!"

"Actually, you think the ball has been in your court this whole time, but the ball has been in mine. You think I was waiting around to find out if you'd say yes or not? I was waiting around to find out if you were worth marrying or not."

I stare at the ground, collapsing under the weight of this all.

Oh my god. He doesn't think I'm worth marrying. I'm not worth anything at all. Once again, I'm kicked to the curb, I'm sent off, I'm...

I think my heart is breaking.

"And you are," he adds simply.

My head flies up. "What?"

"You are worth marrying, Ella," he says.

I blink at him rapidly. "I don't understand. You just said you were going to go marry the Princess of Belgium."

"I'm pretty sure the Princess of Belgium is sixty years old," he says. "And while I do like my older friends, I have to draw the line somewhere."

What the fuck?

"I don't get it. Why would you say all of that to me?"

"Because I wanted to get a reaction out of you."

"You ass!" I try to punch him in the chest again but his hold on me is too strong. "A reaction? You almost broke my heart right there."

Even in the shadows, I can see his features soften. "Then isn't that your answer?"

He's got me. He's completely got me there.

To think of him leaving me and marrying someone else, it nearly broke me just now. So why on earth could I have ever imagined leaving him? Was it because for once I wanted to be in control, to have the power I so often wish I had? Was that my way of asserting myself when it comes to him?

"Look, Ella," he says, letting go of my hands and cupping my face, making me feel cradled and small. He peers at me intently, his eyes glinting. "The situation hasn't changed, but we have. Maybe this wasn't how we saw our lives going, but right now, I can't think of it going any other way. I know you have your reservations and you're entitled to them. I have mine too. I know we've only known each other for a few weeks and I know we're not in love. We're barely in like. But I do know that I want to do this with you and I can only hope you'll do it with me."

My breath is starting to come back to me, my heart is starting to slow, and yet my nerves feel like they've been laced with gasoline and he's about to throw a match on it.

"Question time," he says softly.

My throat feels thick. "You didn't sing it."

"It feels too serious for that," he says. "Ella, will you marry me?"

I try not to think about it.

I just open my mouth and blurt it out.

"Yes."

He grins so broadly it makes him look positively boyish. "Do you mean that?"

Holy shit. I actually do.

"Yes. I do. I mean, I have a list of demands before we actually get married."

"Oh, I've heard you mention it plenty of times."

"And I'm not sure you can meet them."

"I'll meet you on everything, Ella."

Oh hell, I might as well get this hard part over with. "One of them involves sex."

"I am very much into meeting your demands there."

I flash him a quick smile. "I just…"

"Ella," he says reassuringly, his hands trailing down to hold on to mine. "I'm aware this isn't conventional. I don't expect anything of you. Whether on our wedding night or after that. We'll just take this day by day."

I jerk my chin back. "You're serious? That doesn't sound like a Magnus thing to say."

"I didn't say I wouldn't try and seduce you at every fucking turn," he tells me. "Because, believe me, that's exactly what I'm going to do."

The thrill that runs up my spine nearly brings me to my knees.

"I'll be ready for you," I tell him, my voice sounding choked.

He bites his lip as he smiles. "Yeah, you will be."

Then he leans in and places a long, wet, soft kiss right beside my lips. I never knew something so chaste could feel so sexual. "I'll go tell the cooks you're coming down," he says as he pulls away and leaves the room.

It feels like he takes all the air with him.

What have we done?

FIFTEEN

MAGNUS

I'M GETTING FUCKING MARRIED.

A phrase that once would have made me want to be sick now only makes me smile.

Okay, so it's a shaking smile, a nervous smile. I'm smiling on the outside and I'm a pile of writhing nerves on the inside.

But that's to be expected.

Ella and I have been thrust into a whole new world.

The night that she said she would marry me was the last night the two of us had any peace and quiet.

The next morning my mother came over.

It was supposed to be my father too, but he wasn't feeling that well, which of course immediately put me on edge. My mother insisted, though, that he was doing better and that I'd see him soon enough.

So, with Sigurd and a lawyer that Ella had summoned for herself, since she's smart like that, we all gathered in the parlor and spread out the contracts, which now included Ella's list of demands (minus the sex part):

1. She gets to pick where we live (and she's picked this place, which she calls Thornfield Hall for some reason).

2. She gets to open up and head her own non-profit as soon as possible (I told her to call it the Princess Planet Foundation but she wasn't keen on that).

3. In the event of public embarrassment, AKA if I do something stupid like have an extramarital affair (not going to happen) or anything else that makes her look bad, she has the right to leave the relationship, no questions asked. If it happens after we are married, we will divorce, no contest.

4. We get a dog (rescued, preferably).

5. We open a dog shelter (demand number four suddenly spurred on the edition of demand number five, to be added later. I made them add that I can pick the name).

6. She has the option of finishing her university degree in Oslo.

THEN THE CONTRACTS WERE SIGNED AND THE MOMENT that was done, my mother proudly announced to us that she knew that Ella would come around and that she'd already gotten a head start on the wedding plans with the help of my sisters.

In fact, it was then that she handed Ella the sparkling engagement ring she picked out for her. I obviously didn't have one to propose with, though I would have liked to have some time to pick one out myself.

Needless to say, that was the first sign that there would be no gentle transition into this arrangement. Ella and I were to go from two weeks of isolation to being torn in a million different directions by a million different people.

At least we're in it together. Because I'm the one who has had experience in the public eye, Ella has been leaning a lot on me, and I've been trying to shoulder the brunt of it and show her the ropes.

Especially now with our first on-camera interview. It's not even with a Norwegian network but the BBC. You'd think they'd be over that royal stuff by now but it seems they're jonesing for another Meghan and Harry. I think they're claiming Ella as one of their own, though, since she went to boarding school and university in the UK.

"How do I look?"

I'm standing in front of the mirror and adjusting my tie when she appears in the reflection, standing behind me in the doorway. We're supposed to be somewhat dressy for the interview, but the sight of her is making my heart stop.

My hands fall away from my tie, and I have to remember to breathe.

It's just a simple dress, royal blue and sleeveless with a scoop neck.

But the dress is fitted, showing her every curve, and her golden hair is down around her shoulders in cascading waves. I don't think I've ever seen her so shapely, ever seen her hair so wild and free, begging me to wrap the strands around my hand.

I slowly turn around and she shyly walks toward me, stopping in the middle of the room and sticking her hips out to one side, arms raised, as if to say "ta-da."

"I'm speechless," I finally say, licking my lips.

She smiles warmly. "I can see that. Maybe I should dress up more often. Though I do have my dress fitting tomorrow and we do have our engagement photos in a couple of days. Honestly, I don't know why since we're getting married so soon after."

"The pictures are my mother's idea, you know that," I tell her. "But it makes her happy."

She nods and we stare at each other, long beats stretching out between us.

Even though it's been five days since we signed the contracts and two days since the news broke publicly that we are engaged, and we've been together almost every step of the way, there are a lot of little moments just like this one. Moments of slight awkwardness, of sexual tension. This whole thing is so strange and new, and fuck, *scary,* but underneath it all is the fact that I want her like I've never wanted any woman before.

And I know she wants me.

But that kiss we shared at the cabin was the last time— the only time—we were physically intimate in any way. And even though I want to be as respectful of her wishes as possible, I am a hungry, greedy man who would like nothing more than to relieve her of that dress, throw her on the bed, and make her scream my name until the whole house shakes.

"There's a problem," I tell her gravely.

She sucks in a breath. I slowly bring my gaze up the length of her body and focus on her fearful brown eyes.

"What?" she asks.

"You look extremely fuckable."

Those eyes widen, stunned. "That's a problem?" she asks after a beat.

I grin and walk over to her. "Yeah, it's a problem." I stop right in front of her and reach for her hair, letting the smooth strands run through my fingers before brushing it over her shoulder. "You see, according to the story we've been telling everyone, we've been on-again, off-again lovers for a long time. Years. And I finally broke down and admitted my love for you. Swept you off your feet in an extravagant proposal that involved trained peacocks, a flock of doves, and a monkey. And in order for that to be believable to everyone, especially the people at home watching our interview, we have to act like we've been passionate lovers for years and are finally celebrating our overdue love by getting married. You get what I'm saying?"

She does. I can tell from the way she's breathing heavier, the way her pupils are dilating as she stares at my lips, the way she swallows, her throat so pale and delicate I'm suddenly envious of vampires.

I let my hand drift down over the smooth slope of her shoulder, down her arm, to her hand. "The more I touch you, the more you touch me, the more believable this is going to be. If we go out there as we are, where you try to run every time I come near you, it's not going to work."

"I'm not running now," she whispers and meets my eyes. "Try me."

My lips curl into a smile. "I will. Maybe it's best, though, if you try me first." I take a step back. "Go ahead. Touch me."

She lets out an incredulous huff of air. "I can't touch you on demand."

"Sure you can. I give you permission."

She shakes her head. "This doesn't seem right."

"Princess, nothing seems right at this point." I walk around her over to the door and close it.

Lock it.

"What are you doing?" she asks warily. "Magnus, I thought you agreed—"

"Would you just relax," I tell her, turning around. "I'm not making you do anything."

But as I walk toward her, I'm removing my tie and throwing it on the bed. I'm removing my suit jacket and tossing it on the ottoman.

"Magnus," she warns.

I smile and start unbuttoning my shirt. It's wildly presumptuous of me but I've seen the way she stares at my body when I'm parading it around in front of her. I know the thoughts she's had. I know that she's ashamed that she's had them.

I also know that she's somewhat inexperienced, that I intimidate her, that my sexual history scares her a bit.

It's better if I'm the vulnerable one here.

"This is the body you're going to be sleeping next to after we're married," I tell her, my shirt dropping to the floor.

"Actually, that was never in the contract," she points out as I start unbuckling my pants next. "You know I want separate bedrooms."

I'm going to pretend the fact that she's still sticking to that doesn't hurt.

"Then this is the body you're supposed to have been sleeping with for years," I amend as my pants drop to my ankles, leaving me in just my gray boxer briefs. "You better get a damn good look at it. Please. It will be such a waste otherwise. Years and years of marriage ahead of us and no one to admire my hard work."

She's trying not to smile as her eyes drop to my dick.

Hard work, indeed. I've never been stiffer.

I run my thumbs along the waistband. "Want them on or off?"

"On," she says quickly. "I'm having a hard time handling all of this as it is."

"Well, I definitely have something hard for you to handle."

She laughs, her cheeks redder than ever. But when her eyes meet mine, they're sparkling deviously, like she's enjoying this. "So now what? This is your plan for us to get comfortable with each other? Just you standing there in your underwear with your pants around your ankles?"

"Don't forget my hard-on. It's the perfect accessory."

She shakes her head, eyes closing briefly. "Honestly, Magnus. You are such a man-child."

"Definitely all man," I tell her. "Touch me and find out for yourself."

"This is way too weird," she says as I step out of my pants, taking off my socks and pushing them to the side. Now I really am all naked except for my boxers.

"Do you want people to believe we're comfortable with each other physically or not?"

"I..." She trails off, her eyes roaming freely all over me now, like she just gave herself permission to take me in. She licks her lips then says, weakly, "I can fake it."

I don't say anything to that. I'm at the point where opening my mouth isn't doing me any good. I feel like a fucking fisherman with their line dangling in the water, waiting for hours on end to see if the fish will bite.

She comes closer to me.

Hell, it's working.

I keep quiet, holding my breath so as not to scare her, as she reaches out and touches the Viking axe tattoo on my shoulder. "When did you get this one?" she asks.

"When I was twenty," I tell her. "I went to Thailand, as one does. Woke up with it."

She smiles, letting her fingertips trace the outline. My skin comes alive under her touch. "That's not a very romantic story."

"No. Most of my life hasn't been very romantic, to tell you the truth. Just impulse after impulse."

Her fingers freeze, and she gives me a sharp look.

"I mean with travel," I assure her. "Or tattoos. Or spending money. Some days I wake up in other countries. Some days I buy a car and then leave it somewhere I don't remember. Some days I get tattoos. Now mind you, this Viking tattoo was one I wanted for a long time. And Thailand was a place I'd always wanted to go. And I'd always wanted to drive a Ferrari for one day. It's just that these things have an odd way of working out with me."

"Very odd," she says softly, gently squeezing my muscles now. "But I think that's what I like most about you."

"My bulging biceps?"

"Your...uniqueness. How terribly boring it is to be normal. I should know. I'm normal and I'm boring. I'm not even interesting enough to be a basic bitch."

It breaks my heart to hear her say that.

"That is nowhere near true," I tell her, my voice rising a bit. "You're not boring. You're more normal than I am but you're not boring. You're not basic. You're smart as hell. You're interesting. I'm always learning something from you, every single day. You're not afraid to put me in my place, you keep me on my toes. You're gracious, you've got a big heart, and you've fought really hard to become the person you are. I can tell. I know what that fight is like."

She gazes at me with those searching eyes of hers, her face just inches from mine, and I know if I lean in just a bit, my lips will brush her lips. It takes all my restraint to stay in control.

"You're breathing hard," she says after a moment, her fingers resuming their path, this time across my chest which is rising and falling faster than usual.

"You've got me all fired up," I tell her, my voice coming across gruff and low. "I don't want to hear you talk about yourself like that. I will always defend you, even from yourself."

Her eyes go to my mouth and all I can think is *kiss me, kiss me*, and it pains me that I need this to be in her court. I swear to god, the moment she does, all hell will be unleashed. I've got enough pent-up sexual tension to last into the marriage and beyond.

She knows I'm thinking that too. She might even enjoy it. Again she glances at my dick and again her expression turns hot and wanton.

Her hands slide around my other shoulder and she walks around to the back of me. "I'm still not sure what you're trying to accomplish here."

Even though I can't see her eyes, I can feel them on my ass.

"The British royals never touch each other like this in public," she goes on, running her fingers gently over my shoulders. "Maybe not even in private."

"We're Norwegians. We do things differently."

"Savagely," she says, now bringing her hands down my back, her nails scratching me gently.

Oh fuck that feels good.

"Trust me," I growl. "I'm holding back."

"And what happens when you let go?"

I nearly let out an explicit groan. "I don't think you'll be able to handle me."

"Try me." I hear the smile in her voice.

Oh, fuck me.

I manage to swallow. "Do you know what you're asking for?"

A pause. "Then tell me."

This is a side of her I didn't think I'd see so soon. Maybe touching me has riled her up the same way it's made me fucking stiffer than cement.

"Is this an official question?"

"I'm not singing it."

"Well I'm going to answer it anyway."

She moves her hands around the sides of my waist, letting them run over the hard ridges of my abs, down, down. Stopping just at the waistband.

My breath hitches in my throat.

She reaches further and slowly slides her palm down, down, down, over the hardened length of my cock.

My eyes flutter back in my head.

Sweet Jesus.

She grips it, hard.

Helvete.

There is no holding back now.

I whip around and grab her face, her beautiful, sweet face and kiss her more wildly, more violent and desperate than I've ever felt before. Her mouth is warm silk as my tongue thrusts inside, wanting to claim every wet inch, and her skin feels like the best version of heaven.

Valhalla.

A small whimper escapes her lips and into my mouth and her hands are on my bare chest, trying to push me back, but I can't wait. Not anymore.

I grab her roughly, and with a grunt, whirl her around

and throw her on the bed. She bounces on it, her mouth open in surprise.

I reach down and pull off my boxers.

Not hiding anything now.

She's breathless and wide-eyed as she stares at my naked, massive cock for the first time. It's just the reaction I want. Actually, she's looking slightly intimidated, which isn't bad for my ego.

"Do you know I've thought of this every single night from the moment I first saw you?" I tell her hoarsely. "Do you know how badly I've wanted you? Do you know how much I've dreamed of doing exactly this?"

"Stop talking and show me," she says breathily.

I didn't expect her to say that.

But fuck does it ever spur me on, especially in that *fuck me* voice of hers.

Whatever restraints that were holding me back are now snapping loose, and the animal inside is coming out to play, to hunt, to take what's his, what he needs and desires more than anything.

Ella, every way I can get her.

I prowl onto the bed, my cock jutting out, as I put my hands on her thighs and spread her legs, hiking her dress up to her waist.

She's wearing just a thin pair of cotton underwear, the type I could make transparent in seconds. In fact, it looks like she doesn't need much help. She's wet like anything.

I bring my finger to the edge of her panties and pull it aside, exposing her bare, glistening flesh.

"*Helvete*," I murmur, taking her all in. "You're so fucking gorgeous, you know that? Perfectly pink, wet, and, god, I bet you're tight."

She lets out a soft gasp at that, tensing up. Then I can

tell she's willing herself to relax. I don't even know if she's had anyone go down on her before but I guess it doesn't really matter, does it? My goal tonight is to make sure my name is the only name she'll ever remember screaming.

"Does this feel good?" I ask her, trailing my fingers up and up and up until they brush against her clit.

She gasps again, her head rolling from side to side, her hands grasping the blanket.

"Tell me," I demand.

"Yes," she whispers, trying to raise her head to look at me. It drops back down once I start rubbing her in tiny circles. Over and over, tighter and tighter.

Part of me wants to take my time.

The other part wants her to come right now, all over my hand, all over my face.

I know what part will win out tonight.

Without saying a word, I bend down and start licking up her soft naked thighs until she shivers and moans, until goosebumps erupt all over her sensitive skin.

I slide my fingers into her cunt, wet and wanting, just as I'd imagined it would be. She's practically melting into my touch and my fingers melt into her.

"Feel how soaked you are," I moan, kissing briefly down her legs. "God, I want you to come in my mouth, all over my face. I want to drink you all up for days."

At that, she stiffens. She's used to my vulgar mouth, but she's not used to the dirty talk.

Only one way to get her used to it.

"Do you want that?" I ask, pulling my head back to look at her. "Do you want me to keep fucking you with my fingers?" I push my fingers deeper inside her, causing her back to arch. "Or maybe my mouth?"

"Yes," she cries out.

I grin, sliding three fingers in this time. She grips them like a fucking vise.

"Yes what?"

"Yes, god Magnus, everything. Give me everything."

Fuck me.

If she keeps talking like that, I'm going to come right here, right now.

Actually, why the fuck not?

While I lean over and start teasing my tongue up her thighs again, inhaling her sweet, intoxicating scent, I take my other hand and start sliding it up and down my hard cock, my grip light and quick for now.

"Fuck," I moan, and she reaches down and grabs the top of my head, her fingers sinking into my hair as I move my face between her legs. My lips meet her swollen ones and I tease her clit with the tip of my finger before sliding my tongue along her cleft and plunging it inside her.

She lets out an airy, breathless gasp, the most gorgeous sound I've ever heard, and then her hips start bucking against me as I swirl my tongue around her clit relentlessly and plunging my tongue deep inside.

"Yes, fuck my mouth," I murmur against her as she tries to get more out of me, her hips slamming up in building desperation.

This is unreal.

She's so hot, so tight, so wet.

So damn wild.

Her sweet, salty taste on my tongue feels like it's a drug in the slipstream and I'm slowly going mad over it. I want to devour her until there's nothing left. I want to make her scream and squirm and moan into oblivion.

I want her to be the opposite of a princess.

I want to see her down and dirty.

Slumming it with a prince like me.

She cries out, her fist in my hair, yanking hard as she sinks further into me, hips rocking for pressure, for purchase. I give it my all, fingers going in deeper, sliding along the right places, my tongue working her clit overtime, her juices running down my chin.

"Magnus," she cries out, and I know I just need to give her a lick to push her over the edge.

I push.

She cries out as the orgasm tears through her, coming hard into my mouth, her clit pulsing beneath my lips, and I drink her all in, keeping her coming until she has nothing left to give.

I pull back and watch her for a moment, watching as she writhes there, breathless and high, waiting for her to come back to earth.

Then, when she does, I make sure she sees me touching myself, getting off. My fist works my cock faster and faster.

"That's right, keep watching," I tell her, voice breaking from the strain. "Watch me fucking come."

Her dazed eyes are locked to the sight of my fist pumping, my cock growing darker and thicker and that sight alone is enough for me.

My eyes pinch shut as light bursts behind them and I'm going off, explosions along my spine, my cum shooting hard onto her thigh as I let out a loud, long moan.

I keep my fist working, getting every last drop, relishing the triumphant sight of my release all over her bare skin.

Considering how hard I've been around her for the last few weeks, I'm surprised I lasted as long as I did.

She's still got that serene, sated look in her eyes as she stares at the mess I left on her legs. "Don't worry," I tell her. "I didn't get any on your dress."

I slow my pumping down and then start crawling back on the bed over to her.

"That was round one," I tell her, capturing her mouth with mine, wanting her to taste herself. "How about round number two?"

"Already?" she asks, her voice throaty. So fucking sexy.

"Give me a second and—"

"Magnus!" A pounding at the door makes us both freeze on the spot.

It's Jane.

"I can't find Ella," she yells, and I'm glad she doesn't try to open the door, even if it is locked. "If she's in there with you, tell her that the limo is here. We need you downstairs, STAT."

I don't say anything back at Jane, but I stare down at Ella and I smile big as I brush her hair off her damp, glowing face.

I can't believe we just did that.

"Looks like round number two might have to wait," I tell her. "Well, now that you've come in my mouth and I've come all over your legs, I think we might just be a little more comfortable with each other, wouldn't you say?"

~

THE INTERVIEW WENT BETTER THAN EXPECTED.

At least we were a lot more comfortable with each other, comfortable in the way lovers might be if they have to try and behave in a formal setting.

But it wasn't all smooth sailing. The sexual tension was somehow even worse than before. Getting a taste of Ella only makes my need for her stronger, and I think it was the same for her. I mean, I know that orgasm nearly ripped her apart. She was practically squirting into my mouth.

And of course the fact that we both just came like messy teenagers before we left for the interview meant we weren't the sharpest tools in the shed. There were a lot of blank moments, a lot of leaning into each other and giggling. I have no idea what it's going to look like, but at the end the interviewer did say we seemed very much in love.

Which was what we were going for.

But damn if it didn't seem weird to have that term thrown around. All I've been thinking about was the sexual and physical side of our relationship, making that seem believable. I didn't think once about love.

I have to wonder when that's going to change.

"Well, that was nerve-racking," Ella says after we head toward the waiting limo. There's a crowd of people who have gathered outside the studio, taking pictures. I do my usual wave and smile, while Ella looks like she could crawl under a rock.

"You were amazing," I assure. "Not a pro like me but still pretty good."

She rolls her eyes and laughs.

We get inside the limo and Ottar is already there in the back seat.

"How was it?" he asks as the limo pulls away.

I hold Ella's hand up to my lips and kiss the back of it. "I think it went well."

She leans in to me, smiling happily.

Ottar winces. "I'm sorry to do this, Ella, but Magnus and I need to be dropped off at the palace to deal with some arrangements."

"I do? What? Why can't she come?"

"It's nothing to do with her, just things to be read and

some papers to be signed. About you starting to sit on the high council meetings soon. To get you up to speed."

Shit. Forgot about all of that. My first steps to becoming a king.

I've really tried not to think about that, no matter when in the future it happens. But my father reminded me on the phone the other day that it's time to start learning.

I give Ella an apologetic look. "You'll be all right at the estate by yourself?"

"I'll have Jane, and you know she won't give me a moment's peace." She smiles, so damn beautiful. "I'll be fine."

I won't be. I won't even be able to concentrate on what I'm supposed to be learning when all I can think about is her.

She's become my focus in this crazy world.

And I don't mind that one bit.

SIXTEEN

ELLA

"Ella, darling, you are looking radiant," the King says to me as he enters the sitting room where I've sequestered myself with a cup of tea.

I immediately attempt to get to my feet but he puts his hands out. "No, sit. Don't get up. I know you weren't expecting to see me."

The truth is I wasn't. I've been at the royal palace all morning for the sake of trying on wedding gowns. The Queen told me that it would be impossible to go into stores to get it done, so last night I scrolled through my phone and picked off all the dresses I liked.

Then the Queen had to approve them all, because apparently this isn't really my wedding but hers.

In some ways it's not a real marriage either, but I digress.

Ottar drove me out to Oslo early, before Magnus was even awake, and I've been trying on dress after dress after dress here, with the Queen insisting she inspect each one, no matter how horrible it looked on me.

But none of them have been right, so now I'm allowed to

take a little break while she sends out for more dresses and all the while I was told that the King was upstairs sleeping and no one was to disturb him (that was more for the staff than me. I know my place).

But now, the King is awake and on his feet, though he seems a little bit unsteady and has to lean against the back of the couch. I haven't seen him in a few days and I'm relieved that he hasn't gotten any worse.

That said, he's deteriorated a little bit since the first time I met him at dinner almost a month ago. The Queen hasn't mentioned it and neither has Magnus for that matter, but it makes me uneasy to see him getting thinner and paler with time.

"How did your interview go yesterday?" he says, slowly walking around the couch and taking a seat in the deep armchair across from me.

"I think it went great," I tell him.

I hope it did. I can barely remember the whole thing. After what happened between Magnus and I in his bedroom, it was like my brain was permanently scrambled and everything else after that was a blur. In fact, it's still a blur.

When the interview was over, Magnus was sequestered by Ottar for something or other and I was taken back to the estate. I don't think Magnus got home until quite late and I was feeling too vulnerable after what happened to go to his room and check on him.

I'm still surprised it happened. Not that I hadn't thought about it before, but even so, I was shocked that my body craved him that much. All the shyness and inexperience I thought I had that would hold me back from enjoying it had vanished. It was like some other Ella came out to play and she knew exactly what she wanted.

His cock more than anything. His head between my legs...

If only we hadn't been interrupted.

"Are you excited for the gala tonight?" the King asks and I blush, ashamed that I've been thinking about his son like that when I'm sitting here in front of him. Not to mention the fact that he's the freaking King of Norway and soon to be my father-in-law.

Another one of those moments where I realize just how much my life is about to change.

"Yes, the gala," I say with a stiff smile, and of course this is either news to me or it's totally slipped my mind because what the hell, what gala?

He raises his bushy brow a touch and I think he's on to me.

"It's been a busy week, I know that," he says gently. "Tonight's gala will be easy, I promise. It's your first appearance together at an event and it's only for the social elite." He chuckles. "Okay, I think I made them seem pompous, but I promise you that you'll have a good time. Everyone is just so excited to meet you."

I'm starting to remember something about a gala at some museum. Honestly, with the on-camera interviews and the magazine interviews and the photos and the meetings and the wedding stuff, I feel like I'm being spread too thin and barely hanging on. This gala is just another thing to add.

"So," he clears his throat and adjusts himself in his seat, "if you don't mind me asking...how are you and Magnus?"

"We're good," I tell him.

"You know, dear, that we're one of the few people who know the truth. You don't need to pretend with us. We know everything and we certainly know Magnus." He pauses. "He is not an easy man to live with."

"Actually, he's been fine," I tell him truthfully. "Better than fine. No, it's been good. Really. I think we get each other in ways that other people don't."

His eyes seem to brighten. "Really? That's great news."

I give him a reassuring smile. "Magnus is different. And he can be difficult. But I think I like that about him. There's a reason I said yes to all of this. I think if we keep leaning on each other, we're going to be okay."

"Good, great," he says, grinning. I guess he was expecting the worst. "That makes me incredibly happy to hear, especially from a girl such as yourself. I can see you keep him on his toes." He averts his eyes for a moment. "You know, I know this was Magnus's problem to get out of and it had nothing to do with you, so I just want you to know how much we appreciate you. You've been so poised and thoughtful and warm with us all despite everything you've had to give up. The fact that you're willingly wanting to become a part of this crazy family, well, it means the world to us. To me. To Magnus."

Oh. Damn. I didn't expect that level of sincerity to come out of him and suddenly I feel hot tears picking at the back of my eyes. It's not exactly something to cry over, but I have to say it feels so bloody good to be validated like this.

"Don't worry about it," I tell him. "Honestly. It's my pleasure."

The funny thing is, the conversation I've just had with Magnus's father is more than the conversation I had with my father the other day when I told him that the wedding was officially happening. He sounded happy, of course, but there was none of the warmth and elation that I'm getting from the King.

No, my own father still sounded so distant and far away, like the joy and thrill of me being married to the Norwegian royal family had worn off much earlier. It made me feel relieved that, in the end, I was no longer marrying Magnus to make him happy. Yes, it was still a part of it, but that wasn't all of it. It's more for me than anything else at this point.

Soon after the King had his talk with me, the Queen appeared with the next batch of dresses and gently shooed him away. I tried on a million of them—I don't know why royal families are so partial to sleeves—and it wasn't until I put on the last dress that I really, truly fell in love.

It's white, obviously, and has sleeves, except the sleeves are wide and transparent with flowy lace overlaid with small gold beading that comes to my elbow. The rest of the dress is in Grecian style, more form-fitting and drapey with hints of the same gold overlay. It's sexy, it's romantic, it's demure.

It's perfectly me.

"You look beautiful, dear," the Queen says to me as I'm admiring the dress in the mirror. She comes forward and touches my elbow. "Though sleeves this short will be breaking the rules."

"What rules?"

She waves me off. "You don't want to know. I swear, some of the protocol we're supposed to follow seems like it comes from the middle ages. And don't look at me. Remember I married into this family. Sometimes I'm the only one with a damn brain."

She reaches over and touches my hair, wincing. That's definitely not how Magnus touched my hair yesterday.

"Are you going to wear it down or up?"

"I haven't decided yet," I tell her.

"Well, you better hurry up and decide. We have people to book and the wedding is two months away."

Ah, yes. Another thing that she picked was the wedding date. December 23rd. An almost Christmas wedding.

Which brings me to a question I've long since wanted to ask her.

"Your Majesty, Else, if I may ask and I promise I mean no disrespect by it..."

By the flare in her eyes I can tell she's ready for a bunch of disrespect.

"Why the rush for the wedding? Why not take our time and plan a year out? A winter wedding in Norway doesn't seem all that ideal and if we did it in the summer..."

"Ella," she says rather sharply. "This is the way it is. The sooner the better. Trust me. Especially with you two."

"What do you mean?"

"Look, dear, I know my boy far better than you do at this point. I am sure that will change as your marriage goes on but for now you just have to take my word. He...has issues. Problems. And one of his problems is that he can't seem to stay focused on much for long and that includes women. We've got him to agree to this wedding right now and he's in it and he's focused, but what happens in a year from now when his attention strays?"

I can't explain how much this hurts to hear but it does. Maybe because I know it's the truth and it's a truth I've tried to ignore.

"Surely you've seen him take interest in one thing and drop it the next?"

I think back to the billiards table he wanted, then the dog—which we still haven't gotten—then his brief obsession with gin and wanting to open a distillery.

"And he does this with women too. I just don't want you both to get engaged and have all this planning go into it and then have him change his mind. He's fickle and he doesn't always make the right decisions, and I would hate for you to be a casualty of that."

"But what if he changes his mind after we're married?" I say softly, barely finding my voice. Suddenly the dress feels two sizes too small.

"Then he's stuck with you," she says. She puts her hand on my arm. "I mean that in the best way possible. I think marriage will teach him to appreciate the things he has once he learns there is no easy way out."

Except for that clause in the contract I signed, I think.

She claps her hands together. "Okay, enough of that sort of talk, right? Let's get you out of that dress and into a new one."

"A new one?" I ask absently.

"Yes. For the gala tonight at the museum. You're going to want to shine, my dear, and believe me, I have a lot of options. And guess what, none of them have sleeves. How scandalous!"

～

I'M NERVOUS.

I can't decide if I'm nervous because it's this damn gala, if I've been sitting alone in this parlor for too long, or because I haven't seen Magnus since the interview and so much has happened since then.

It's probably all of those things.

I keep looking at the old, ornately-carved grandfather clock ticking in the corner of the giant room, counting down the minutes. I was served a small glass of champagne by the Queen's butler a little while ago but other than that I've been sitting in my fancy red silk gown in silence.

"Ella."

Magnus's rough voice comes from behind me and I turn around in my seat to see him in the doorway. I don't think I've ever been so glad to see him, and it makes my stomach do trampoline flips.

I get to my feet as he strides right over to me.

I thought maybe there would be some awkwardness since this is the first time we've seen each other since the interview. That maybe he regrets what we did or maybe he fears that I would.

But it's nothing like that.

He grabs me by the waist and pulls me to him, longing and fire dancing in his eyes as they meet mine, and then he kisses me.

I'm immediately swept away, out of this room, into a little universe that consists of just the two of us. I kiss him back, eagerly, hungrily, because I want him to know how I feel, I want him to know that I've missed him, that I need him by my side through all of this.

"I am so sorry," he says, pulling his lips away, his hands cupping my face. "I should have been here. You left so early this morning, I didn't even get a chance to say hello."

"It's fine," I tell him, my fingers curling over his wrists.

"If it's fine, then you're a fucking trooper," he says, leaning in again to kiss me. And then kiss me again. And again.

I know I should push him away, that we're in his parents' royal palace, that this isn't proper, but I can't. His mouth against mine is like shock paddles to my heart. I need more and more and more. My lips hard against his, our tongues dancing through silk.

To think I'll be kissing this man for the rest of my life.

I've thought that thought many times already, but this is the first time it doesn't scare me.

Finally, he pulls back and rests his forehead against mine, gasping for air. "This is why I should have been here. Ella, I need you like I've never needed anyone. Why didn't you come to see me last night?"

"Why didn't you come to my room?" I ask him. "You're the one who got in late."

He presses his fingers into my cheek, his eyes searching my face. "I wanted to. I stood outside your door after I got back, like a fucking creeper. I just, I didn't know how you felt after what happened. I didn't want to push you in any way, but god how I wanted to push you."

I smile, my hand going to his hair and running my fingers through it. This man has the best damn hair in the world. "So, then next time, you know. Push me."

He grins right back. "If you're still considering having your own room, you know I'll do my best to change your mind."

"Magnus," his mother barks.

Immediately our hands drop away from each other and we turn toward her. She's standing with her hands on the hips of her long glittery dress, Tor her butler behind her, and if I'm not mistaken, beyond them I see the four blonde heads of his sisters hovering in the background.

The funny thing is, I feel like we were doing something we shouldn't have, as if this engagement and marriage was supposed to stay a sham and never evolve into anything more.

Or perhaps I feel that way because of what the Queen had said to me during my dress fitting.

He's fickle and he doesn't always make the right decisions and I would hate for you to be a casualty of that.

I push that thought out of my head. It won't do me any good.

The Queen comes forward and introduces me to Magnus's sisters, Cristina, Britt, Irene, and Mari, whom I already know.

They seem really nice, really pretty, really blonde, and really happy that I'm here, which is nice. At least with this family there's none of that opposition that you always hear about with weddings like this.

And I'm also relieved that all of us are going to the gala together—it takes a lot of the pressure off the two of us.

Magnus doesn't let go of my hand for the entire limo ride to the museum and he's always pulling me close to him. I know I like him for a lot more than his looks and his body but the fact that he's ripped as shit—and I now know what all that feels like under my fingers—and built like a mountainside, makes me feel wonderfully protected. Secure. Safe.

And that feeling is needed because the moment we step out of the limo and into the lens of the photographers lining the red carpet into the museum, I feel anything but safe.

This. Is. Insane.

All I see are the flashbulbs of cameras and a range of different accents shouting my name.

"Ella!"

"Princess Ella!"

"Your Serene Highness!"

I have never been subjected to anything like this before, like I'm a bonafide celebrity when all along I'm just me.

But I keep holding on to Magnus's hand.

I do the wave that the Queen taught me during my fitting.

I do the smile that Mari taught me in the limo (press your tongue to the roof of your mouth).

And I never look directly into the cameras.

I taught myself that one after the first time I posed because I think I was legally blinded by that flash. In fact, the only reason I'm making it up this red carpet is because Magnus is confidently leading the way.

My god, he looks fantastic. I don't care what he says about hating the paparazzi. In practice it looks like he loves them and they certainly love him.

And how can they not? He doesn't just do the smile and the wave. He somehow gives a piece of himself with every single camera flash. His smile makes everyone automatically smile back, the way he plays to people with his winks and nods. He's flirting with every single person here, and they love him more for it.

The thing is, for all the shit everyone puts him through, for all the shit that he puts himself through, the world adores him. There's no one else quite like him out there. He's charming, he's real, he's one of a kind.

No wonder it's so easy to love him.

The thought only stuns me for a moment. I don't know if I love Magnus but I'm definitely falling in that direction. Even with the words of his mother ringing in my ears, even with those fears, I know the fall is inevitable.

Please take it easy on me, I think as I stare at him as he smiles for the cameras. *Please let this work. Please don't break my heart.*

As if he hears me, his eyes are brought to mine and his smile deepens.

I feel like every doubt I had in my chest is giving way to butterflies.

His grip on my hand tightens, and as soon as we've made our way into the building, his hand slips to my lower back. I've been told that, in public, hand-holding should be the only public affection we show, but fuck it. This whole affection thing in general is new to us and we're going to indulge in it every chance we get.

The gala itself isn't as bad as I thought it would be. I mean, I don't really know what a gala is anyway, but at least the paparazzi weren't invited. There are some photographers, of course, but they were hired by the event and are very courteous, always asking before they can take photos.

Of course there is no hiding from the fact that the whole reason for the gala is to celebrate our engagement. Naturally, a lot of the attention is on us.

Okay, *all* of the attention is on us.

Magnus and I go from person to person, letting them give us their well wishes and congratulations, posing for photos, making small talk. Even though he's by my side the whole time, it seems I won't have a second to talk to him in private.

"Your Serene Highness," a voice says from behind us, and Magnus and I interrupt our conversation with one of Finland's diplomats to see the prime minister of Norway standing behind us.

"I am so delighted to meet you," he says.

The prime minister is tall, with glasses and a shock of black hair that's so obviously dyed. His smile couldn't be faker but, hey, I'm getting pretty good at faking it too.

"Delighted to meet you too, Mr. Prime Minister," I tell him, shaking his hand.

He shifts his cold, beady eyes to Magnus and that's when it hits me that the whole damn reason why Magnus and I are even together right now is because of him. Because Magnus has to prove to him that he's the future king and not some twenty-eight-year-old who got carried away with his daughter.

"Do you mind if I steal him away?" the prime minister says, putting his hand on Magnus's shoulder.

I briefly meet Magnus's eyes and they're sparking with fear.

"No, of course not," I tell him because what choice do I have here. If the Prime Minister of Norway needs to talk to the country's future king, the future queen isn't going to stop him.

But as the two of them walk off, the prime minister already deep in conversation about something, I'm not alone for long. Mari comes up to me, handing me a glass of champagne.

"What was that about?" she asks me nosily.

"I have no idea," I tell her. "Is it just me or is the prime minister kind of, well..."

"Icky?" she offers with a nod. "He's super icky. He wasn't even supposed to be the prime minister but our old one, a woman, withdrew at the last minute and there wasn't anyone to take her place. I just hope Magnus isn't in any more trouble. You would think that the public apology he made would have been enough."

"You'd also think this marriage would be enough," I say wryly before I sip my champagne.

Mari smiles as she looks me over. Something about her gaze is very disarming. It reminds me of Magnus. Always seeing more than you want them to. "You know, I think you and Magnus make a good match."

"Well, I hope so." I look around, making sure no one else is in earshot. You never know who is listening.

"I mean it," she says. "He needs someone—"

"To keep him on his toes," I finish.

"No," she says. "To talk to and to listen to. I don't know, maybe I'm too young and I don't know what I'm talking about—that's what I'm told anyway. But I think all people are looking for is someone to talk to *and* someone they want to listen to. It sounds so simple but it's actually really hard to find both."

Huh. That's definitely food for thought.

"I'll be right back," she says to me, touching my arm briefly. "Cristina looks like she's about to get into an argument."

I laugh and watch as Mari hurries across the floor to her oldest sister who is yelling at someone about something. Then I decide I should probably go to the bathroom while I have a chance.

I pick up the ends of my long silk dress and make my way across to the bathroom, but it's locked. I see signs that there's another one upstairs. I really don't want to make my way up them since the heels I'm wearing are stilettos and the steps are all granite and my feet are already killing me, but I do so anyway.

Upstairs I find the other set of bathrooms, completely deserted, as well as a wing of the museum. I quickly go pee but when I get out, I decide to snoop a bit.

It's an art gallery with a few sculptures scattered here and there. There are a few lights in each exhibit illuminating the paintings, but for the most part it's dark.

And creepy.

In fact, the longer I stand here staring at the paintings in the dim light, the more I think they're actually looking at me.

I shudder and turn around.

And almost run right into another person.

Thankfully my scream chokes in my throat.

"I'm sorry," I apologize, giggling nervously at almost losing my shit.

The person I bumped into is a red-headed woman in a pink tulle gown. She's about my age, very pale and skinny, with a wide mouth and dark eyes. Her hair is long and parted on one side, this deep red with a tinge of orange, the kind that's so vibrant you can't be sure if it's real or fake.

"I didn't mean to startle you," she says with a very big smile, the kind of smile that doesn't match her eyes. "It's pretty dark in here."

She's so chipper that it puts me on edge. She's also speaking English to me with a very refined accent, so she obviously knows who I am.

"Yeah," I say, looking around so I don't have to be sucked into the strangeness of her eyes. They're both wild and vacant. "I would have thought they would have sectioned this all off."

"I suppose they trust the people that come to this sort of thing to have a certain level of class, don't you think?" She tilts her head and purses her Lana Del Rey lips.

For some reason I feel like that was a dig at me. I mean, I don't pull out my status card very often, but I am a freaking princess.

"I guess they know what they're doing," I tell her with a quick smile and then move on past her.

"You know he loves me, right?"

I stop dead in my tracks and slowly turn around. "What?"

What the hell is this girl talking about?

"With all due respect, *Princess*," she says, slowly coming toward me, "he's always loved me. I don't even know where the hell you came from, but it's time you backed the fuck off."

I let out a huff of air and I think my eyebrows are on the

ten-foot ceilings. "Excuse me, but I have no idea what you're talking about, and I have no idea who you are."

She rolls her eyes and examines her nails like she's playing the part of bitchy sorority girl number three in a movie. "She says she has no idea who I am," she says to no one. Her eyes go to mine. "Likely story."

I try and think. The girl seems to be a bit unhinged and she knows who I am and I guess she's talking about Magnus, so...

"Are you one of his ex-girlfriends?" I ask carefully.

"Oh, that's real funny," she says. "Ex-girlfriend? I was his ex-*everything*. We were supposed to be together until everything got fucked up. It's not my fault that my phone was hacked."

Oh my god. Is this the prime minister's daughter?

What the hell do I do?

I clear my throat. "I'm sorry but I really think whatever you guys had is over. Maybe you just need to move on."

Her eyes flash. "Move on?" she says in an eerie hiss. "I'm not moving on because I know about your sham marriage."

"Sham marriage?" I repeat nervously.

"Don't pretend you don't know English," she says, walking over, approaching me like she's sizing me up for dinner. "I saw him, just a few weeks ago. At his apartment. Did he tell you about that? Or had you not been *invented* yet?"

She then saunters past me to the stairs and starts going down them. She says over her shoulder, her long red waves cascading down her back, "Ask him about it."

And then she's gone.

Ask him about it? Oh I fucking will.

SEVENTEEN

ELLA

I'M TOO ANGRY TO HEAD BACK DOWNSTAIRS TO THE gala though I do feel like running after that red-headed twat and pushing her down the stairs, which means I should probably wait to calm down. I'm not quick-tempered—at least I never thought I was—but ever since I've been thrust into Magnus's life, I find myself wanting to boil over at least once a day.

What the hell was she talking about? A few weeks before we met? After we met? Had Magnus been seeing this girl when he was leaving the estate at night? He said he was going to Harold's but was that just a lie?

Then his mother's words are slicing through my head, razor sharp and leaving wounds.

Surely you've seen him take interest in one thing and drop it the next?

Has he already started? Does till death do us part mean anything if it started under a lie? I might be marrying him but where is the guarantee that he'll be faithful? At this point, how could I expect him to be?

"Ella?"

I don't know how long I've been stewing in the dark, staring absently at a Monet, but suddenly Magnus is here.

I turn around, feeling the fire roll through me again as he strides toward me, looking like a rough and rugged James Bond with his scruff and his wild hair and his massive frame that seems like it can barely be contained.

"What are you doing here?" he asks, his pace slowing when he sees the expression on my face.

"Did you run into her on the steps?" I ask. My voice is cold.

He frowns. "Run into who?"

"Don't play stupid," I tell him. "You're so good at that."

He stops and raises his palms. "Hey now, I like you nasty but not without reason. What's going on?"

"I saw her. That girl you fucked!"

He raises his brows, and I know he's thinking, *that could be anyone*.

"Who, specifically? There are a lot."

"You're such an asshole."

"Why, because it seems like I've had sex with everyone but you?"

I feel like my head is about to explode. "What?!"

He narrows his eyes at me. "If you don't fight fair, I won't either. But, hell, I'd sure like to know just what the fuck we're fighting about. Who did you see?"

"That girl! The prime minister's daughter."

"Oh god." He runs his hand over his eyes and then gives me a cagey look. "She's here? Heidi?"

"Yeah, she's here. She ran into me up here after I came out of the bathroom. Like she was stalking me."

"That's what she does."

"I didn't know *who* she was, she was just babbling on about how you still love her."

"You didn't know who she was? Didn't you recognize her from the sex tape? I mean, she made sure that camera was getting all her best angles."

"I never watched that stupid video! And nice way to gloss over the fact that she said you still love her."

He sighs heavily. "Because that's her. That's a thing she would say, just like stalking you to the bathroom is too. Ella, she's nuts. And not in a good way."

"She says she saw you at your apartment a few weeks ago," I say, wishing my heart wasn't racing so fast. I need to keep it together. "Is that a lie too?"

Magnus shakes his head. "Yeah, I saw her. *Outside* of my apartment. She'd never been there before but somehow she found out where I lived. Ella, she leaped out of the bushes at me. Einar was there, he can back me up."

I cross my arms, still on edge. "When was this?"

"A few days after we first met. The night before you came back and told us you wanted two weeks."

"Why didn't you tell me about it?"

"Why would I have?" He looks confused.

"Because it's important."

"But it really isn't," he says. "I'm sorry that she got to you tonight but you have to take everything she said as a fabrication. I'm not in love with her and she was never in my apartment. She's nothing."

"She's not nothing! It was her sex tape with you that got you into this mess with me!"

He frowns, his jaw tensing as he stares at me. "Right. This *mess*."

"You know what I mean, don't twist it around."

"I just don't know what your problem is. She's nothing, okay? Yeah I had a few nights of fun with her and yeah I made one hell of a stupid mistake with her filming us, but that's all done now. I'm moving on. With *you*."

"I suppose I should enjoy it while it lasts."

"Fuck, Ella," he snarls at me, coming over and grabbing my arm. "What is going on? I mean, what's *really* going on here? You're usually so logical and rational and I'm supposed to be the one flying off the handle with crazy thoughts."

"I am not flying off the handle!" I yell at him. "And I am not having crazy thoughts. These are valid thoughts."

"Then tell me what these damn thoughts are and quit your squawking."

"Squawking?" I repeat, my voice going higher.

"Yeah, you sound like a fucking chicken right now."

"Fuck you!"

"That's right," he says, gritting his teeth into a wolfish smile. "Yell. Swear. Lay it on me if it makes you feel better." His hand goes to the back of my neck, gripping me there. "The only thing you really need is some good hard dick."

I stare at him, my mouth dropping open. "What?"

"You heard me," he says, his heated gaze going to my lips, the grip on my neck growing tighter. "You need to be royally and thoroughly fucked. That's your biggest problem. That's why you're so snappish and tense tonight."

"Of course you would assume every problem can be solved by sex," I sneer at him, trying to ignore the heat building in my core.

"I think your problem can be," he says. "And I'm more than *up* for the job."

With his free hand he takes my wrist and places my palm flat against his erection. My breath hitches as I feel how hard and warm he is, and my hand instinctively grips his length, which brings out a low moan from him that I feel reverberate down my spine.

Maybe he's right. Maybe this is exactly what I need.

Him.

Inside me.

But no. No, I'm still mad. I'm still mad that he slept with that crazy girl even before he met me, I'm still mad that his mother told me those things, like she has zero faith in his feelings for me, feelings that I'm not even sure exist. I'm still mad...

"Question time," he murmurs as he leans in and slowly brushes his lips against the rim of my ear. "Do you want me to fuck you?"

I swallow. The pressure between my legs is indescribable.

"Answer carefully," he murmurs, the heat of his breath and growl of his voice sending shivers from my head to my toes. "I'll find out the truth in a second. I can practically smell how fucking wet you are."

His mouth goes to my earlobe, nipping it between his teeth and giving it a tug that makes tiny explosions go off around my body.

Oh, *god*.

"What was the question again?" I whisper, my eyes rolling back.

"Do you want me to fuck you?" he says into my skin as his lips slowly slide down my neck, setting me on fire. "Princess?"

"You tell me," I manage to say, playing the game, wanting it so damn badly.

Because yes, I want to be fucked. By him.

Roughly.

Royally.

Fucked.

And now I'm mad that I can't stay mad at him.

"I like this version of you," he says, stooping over slightly to place his hands under my dress and slowly slide them up my inner thighs, just as he did yesterday. The heat from his wide palms makes me feel like I'm about to combust right here on the spot.

"We shouldn't do this here," I manage to say, already feeling dizzy and breathless as his hands go higher

"It's already started," he says. "Can't be stopped. You said for me to push you, so I'm pushing you."

His hands slide up and up and now I know he can feel how wet I am. The sensation of his skin against mine makes my world spin.

"Helvete," he swears, his voice hoarse. "You're soaked. And you're not even wearing underwear."

"I didn't want pantylines with this dress. I—" My words fail me as he slides one long finger right over my swollen flesh. I moan, unable to keep composed and my hands grip his arms to keep myself steady. "Magnus," I gasp.

"Fuck, yes. I love hearing my name like this," he says gruffly, taking a nibble of my neck. "I don't think I ever want to hear anything else."

He slowly begins to rub the tip of his finger over my clit.

My body feels like it's going to explode. "Figures you'd love the sound of your own name," I say, trying to catch my breath.

"Only when your cunt is drenching my fingers like this," he says in a near growl. I have to admit, his dirty talk caught me off-guard yesterday but it's definitely starting to have an effect on me.

A good effect.

The kind that makes me want to give in, to be absolutely

263

wild and free with this man. To be the person I've been afraid to let loose.

To be completely uninhibited.

Completely his.

"Kiss me," I whisper.

He raises his head and looks at me in surprise before a wicked smile curls the edges of his mouth.

He does as he's told.

The kiss is far more than I remembered from the other day. It almost knocks me off my feet, my heels starting to wobble. His tongue is insatiable, explicit, as it thrusts into my mouth hungrily, his lips crazed and needy. It's wet and violent and makes the want inside me throb, tighter, harder. His hand at my head is gripping my hair as if he's holding on for dear life and each tug shoots fire down my nerves. Every part of my being feels alive, soaking it all in, desperate for more of his touch, more of him, more of everything.

He pulls back half an inch, just for a second, just enough time to let out a moan while his other hand holds my face captive. His heavy-lidded gaze fixates on my eyes, then my lips, as if I'm some sort of apparition.

Then I grab the lapels of his tux and yank his lips back to mine. The need in me builds and builds and I'm dying to wrap my legs around him, to feel every inch, to feel his want for me. I think I whimper. I gasp. I kiss him with the same kind of abandon as he's kissing me with, his mouth devouring me as if wanting to swallow me whole.

The sound of footsteps echoing on the stairs makes us both freeze. My heart is pounding so loud, I wish I could quiet it.

Shadows appear on the walls of the curved stairwell and Magnus quickly takes my hand and pulls me into another darkened room full of paintings. From here no one can see us.

Whether they can hear us or not, that's another story.

"Magnus," I whisper, but he places his palm over my mouth.

"Shhh." His eyes are wicked as he stares at me. "We have to be quiet."

He pushes me up against the wall between two Edvard Munch paintings as his lips close gently around my earlobe, teeth razing my skin, the heat from his breath lighting firecrackers down the expanse of my neck. His hand falls away from my mouth and his fingers curl around the edge of my dress, pulling the silky fabric up over my hips so it's bunched around my waist. I'm between both of his warm, strong hands and he stares down at my nakedness.

He licks his lips and I want him to put those lips between my legs, I want to make him do what he did to me yesterday. But I'm also dying to finally feel what he feels like inside me. A little bit scared, too.

His grip on my hips intensifies. He lifts me up effortlessly, placing me back against the cold wall, and moves forward between my legs, my heels hooking around the back of his thighs.

He places his hands on either side of my face, holding me in place, his nostrils flaring as he breathes in hard. It's as if he's trying to restrain himself, and I want him to let go and unleash it all on me, everything that he has.

It's all come to this moment.

All come to this.

A line between his brows deepens as he tries to drink me in with his intense eyes. I'm holding my breath, wanting *so* much, and he keeps searching me, trying to read me.

Just take me, I want to say. *Fuck me here. Fuck me wild.*

My mouth parts, the words teasing on my tongue.

Fuck me wild.

The old Ella would never think that.

The new Ella is engaged.

And she knows what she has.

She knows what she wants.

His eyes drop to my lips and his gaze burns both brighter and darker, carnal and hungry. I see the restraints inside him let loose.

Magnus pulls my face forward and his lips crash against mine, fevered, crazed and wilder than before. His hands sink into my hair and my hands fumble for the buttons on his shirt, desperate for his skin. Our mouths are lost to each other in a race, a battle, where both of us win. It's breathless, greedy. It's a battle for our bodies and souls.

My toes curl.

My heart somersaults.

I'm pressed back between two priceless paintings, drowning under the onslaught of his tongue, each hot, torrid stroke inside my mouth making me absolutely drenched. I feel wet to my thighs and he must know it too.

I'm starting to slip just a bit so I wrap my legs further around his waist eagerly, and he presses up against me. We both moan into each other's mouths. He's as hard as cement and pressing against me in all the right places. With just the slightest movement, the fabric of his pants brushes over my clit and I almost lose my mind.

One hand makes a fist in my hair, tugging at it, messing it up, while his lips bruise me, our mouths messy and hard, teeth hitting teeth in our uncontrollable need to devour each another right here, right now. In the middle of a museum at a gala meant for us?

Sure, why not?

This is Magnus we're talking about.

And I'm absolutely crazed for this beautiful man.

My fiancé.

My Prince.

With his white shirt unbuttoned, I drag my nails over the hard planes of his chest and the edges of his tattoos. I reach down to the waistband of his pants and undo the button, while his mouth goes for my neck again, sucking, biting, and I throw my head back to give him better access.

I deftly undo the button and zip down his fly before sliding my hand over his hardness. Holy shit. He's not wearing underwear either. The long, heated length of him pulses beneath my palm and he lets out a low, rough growl that vibrates down my spine.

"Oh, Ella," he groans, breathing hard into my neck. "I'm already going to explode."

"So am I," I tell him. He's so fucking huge, and just touching his cock is bringing me to the edge. I don't know how I'll survive it inside of me—it's been so long since I last had sex with someone—but I am more than willing to try.

I wrap my hands around firmer and free it from his pants. I curl forward, glancing down to see. He grows harder in my hands, the tip dark, flushed, and gleaming. Oh god, I just want to put it in my mouth, all of it, sucking, tasting every inch of him.

The wild, dirty thoughts take me by surprise but I have no choice but to embrace them.

This is what he does to me.

This is the woman he's slowly letting out of her cage.

But as much as I want to taste him, what I want, what I need more, is him deep inside of me, as far as I can take him, even though he could break me open.

I want that enough to let him screw me for the first time right here in public.

I start stroking him, running the precum over his silky hot ridge, pausing at the round and full tip, before going back down again.

"Jesus," he says, raspy, sucking in his breath. "You need to stop that or I'm coming."

I bite my lip and smile at the effect I have on him. I want to ruin him and I want him to ruin me. The need, the power, is intoxicating.

One day he'll rule this country.

Right now I want to rule him.

See what it's like to bring Magnus the Mad to his knees.

He pulls back for a second, watching me with a delirious look in his hooded eyes as my hands work him up and down. His scrapes his teeth over his lower lip then slowly looks up at me. "Princess," he warns.

I pause and grip his gorgeous dick tighter. His eyes roll back in his head, and the muscles in his neck are straining as he tries to hold back. "Yes, Your Highness?" I tease.

He grunts and moves back into me, pulling the neckline of my dress down. My nipples are as hard as pebbles, and he cups my breast, licking a path to the center. He takes one in his mouth and I'm swept away by the warmth, by the fire-laced nerves that radiate out from me.

"Oh god," I cry out softly.

He makes a noise of agreement against my breast, causing more nerves to incinerate. He slips his hand below, sliding it over my clit which is beyond wet and slippery.

"You're soaking me again," he says huskily before taking my nipple between his teeth and pulling slightly.

I moan as he pushes one big finger inside of me, the roughness igniting my sensitive skin. The penetration seems to roll through me and I automatically jerk my hips forward, bringing his finger further inside.

I think I want more.

No, I need more.

He makes a low, guttural sound and pulls out slowly before adding another finger. I bite my lip to keep from yelling his name as he expertly slides his fingers over the swollen bundle of nerves that threatens to destroy me from the inside out.

"Magnus," I say through a moan, my mouth open and gasping as my senses are nearly blinded. "Don't stop."

"Never," he says before flicking my nipple with his tongue. He pulls his fingers out and then pushes three in and I'm breathless and shaking. His fingers are so thick that it's nearly unbearable and he plunges them in and out, fucking me with his hand.

"I want you to come all over my hand," he says through a grunt.

"I want to come all over you," I tell him. "Please, I need you inside me. All of you."

He pauses and takes his mouth away from my breast, his stubble wet with moisture as his heavy eyes gaze at me. "Is that an official command?"

I'm breathing hard, my hand going to the back of his neck that's already damp with sweat. "What do you think?"

"I think you're greedy," he mutters. He shakes his head slightly, a hint of a smile on his glistening lips. "I think you're a greedy little Princess."

"I think you need to give me the royal treatment," I say, leaning forward and grabbing his lower lip between my teeth and tugging. "Fuck me, my Prince."

"Jesus," he curses roughly, the heat in his green eyes growing hotter. "Where did this Ella come from?"

I bring my mouth to the soft spot where his jaw meets his neck, the stubble brushing against my bruised lips. "I think you brought it out of me the other day."

"Then I hope she's here to stay," he says between moans as I suck at his neck. "Because I don't think I'll ever get my fill of you, Princess."

He pulls back slightly and reaches into his pocket, his pants slung low on his hips, his throbbing cock beating against me in time with his heart. He pulls out a condom. The foil crinkles as he tears it open. "I am clean," he says. "But are you on the pill?"

I shake my head. "No. But I'm signing up right after this."

I watch eagerly, holding my breath as he slides the sheath on, loving the ease in which he handles himself. His pants fall to his ankles and he positions his tip against my wetness, hesitating, teasing. He grins at me, biting his lip, sly eyes appraising me, as he rubs his engorged head up and down over my swollen skin.

"Stop being a tease," I whimper, my hands going around the hard lines of his waist, grabbing onto his ass.

I don't think we have a lot of time.

With a hiss, he pushes his cock into me with one sharp, searing movement. If I wasn't so damn wet, there is no way I'd be able to accommodate him, and even now I feel so full and strained, I might burst.

"Ella," he says with a raspy groan. "Fuck."

I can only gasp, feeling my toes curl as he slides in further.

It's better than I imagined.

With each thrust, his cock drawing in and out, I'm pushed harder against the wall. He puts his palm behind my head, firmly holding me in place, allowing him to go deeper and deeper and deeper.

I just hope those paintings are secure. We may be getting away with screwing unnoticed in this darkened section of the museum but one slip-up and our cover is blown. I'm not sure sex is worth destroying fine art.

Then again, maybe it is with Magnus.

My mind is reeling with the sensation of having him so connected to me, so thick and all-encompassing, it takes over my every thought and makes me lose all logic. I am raw, primal, desperate with need. And I want more. So much more.

Greedy Princess indeed.

I grab hold of his biceps, hard as concrete slabs, as he works me in and out. I hold him, still in awe, desperate to hold him close to me. This man is all mine, and I'm going to have to work hard to be worthy of a prince like this.

His mouth joins with mine, moving together in deep, searing kisses in a rhythm that his body matches as he thrusts his hips forward, his cock driving deeper and deeper inside. Every nerve in my body is being pulled inward, swirling into a hard knot, live wires needing the slightest hair trigger to set me free. Each deep shove of his body threatens to undo me.

I run my fingers down his forearms, feeling the tense muscles through his tuxedo jacket as he holds me in place, then I brush my hands back up to his biceps, to the roundness of his shoulders, down his chest, then trail further to his shaft. I grip him there at the base, wet with my own desire, and he groans with wild lust.

This wild heir.

With one hand, he reaches down and rubs his fingers up

and down over my clit. I'm so ready to go that I whimper helplessly, knowing I can't hold back anymore.

"You said you wanted to come with me inside you," he whispers into my ear. "You're going to right now. And you're going to stay quiet."

He rubs his fingers faster and he pulls his head back to watch as he takes me to another level.

"That's it," he says quietly. "Let go."

It spreads slowly at first, a spark traveling from my core and out through every nerve in my body. Then I implode with a jolt that almost makes me scream.

He places his palm over my mouth at the last moment and I open my mouth to it, crying out softly, breathing in his skin.

The orgasm just keeps coming. I'm fireworks blasting off, shuddering, shaking, quaking in a cascade of flames. I can't control anything and I'm grateful his hand is keeping me quiet. My heart fills to the brim then floods over with emotion that nearly brings tears to my eyes.

He removes his hand.

"Oh my god," I cry out softly against him, my head buried in his sweaty neck, holding his body against me, as if I would sink into the ground if I didn't. My heart is beating so hard I think I might be having a heart attack.

Can you die from good sex?

But he's not done.

He pumps into me harder, faster, and I'm holding my breath now watching those paintings as they rattle, and then he's grunting hoarsely with every deep shove.

"Fuck, I'm coming too," he whispers, words broken up and hoarse and he's shaking over me, my name raspy on his lips. He groans and the pumps of his hips slow against me as he empties himself into the condom.

He practically collapses against me and I run my fingers through his long hair, feeling him, feeling everything.

I can't believe that just happened.

I can't believe we did that.

He's breathing hard still as he leans back and pulls himself out of me and gives me a lazy, sated smile. "And here I was thinking museums were boring."

I let out a shaky laugh as he lowers me to the ground. I wobble on my stilettos for a moment and he grabs my arm to steady me. "Looks like I fucked you off your feet."

"You did something all right."

He pulls the condom off and says. "Let's go dispose of the evidence and head back to the party. Someone might have missed us by now. Can you walk?"

I giggle and take a few steps. I think I'm going to be feeling all that tomorrow.

"Don't flatter yourself."

"I don't think I need to when I got you to do it for me," he says, holding out his arm.

With a dazed grin, I take it and we join the party.

EIGHTEEN
MAGNUS

AFTER THE GALA WE WERE ALL TAKEN BACK TO THE palace to stay the night, my sisters included. Usually after this kind of event that we do as a family, my sisters and I stay up late talking in the sitting room, drinking coffee and cloudberry liquor, and eating cake.

But even though everyone went straight to the sitting room to carry out this tradition as we normally do, Ella and I were excused.

Thank god.

Fucking her in the museum was long overdue but instead of relief at having finally been inside of her, now I only want more. For the rest of the night, I couldn't stop touching her, thinking about her, smelling her on my fingers.

And even though there was nothing hotter than screwing her standing up in that art wing, with her legs wrapped around me, the adrenaline flowing through me over the fact that at any moment someone could have walked in on us, it's not enough.

I want her in my bed.

I want to strip her naked and go over every inch of her body with my tongue.

I want to slowly sink into her and watch the expression in her eyes change as she takes me in.

That was fast and rough. Now I want it sweet and slow.

Okay, maybe still a little rough.

My family gives me sly little waves and smiles as Ella and I depart the scene, hand in hand. This is all sorts of fucked up but I'll take it.

We walk through the palace and take the elevator to the third floor and I'm so tempted to grab her and press her against the walls but I manage to refrain.

"We're not really going to bed, are we?" she asks as we pass the blue room which she normally stays in when she's here.

I give her a wry smile, squeezing her hand tighter as I lead her to my old bedroom. "I love it when you play naïve."

Her eyes dance. "I thought you loved it when I played nasty?"

I think I love every part you play.

Shit.

Glad I kept that one inside.

I pull her into the bedroom and like I hadn't just ravaged her earlier in the museum, I'm pulling her dress off over her head while tearing off my own clothes.

I attack her, tongue, lips, mouth, teeth, my hands roaming all over her bare body for the first time, hungry and greedy and just a bit desperate.

"Lie down," I tell her, and I manage to pull myself away. "Get on the bed and let me look at all of you."

She no longer looks embarrassed at this type of request. She goes to the bed and I watch her, drinking her all in. I watch as she lies down on the mattress, everything from the perfect pink of her cunt to the sharp peaks of her nipples and perky breasts is on display for me.

I can't believe my luck.

I can't believe I get to marry this woman.

Whatever I had once said to my father about having sex with one woman for the rest of my life, well I obviously had no idea it would be this woman.

This woman is my fucking queen and I will never ever lose sight of that.

"If only you knew how beautiful you look to me," I murmur to her as I step over to the bed and gaze down at her. "I could tell you but I don't think it would be enough. The only thing I think might work is if I show you." I pause. "Do you want me to show you?"

She doesn't answer. She gives me a wicked smile and opens her thighs.

Helvete.

I move between her spread legs. It's almost painful, this desire, this need to make her see what she does to me, how she makes me feel. Seeing my bare cock hard and ready, her cunt open, pink and soft—I feel like I'm going mad with desire.

Slowly, so slowly, I ease myself into her as she raises her hips, pushing toward me herself, wanting that deeper purchase. Her mouth opens wider the further I get, her skin sliding against my skin like endless silk.

This feels too fucking good.

Too perfect.

I kiss her, melting my mouth into hers, wanting to be as close as possible.

"What about the condom?" she whispers.

"I'll pull out."

"Come all over me again?" She raises a brow.

Fuck, that couldn't sound sexier.

Our faces are just inches apart as I slowly pull out and ease myself back into her. Our gaze never breaks. Hers is full of lust and wonder, as if she's seeing me for the first time. In the museum it was dark and rushed, but now we are intimate, now we can really take each other in. I can only hope she likes what she sees, that I'm enough for her.

I'll do anything to be her king.

When our hips meet, it makes me still, and I have to suck in my breath to regain control. There's something about her that makes me want to completely lose it and, honestly, I think I've been losing it since the moment I first saw her.

She wraps her legs around my waist and rocks her hips, each movement pulling me further and further into her. Her hands are at my back and pushing into my muscles. Our skin moves against each other like we are one.

"Fuck, Ella," I croak out, sucking along her neck, to her breasts. My tongue teases around the hardened peak of her nipple and I pull it into my mouth with one long, hard draw. Her moan is so loud, so uninhibited that I feel like the king I want to be, and for once we don't have to hold anything back. I groan loudly, falling into that intoxicating warmth of being really, truly inside of her, of feeling her in every way I can.

"Harder," she says, arching her back. "Please."

Please? Lord, she is so fucking cute.

"Your wish is my command," I tell her, my voice straining. "Though I should be addressed as Your Highness."

"Please, Your Highness. Fuck me harder."

God damn.

I piston my hips to drive into her deeper, pumping harder and harder. Her perfect tits bounce with each thrust, and suddenly there are no thoughts. Nothing but feeling. That feeling of falling, of realizing how good it can fucking be when you actually care about someone.

I've never had sex with a woman that I had feelings for.

And this is so much more than just feelings, so much more than that.

"Magnus," she whispers to me. "More."

I give her a look of surprise.

She wants more?

I'll give her fucking more.

I grab her by the waist and flip over so that she's riding on top of me now. My grip tightens as she sinks onto my cock and I'm grunting hard from having to hold back.

"God, you're so fucking amazing." She starts rocking back and forth on me, finding her rhythm. "Ride me harder, Princess. I want to see those tits bounce."

She bites her lip as she gazes down at me, leaning forward on my chest for a moment before she starts putting her back into it, her hips bucking back and forth against mine.

"God yes, look at your cunt juicing all over my cock," I moan, my eyes glued to where my wet shaft sinks into her. "Fuck, keep going, don't stop."

A flush starts on her face that spreads to her chest, and her legs quiver around my waist. Her back is arched, nipples pointed at the ceiling, her head back as she gives into me.

I go to slip my hand over her clit, to give her the push, but she's already there. She cries out loudly, hips jerking upward, body shaking like an earthquake. She's so unbelievable when she's coming, this pulsing, writhing, sexual being and I'm the cause of all of it. I'm the one who brings this Princess to the edge.

As she comes, her rocking slows, and I hold on just long enough to flip her back over onto her stomach, pulling out as I do so. I straddle the back of her thighs, grab my cock and give it a few pumps before the orgasm is rolling through me and my world explodes.

"Ella," I cry out. "Oh, fuck."

My words are wrenched out of me.

I manage to watch as I come, shooting all over her back, all over her round ass, my heart a drumbeat in my ears. I keep my wrist going until every last drop is milked out of me, then I collapse on the bed beside her.

"*Helvete*," I manage to say after a few minutes. It feels like a dump truck ran over me.

"You could say that again," she says. "What's the Norwegian word for thoroughly fucked?"

～

EVEN THOUGH I KNOW IT MUST BE THE MIDDLE OF THE night, and my body is physically spent from the orgasms, I can't sleep. Whatever focus and peace I found while I was deep inside Ella has scattered and my mind won't stop tripping. When it gets like this, it's like I have a race car brain with bicycle brakes. Nothing can slow it down.

It doesn't help that Ella is asleep beside me, her back turned to me. Even though I've been wanting to sleep in the same bed as her for a long time now, for some reason I feel cold and alone.

I hate this feeling. If I was a real shitbag I would wake up Ella just to talk to her, just to get some distraction from this feeling, but I'm not about to do that. We're both so exhausted, not only from the gala but from the last week, and she needs her sleep.

I slowly get out of bed and walk over to the window, pulling back the curtains and peering outside into the dark night. This is my old room, the one I had while growing up, and the view remains unchanged. From here I can see straight down the long palace square, the statue of King Charles John lit up in the middle by streetlamps. In the day, the square is crowded with tourists but for now I only see one homeless person slowly pushing a cart across.

The sight makes me feel even lonelier, and as usual, my head starts to spin from the feeling.

I shouldn't feel this way.

What's wrong with me?

I have a beautiful fiancé in that bed.

The person I'm to spend the rest of my life with.

Is that it? Is it the threat of a lifetime that kills me?

Is it being tied down?

Or is it that I'm feeling something for her that I've never felt for anyone?

I don't know what to expect from it.

I don't know what to expect from her.

I don't know how to handle anything.

How to be a good husband.

How to be a good king.

How to be a good person.

This is out of my hands.

This is out of control.

I have no control anymore.

I'm barely here.

I'm not here.

I just need to focus.

I can't focus.

I can't.

I can't.

I can't.

Help.

"Magnus."

I hear words, but they aren't here, I'm not here, I'm just flipping through the channels of life at lightning speed and there is no past and no future and there's barely a right now.

"Magnus."

The voice is firmer now and there's a hand on my shoulder and there's familiar pressure and it's bringing me back to reality.

I stop, just realizing now that I've been pacing back and forth in front of the window.

I'm staring right at Ella who is standing in front of me with a loosely tied robe, her eyes wide with fright with the dim light coming through the windows.

"Magnus," she says again. "Are you okay? My god, you're sweating."

I look down at myself. Not only am I completely naked but I'm drenched with sweat. There are strands of hair in my hands, as if I've pulled them out while I've paced about like a madman.

Holy fuck.

I never wanted her to see me like this. I've been so fucking good until now.

"Come here," she says, taking my arm and leading me over to a couch in the corner of the room. She sits me down, then goes into the bathroom and comes out with a robe and throws it at me. "Put that on."

She then disappears into the bathroom again, and I hear the tap running. She brings out a glass of water and a damp cloth and sits down beside me on the couch, handing me the water and dabbing the cold cloth over my shoulders, my chest, my forehead.

"Drink it, you're dehydrated," she says softly, gesturing to the cup.

Now that my heart rate has slowed and my breathing is getting normal, I down the glass of water in one gulp.

Ella isn't saying anything, just keeps running the cloth over me. I glance at her nervously, afraid to see her judgement.

But this is Ella we're talking about here. She's never judged me. Unless I've said something terribly stupid. Which does happen a lot.

This is something else, though. I don't think I've ever felt so exposed and vulnerable before. It's like she's finally seen the real me and...I'm ashamed.

"You think I'm crazy, don't you?" I ask her quietly.

She gives me a small smile. Her eyes are gentle. "Not at all."

"Maybe I'm sick. I certainly feel like I'm running a fever."

She sits back and watches me for a few moments and then says, "You're not sick, Magnus. I'm guessing this has happened to you before."

"Not really lately..." I admit.

"You're under a lot of stress, it's okay."

I nod. "Yeah. I'm not the best when it comes to that. Emotional stress especially."

She almost flinches at that. "I hope it's not because of me."

I grab her hand and kiss her knuckles, staring deep into her eyes so she understands. "It's not you. You're the only thing that's making sense right now. The only thing that gives me focus. It's everything else around us. The marriage, the wedding, becoming a king. Getting ready for that. I'm not ready for that."

"You will be."

I shake my head. "Not when I'm like this."

"So, what happened?"

"Same as always. Sometimes I can't sleep. I can't shut off my brain. It's like it holds me hostage and puts me in the passenger seat. Chains me there. Then starts driving faster and faster through the dark, in the rain, no headlights. No wiper blades. Eventually I crash."

She looks me over, her eyes taking in every detail of my face in this darkened room. Finally, she says, "I'm going to ask you something and I don't want you to take offense."

I give her a lazy grin. "You know it's pretty damn hard to offend me."

"I know. But that doesn't mean you're not sensitive. Some things I know roll right off your back and you don't pay it a moment's attention. Other things, well I think they hit deep and they stay there, whether you want to admit it or not."

I swallow thickly. She might be right about that.

"Okay then. Is this a *question time* question?"

"This is an 'I'm going to be your wife and I have a right to know,' question."

Oh shit. Those have to be the worst.

"Okaaaay."

My heart has started to race again.

"Have you ever been diagnosed with anything? Particularly ADHD?"

I stare at her blankly. "No."

"Does it surprise you that I'm asking that?"

I don't even have to think about it. "No..."

"Have you ever looked into it?" She squeezes my hand. "I'm no doctor, obviously. I nearly faint when I see blood. But I knew some people at school who have it and not the 'faking it so they can get Adderall' version, but the real version. From what you describe about your brain to the way you only focus when you're knee-deep in adrenaline, it just sounds like that's what you could have. It's common and I know it's underdiagnosed in adults. Nothing to be worried about."

I shrug. I'm not sure if I should be telling her that she's wrong or that this sounds impossible or there's no way I could possibly have *that* but everything she said makes a lot of sense. "When I was young I was definitely hyperactive and always thumbing my nose at authority. I thought that was my personality."

"That is your personality, Magnus," she says. "You were probably a little *drittsekk* when you were a kid." I laugh. "But maybe you had a hard time concentrating on school, on math, on books. That would be part of the disorder. It's complex, and it's part of who you are."

"I guess Magnus the Mad was a pretty accurate nickname."

She lets out a soft laugh. "Just because it's classified as a disorder, it doesn't mean you're crazy. It doesn't even have to be a disorder, it's all how you look at it."

"How do you know so much about this?"

"I had a beloved professor last year who had it. He was very open about it. Actually, he taught some of the best, most engaging classes. Nothing was boring about the way he approached life. Same goes for you."

"So, what, you think I should see a doctor and go on medication?" The thought makes me grind my teeth together.

"I think you should do whatever you want to do," she says. "If it gives you peace of mind, then yeah. You have to ask yourself if you're happy the way things are inside that brain of yours. If you are and you feel you're doing just fine in life, then just keep on keeping on and I'll be there by your side. But if you feel there's room for improvement, if you need help concentrating on things in the future, if you hate the way your brain feels, especially on nights like this, well maybe it's worth looking into."

"I don't want to be a different person," I tell her.

"I don't think that's how it works, Magnus. You'll still be you. You'll still be funny, quirky, smart...and devastatingly handsome."

I grin at her. "You really know all the right things to say."

"I hope so," she says. "That's why I'm here. Now, is there anything I can do to help you fall asleep?"

From the wicked glint in her eyes, I know she means something sexual. But actually, for the first time *ever*, that's not what I'm craving right now. That's not what I need. I need something more intimate and meaningful than another roll in the hay, if that's even possible.

"That might make me more hyped up," I tell her. "But there is something you can do."

I get up and walk across to the bookshelf which has had the same books in it since I was a kid and pull out the three-volume hardback set of *Lord of the Rings*.

"Come on," I tell her, heading over to the bed. I switch on the bedside lamp and climb under the covers.

She gives me a curious look and then comes over and gets in bed beside me, taking the book from my hands. "It's in English," she remarks, turning it over.

"It took me years to read the trilogy when I was younger," I tell her. "Even though they're my favorite books, I couldn't understand why I was so slow. Maybe now I do. Anyway, when I finally got through them, I decided to read them again on audiobook. Worked so much better." I tap the cover of the book. "I bought the English edition when the movies came out. Would you mind?"

"You want me to read to you?"

I nod, feeling uncharacteristically shy all of a sudden. "I think it will help. Transport me to that world for a bit." I take in a deep breath. "I want to fall asleep to your voice."

And there it is. I think I just uttered the most vulnerable and nerdy words that have ever come out of my mouth. The Magnus of a few months ago would kick my fucking ass for that. But that Magnus wasn't a man who was falling in love.

Ella stares at me, not with pity but with this sweetness that does something to my heart, melts it ten times over. "Of course, I'll read to you." She clears her throat and starts flipping through the pages. "Prologue. Concerning Hobbits..."

And as Ella reads on, my eyes close and I'm lost.

Not in a racing mind.

Not in the world of Middle Earth.

I'm lost in my feelings for her.

And for the first time, I don't want to be found.

NINETEEN
MAGNUS

Time flies when you're having fun.

Time also flies when you're about to be married and there are millions of things left to do, a million places you have to be, a million things you have to say.

The last few weeks have been crazy, or as Einar would say, as sticky as a polar bear's hairy asshole. I don't know what those Northerners are doing up there but there are some things I'd rather not know.

In addition to Ella and I being the constant talk of the town and doing countless engagements around the country as well as the regular interviews, Ella is dealing with wedding plans that seem never ending. Even though my mother is still at the helm of all of them and acting like a major Bridezilla, Ella is stressing out pretty hard. She's taken to drinking a few fingers of scotch with me at night now, which is a long way from those dainty bird sips she used to take.

As for me, I've been busy with my own things. For one, I've started seeing a psychiatrist. He comes to the house once a week and we go into the study and we just talk things out. I took a few tests for ADHD and passed them with flying colors, which means to say I got about a ninety-five per cent on all of them. I know there's a spectrum of it all and every individual is different but I'm definitely part of that club.

Honestly, it's a relief more than a hindrance. I've always felt different in countless ways and now I know the reason why. Now I can step back and look at the way I work a little differently. Most of all, I can stop beating myself up and give myself some slack. And just as I've gotten hyper-focused and obsessive about certain things before, I'm learning as much as I can about this to come up with a game plan moving forward.

I'm not sure yet if it will include medication, though I'm sure it will as the years go by. For me, exercise, vitamins, meditation and counselling will only go so far. After all, right now my decisions don't affect the whole country, but one day they will. When that time comes, then I might have to go that route. I just hope I won't be too stubborn when the moment arises, when I become king. I may be changing in some ways, but at heart, I'm still one stubborn shitbag.

I've also started going to the high council meetings with my father. It's an adjustment for sure—I stick out like a sore fucking thumb among all the politicians and officials—but I'm just trying to soak it all in.

What I'm not trying to do is let myself focus on my father's health. It's hard. Even though he's going to these meetings, I can see him slowly deteriorate and I think the others can too. He's putting on a brave face and thankfully his wit and warmth is as bold as ever, but it takes a lot out of him. One meeting, and he has to sleep for the next two days.

He hasn't been doing any public appearances either, though he assured me he will for the wedding. That scares me the most. I don't want the world to speculate about him, because I know, once they see him they will, and my father doesn't deserve that. Sure, it comes with the territory of being the king but I'm the one people should gossip about. I'm used to it.

"So, have you talked to your father yet about him walking you down the aisle?" I ask Ella just as the plane's wheels touch down. Another part of our engagement blitz is having to go to various nearby countries and meet with other royals and leaders. It's all just public relations, but apparently it must be done.

Thankfully, today is our last day of doing that, and we're actually visiting a man I call a friend, King Aksel of Denmark. Actually, he might be greeting us as we step off the plane.

"I've tried," Ella says with a heavy sigh, staring out of the plane's window at the runway. "Schnell said to try again tonight."

Ella has been having some issues getting in touch with her father. Even though he's repeatedly talked to my father on the phone about the wedding and everything, he hasn't talked to Ella. Of course, given their history, Ella is taking it all very personally.

Actually, we did attempt to make a stop in Liechtenstein to say hello to her family and make a public appearance before her own people, but we weren't able to set anything up in time. I just hope, for her sake, she gets to talk to him tonight because I know this wedding is extremely stressful and hard on her, and all she really wants is her father to be there and show a bit of love and support.

It's funny, sometimes I completely forget why this is happening. Things with Ella, our actual relationship at this point, has felt so easy that I trick myself into thinking that I had actually proposed to her because I was in love, that we met under normal circumstances and this is how our lives are naturally playing out.

But of course, that's not the case at all.

It doesn't matter what I feel for Ella at the moment, I still can't forget that this whole upcoming marriage is a publicity ploy to make me look good in the public eye. And that fact looms over me, looms over us, whenever I take a moment to think about it. It's a heavy weight to carry.

What we have is based on a lie, and it's a lie that the both of us will have to take to our graves. I'm trying not to think about it too much because it honestly does scare me, but I worry that whatever real feelings I have toward her will be overshadowed by how fake everything else is.

I used to be so fearless.

Then I met Ella.

Then I realized how much I really stand to lose.

"Are you okay?" Ella asks me, placing her hand over mine. I hadn't noticed that I was gripping the arm rest. "We're here. We've landed."

I give her a quick smile and pass it off as nervous flying.

We head out of the plane and onto the private air strip outside of Copenhagen. It's as cold as a polar bear's balls (I don't need Einar for that one), but there's no snow yet.

King Aksel stands beside a row of official vehicles, flanked on all sides by his royal guards. He's wearing a long black coat and a black hat, and I'm reminded of some emperor or perhaps a villain from *Game of Thrones*.

"Wow," Ella whispers from behind me as we go down the stairs. "He looks so impressive."

I won't let myself get jealous over that remark. King Aksel is pretty impressive. Aside from the dramatics of his clothes, he's got that classic Danish face that is both sharp-jawed and austere and rough at the same time. He's also forty, which is pretty damn young for a king.

We approach him, and he gives me a nod as I bow to him.

"Magnus," he says to me, holding out his hand. "Glad you could make it."

I shake his hand. "I've been looking forward to this. You're the only royal on this continent with a decent scotch collection."

He nods. "I brought some aquavit in just for you."

Oh yes, that's the other thing about him. He doesn't smile. At least, I haven't seen him smile in years. He's got his reasons though.

But I step back and introduce Ella to him.

She, of course, has that smile that brings me to my knees if I'm not careful.

It has zero effect on him, which puzzles her, but she takes it in stride.

We get into his SUV and I do what I do best, which is to talk everyone's ear off because I can't stand uncomfortable silences. Aksel listens because that's what he's good at (and probably why we get along so well), and Ella interjects a little here and there.

I'd warned her ahead of time not to mention the Queen or a wife since his wife died suddenly last year, and it's a sensitive subject. You'd think that would be the reason why he's so emotionless and quiet, but he was like that before she died. Now it's just increased ten-fold.

During the winter the King stays at the Amalienborg Palace, which is absolutely huge and way more opulent and grandiose than my family's. Sometimes I think the Danes and the Swedes are always trying to one-up us. I guess that's what we get for getting all the Viking love and recognition.

Even though this is a friendly visit, it's also one that my father and mother set up to try and facilitate a more professional relationship with the Danish public. When it comes to Scandinavian countries, all the royals are fairly close with each other and can treat each other like family, hence my relationship with Viktor as well as Aksel.

The thing with Aksel is, he is a king, and he is a bit older than me and because of that, I don't quite have that same dynamic with him as I do with Viktor, who is a prince my age. In the past, that would sometimes put distance between Aksel and I, depending on how much I was hating formalities and authority at that time. But now, now I feel like I can learn a lot from him.

But that will come later. For now, there's a fancy dinner at the palace with Danish politicians and officials, so the moment we arrive, Ella and I are shown to our room where we get ready.

"He certainly is the silent type," Ella says as she pulls her dress out of her suitcase and inspecting it for wrinkles.

"He's not so bad when you get him going," I tell her.

She cocks a brow. "Is getting him going another way of saying getting drunk?"

I laugh. "Pretty much."

"I feel awful for him to lose his wife like that."

"And leave him with his two young daughters."

Her eyes go round, and she lets out a soft gasp. "Daughters? You never told me he has kids."

I take out an assortment of colored ties. "Yup. Sweet girls too. You know, as far as children go."

She pauses, putting down the dress for a second. "You're not a fan of kids?"

I shrug because I haven't thought about it either way, and then I realize who I'm talking to.

My wife to be.

"You just shrugged..." she says.

"Sorry," I tell her, giving her a quick smile. "I've honestly never thought about it."

"You've never thought about it?"

I shrug again, and I can tell that's driving her crazy. She's getting that fiery look in her eyes.

"I don't know what to say," I tell her. "It's just never been on my agenda. What, has it been on yours? You're only twenty-two."

She puts her hands on her hips. "What's that supposed to mean?"

I frown. "That you're young, and you shouldn't be thinking about shit like that."

"Shit. Like. That?" she repeats slowly, and now I know I've entered the danger zone.

No choice now but to back away slowly.

I pick up a purple tie and start waving it around. "This is a white flag. I surrender. Let's not argue."

She narrows her eyes at me. "It's too late for that. The door has been opened and I am stepping in."

I give her an odd look. "That's not the wittiest saying you ever had..."

"Magnus, just because I'm young doesn't mean I haven't thought about having children, because I have." I open my mouth to speak, and she raises her finger to cut me off. "And before you say anything ignorant, it's not because I'm a woman either. I just happen to want them, and I know that already."

Oh. There's no reason for that to surprise me at all and yet it does. Goes to show I probably should have had this on my radar. "Okay. Good to know."

She shakes her head slightly, looking pained. "I can't

believe I didn't think to discuss this with you before I signed the contract."

"Why? What would you have done? Put a baby in there with one of the clauses? First house, then dog, then baby?"

"Oh, come on," she snaps. "You know it would have been good to at least discuss it. I eventually want kids. Don't you?" She quickly adds, "And don't you dare shrug."

I mentally will my shoulders to stay down. "To be honest, Ella, I never gave it any thought."

"But you're the heir to the throne. Your whole, I don't know, business is based on handing down this position to the next in line. Who does it go to after you?"

I manage to get one shoulder up in a shrug before she spears me with her eyes. "I don't know. Cristina? Irene? One of them."

"Magnus."

"What?" I throw my arms out. "What do you want me to say?"

"Didn't you think you'd get married?"

"I never thought about it either."

"You just assumed you would stay single for the rest of your life?"

It sounds dumb when she says it like that, but, "Yeah."

"I can't believe you," she says softly, staring blankly down at the ties.

"Wait, what? I just never gave any thought about the future before, it was like it didn't exist. Ella, you can't get mad over things I thought before I met you. That's not fair."

She looks at me with forlorn eyes. "But you only met me six weeks ago."

"Things change. They've changed big time. We're getting married!"

"Because you have to!"

"No. No, because I want to. You should know that by now, please."

She's shaking her head, pressing her lips together until they're a thin white line.

I sigh and come around over to her, grabbing her hands, making her drop the dress. "Ella. Look at me."

Reluctantly she raises her head.

"We'll get through this," I tell her gently.

"Through what?" she asks, searching my eyes. "There is so much for us to get through already."

"I know this has been really stressful and hard on you and you're handling it so well, but you just need to handle it for a little more. In two weeks we'll be married."

"In two weeks I might be married to a man who doesn't want children."

"That's not fair."

She moves out of my grasp. "No, it's not fair. I always thought I would have kids one day, especially if I got married."

I bite my lip, staring at the carpet for a long beat. "Yeah, but..." I look back at her. "Didn't you also see yourself having kids with someone that you loved?"

And there it is.

There's the elephant in the room that has been following us from room to room to room throughout our entire engagement.

She doesn't say anything to that, just moves away to the bathroom and shuts the door.

I sigh and sit on the edge of the bed, my head in my hands. This is still so messy, still so complicated. I thought it would get easier with time but so far, it's not.

And a part of me is afraid getting married won't fix a thing.

We end up going to dinner not on speaking terms, which makes things fucking awkward as anything. Luckily, we've gotten so good at faking things so far, that any strain between us isn't apparent to anyone else.

Well, except for Aksel. I can't read that man very well, but I can tell he thinks something is a bit out of whack. I'm just not sure if he's picking up on the fight or something else. The whole sham marriage thing.

It isn't until after the guests leave and we've put on our last fake smiles that Ella says she has a headache and quickly excuses herself, going to the room.

Aksel and I are sitting in the lounge (one of them, anyway, there's, like, ten in this palace) with glasses of aquavit and he's staring at me curiously.

I look around the room, avoiding his eyes. "So which room out of all the rooms is your favorite? Must be hard to choose."

"Why didn't you go after her?" he asks.

I stare at him. "What?"

"Your fiancée," he says. "She didn't seem well."

"She's fine. Just a headache."

He takes his time digesting that as he takes a sip of his drink. "How long have you guys known each other again?"

I can't tell if there's more behind that question than he's letting on. "Why?" I ask carefully. I may have told Viktor the truth about us but I'm not sure how honest I should be with Aksel.

He shrugs with one shoulder. "I don't know," he says smoothly. "I know we don't talk often but it does feel like this came out of left field. In other words, Magnus, this isn't like you."

"Maybe I'm growing up," I say, wincing as I take a sip. Good lord it burns, it burns. "You know, I got diagnosed with ADHD and I've been learning to handle myself better so maybe that's what you're picking up on."

"You don't say," he says wryly. "And don't change the subject. When did you meet her? How long have you known her?"

"I'm not changing the subject," I counter. "I just want to know why you're so suspicious of my fiancée."

"I'm not suspicious of her," he says. "But it's obvious you two don't know each other." He pauses. "Is she pregnant? Is this a shotgun wedding?"

"Maybe you should slow down on the aquavit there, Hamlet. She's not pregnant. In fact, we were just arguing over kids upstairs."

Oh, I think I've said too much.

"You do know Hamlet was the Prince."

"And he was also the father. King Hamlet. Hey, I paid attention to Shakespeare in school. I thought he had the lowdown on what the real royal life was like."

"Why were you arguing over kids?"

"Why are you suddenly Mr. Talkative? What happened to Mr. Quiet and Mr. Brooding?"

"Nothing happened to him," he says. He grows quiet and then seems to brood into his drink right in front of my eyes. "I haven't really talked to anyone in a while."

Well, shit, now I feel bad. And I certainly don't want him to feel worse.

"What happened with your nanny? I thought you were getting a new one."

For the first time I see a smile creep on his face. A small one, invisible to the naked eye, but it's there. "I did get a new one. She's actually more of a governess. From Australia. The girls love her."

I raise my brow and take a drink before I ask, "What's her name, this Australian governess?"

"Aurora," he says.

"Pretty," I comment.

"She is," he says. Then he clears his throat. "So, you don't want kids...?"

"I never said that. I told her I'd never thought about it."

"You never thought about having kids and yet you asked this woman to marry you? Magnus, you have to come up with a better story than that."

"It is *not* a story," I say in overblown defensiveness, like how dare you insult my sensibilities.

But I don't have the energy to keep this up around him.

"Okay fine, here's the truth. Ready, King Hamlet?" I exhale loudly. "I fucked up with that sex video. Everyone hated me. Pretty sure that included my own family. I had to get married to someone royal and nice to improve my image. I was arranged to meet Ella. She reluctantly agreed to marry me. Now we're getting married, everyone has forgotten about the video, and appears to love us all again, and that, my friend, is that."

"Uh huh," he says slowly, sitting back in his chair and steepling his fingers together. "You left out the part where you've fallen in love with her."

I stiffen. "That's neither here nor there. And damn you for assuming that."

"I don't know how you can possibly be ashamed of it."

"Who said I was ashamed of it?" I look at him sharply.

"Look. I was married to my wife for a very long time. Over those years I learned a lot about being in a marriage. I learned how...easy it is to fake love. I also learned how easy it is to spot the real thing, or at least the lack of it. For heaven's sake, Magnus, you're marrying this woman and you love her. Go and tell her."

"How do you know I haven't?"

"Because she thinks whatever you're putting out there, you're faking it. I'm telling you, I know. Don't let her become a fool."

Hold on. Does this mean that there was a lack of love between him and his ex-wife, the do-gooder Queen that captured the hearts of the nation, of the world?

But of course, I don't ask him about that. This isn't about him. This is about me. And I'm afraid he has a point.

I get to my feet. "Well, then I'm sorry to love you and leave you, Aksel. But I think I have something to tell my future wife."

I leave the room and head up the many stairs to our floor, get lost a few times, and then finally find our bedroom.

I open the door to a darkened room and use the flashlight on my phone to shine the way forward.

Ella is lying on the bed, still in her dress from earlier.

Crying.

I hear her sobs before I even see her.

"Ella," I whisper, coming right over to her. My heart is in my throat, slowly melting. I've never seen her cry before, and the sound of it is already doing a number on me.

I put the phone down on the bedside table and flick on the light. She's face down on top of the covers, her own phone beside her.

"Ella, I am so, so sorry about earlier," I tell her, hand on her shoulder, wishing I could make it stop. "I hate arguing with you."

She just sniffles and sobs and buries her face deeper into her pillow.

"Baby, please," I tell her, running my palm over her arm.

"I'm here. Talk to me."

Silence. Then more sniffling.

I take in a deep breath, trying to feel emboldened by Aksel's words. Doesn't stop me from feeling nervous as hell though.

What if she doesn't feel the same way?

I have no choice but to ignore it.

No choice but to solider on.

It's that moment before I make the jump.

"Ella, I'm sorry about what happened. About what I said. It was the truth, but I could have handled it better. The real truth is, I needed a moment to think about it. I'd just never thought I'd meet someone like you, someone I wanted to be with, someone who wanted to be with me. Forever. But that's you. I know that's not what we were expecting from this when it first started, but that's the truth of the matter now. If you want babies, Ella, I will give you babies, and I will do it gladly because I *want* that life with you. I want any life with you."

The sniffling stops. She's listening, breathing hard.

I reach over and gently smooth her hair against her head. "Sometimes I might seem brash or confused about things but it's never to do with how I feel about you. That's the one true thing that hasn't faltered. Things are tough, and they'll get tougher and our relationship and our marriage was never meant to be conventional and neither is the way I feel. Least not to me. Because I never imagined in a million years that someone could see me the way that you see me and make me feel that I'm worth something. And I hope, beyond all hopes, that I do the same for you."

Slowly she lifts up her head and rolls over to the side, blinking up at me with tears swimming in her eyes.

"You mean that?" she whispers.

I can't help the lovesick puppy smile that I know is spreading across my face. "I mean it. I mean it with every beat of my Viking heart."

"A savage heart," she whispers. "A warrior heart."

"A heart that's all yours. Ella, I fucking love you."

I thought my words would hit her slowly, but instead they drop on her like a bomb.

She bursts into the saddest, most beautiful smile I've ever seen, the kind of smile that leaves a mark on your heart. "I love you too."

But those words take a moment to sink in.

She loves me.

I never really imagined anyone loving me, but here it is.

The woman that I've fallen for, stupidly in love with, loves me back.

Loves my heart.

She's seen the real me and all my dark and devious places and she *loves* me.

I swallow, my throat feeling thick with emotion. "You don't have to say that because I did."

"I didn't," she says softly. "I love you." She pauses. "Do you really think I would say that to make you feel better?"

I smile. "No, I suppose you wouldn't." I sigh, feeling both elated and still terrible over our fight earlier, for making her cry. "I just want to apologize again, I know we like to fight sometimes, but I could tell that one cut deep."

She nods, holding onto my hand. "I know. And I overreacted. I want kids, I know I do. I was just so damn afraid that maybe you wouldn't. It reminded me of things that I don't want to be reminded of. Of how we started. And I know I need to stop thinking about that because it's not about how we start, it's about how we end. It's about everything in the middle."

"I hate to be the one to make you cry."

She closes her eyes and blows a strand of hair off her face. "No, it wasn't just you. I called my father, and, well, I got him on the phone."

Uh oh. "And?"

"And he was short with me. I mean it was fine, he said he was coming to the wedding and that he'll talk to your father about it. But he was off the phone with me so fast, it was like his castle was on fire or something. I really thought he would have been more receptive but...I dunno. Maybe this doesn't change anything."

At this point I'm not sure what I'm going to say to my future father-in-law when I finally meet him because he's put Ella through the ringer enough times by now.

"It's going to be okay," I tell her. "I promise."

"How do you know that?"

"I don't know, I just feel it. It's a royal wedding. No matter what, everyone is going to be on their best behaviour."

"Great. So that means I'll have my father there pretending that he cares about me."

"Ella, you can't go into this like that. You'll just set yourself up for disaster. It's not about him anyway. It's about us. And I promise you when that day comes, and we stand before each other at that altar, there will be only truth between us. Okay?"

She nods. "Okay." She sighs, and her eyes start to droop closed. "What happened to the old Magnus?"

I stiffen. "The fun one?"

"You're still the fun one. I mean the man-child. I only now see the man."

I lean down and rub my lips along hers. "Oh, I'll show you the man, all right."

TWENTY

ELLA

"Here comes the bride, all dressed in white!"

Welcome to my new alarm clock.

Apparently, it's Jane, sneaking into my room in the wee hours and singing this song. But before I can laugh at how horrible a singer she is and how obnoxious she's being and how much I want to keep sleeping, it all hits me like a hot frying pan to the face.

Today is the day.

I'm getting married today.

It's actually happening.

I open my eyes to see Jane holding a tray of food and coffee.

I slowly sit up. "What is this?"

"Well, since this is the first morning in over a month that you've slept in this bed here and not with your husband-to-be, I decided to take advantage of that and bring you breakfast in bed."

She places the tray down on the bed and then hustles over to the windows, opening the curtains. It's been snowing for the last few days, though today the sun is out, and everything is blinding and bright.

This should be a good omen.

As is Jane bringing me food.

I stare down at the tray, eagerly going for the cup of coffee and slice of cake. I turn my nose up at the pickled herring strewn bread in the corner. "Jane?" I gesture to it. "I'm not eating that."

"Sorry," she says cheerfully, snatching it up and cradling it in her hand like it's a precious gem. "This is for me."

"Since when do you eat pickled herring?"

"Since I decided to become as Norwegian as possible," she says, taking a large bite. I grimace and turn away. "Today I'll stand before the public as your maid of honor, and I want them to know I'm fully embracing their culture."

"Well, then I'm sure they'll appreciate your culinary sacrifice," I tell her as I take a sip of coffee. I close my eyes. It's bliss. I feel like I've gotten no sleep these last few days and it was only last night when I went to bed early that I was able to get some shut-eye, AKA my beauty sleep.

It helps that Magnus stayed at the royal palace in Oslo last night as part of the tradition of the bride and groom not seeing each other before the wedding. I love that man, but my god does he tire you out sometimes, especially in the bedroom. He can go all night. I can go once, okay, usually twice when he's working his magic. But then I need to sleep.

"Are you nervous?" Jane asks. "How do you feel?"

I give her a dry smile. "What do you think?"

"I think you're handling all of this rather calmly. The last few days with all your fittings and that damn drama with your tiara, you've been taking it in stride. I'm impressed."

That damn tiara. It's customary for those marrying into the royal family to wear their own tiara at the wedding, given to them from their own country or family. I'm not sure what the protocol is if you're not of royal blood but in any case, I had to get Schnell to send it from Liechtenstein. Only it was never sent.

Now, he and my father arrived in Oslo last night and are also staying at the royal palace and apparently have the tiara with them. I just hope I get that thing on my head before I'm walked down the aisle.

I really should just be grateful that my father came at all. I know it would have been in very bad taste if he didn't —he really does care about a better relationship with Norway—but I hate the feeling that I was pulling teeth with him. I mean, my brothers aren't coming, and they were invited.

I sigh. I'm not upset that they're not coming, per se, but I do feel slighted. They've never given a damn about me and maybe it's because I was sent away from them so young, it was easy to forget I existed, but even so it brings back all those feelings of being not wanted and not good enough.

"Oh, come now," Jane says, coming over to me. "Keep your chin up."

I look at her fearfully. "I am nervous, obviously. It's not just this whole family drama. It's the fact that this is a wedding, my wedding, and there's a lie underneath this whole wedding and then there's the fact that it's going to be televised! I mean, people in Norway have the day off today because of this! This lie is a fucking national holiday!"

"Calm now," she says, taking the coffee from my hands and putting it on the tray. "You're spilling your drink."

305

"I am calm," I try to say, but the words come out shaking.

"Yeesh, I shouldn't have asked you. But listen, now that we're talking about it I just want you to remember one thing. This isn't a lie anymore, Ella. You love Magnus. He loves you. You are getting married now because you love each other. It may have not started that way, but that's what it's become. There is no shame, no wool over the public's eyes. Maybe you have to lie about how you met, but you will never *ever* have to lie about the way you feel about him. You got that?"

I nod. I know she's right. I know we love each other. Ever since he opened up and told me how he really felt while at King Aksel's in Copenhagen, I've fallen even more madly in love with him. And he, well, he loves me with the same kind of focus and intensity I'd come to expect from him. Every day we're together he's making sure I'm a part of his world, a part of his heart. Even now, being away from him this morning, feels unbearably wrong.

But even with all that, there are some things I'm having a hard time letting go of. The fear that the truth might one day be exposed. The fact that I'm about to enter a life that I've had no preparation for. And, unfortunately, his mother's words to me. That there already seems to be a time limit to this relationship, and it's not a question of if, but when, his intentions begin to wander.

"I suppose this isn't the time to tell you some bad news," Jane says.

"What?" I whisper. My heart feels like it's getting a workout lately. "What bad news?"

Oh my god. Today? She's giving me bad news *today*?

"It's about the guest list," she says, cringing as she looks at me.

"What about it?"

I didn't have a hand in the guest list. I mean, I did but there's really only my father, my brothers who declined, some cousins who I think are showing up, and Jane. It's sad that my side is so lacking, but that's the way it is. The rest of the list was handled by the Queen.

"I only found out this morning while talking to Her Majesty," she says. "But Heidi will be there."

"What?!" I nearly knock over the tray. Jane quickly removes it before I can do any damage. "Heidi Lundström, that crazy bitch of a prime minister's daughter?!"

"Yes, that's the one."

"No!" I cry out, throwing back the covers and getting out of bed. "She can't be there! She's going to try and ruin the wedding! Why would the Queen invite her after everything? Doesn't she know how that looks?"

"I guess she didn't really have a choice. Heidi is the prime minister's daughter and he will obviously be there."

"But the sex video! Everyone will be talking about it!"

"Everyone will be talking about how gracious you all are for allowing it. The Queen thinks it will make us look like there are no hard feelings, and we're taking the high road."

"Fuck the high road! And there are hard feelings. Jane, that bitch leaked that sex tape, I know it was all her. She's crazy, she's obsessed with him, she's going to do something."

"Your language has really become quite colorful after meeting Magnus."

"Jane!" I point at her. "This is serious."

Jane tries to smile. "I know. I know she's daft and I agree she shouldn't be there after all that. But there's nothing you can do about it."

"I can talk to the Queen."

She gives me a caustic look. "Oh really. You know this is

more about the Queen today than it is you? It's about her son getting married and stepping up in his role as heir apparent. You aren't going to win arguments today."

I growl angrily, snatching the cup of coffee off the tray and downing it. I think I need something a lot stronger than this.

"You know I'm right, Ella. So instead of being angry about the things you can't control, why not just sit back and enjoy the ride."

"Enjoy the ride? This is a wedding, not a theme park."

"Actually, I'd say it's closer to a rollercoaster."

"Closer to a shitshow."

"I mean it," Jane says sternly, taking my hand and squeezing it. "Look, you've got me, and I've got you. You've got Magnus. You've got the man you love and you're about to become the Princess of Norway, a title you can wear proudly. You're about to embark on a new life, one that you do have control of. So just sit back and relinquish what little control you have over today. Let everyone else worry about everyone else." She cracks a smile. "You don't think that the Queen hates the idea that Heidi will be there? Believe me, it's going to eat her up. Today all eyes are on the Norwegian royal family, on Magnus. They know nothing about you, so you have nothing to lose and everything to gain. So just let it play out and have faith knowing that everyone else is trying to make this the best day possible. For crying out loud, you get to be paraded in a horse and carriage around the streets of Oslo."

"I'm going to freeze my ass off," I tell her.

"And I'm sure you're going to look very chic while doing it," she says. "Now come on. We have to make you into a blushing bride, not an angry one."

~

THIS IS SURREAL.

I'm standing in my wedding dress in an ornate and gilded room in the royal palace staring at myself in the reflection of a floor to ceiling mirror.

I'm alone.

I requested I be alone.

I needed a moment to just let everything sink in. Otherwise, I don't think I'll remember a single moment of the day. It's hard when there are a million people rushing about you like there has been all morning.

There were copious amounts of hairdressers and makeup artists and wardrobe ladies. Photographers who captured every moment of the getting ready process. Well-wishers whom the Queen led into the room just to get a peek at me and say hello.

I felt like a mannequin on display, nodding here and there, especially as a lot of the time they were speaking in Norwegian and I couldn't understand a word that they were saying. I can only hope it was good.

But now, now I have a moment to breathe.

A moment to take it all in.

I have to admit...this is the best I've ever looked.

There was a team of beautifiers, so I can't take any of the credit, but my skin has never glowed like this before, my eyes have never looked so sensual and expressive, my lips never been so supple. My hair is piled into an updo with a few strands framing my face. My dress fits me like an absolute glove.

The only thing missing is the tiara.

I take in a deep breath.

Was there even a back-up plan in the event that he

didn't show, or he forgot to bring it? I mean neither my father or Schnell are getting any younger, it's possible they forgot to even dig that crown out of storage.

Breathe, I remind myself. *Remember what Jane said. Go along for the ride.*

I take in a deep breath.

Let it out.

There's a knock at the door.

I give myself one last look, smoothing out my dress, and say "Come in."

"Ella?"

The door opens a crack and my father sticks his head in.

Oh my god.

It's him.

"Father?" I say, taking a step forward.

I can't believe it.

Surreal indeed.

My father opens the door wide, a tentative smile on his face, the tiara shining in his hands. He's wearing a black tux with a long jacket and a red sash across the front, his most formal outfit.

I know I saw him about a year ago, but somehow, he looks different and it's not just the formal garb. He somehow looks less intimidating, if that's even possible.

My father isn't as old as Magnus's is, he's in his early-sixties, but I've always built him up in my head to be this aging overlord or something. Perhaps because all of his official photos seem to take this sinister slant and when you spend half your life living away from him, those photos become default memories.

But here, as he stands before me, he looks spritely and younger.

And kinder.

Maybe it's because he's looking at me with a tenderness I've never seen, maybe it's because he's holding a tiara in his hands, one meant for me.

"I'm sorry I didn't come earlier," he says and while I know that we're not making any moves to embrace each other, I'm still touched that he's here. "King Anders has been talking my ear off since the moment I arrived."

"He'll do that." I pause. "How does he look? He's been sick..."

I haven't seen him lately and I know Magnus has been worried about how he's going to handle everything. Thankfully, he doesn't have to do anything formal during the ceremony except stand when I come down the aisle.

"Oh, he's been better," my father says. I get the feeling he wants to tell me more but that's not his nature. "I think he'll do just fine today, however." He takes a step toward me and holds out the tiara. "This is for you. I'm sorry it's late."

"It's not late," I tell him. "It's perfect timing." I give him a shy, hopeful smile. "Will you put it on?"

"It would be my pleasure," he says, concentrating as he raises it up and places it on my head. "Oh, I really hope I'm not messing up your hair."

"I'm sure it's fine."

"You know this is your mother's tiara originally."

This takes me by complete surprise. "I didn't know that."

He nods, frowning as he tries to get it in just the right position. "I guess there's a lot you don't know about her." He steps back and smiles, and I swear I see tears in his eyes. "There. You look just like her."

We have so much to talk about. Now that he's here and he's here for me, I just want to sit him down and ask all about my mother, ask about my childhood, ask about him. Everything. Just start over.

But time isn't on our side today. I am more than grateful that he's here right now and he's going to walk me down the aisle, but what happens when this day is over and he goes back home? Where does our relationship go after that? Will it evolve now that I'm an official princess, a future queen? Or will it fade away as it always does? After I see him at Christmas, we're always back to our old distant ways before the Christmas decorations are even taken down.

I don't have time to ponder that.

There's another knock at the door.

"Come in," I say, wondering who it could be now.

The door opens and a gaggle of blonde heads in light-blue gowns scatter into the room, followed by Jane. It's Magnus's sisters, my bridesmaids.

They all stop the moment they see my father.

"Oh," Mari cries out, automatically curtseying. "I am so sorry, Your Serene Highness."

My father waves her away. "No need for that formality, we've already met."

"What's going on?" I ask them.

"It's time!" Jane barks, pulling down at her sleeves. "Bloody hell, I think my arms got fatter since the last fitting. It's like they're wrapped in sausage casing."

I'm too nervous to roll my eyes. Jane's actually lost some weight since coming to Norway. Must be trading in all the British pies for all that herring.

"Are you ready?" Mari asks, looking me up and down. "You're absolutely gorgeous."

"Magnus is going to die when he sees you," Britt says.

"Not literally, I hope," says Irene.

Cristina rolls her eyes at her.

My father looks at me and holds out his arm. "Shall we get going then?"

I gulp, my heart beating faster than ever.

It's show time.

My bridal party and I are taken by limo through the streets of Oslo to the Cathedral. Though the Cathedral itself is pretty, especially as it's all done up for Christmas as well, my jaw drops at the sight of the people crowded around outside, held back by barricades. There must be thousands of them all bundled up in the cold and waving tiny Norwegian flags.

They're here for me? For us?

Holy hell, now I'm even more nervous than before. So nervous that I think I'm going to pass right out.

"You're going to be fine," Jane says, patting my arm. "Trust me."

I don't have a choice.

I take in a deep breath and exit the limo.

Everything after that happens in a blur.

There are flashbulbs and cheers from the crowd.

Music inside starts playing.

Jane and the sisters start walking down the aisle.

My father appears at the doorway of the Cathedral and offers me his arm again.

I take it and my other hand is shaking as it holds onto the bouquet, a mix of yellow lilies, Liechtenstein's flower, plus some tiny white flowers that symbolize Norway.

We start walking down the aisle.

Everyone stands.

The music plays.

A TV camera records it all.

And there, standing at the altar, looking absolutely dashing in a black uniform with red sash and medals, is

Magnus. I can see his beautiful smile, feel his burning eyes from all the way across the Cathedral, shining like divine light.

The minute I see him, I know I'm going to be okay.

As long as I have him in my sights, I'm going to be okay.

I hold onto his gaze the entire time until my father has given me away at the altar. It's only then I notice Viktor, his best man, standing proudly beside him in his own country's military uniform, nodding at me with a big smile on his face.

Then I notice the elderly Bishop standing between me and Magnus.

I flash him a quick smile—I met him at the rehearsal ceremony—but then my eyes go back to Magnus.

I never want to look away.

He looks just as excited, nervous and elated as I feel.

He can't stop smiling at me.

I can't stop smiling at him.

But, eventually, I do.

Because the Bishop blabbers on, and on, and on. This isn't one of those quick weddings where we go straight to our vows and be done with it (which is, frankly, what I would have wanted) because the Queen wanted to drag this out as long as possible. I guess if it's a national holiday, you have to make it worth their while.

So, my gaze starts to wander over the crowd. There's a staggering amount of people in here, packed to the pews. The entire front section seems to be taken up by royalty of sorts. There are Kings and Queens and Princes and Princesses and Dukes and Duchesses of Monaco and Belgium and the Netherlands and Spain and so on.

There's Magnus's parents, the King looking better than I expected, the Queen I think might even be crying. I see Maggie, Viktor's American fiancé, sitting with the King and

Queen of Sweden. I see King Aksel. Then behind that row of royals, I see the prime minister, looking especially greasy today. Then a spindly-looking woman I assume is his wife. And then...Heidi. Her long, red hair side-parted with movie star waves, wearing a demure black dress with a high collar.

Our eyes lock and she stares at me with that blank, vapid expression.

I hate to admit it, but it's getting to me.

Don't let her win. There's a reason why she's sitting there and she's not up here.

I bring my focus back to Magnus.

Magnus.

His beautiful face.

Those fathomless dark eyes that seem to hold a world of love for me.

How did I ever get so lucky?

That keeps running through my mind, even as we say our vows, even as we slide the rings on each other's fingers and promise to be there and love each other until the end of time, even as the tears come to my eyes.

So, so, lucky.

"Now," the Bishop says with a smile, addressing the crowd, "if anyone should know of a reason why these two should not be married in holy matrimony, speak now or forever hold your peace."

Normally no one ever pays attention to this part of the wedding.

But now these words have weight, a weight that I know both Magnus and I are feeling at this very moment, a weight that could threaten to undo everything we've worked hard for.

My mind trips back to when I saw Heidi in the museum.

When she said this was a sham marriage.

When she said I had been invented.

How had she known that?

Was it just a guess?

Good lord, is she going to say something?

I look at Magnus, trying to hide the fear in my eyes, but he picks up on it. As subtly as we can, we both look over at Heidi in the crowd.

She's staring right at us.

And grinning.

I don't think it's her blessing.

"Then, by the power vested in me," the Bishop says, and his words bring our attention back to each other, "I now pronounce you man and wife. You may kiss the bride."

And just like that, crazy Heidi is forgotten. She stayed silent. And now our love is speaking the loudest.

Magnus steps forward, takes my face in his hands, tells me he loves me, then places a deep, passionate, searing kiss on my mouth, the kind that I'll never, ever forget.

Everyone starts applauding and cheering, but I don't hear it.

I only hear his heartbeat and mine.

~

THE FACT THAT WE DID IT, THAT WE MADE IT, THAT we're married, doesn't actually hit me until later, after we get in the horse-drawn carriage and are paraded around the snow-covered cobblestone streets, bundled up with faux furs, waving to everyone as we pass.

It all hits me when Magnus and I are standing on the palace balcony in front of the palace square and waving at the thousands and thousands of citizens, tourists and well-wishers who have gathered below.

With bands playing and champagne corks popping and cannons firing and a whole nation celebrating, that's when I realize that I'm Magnus's wife.

The Crown Princess of Norway.

Eternally his.

I turn to him and pull him toward me, kissing him hard, the crowd going wild.

But it's not for them.

It's for him.

"My husband," I whisper to him as I pull away.

"My wife," he whispers back.

TWENTY-ONE

ELLA

"Do we really have to go home?" I whine.

I never thought I'd be much of a whiner and I hate the fact that I've only been a wife for a few weeks before I started but the truth is...

I *really* don't want to go home.

Right now, it's cold and snowbound in Norway, and here on a yacht anchored off Tenerife in the Canary Islands, it's warm and sunny and majestic.

Granted, this honeymoon might feel especially warranted as it was a bit delayed. After our wedding, it was just a few days before Christmas, which meant a lot of time spent with the new family between our estate and the royal palace while we celebrated the holidays.

Now, it's finally January and everything is off to a fresh start.

Helps that my royally hot prince of a husband has been lounging around on the deck beside me in next to nothing, his skin all oiled and glistening from the sun.

God, I love this man.

I love how much closer we've gotten since we've gotten

married. It's like we finally passed the test and now we can just relax with each other and enjoy the relationship we cultivated for ourselves instead of the one the public knows about.

It doesn't even bother me anymore how we started out. The way I look at it, it's just the way that we met—in an extremely unconventional way. Maybe it's not the way everyone knows, but it's our way and it's still valid. What counts is how we feel for each other now.

And what I'm feeling at this moment, is well, kind of frisky.

Magnus is lying on his back, a towel covering his face from the sun, his body on full display. As we've been stationed on the yacht, there hasn't been any paparazzi around. I think it's because the actual royal yacht is currently sitting off the coast of Greece with Cristina and her boyfriend who, at a far away glance, resembles me and Magnus. They're the perfect decoy and it's worked for our entire honeymoon, giving us all the much-needed privacy in the world.

And it's needed. Just lying here and staring at my husband in all his sculpted, muscled, sun-kissed glory, I have a hard time keeping my hands to myself.

I move on over, sidling up to him.

"Magnus," I whisper so that I don't surprise him.

"Mmmm?" he asks lazily from under the towel.

I place my fingers on the hard, taut planes of his chest and slowly, teasingly run them down until they're skimming over his rigid abs, the oils from his suntan lotion making his skin slick.

"Do you want to go for a swim?" I ask, my voice throaty, craving him. I think marriage and this sunshine is a lethal combination.

He clears his throat. "I guess I am burning up."

My hand goes lower, sliding over the bulge of his swim shorts and I can feel his dick twitch, growing harder under my palm.

"You certainly are."

He lifts the towel off his head and tilts his head toward me, my own brazenness reflected in his aviator shades. "Where's Einar?"

A throat is cleared from the cockpit. "Right here, sir."

Ah yes. Exactly why I wanted to go for a swim. It's too hot below and when you're on deck, well, Einar seems to be everywhere.

Magnus lifts his head and looks at him. "Yes. There you are." He looks to me. "Shall we?"

We both get up and before I can even think about what's next, Magnus is running down the deck and launching off the side, doing a full summersault before he splashes into the ocean in a perfect dive.

Show off.

I go to the edge and look over. "Were you a gymnast in another life?"

He's treading in the aqua-blue water, his hair slick off his forehead as he stares up at me. "I don't know." He looks down the yacht toward Einar. "What would you rate that?!" he yells at him.

"Eight out of ten, sir," Einar says.

"Only eight?" Magnus decries. "That was a perfect landing."

"You went in with your sunglasses, sir, which are no doubt sinking to the bottom."

"Shit," Magnus swears. He looks to me. "Ella, come in before I make Einar throw you in."

"You wouldn't dare!" I tell him.

"Einar," he commands.

Einar gets up, makes a motion to walk toward me.

"Okay, okay, I'm going," I tell them quickly, carefully stepping over the railing. No way that man is throwing me overboard.

I stand on the edge, take in a deep breath, and jump.

The water is colder than you'd think, especially with the temperature outside being so hot, and it's a shock to my system. I also feel like I'm sinking way further than I should, but then I feel Magnus's hand on my arm, pulling me up to the surface.

I yelp once I break through, spitting out water. "Gah, it's cold!"

"Stop being a wimp," Magnus says.

"I'm not a wimp," I protest, treading water around him. "You've got crazy Norwegian blood."

"I also have a crazy Norwegian cock," he murmurs, wrapping his arm around my waist and pulling me toward him. His eyes have gone from being light and teasing to half-glazed with arousal.

I grin at him. "You missed out on a serious Norwegian Wood pun. I'm very disappointed in you."

"You're right. Guess I was a bit distracted." He looks over my shoulder and up at the boat, judging to see if Einar can see us our not. To be safe, while he's still got a hold around me, he starts swimming backward until we're just beside the anchor at the stern.

"Now, where was I?" he says, his eyes dropping to my lips.

It's funny how just a look from him can get my body revved and running. I wrap my legs around his waist, and he slips his fingers to the front of my bathing suit, rubbing them against me.

"Here?" I ask, looking around. Even though Einar can't see us, it doesn't mean passing boats can't. I know that the paparazzi hasn't discovered us in the Canary Islands yet, but all it takes is one photo.

That said, I'm sure a couple having sex on their honeymoon will be forgiven.

"Hold onto the chain," he whispers, leaning over and taking my lower lip between his teeth and tugging on it.

A small moan escapes from my lips, the pressure from his fingers growing harder. He reaches down with his other hand to free his cock from his shorts while I grab the anchor chain.

"No, up high," he says.

I raise my arms above my head and hold onto the chain that way.

"God you're fucking sexy," he growls, staring at my breasts as my chest is thrust forward. Then he grabs the chain with one hand, just below where I'm holding on.

"You got it?'" I ask as his lips go to my neck, sucking the salt water off me.

"Mhmm." He pushes aside my bikini bottom and runs the tip of his cock up and down my slit, teasing oh so slowly.

I've never had sex in the water before—before Magnus, I'd never had sex standing up before, let alone in public—and I'm grateful that he gets me wet and greedy so fast, because when he starts to push in, I feel *everything*. I suck in my breath, my fingers clamping around the chain, trying to hold on.

"You're making me see stars," he tells me, licking my earlobe. "I'll take it slow until you tell me otherwise."

I nod and let out my breath, feeling myself expand around him. The pressure of his fingers on my clit fills me with an aching hollowness, like I need more of him inside, like I'll never have enough of him.

"That's it," he groans, mouth at my neck. "Fuck yes. Oh, Ella. Tell me how this feels to you. How fucking hard and thick does my cock feel? Do you want me deeper?"

I fumble for words. I make a sound of dazed encouragement and try to breathe, my head back to the blue sky above. He starts pumping into me faster, deeper, controlled jabs of his hips against mine. The friction of the water seems to slow down time, making me feel every single inch of him as he thrusts in and out.

I don't know if it's the turquoise water of the Atlantic that envelopes us or the stark sunshine that illuminates everything, but I've never felt so alive and free and wild. I'm being thoroughly fucked by my husband, by my world, and I think with every thrust he's imprinting himself on me.

Magnus looks up from my neck, staring right into my eyes, his wet hair slick. His breath is ragged and rough as he moves in and out of me, picking up the pace. But his brown eyes never break from mine and I watch as the fire inside them builds, just as it builds inside me.

I can't hang on anymore. Either onto this control or onto the chain. "Oh, fuck, Magnus," I cry out softly. "I'm coming."

"Fuck," he swears, his eyes snapping shut as he thrusts in harder, deeper, his fingers on my clit rubbing me to completion. My fingers slip away from the chain and I'm holding onto him desperately as my legs convulse, trying to keep from drowning as I let go and he pumps into me until he's grunting and cursing into my shoulder, finding his own release.

When I've finally caught my breath, I lift my head and give him a lopsided smile. "Happy honeymoon to me."

He kisses me softly on the lips before he slowly pulls out of me. "Happy honeymoon to both of us." He tucks himself back into his shorts. "How would you rate me on that one?"

I grin happily. "Ten out of ten."

"You hear that Einar?!" he yells. "Ten out of ten!"

~

EVEN THOUGH WE WERE ONLY AWAY FOR A WEEK, I feel like a different person by the time I return to Thornfield Hall. Not only are Magnus and I both tanned and glowing (okay, so I'm still a shade of pale with the addition of a few freckles), but I feel like a giant weight has been lifted. Now, looking around at this place, it feels like ours and ours alone.

Well, aside from the fact that we share it with Jane and Einar and Ottar and a bevy of cooks and drivers and cleaners. But even so, it's ours and we're putting our own stamp on things. Literally, too. We got our own official stamp after we got married, not to mention a coin.

I have so many plans to get started on. I want to get a dog, I want to start redecorating some of the rooms, I want to start horseback riding lessons, I want to start planning my non-profit organization. I want to jump into this new life with both feet.

Today, though, it's all about sitting together with Magnus in the parlor room and going through all the wedding gifts and writing out thank-you cards.

With the snow falling lightly outside, hot cocoa drinks at our sides and a roaring fire, it's actually quite enjoyable.

For me, anyway. I can tell this is boring Magnus to tears, having to sit here and do this.

"We can make it a game," I tell him. "To make it more interesting and fun."

He sighs dramatically. "No. It's fine." He pauses. "Can't you just forge my signature?"

"No," I tell him and then watch as he reaches behind a couch pillow and pulls out a bottle of something and pours it in his hot chocolate. "What is that?"

"Medicine," he says. "To keep me from dying of boredom." I roll my eyes. I can smell the whisky from here.

He picks up what looks to be a paper-mache crown out of a box and glances at the card. "I mean what is this? And why did the Duke of Cornhole send this to us?"

I snatch the paper-mache mess from his hands. "It's Duke of Cornwall. As in Prince Charles, you shitbag. Have some respect."

"Respect? You're the one who just called me a shitbag."

"I always call you that."

He sighs again and scribbles something on the card then hands it to me. "Exceptionally yours?" I read it out loud.

"That's my calling card."

"You could just write thank you."

"I could but that has a better ring to it, don't you think? Exceptionally Yours, His Royal Highness Crown Prince Magnus of Norway."

"That's quite the mouthful."

He wags his brows at me and gives me a salacious grin. "You know I am."

Suddenly a loud, frantic knocking at the door makes us all jump, including Einar who has been sitting in the corner of the room and doing his best to ignore our bickering.

"Are we expecting anyone?" I ask as Einar strides across the room and disappears into the hall. Jane went into town with Ottar, but they shouldn't be back for another few hours.

"God, I hope it's not the Duke of Cornhole," Magnus says, getting to his feet. "With those ears, I bet he hears everything."

I hear the front door open and Einar talking to someone in Norwegian. He sounds rather gruff and angry and I can't understand what he's saying.

"What is he saying?" I ask Magnus, but Magnus is already heading out into the hall. I catch a look of fear in his eyes.

This isn't good.

I get up from the couch and hurry after them.

I round the corner into the foyer and stop dead in my tracks when I see who is at the door.

Heidi Fucking Lundström.

Standing there in a big, furry coat that makes me cringe thinking how many bears probably died for it, holding a manila envelope in her hand. Behind her in the driveway is a waiting car with the prime minister's insignia on it.

Her eyes are wild and dark as she looks at Magnus, shaking the envelope at him and the moment she spots me, they seem to turn into something more wicked.

"I guess you need to hear this too," she says in English.

Magnus gives me a wide-eyed look, his jaw firm, shaking his head for me to stay back, but there's no way that is happening.

I go over to them. "What is this? What's going on?"

Heidi looks up at Einar. "I don't think you should stay for this. Unless you think I'm a threat."

Einar glances at Magnus, waiting for his instruction.

Magnus just gives him a solemn nod.

Einar walks off, though I know he won't go very far.

Which makes me wonder, she said she wasn't a threat but usually people who say that are. Is she carrying a knife with her?"

"How did you get in here?" I ask.

"Took my father's car," she says with a shrug. Then her eyes go all blazing hot again and she looks at Magnus. "So nice of your mother to invite me to the wedding. I know that had nothing to do with you."

"What do you want, Heidi?" Magnus says, crossing his arms and taking a wide stance with his legs.

She's not intimidated. "What do I want? What do I want?" She lets out an acidic laugh. "I want a palace, just like this one. Maybe this one. I want prestige and money and adoration. I want my face on a coin. I want a title. I want the power that my father refuses to give me. I want every single thing that Princess Ella here has. Including you, Magnus. Especially you."

And this chick is on the one-way train to Crazy Town. Next stop, Delusionville.

I look at Magnus, brows raised, my mouth open. I would laugh but there's something about her delivery, something about the fact that she's actually *here*, having, what, stolen her father's car, that makes me think twice.

This isn't funny.

This isn't going to end well either.

"Heidi," Magnus says as gently and sternly as he can, "you know that what we had is over. I'm married to Ella now. She is my wife. We are very happy. I know you tend to get, uh, wrapped up in things and feelings, I know you have your issues you need to deal with, but I promise you, this isn't the answer. We had a nice time. It's in the past. I moved on and you need to too."

She stares blankly at him, her lower lip trembling for a moment.

Then she tilts her head and says, "No."

"You need to leave," Magnus says after a beat, seeming a bit taken aback by her reaction, just as I am. "If you don't leave, I will have to make you leave."

"I'm not leaving until you know the truth," she says, then looks at me. "Until she knows the truth."

She slaps the folder against Magnus's chest.

"What is this?" he asks.

"It's a paternity test."

My stomach sinks.

Oh my god.

No.

"A...what?" Magnus asks, quickly fumbling to get the papers out of the folder.

"A paternity test," she says. "I'm pregnant, Magnus. And you're the father."

No.

There is no way.

"She's lying," I manage to say, my words choked, my hand at my chest as if to keep my heart intact. "This is impossible."

She gives me a sharp smile. "It's not impossible. We last had sex in mid-September. That was four months ago." She reaches forward and taps the folder. "That proves everything."

I can't believe this is happening.

This can't be happening.

My chest is constricting, I don't think I can breathe.

Magnus looks absolutely dumbfounded, his face growing pale. "I never gave you my DNA."

"If you think my father doesn't have your DNA on file somewhere, you would be sorely mistaken."

"You're not showing..." I say, but I trail off as she opens her coat and pulls up the sweater she's wearing. She's a thin girl but her belly is definitely sticking out and round, more than the beginning of a bump.

Holy fuck.

I can only shake my head and try to process it.

But I can't.

I can't.

This can't be happening.

This is going to change everything.

Everything I have is going to disappear.

"You're lying," I tell her again, finding my voice, the last shred of hope I can cling to. "You're lying just like you lied about the sex video. You leaked it, you shared it. You wanted the publicity. This is the same. Well I'm telling you, it's not going to work."

She bares her teeth at me in the nastiest smile. "It's working because it's the truth. And soon, every single person will know that I'm pregnant with the Prince's baby, a baby conceived while the two of you should have been together. If you think I'm going to just let Magnus off the hook, oh boy, you poor little girl, you're sorely mistaken."

Magnus is silent, stewing, simmering. His eyes are flickering with a mix of rage and shame. "What do you want?"

She laughs. "Isn't it obvious? You." She points at me. "Her. I want her life. And I want her out of the picture."

"That's not going to happen," he says in a calm, measured voice. "She's my wife."

"And I'm going to fuck shit up for both of you, so you might as well let her go before I do."

"I'm not letting her go," Magnus says. "We just...we just

329

have to figure something out. Money. That's what you want, it's money."

"It's you. I have money."

"Listen, Heidi. I'm sorry..."

"Are you telling me that the Crown Prince won't support his child? Is that the kind of father you want to be? The world is going to judge you on this, but you should be judging yourself. This child is going to grow up without a father's love."

Oh my god. I'm going to be sick.

This is actually happening.

He's going to be a father, a father of someone else's baby.

I can't handle this.

"Heidi, have some compassion," Magnus says, his voice barely a whisper. He's losing the fight and he knows it.

I know it.

Oh god.

"You have some compassion for me," Heidi says. "I'll let you keep these files just in case you don't believe me. Trust me, I have more than enough copies at home, you know, in case my father or the press wants to see. Perhaps your father, hmmm?"

"Look," Magnus says, gasping for air as he runs his hand through his hair, tugging on the ends in frustration. "Let's just...I need to process all of this. So does Ella. Give us a few days and then we can figure something out."

Heidi crosses her arms and looks between the two of us, smiling at our stunned and staggered expressions. Smiling because she's winning.

"Okay. I'll be back. But just so you know, there isn't much to figure out, Magnus. Everything going forward is all about you and me. It's that simple."

Then she turns around and flounces out of the door and down the stairs.

Magnus barely has enough strength to close the door behind her and collapses against it, staring at the tiled floor in a daze. "This isn't happening," he says. "This can't be happening to us. Not now. Fuck, not now!" He yells and pounds his fist against the door.

I should calm him down but I'm equally as mad, and as the seconds go by I find myself growing more mad at him.

"Say something," Magnus says, glancing at me through his hair in his eyes. "Please. Ella. Say something."

My mouth opens, trying to find words. Heat builds behind my eyes. "I can't believe this."

"I know…"

"I can't believe you."

He glances at me sharply. "What? Me?"

"Why did you have to sleep with her of all people? Aren't you picky at all? Don't you have standards?"

He frowns, incredulous. "What does that have to do with it?"

"Because you slept with her and you probably knew she was bad news. Now she's here, trying to ruin our lives. Oh my god, Magnus. We're newlyweds. We just…this isn't fair. I didn't…I can't do this," I tell him, doing everything I can to hold back the tears. "No, I can't handle this, not right now."

"Ella, please. Don't do anything."

"I need to think. I need to…Magnus. Don't you know what position this puts me in?"

"Don't you know what position it puts me in?"

"Yes. As a father. Because you reap what you sow," I say bitterly, practically spitting out the words.

"Excuse me?"

"You heard me. You fucked her, over and over again, not

caring that she was nuts. You make this god damn sex tape. You do all these things because you don't have a fucking brain, because you're reckless, you're irresponsible, you're selfish." I know what I'm saying hurts him, but I can't stop, the frustration and fear is too strong. "It's your inability to think about any consequences that got us into this mess!"

He stares at me like I just slapped him in the face. His nostrils flare as he inhales. "Fuck. You."

"It's the truth, Magnus. If you had just given it a moment's thought, this never would have happened."

"If I hadn't fucked up and gotten myself in this mess, you wouldn't be here!"

"Yeah, well maybe that would have been for the best."

He blinks at me in awe. "What are you saying?"

I need to stop talking. I need to get a hold of myself. I'm hurt, and confused, and I'm scared. So scared of where this is going, so scared that in the end I'll be tossed aside. It doesn't matter that we're married, he could still discard me, he could still end up with her.

I press my lips together, afraid to say something I'll regret, but instead I start shaking and quivering inside like a volcano ready to blow.

"What are you saying?" he asks again. "Don't tell me you're considering those clauses. Don't tell me that's how you're going to handle it. Turn into a little girl and run away."

"I am not a little girl! I'm your wife and you're having a baby with another woman. How the fuck do you think I feel? How do you think I'm supposed to act?"

"It's not a choice, Ella! I'm stuck with this fucking problem too. What do you want me to do? Turn my back on a child that's mine? Cast her out when I'm also responsible for what happened?"

Yes. That's exactly what I want to happen.

And I hate to say it, I hate to be that person.

It would be better if we could pretend that Heidi didn't exist, that there was no child on the way.

But if Magnus did that, if he chose to not be a part of it, then he's not the person I thought I married. The man I married would always do the right thing, even if it hurts.

No matter what happens to us, we lose.

I feel like my heart is being obliterated the more I stand here and think about it.

I can't deal with this here, with him.

We won't get anywhere.

I turn around and head upstairs to our room.

"Where are you going?" Magnus yells after me.

I don't answer him. I grab my purse and make sure the essentials are in there and then I head back down stairs.

Einar is standing by the front door, Magnus walking toward me.

His face falls when he notices my purse.

"Where are you going?" he asks, reaching for my arm.

I rip it out of his grasp, not wanting to look at him anymore.

"Home!" I tell him. "I'm going home."

I pass by Einar in the hallway. "When you see Jane, tell her I'll send for her in a few days."

He gives me an apologetic smile. "Yes, madam."

I walk down the stairs and into a car as a driver runs out of the house after me, hurrying to the driver's seat.

"Where to?" he asks.

"The airport," I tell him.

I tell myself I won't cry on the property. I won't let my tears tinge that estate. I won't let this bury the life that I've built here.

But the moment the car passes through the palace gates, I burst into tears.

I cry and I cry and I cry, as if my heart is being emptied out.

And all that's left is the lie we built our love on.

TWENTY-TWO

MAGNUS

It was the wedding band that set me off.

Ella's wedding band, sitting in a silver dish beside the bathroom sink.

It's been a day since Ella left the house.

A day since Heidi appeared with the paternity test, telling us she was pregnant with our child.

A day since my entire life collapsed in ruins around me.

It's been a hell of a day to say the least.

But I was managing it the best I could.

I think I was more in a daze than anything. Pretending that Ella went around the corner instead of who knows where she went. Pretending that Heidi was mistaken. Pretending that everything in my life didn't drastically change forever.

But that wedding band, that did it.

I picked it up in my hand and felt the complete absence of her.

The fact that she had left me.

She *left* me.

The fear that she might not ever come back.

And who could fucking blame her?

I apparently have some demon spawn with Heidi and that's something you don't get to come back from.

So, when I saw that ring, the fact that she took it off as if she was discarding our marriage, I did what I do best when I get into these panicky situations.

I completely trashed my room.

I mean, yelling, screaming, punching the wall, kicking things over, throwing shit. It was ugly.

Just acting like a complete barbarian with a peanut brain.

And even though Ottar is used to these kinds of outbursts from me from time to time, when my temper and frustration levels and my race-car brain can't be controlled, this time he's barging in the room like he's ready to wrestle me.

"Bring it on, little man," I snarl at him as I turn around, doing my best Wolverine impression.

"What the hell are you doing?" he asks, looking at the mess and chaos around him. Feathers from the down pillows I kicked are floating in the air. "Don't you have any self-control?"

"You know I don't," I say, still trying to catch my breath. Somehow, I don't feel any better though, and now the room is all fucked up. "You should really know I don't by now."

"Sir, listen," he says as he slowly approaches me, as if I'm going to pick him up and throw him through the window. That's when I notice the envelope in his hands.

The paternity test.

The sight of it nearly sends me reeling again.

"Get that thing out of here," I grind out.

He shakes it at me. "No, listen to me. I don't think this is legit."

That makes me pause. "What do you mean?" I can't ignore the hope building through me and if it's false hope I'm going to kill him. "Tell me you know something."

He comes on over and shows it to me. It looks the same as it did before.

"Look," he says, running his fingers over some lines at the bottom. "See the doctors that signed it?"

I squint and read the list of three names below their signatures. "Yeah, so?"

"Well I thought the name Gunnar Hamundarson sounded familiar," he says. "So I Googled him."

"Yeah. And?"

"Well he's a famous Viking from Iceland. From the tenth century."

I stare at him.

"So then," he continues, "I Googled the rest of the names. They're all dead Vikings. Magnus, these doctors don't exist. The thing is a forgery."

"Are you sure?" I ask carefully. "Please be sure about this."

"Positive," he says. Then he flashes me a smile. "Besides, you said she got your DNA from her father? That's a load of shit. The prime minister doesn't have people's DNA on file, he's not a criminologist or whatever. I doubt anyone has your DNA. You'd have to know about it if they did."

"Soooo," I say slowly.

"So, Heidi Lundström just royally fucked herself."

"But her stomach?"

He shrugs and puts his hands on his own round belly. "Maybe it was a food baby. Either way, it doesn't matter what it was. That test is a fake and therefore you're not the father. Rest easy, Prince Magnus. There shall be no red-headed ginger babes."

I should be relieved.

I mean, I *am* relieved.

Relieved but I also feel completely foolish for taking Heidi's word at face value and on top of that I feel like a total ass for losing my temper like this and having a yelling match with Ella last night which prompted her to leave.

But I'm also still angry.

Only it's a righteous kind of anger.

Driven by justice.

"Oh hell," Ottar says. "You're getting that look in your eyes, Magnus. You know the look. This can't be good."

I grin at him. "You're a good friend, Samwise. Been here through so much of the journey."

"Please don't start, sir."

I ignore him. "But we have to do this together. We have to put an end to this battle once and for all. Or at least, you can come along for the ride."

I grab a sweater and leave the room. I'll deal with the mess when I get back.

"Where are we going sir?" Ottar asks with a weary sigh before eventually following me. "Or maybe I don't want to know."

"We're going to see Sauron."

"Fucking knew it," Ottar swears.

We pass by Jane on the stairs. "Jane, tell me where Ella is."

She pauses and leans against the railing and rolls her eyes. "I told you. I think she went to Liechtenstein."

"Think? How come you don't know? You know everything."

"Because I've tried calling her too. She won't answer. I think she's just figuring stuff out. Maybe she wants to be alone. I certainly don't blame her when she's surrounded by a bunch of twits all the time."

"Well keep trying her. Tell her to call this twit, please."

She sighs. "Will do. You know, I don't like being put in the middle of your marital quarrels. I don't think it's fair."

Ottar laughs nervously. "Welcome to the rest of your life, Lady Jane."

We get into the car with Einar behind the wheel and he drives Ottar and I into the city. I call Ella numerous times, trying to tell her the news, but she never answers, and my texts don't seem to go through either. Not that I was about to text her: **Surprise! No Demon Baby! Come Home!**

Einar drives us straight to the prime minister's office, which actually is just a few blocks from my parent's palace. I think I'll pay my father a visit after but for now, I have one thing I need to set right, even if it hurts me.

Of course, I don't have an appointment with the prime minister, but I use my status and smile to get the secretary to send me on through, Ottar at my side.

"Your Highness," he says as we step into his office. He gets to his feet and gives me a slight bow, which already makes me feel like I have the upper hand. "To what do I owe the honor? I wasn't expecting you."

"I have something I need to discuss with you," I tell him, leaning against the edge of his desk. "It's rather personal and sensitive."

He nods slowly and eyes Ottar. "Should he be here then?"

"He's here for backup," I tell him. "You see, this concerns you. To be more specific, it concerns your daughter."

Oh, it's so hard not to call her the "psycho-hose-beast,

stage-five-clinger, batshit barnacle of a daughter" but I manage to bite my tongue.

"What about her?"

Uh oh. His eyes are already narrowed. This won't be easy.

But hopefully it will be satisfying.

"First of all, I want to apologize yet again for that video that leaked out into the world. It was never meant for anyone else's eyes and I'm still very mad at myself that I let it happen," I say.

His eyes soften, just slightly. "Oh. Okay. Well that never hurts to hear again."

"I should have never put myself in that situation. I never should have gone out with her and I never should have let her film us. It was a bad idea and being a prince, being the older one, being the man, I should have put a stop to it. I didn't, and I accept that as a lack of responsibility and control. It's something I will forever aim to make better."

He was nodding during this but now he's stopped. "You make it sound like it was her idea. She would never..."

I try not to smile. "Yeah, well, here's the thing. It was her idea. I should have said no, I should have known better, but it was her idea. And I think she leaked the whole thing as well. There was no hacker. It was just her, sharing it with the world."

His eyes spark as he looks to Ottar and back to me. "That's insane. More than that, it's terribly inappropriate, horrific even, to accuse my girl of that. How dare you!"

"Once you know what else she's done, I think you'll come to the same conclusion," I say, jerking my head toward Ottar.

Ottar comes forward and places the paternity test papers on the desk, sliding them toward the prime minister.

He eyes them but makes no move to pick them up. "What are these?"

"This is a paternity test. Your daughter borrowed your car yesterday and came to see me at Skaugum Estate. Did you know that?"

Now he looks completely taken aback. "Oh, well I. Uh, no. She said she needed it but..."

"She came to see me and Ella and gave me this. A paternity test that says she's pregnant and I'm the father."

"What?" he barks, his beady eyes flashing. He snatches up the paper, his hand starting to shake as he reads it over.

"Yes, that was my reaction. Said it must have happened back in September. Maybe that tape was supposed to have captured it all for proof, I don't know."

"She can't be pregnant," he says softly. "Especially with you." He glares at me, his words turning harsh at that.

I shrug. "That's the game she was running. Until Ottar, wonderful, suspicious Ottar, who was further removed from the situation and able to look at it unemotionally, decided to examine it further. First of all, all those doctors who signed it are dead Vikings. So, that's weird right? Second of all, she said you personally have my DNA on file somewhere and that's how she obtained it."

"I don't," he says, his voice now breaking a bit, like he's losing it.

About time.

"That's what we figured. Look, I understand it's a lot to take. But you have to know that even though I have royally fucked up before, many times, that is all in the past. I learned my lesson. And I found love. I'm not saying I won't fuck up again, but you can be damned sure it won't be like this. I am the future king and from this moment forward, I will be behaving as one." I pause and stand up straighter. "I think it's only fair you treat me as one."

He stares at me for a few long, awkward seconds and I have no clue what he's going to say. Finally, he says, "I'll treat you like a king when you act like it."

"Fair enough," I tell him. "I didn't expect much otherwise. But just so you know, I don't take being threatened lightly. The fact that she told me she would extort me and slander our family name is something we all take very seriously. I don't know what she's going to say and given that she's probably not pregnant with anyone's baby, I don't know how far the charade was going to go on for. But she meant to do as much damage as possible with that document." I clear my throat. "I should probably take legal action against her. And perhaps you, for allowing this to happen."

Now I've got him.

Oh, how the tables have turned.

"Come now, Your Highness," he starts babbling, wiping sweat off his greasy brow. "I had nothing to do with this, I don't know what goes on with her. I mean, you can't be serious. We can talk this out. There is no reason to take it to that level."

I shrug. "I don't know. Considering the mess she aimed to cause, I think it should be. This is an offense I'm sure, forging something like this, and it's a greater one to threaten royalty. If this got out into the public, why I'm sure your entire reputation would come crashing down in a hot second."

"Magnus, Your Highness, please. Just sit down. Let's talk."

"I don't need to talk," I tell him. "And I won't say a word of this. I'll sweep it under the rug." I pause, pointing my finger at him. "Just promise me that *you'll* deal with your daughter. Honestly, and I mean this from a good place, but she's not right in the head. She needs help. Professional help and *lots* of it. I think she's lost and lonely and feels ignored when it comes to you. She feels victimized and forgotten. You need to start being there for her more and you can start by getting her the help she needs before she goes off the rails for good."

He just nods, staring into space. "Yes. Yes. Of course."

"Are we good, sir?" Ottar says to me.

I give him an appreciative, triumphant smile as we start toward the door.

"Oh yes. We're good."

～

I'M STARING DOWN AT MY PHONE, WILLING FOR ELLA to call me, when my father beside me stirs. I've been sitting next to him for nearly an hour now, patiently waiting for him to wake up. I know I shouldn't unload anything on him, I know he needs his rest and, as my mother has been saying, only happy thoughts and happy things are to be discussed with the King, but of course that doesn't seem to apply to her since she's still the number one complainer in this royal household.

But I digress. I need to talk to him. In the past I would have kept my father out of whatever messy thing was going on in my life. When it came to the whole sex tape thing and marriage, well that was him reeling me in, not the other way around. If I could have, I would have pretended nothing happened.

But I don't want to live like that anymore.

Today, talking to the prime minister, I felt more like a

king than anything else. Emboldened and authentic and real. For the first time, I really felt like I owned up to my title of heir, that I was worthy of it.

And kings don't shrink from the hard conversations.

My father never did.

And I won't with him. I have to speak with him, I have to let him know what happened. Pretending it never existed won't do me any good. I need to own it before it's swept under a rug.

He groans lightly and opens his eyes, blinking at me. "Magnus?" he asks, his voice hoarse.

"It's me," I tell him, grabbing his hand softly. "I just wanted to say hello."

His eyes close but he smiles. "Well hello to you too. How long have you been there, watching me snore away?"

"Long enough."

"I have to say, with your condition, that must have been very boring for you." He opens one eye and spears me with it. "What brings you here today?"

I take in a deep breath. Suddenly I'm afraid. I'm afraid that he'll lose respect for me. I'm afraid that he'll think I've regressed in some way.

"What is it, Son?" he asks. "I can tell it's something big. Do I need to call for a nurse?"

I shake my head. "No. No, I think it's okay. It's okay because everything turned out okay in the end. Just, uh, remember that. That everything is fine now."

He sighs, his chest rising and falling. "Well that's good. Fine is good. They say greed is good, but fine is good too."

Hmmm. He may be a little loopy.

"Ella left me."

Boom.

There it is.

"She what?" he says, moving around to get a good look at me. "What are you talking about? I thought you guys were writing up your thank-you cards just yesterday. Oh, and by the way, don't bother with Prince Hans of the Netherlands, I didn't care for the way he looked at your mother at the wedding."

I ignore that. "We were doing that yesterday. After that, well...a bomb went off. It wasn't pretty."

"Well what was it?" He pauses, watching my face carefully. "Magnus, what did you do?"

"Heidi Lundström came to our door."

"Oh, dear."

"Yeah. Oh fuck was more like it, but yeah, oh dear works. She told me she was pregnant with my child and had a paternity test to prove it."

His eyes widen. "Oh, fuck," he says after a beat.

"There you go."

"I can see why Ella might have left," he surmises. "What did you do?"

"Well I pulled my lovely hair out and commenced losing my mind. She said she was four months pregnant, she had the stomach to prove it, and the paternity tests, which she left in my care."

He frowns thoughtfully. "Wait. How on earth did she get your DNA for a paternity test?"

"She said her father had it on file."

"That's simply not true."

"I know. I know that now. Thanks to Ottar who took the documents and examined them closely. Heidi isn't very smart, and she isn't very thorough. Conniving yes, but that's not the same thing. They were forged."

"What about her stomach?"

"Well aside from wanting to punch her in the gut to find

345

out, I'm guessing she was just sticking out her stomach. The bump was there but it wasn't huge and it's not like I got a chance to inspect it."

My father shakes his head. "This is unbelievable. I'm sorry you had to go through that Magnus. But surely this isn't the end of the world if Ella knows it was all fake."

I sigh and rub my hand down my face, suddenly so tired. "She doesn't know because she's not talking to me. According to Jane, she's in Liechtenstein, but Jane hasn't been able to talk much to her either."

"So, did you tell Heidi?"

"I marched right down to the prime minister's office and told him."

My father grows silent. Then, "You what?"

"I know it's not the protocol with dealing with him, but he has to know what his daughter is up to. And I refuse to be bullied and intimidated by him. I am your son. One day I will be king. There are lines that shouldn't be crossed, but there should always be respect, and that man has no respect for me. But I think he does now."

I can tell my father is thinking the worst. That I went into his office and embarrassed myself. But I didn't.

I go on. "I owned up to my mistakes, but I refuse to own up to things that aren't of my own making. I chose Ella and we are married and that's the life I want to pursue. The man I was before isn't gone, but I feel the king in me is stepping forward. People can deal with that however they wish, but it's the new truth."

My father sighs. "Well then. I see."

I swallow hard, feeling pained for bringing it all up. "I didn't want to make you upset, but I had to be honest with you and let you know. I'm sorry for the things I've done in the past, I'm sorry it took me so long to live up to my potential. But it's better late than never."

"Oh, Magnus," he says to me. "You're my world, you really are. My world, my son, my heir and you're exactly who you're meant to be and where you're meant to be. I'm very proud of you for standing up to him, and her, and I'm grateful that you chose to tell me the truth when I probably would have had no idea. I don't like to rule like that. Ignorance is no way to run your life, let alone a country."

I give his hand a squeeze, feeling overly emotional for the second time today. "Thank you," I whisper.

He smiles but his breathing suddenly becomes more labored and his face seems to pale.

"Are you okay?" I ask him, my pulse quickening.

He nods, takes in a few deep, shaking breaths and clears his throat. "I'm fine, Magnus. I just feel...anyway, I'm happy that everything is sorted."

"Well, I still don't have Ella."

"I'm sure she just needed time to think."

"I found her wedding band by the sink."

"That doesn't mean anything."

I feel like if I mention it, it will come true, but I can't ignore what's really worrying me. "Father, the clauses she put in the contract. What if she's going to use them?"

"And ask for a divorce?"

"Yes."

"Over a fake pregnancy?"

"No. But she never really got to know me before we married. There's so much baggage behind me. What if something else one day raises its ugly head? What if she discovers that she can't handle being with me? What if she decides that marriage with me was a mistake?"

My father chuckles softly, which then turns into a

347

wheezing cough. When he finally recovers he says, "That's called divorce, Magnus, and it's available for everyone. Not just you. Those clauses are there because Ella had to have some sort of control over this situation. You can't blame her. And she's young. She's so young to be thrust into this new role, she has no idea how to handle this and neither do you. You just have to trust that what she feels for you is genuine and let everything else go."

I look down at my hand on his. "What if she stops loving me after this?"

"She won't. I promise. It's a hurdle that will make your love grow stronger. Take it from me. You're going to have a lot of hurdles."

"What if...?" I trail off. I could go on and on.

"Ignore the what ifs," he says. "Ella is complicated and passionate and fierce. Just like you. You have a fierce Viking heart, handed down from your ancestors. So, love fiercely, Magnus. Love bravely. Love her with everything you've got."

It feels like I have a brick in my throat. It all sounds too simple and yet I know there's nothing simple about love at all. But I can continue to be brave with my heart.

"Thank you for listening," I tell him, taking in a deep breath. I glance up at him. "It means the..."

Something stops my words.

My father's eyes are closed.

His face seems more ashen than it was seconds ago.

He's not moving.

He's suddenly so unnaturally, eerily still.

No. No. *No.*

I squeeze his hand. "Father?"

Nothing.

Oh god.

I lean over him, peering at him. "Father? Wake up. Wake up."

No response.

"No, no, please!" I cry out, feeling his neck for a pulse, trying to see if he's breathing. I can't find it. His chest isn't rising.

"Nurse! Someone! Help!" I start yelling, frantically grabbing his other wrist to check, lightly slapping his face.

No, this can't be my father dead.

This has to be a dream.

This can't be real.

"Help!"

The door bursts open and the nurse rushes in, followed by Sven and Tor. Tor pulls me out of the way while the nurse checks for vitals.

"We need an ambulance, now!" she yells, and Sven brings out his phone, dialing it.

Then my mother is in the room, panicking, and Mari, crying, and I've never felt so alone so suddenly before, like everything beautiful and light and joyous in my heart was suddenly sucked out like a vacuum, like my father was taken with it.

Mari comes to my side, tears streaming down her face and I put my arm around her, holding her close to me, holding on for dear life.

Soon the medics come, and the stretcher, and I'm escorted out by people I don't know, and I'm lost and I'm surrounded by people but I'm alone and my father...

God, please don't take him.

I'm not ready to lose him.

I can't imagine life without him.

As he's taken out on the stretcher to the ambulance, I

lean against the wall in the hallway and slump to the floor, the sorrow inside me flooding up like a tidal wave.

For a moment the numbness and the confusion fades.

For a horrible moment I feel everything I have lost.

The tears that I had held back can no longer be tamed.

I cry, tear drops splashing to the palace floor.

I never had the chance to tell him how much I loved him.

My father.

My king.

TWENTY-THREE

ELLA

"You're not wearing your wedding band," my father comments.

I look over to him in the same daze I've been trying to shed for the last twenty-four hours. "What?"

"Your wedding band," he says again. "Where is it?"

I swallow uneasily. "Oh. It's by the sink. It's a bit loose so I always take it off to wash my face."

"Here?"

"At home."

Home.

It's a word I've been trying to avoid. It's a word that I've tried to lend to this place I'm in, the Vaduz Castle, the official residence of my father in Liechtenstein and the place where I grew up.

But now that I'm here, I know it's not home.

As much as I've wished it could be since I was thirteen, as much as I've glorified and romanticized this place, it's not at all what I remember it being. They say you can't go home again, and it couldn't be more true.

But it's not because the place you used to call home changes.

It's because you change.

This place, this castle, it's the same as it always was. It's drafty. It's dark. It's both gaudy and opulent and dank and depressing. Jane always says this place suffers because men always rule here, not women, and that could definitely be the case. And after my mother died, I guess things just became a little colder.

But when I was growing up, it was the only home I knew, and I loved it as such. When I was sent to boarding school it's not that my new life was awful, although it was a bit lonely, it's that I associated home with love and if I wasn't at home, if I was sent elsewhere, I wasn't loved. I longed after it, after my family, like someone longs after a lover when they've been given no closure. You always wonder what if.

Now I'm here.

I came right here after I left Magnus because there really was no other place to go. The university was no longer my home, which meant this was the only place that hadn't changed.

But I've changed and now I can't fit my parameters of my new self around this place and it can't fit around me. I came here looking for support and love, something to bolster me after losing the life I had planned with Magnus. But that just doesn't exist here.

It only exists in myself.

It always has.

Now I'm sitting with my father at dinner and while I've appreciated how kind he's been with me and how I'm able to talk to him now more than ever, that we're relating to each other in a new way, as adults instead of a parent and child, I know that he can't give me what I'm missing.

Only I can.

"I'm sorry your brothers couldn't be here," my father says, dabbing a napkin at his face while a servant comes and takes the plates away. "They're rather busy."

"So busy that they couldn't come to my wedding?" I ask. I know I'm being blunt and judging from the expression on my father's face, I know this is a new side of me too.

"Yes, well," he says and then sighs. He gives me what can only be described as a wince. "I'm sorry about that too. I know if your mother were alive, she would have hit them all upside the head and forced them. Actually, I believe if she were alive, she wouldn't have had to force them. They would have gone because they wanted to. I'm afraid it's my fault."

"Your fault?"

He nods slowly, tapping a finger on the table. "Yes. I suppose so. You see, I...never really learned how to become a father. I was always a ruler of this land first and a father second and it was your mother who kept me in line and accountable. After she died...that fell to the wayside. I know I wasn't a great father to you, and I wasn't a great father to the boys. I taught them how to be rulers, but I don't think I taught them to be good sons, or brothers, or men in general. And you, well I didn't know what to do with you. I just wanted the best for you. You weren't like them and I knew you wouldn't rule, so I sent you away. And for that, I'm sorry. So many years I've missed."

I'm going to cry.

Again.

For the millionth time in the last day.

Somehow, I manage to hold it together. "So, there was nothing wrong with me?" I ask, my voice breaking.

"Heavens no, Isabella. You're such a bright and shining star in my life. I guess I just feel because I've missed so many years with you, I don't know how to relate to you, I don't know how to be a father. But I promise you...I'm willing to try."

I know it's not part of the proper etiquette or decorum, but I abruptly get out of my seat and walk around the long table to him on the other end, lean over and hug him from behind.

"Thank you," I tell him. "I promise I'll be a better daughter."

He pats my arm and chuckles. "You can't get any better, Isabella. Just be yourself. And for heaven's sake, go back home to your husband."

I let go of him and straighten up. "What?"

I hadn't told my father I had come because of Magnus, but I guess it was a little more than obvious when I showed up with no luggage and no wedding ring. Though I swear I didn't leave it behind on purpose.

He cranes his neck around to stare up at me. "I was married, you know. I know what it's like. It's work. Sometimes it's fun work, sometimes it's hard work, but a lot of the time it's work. You just have to buckle down and get through it and come out the other side. Work makes a marriage stronger and more than that, it makes you stronger."

Suddenly I feel horrible about missing all of Magnus's phone calls, for turning my phone off. I still don't know what we're going to do, and it still eats me up inside and makes me sick to think about it. But I took a vow that said we had to stay together for better or worse. This is worse than worse, but shouldn't I stand by his side through it all? Wouldn't he do that for me?

"Well you're being a father already," I tell him, patting him on the shoulder. "Giving out marriage advice."

"Sir," Schnell appears in the doorway of the dining room with a mobile phone in his hand. "I'm afraid it's an emergency."

He rushes in and gives my father the phone, giving me a sympathetic look as he does so. The kind of look that makes my heart still.

I can't imagine what it could be this time.

"Hello?" my father answers in German. "Yes," he says, switching to English. Then he looks right at me. "Oh, no. I see. That's terrible. Thank you for telling me. Yes. I will. Send my regards."

He hangs up.

"What?" I ask, my stomach sinking fast.

"It's King Anders. He's on his deathbed."

❧

As soon as we got the news, I took the quickest flight back to Oslo. Luckily, already being in Liechtenstein, I was able to fly on my father's private jet and he came along with me for moral support.

I'm a little bit nervous over the fact that I'm seeing Magnus again, that I'm walking back into a messy, horrid situation that I have no control over, but for the most part, that is buried by my absolute worry for the King.

According to Mari, whom I talked with on the phone on the car ride to the hospital, his organs have started to fail, and he went into shock, apparently right in front of Magnus.

My heart breaks for him, it breaks for his whole family, for the country. I know how well-loved the King is. He's been so welcoming and good to me, and even though we didn't see eye-to-eye at the beginning, he's more than made up for it. He's the type of person who reigns effortlessly and with a lot of love and that's how he conducts his life as well. He's always coming from a good place, even if you don't agree with his tactics.

And at this point, how could I ever be mad at him for what he did. If he hadn't told my father that Magnus had proposed, that would have never forced me into this situation with his son.

Which means that no matter what happens, no matter what has happened, having Magnus in my life means more than anything else. He is my life now and I know I'm his and whatever is thrown our way, I know it's better to stay by his side and weather it, support him, love him, stand by him. I won't walk from this marriage, I won't run from him, even if it gets harder from here on in.

We get into the hospital and are quickly escorted to the private ward. It's both heartening and horrifying to see so many people, including hospital workers, crying over the news. The further we get into the situation, the more I think that all hope is lost.

And then we're shown to the ICU ward where he's being treated, and I see the family at the end of the hall. Mari, Cristina, Irene, and Britt. The Queen. They're all sitting down, some of them crying and leaning against each other, others, like the Queen, looking in total shock.

And then there's Magnus, halfway between us and the rest of them. Slumped against the wall, his back to me. Even though it's just his back I can see a range of emotion in it. His devastation devastates me.

I break free of my father's arm and run down the hall to him.

"Magnus!" I call out.

He turns his head to look at me, his blank and bloodshot eyes blinking a few times until he realizes it's me and that I'm here.

"Ella," he cries out hoarsely, opening his arms for me.

I run right into him and he envelopes me into a long, hard hug.

"Ella," he says again, his face buried in my hair. Then he starts to shake. He starts to cry. He breaks down.

Everything breaks inside me.

To see him like this.

To hold him like this.

My beautiful man is suffering, ravaged by loss and sorrow.

I keep my hold on him, tears falling from my eyes now, feeling his body pressed against mine, wanting him to know that I'm here and though I can't take away his pain, his heart is safe with mine. It always was.

"I am so sorry," I tell him, meaning his father, meaning everything.

He nods but continues to cry and I continue to hold on to him as tight as I can.

I'm not sure how much time passes in that hospital hallway, but grief and shock have a way of playing with it. It feels like minutes and hours and days.

But at some point, Magnus calms and regains his breath. By now my father is at the end of the hall, talking to the family.

"I am so sorry," I tell him again, running my hand over his head. "I know it doesn't matter right now, but I want you to know I'm here for you. I should have never run away. I'll never run away again. I'm sorry I said terrible things and I should have behaved more like a lady, like a wife."

"Ella," he whispers against me. "It's okay."

"It's not okay," I tell him. "It's not. I realize I have a lot of growing up to do."

"So do I."

"Then we need to do it together, not apart. No matter what happens, I'll be by your side. I'm standing by my marriage and my man." I take in a shaking breath. "How is your father? Is he...?"

He glances up at me with pained eyes. "They're doing everything they can," he says, his words cracking. "It happened so suddenly. One minute I was talking to him, the next...I guess he went right into shock. Ella, it was horrible. I can't get it out of my head. All the things I could have said to him."

"He's not gone yet," I tell him. "You can still say all those things."

"I knew he was sick and I knew that one day this day would come, no matter what, but...I'm not ready. I'm not ready to say goodbye. I can't imagine living a world without him in it, and fuck, I am such a fool for wasting so many years just being selfish and doing whatever I wanted."

"You weren't selfish, you were just dealing with yourself. We all go through that. Don't hold yourself accountable."

He shakes his head, his hair flopping in front of his eyes. "I should have been more involved in my role. I should have been learning from him. Ella, I've missed so much."

His words remind me of my own father's words.

"Magnus, it's never too late to make things better. It's never too late to learn. No matter what happens, you can still learn from him. My mother died when I was young but through my father I'm learning all there is about her, life lessons, other lessons. How to be a better daughter. This doesn't mean the end of that relationship."

He exhales a shaky breath. "I'm hurting, baby."

"I know."

We stand like this, holding onto each other, feeling that hurt and that pain because there's no use running from it. It will find you anyway.

Then a couple of doctors step out of the room and everyone gets to their feet.

Magnus and I break apart, holding each other's hands tight as we face them all.

The doctor says a bunch of something in Norwegian. There's a pause and then he continues, and everyone gasps.

But they're smiling.

Elated.

Relieved.

"What did he say?" I ask Magnus who is now giving me a tired, happy smile.

"He said that he had an infection that caused him to go into shock or something, but they stabilized him and that he's already showing signs of improvement with antibiotics. They said he may also need a kidney transplant when he gets a bit better, but they'll have no problems matching him. I'd give my own, but I guess that's a last resort to ask someone who's alive."

I breathe out a long sigh of relief. "Thank God."

He puts his arm around me, holding me close. "I don't know what I would have done. I really don't."

"But now you know what you can do. Learn from him Magnus. I'm sure he has a whole world he wants to teach you about."

He glances at me and then a look of realization seems to

come across him, like he's remembering something. "I tried calling you, you know."

"I know," I say sheepishly. "I turned off my phone after a bit. Chalk it up to being immature."

"So, you haven't talked to Jane yet?"

"No. Why? What's wrong?"

"Nothing," he says. "Nothing is wrong at all."

"I don't get it."

"Heidi," he says.

Oh shit. *That*.

"What about her?" I ask cautiously.

He grins at me and lets out a laugh. "She's done for."

"What do you mean?"

"Get this, so Ottar being Ottar, and man I don't give Samwise much credit, anyway, while you and I were losing our minds, he used his brains and investigated this so-called paternity test."

So-called? I like where this is going. "And?"

"It's a fake!"

"What do you mean...a fake?"

He gives me a wry look. "It means exactly what I said. She faked it, Ella. She faked the whole fucking thing. I can't believe we didn't even think to question it."

Oh my god. This changes everything.

"Well I don't know," I say slowly. "I've never seen a paternity test before, how would we know?"

"It doesn't matter though, because it's fake. She forged it using dead Viking names."

"So...now what?"

He nods excitedly. "So, Ottar and I took the faked paper, and we went straight to the prime minister."

"*You what?*"

I can't imagine that going well. Those two seem to be mortal enemies.

"We had a little chat and made him realize that his daughter needs help. I may have also threatened him with some legal action, slander and extortion and all that jazz, but it worked."

"So, for sure she's not pregnant?"

"No. Maybe with someone else, but it's not me. Probably just a food baby. And she won't be bugging us again, that's for sure. I feel like her father has no choice but to get her the help she needs."

"I wish I could see her face when he tells her what he knows, that she's a big fat liar."

"Yeah, but you know people like that are pathological narcissists, they don't even see where they went wrong even when it's rubbed in their face. Believe me, I want to be petty about it too but for now I'm just so fucking happy it's *over*."

I shake my head. Even more relief is flooding through me, to the point where I can hardly stay on my feet. "I am so relieved. You have no idea."

"I think I have an idea, Ella. That was something no couple should ever have to deal with."

I grab his hand, squeezing it. "I am so, so sorry I acted the way I did."

"So am I. I don't mind fighting with you, but I don't want you leaving."

"I know. I wasn't thinking."

"I know. Neither was I. You know I saw your wedding band. That fucking killed me, Ella. Killed me. I can't stand to lose you like that. You're everything to me."

Oh god. More tears are coming. I blink them back.

"I'm not going anywhere, I promise. For better and for worse. I will never leave you. I will be a leech."

"As long as you're not a barnacle," he says.

"And the ring, I always take it off to wash my face. I just forgot to put it back on. Believe me, the ring is pretty, but you've imprinted yourself on my heart and that's something that can't be taken off."

The corner of his mouth tilts into a smile and he cups my face in his hands. "I think the greatest thing my father has taught me already is that I have a Viking heart. And with this heart, I can't be afraid to love you bravely and boldly. Ella, I have fierce love for you, the kind that eats me up inside, the kind that influences everything I do. This fierce love might scare the both of us from time to time but it's mine and it's yours." He pauses, his smile deepening. "Exceptionally yours."

I laugh. "Not that again."

"But doesn't it make more sense now?"

I sigh happily and rest my head against his chest.

Everything makes sense now.

TWENTY-FOUR

MAGNUS

I RUN THE SILKY BLINDFOLD THROUGH MY FINGERS, biting my lip at how Ella is going to react to all of this.

She'll never have seen it coming.

Literally.

"Close your eyes," I tell her, standing right behind her.

"They're closed," she says as I bring the blindfold around her face and tie it behind her eyes.

"You can't see out?"

"Not a thing," she says.

"Perfect." I grab her by the shoulders and turn her around. "God, you look sexy with that on."

She grins, her cheeks making the blindfold rise. "I told you I was up for anything."

"Okay, now I'm going to put you in the car."

She flinches. "Okay. Wait. I thought you had a surprise for me?"

"Yeah, but you need to get in the car, so I can take you there. Come on." I take her hand and lead her out of the parlor room and through the front door that Einar is holding open for us. I exchange a knowing look with him and he actually smiles in return.

It's been three months since Ella and I had our first major fight, three months since my father nearly died in front of my eyes. Three months since both Ella and I have started to carve out a bright new life for ourselves.

Even though the shit with Heidi was crazy, it served its purpose. It brought us closer together, to know that even if something that destructive is dropped on our lap, we love each other enough to navigate through it. Our marriage might be new, it might have developed under unconventional circumstances, but it's ours to mold and to keep. We may be young, and we may make mistakes, but we're in it all together to the very end.

As for Heidi, well the last I heard she moved up north to Trondheim after a bout of psychological treatment. I don't ask the prime minister about her often because she's honestly just a speck inside my brain, but when I do, it also subtly reminds him that I'm not someone to be trifled with. Not even a little.

My father pulled through and had a kidney transplant just the other week. He's back in the hospital over that, but he's in great spirits and we're all hoping this means he'll make a full recovery. I'm just fucking lucky that I was able to tell him all the things I meant to tell him.

Of course, being my father, he said he already knew how much I loved him. I'm glad I'm not that hard to read. Sometimes being an open book is a blessing.

But I'm trying not to be an open book today, not with the surprise I have planned for Ella.

I help Ella down the stairs and get her in the backseat. Ottar and Lady Jane get in as well, but they don't say anything. The point is for her to think we're going alone.

Only half way through the drive into Oslo, Ella starts sniffing the air.

"I smell herring."

Oh shit.

I think she's gotten enhanced sense from the blindness.

Jane is wide-eyed in a *who me?* expression even though Ella can't see it.

"Herring and Old Spice."

Now Jane and I are looking at Ottar. He shrugs.

"Oh wait, now I smell...what is that...bullshit and lies?" Ella reaches out for me and manages to smack my thigh. "You told me we were going somewhere alone."

"I had a change of heart. Just don't lift up the blindfold, you'll spoil everything."

"Ottar, Jane," she says. "That's you, right?"

Jane tries to stay quiet, shaking her head but then bursts out laughing. "I'm sorry. I'm sorry I had lunch right before, even though you said not to Magnus."

I'm running a finger across my lips, telling her to zip it.

"Why couldn't she have lunch?" Ella asks. "Magnus, where are you taking me?"

"You know, the best part of this whole experience is the thrill of the unknown."

"Oh my god, you're not making me do skydiving are you, because I will murder you, I swear I will."

"Calm down, will ya? You're so untrusting."

"Because I'm married to someone who probably thinks blindfolding someone and pushing them out of an airplane is a good time."

"That's not what's really happening, is it?" Jane whispers.

I give her a look to shut up. "No. It's not. Okay, how about we all sit in silence until the ride is over."

"Agreed," Einar says from the driver's seat. "You people never shut up. No offense, sir."

"None taken." I always knew one day Einar would snap.

The silence is short-lived because before long we're pulling up alongside Oslo's harbor. Even though it's April, it's still fairly cold out and the harbor is pretty quiet, just a few tall ships and fishing boats.

I help Ella out of the car and lead her down along the cobblestones of the harbor's edge, past the Nobel Peace Prize Museum. Seagulls cry out and whirl above our heads.

"We're by the ocean," she says, breathing in deep with a smile on her face. "Ahh. It smells like spring." She pauses. "Are we going sailing?"

It's at this point I know that I'll have to take the blindfold off.

I glance down at the docks below us.

Right there at the end of the dock is a black inflatable-hull boat, about twenty-feet long, with rows of seats and storage compartments at the back, as well as a giant propeller motor that must weigh a ton.

"Are you ready?" I ask her, positioning her so that she's facing the water and the boat. "Just keep in mind if you step forward any more, you're going to tumble into the sea."

She stiffens. "What?"

"Relax," I tell her, slipping one arm around her waist. "I've got you." With my other hand I pull loose the blindfold and it's swept away by the breeze. Damn it. I could have used that later.

She doesn't know where to look for a minute and then she gasps, probably because she's on the edge about ten feet above the docks. I hold her back against me so she's not going anywhere and wait for her to really see it.

When she does, she gasps.

"Oh my god!'

"Surprise!" I tell her, kissing her cheek. "There's your first official boat."

The boat has the logo of her environmental organization at the front of the ship—Ocean Crusaders. At the back of the boat, there's the actual name of the vessel.

Princess Planet.

She bursts out laughing when she sees it. "You didn't!"

I grin at her, so happy this is her reaction. "I did."

She turns around to stare at me with wide, awestruck eyes. "Magnus. I can't believe you did this."

I'd been planning on doing it for a while. Ella just started up her organization and while she's knee-deep in sorting everything out and hiring people and figuring out the next plan of action, I wanted to show her how much I support her goals and her dreams. She's out to make a difference in the world, and I'll do everything I can to help her do that, personally and politically as well.

"I know you're just getting it off the ground and probably won't need a boat for a little while longer but when you do, whether you're going to go free Willy or yell at tourists for getting too close to endangered rocks or something, this is your vessel."

"Congratulations," Jane says, clapping. "Now, do we get to go on it?"

I raise my hand. "I'm driving."

"Oh, hell no," Ottar says. "Einar should drive."

"Actually, *I'm* driving," Ella says, holding her hand out for the key.

"Is that so?" I ask while I reach into my pocket and pull it out.

"It's my boat," she says smartly. I place it on her hand

367

and she snatches it up with a grin. "This will be the closest I'll get to your adrenaline sports, Magnus, mark my words."

We'll see about that, I think, following her down the gangplank to the docks.

"Hey, does sex count as an adrenaline sport?" I ask.

She shakes her head. "Honestly, Magnus."

"Yeah, honestly Magnus," Jane adds.

I sigh.

EPILOGUE

ELLA
A year later

"I NOW PRONOUNCE YOU HUSBAND AND WIFE, AGAIN," Erik says. "You may kiss the bride."

I grin at Magnus as he leans in, cupping my face with his palm. His eyes twinkle with love and adoration and a hint of something wicked before his lips press against mine and he envelopes me in a long, slow kiss. A sweet spring breeze picks up and flows through us, bringing the smell of glacial water and flowers.

Everyone claps and cheers.

And by everyone, I mean everyone that matters the most to us.

There's Jane.

Ottar.

Einar.

The King.

The Queen.

All of Magnus's sisters.

There's my father, and, low and behold, my brothers, most of whom spend their time ogling Magnus's sisters, even after being told off by Cristina, but hey, at least they're here.

There's Viktor and Maggie.

There's Harold, Maud and Guillermo.

And of course, Slender Man, our officiant. Apparently, it became a side business of his right after I first met him.

There are even two wedding photographers, Russian twins that Magnus likes to call the T-1000. I guess because they tend to be everywhere, Magnus just went right ahead and hired them, just to make it official. If you can't beat them, join them.

Or hire them, as it were.

We've all been gathered on the top of Kjerag mountain where Magnus usually does his BASE jumping. And even though that's not out of the question today, the reason we were really here was to renew our vows.

Yup. We've only been married for over a year, but Magnus had the crazy notion a couple of months ago that we should do it right this time.

Now, I happen to think that the nationally-televised wedding we had was doing it right, but I saw where Magnus was coming from. Mainly, he wanted this to be something that the both of us planned, that was under our control. Most of all, he wanted to get the proposal right all over again. I'm not sure that *question time* was all that official.

So, he got down on one knee and proposed and gave me a ring that he picked out himself—diamonds and orange garnets—and with that, we were doing things honestly. We're not starting over, far from that, but at least it got to be on our terms.

The truth is, a lot has happened in a year.

My non-profit organization, Ocean Crusaders, managed to stop illegal fishing vessels off the coast of Iceland and we started a campaign to eliminate whaling in Norway by 2025. It's been a slow process and there's a lot of opposition, but that doesn't stop us or scare us. In fact, one of the things that keeps us going is the youth in this country. They're numerous, passionate and progressive and it's through their voices, particularly through the high schools, that a lot of the changes have already begun.

It just gets me so excited to get out of bed every day and see what kind of challenge I'll be up against with all these like-minded people at my side. It gives me hope and light and peace to know that surely but steadily I'm making a difference and I'm giving a voice to the powerless. This is exactly what my dreams have been made of and now I'm finally living it, with the man I love at my side.

We still don't have a dog yet. But I'm working on it.

As for my father, we're definitely closer. I visit him every few months for "diplomatic business" which is really just hot-air ballooning with him and Schnell (it's his new hobby). We talk a lot, sometimes about business, mostly about my mother. It's nice to know that I have that relationship with him but it's also nice to know that I don't need it to validate me.

On the other side of the family, the King has made a full recovery, but Magnus has really stepped up in his role of heir. He's balancing his ADHD with mild medication and spending a lot of his time focusing on that aspect of his life. He's attending all the high council meetings, as well as meetings with the prime minister. They still don't get along, but at least there is respect. He's also acting as King Regent and traveling on behalf of his father when he doesn't feel up to going.

I couldn't be more proud of him, taking on the new responsibilities with the same kind of zest and gusto that he has for other things in life.

But of course, he's still Magnus.

And we wouldn't be up here at the top of this cliff if he didn't have some dastardly plan to jump off of it.

"As you all know," Magnus says to the small crowd, "this is a very special place to me." We're gathered about twenty-feet back from the edge. It's been a hell of a climb to get here so there wasn't much to the actual ceremony because we couldn't transport anything up the mountain (except for all the old folks—they were dropped off by royal helicopter) and all of us are wearing layers of warm clothing to deal with the high altitude.

But Magnus just renewed his vows in a flight suit and it seems that Viktor and Ottar are wearing the same thing.

I shake my head. They can't all be going, can they?

"So special you have to launch yourself off of it," the King says dryly.

"You are correct, Father." Magnus nods. "Originally I thought that it would be fun to renew our vows and then jump off together." He glances at me and my unimpressed expression. "But, of course, Ella here quickly shot down that idea."

"I have my reasons," I tell him.

I've told quite a few people here of my reasons too.

He'll find out pretty soon.

"Anyway," Magnus goes on, "I did convince Ottar and Viktor to do it with me. The rest of you are still welcome, I have some extra suits."

"You know the cliff didn't get any shorter," Mari points out. "It's still the most dangerous sport in the world."

"Not any more dangerous than marriage," Magnus says to me with a wink.

I have to laugh, even though I'm a bit nervous.

It's not about him jumping. No, I trust that he knows exactly what he's doing.

It's about everything else.

Nervous in the best way.

While Magnus makes his way to the edge, Viktor positions himself beside him.

The truth is, Viktor isn't jumping. He's suited up for it and everything, but Maggie made him promise he wouldn't, and I don't blame her. Not everyone is cut out for this.

But he does have his purpose to be standing there beside Magnus, with Ottar on the other side of Magnus.

"You're jumping first," I tell Magnus.

"Damn right," he says, slapping his goggles over his eyes. "The first one off gets the best wind."

I don't even know if that's true. It doesn't matter.

He stands at the edge of the cliff, toes hanging off, staring down into the wind and the drop, the fjord snaking three thousand feet below him.

He's taking in a deep breath. Everyone else has their phones out, ready to take pictures. The Queen has her eyes pinched shut.

He's about to go.

I speak up.

"Hey Magnus," I call after him.

He turns his head to look at me, maybe annoyed I got him right before he got in the zone. "What?"

"On the way down, try and think of baby names."

He frowns. "Wh-what?"

I give him a big smile, the kind of smile that shows him exactly what I'm talking about, all the joy I'm feeling.

"I'm pregnant," I tell him.

I've been holding onto that one for a long time.

People around me gasp happily.

Someone claps.

And I'm watching his expression change from one of confusion to one of absolute elation. His mouth drops open into a huge grin.

"You're what!?" he exclaims happily. "For real?"

I nod. "Let me know what you come up with."

"Huh?"

Just then both Viktor and Ottar put their hands on to his shoulders and shove him off the cliff so he goes flying backward and we hear this long "*Aaaaaaaaaaaaah*!!" as he freefalls to the fjord below.

Of course, then we all run to the edge, or at least as close as we can go without getting vertigo and see the bright yellow chute of Magnus's open and he starts floating down to safety. Instead of screaming now, he's hooting and hollering for joy that echoes off the mountains.

He's happy.

So bloody happy.

We're having a baby.

I don't think I've ever felt so much hope before.

"Your turn," Viktor says to Ottar.

"Are you kidding me?" he says. "I'll walk down thank you. Let's go see how his Royal Highness is dealing with the news."

But as we walk down the mountain and continue to hear Magnus's cries of joy bouncing off the cliffs, I know he feels the same way that I do.

He's dealing with the best news he's ever gotten.

~

I HAVE THAT DREAM AGAIN.

I'm on the desolate, cold beach, pebbles strewn at my feet while the giant, black bodies of pilot whales are washed up on the shore.

As usual, the wind bites into me and the whales are crying for help, crying for me to do something, anything.

I know the oil is going to start rising fast soon and as soon as the thought hits me, the black liquid starts to bubble out of their blowholes, staining the sea.

Then the man appears.

Walking right into the water.

At that moment I feel like I have a choice. I can try to save the whales. I can save him. Or I can save myself.

But as he disappears into the oily waves, I realize he's trying to move the whales back out to sea.

He does need help, but not in the way I thought he did.

The oil rises quickly, as usual, to my knees, but instead of letting it swallow me, I start walking out there. I join the man and put my hands on one side of the whale, trying to push it.

With the rising oil, the whale is able to float.

But so are we.

And we keep working, helping each other keep our heads above water, helping each other push the whales out.

Until one by one, they're free to swim away.

Leaving the man together with me in the water.

Now I look at the man and his face is no longer blank.

It's Magnus.

I think I always knew it was him.

And he's here beside me, through thick and thin.

Keeping each other afloat.

THE END

Thank you so much for reading The Wild Heir.

Want to read about the brooding and moody, widowed King Aksel and his forbidden romance with the nanny?

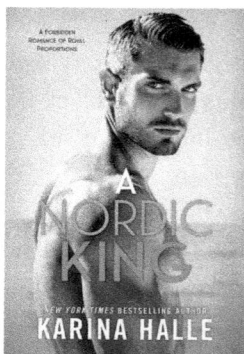

YES YOU DO!

Check out A Nordic King - available HERE after September 20th, 2018

When I first applied for the job I thought it would be like all the others: working as a nanny for an aristocratic family.

Then I got the job and found out how wrong I was.

Now I'm the new nanny for two adorable little girls who happen to be princesses.

Their father is the widowed King of Denmark.

And my new home? The royal palace in Copenhagen.

Adjusting to my new life isn't easy but the hardest part hasn't been the girls who still grieve over the loss of their mother.

It's their father.

Cold, mysterious and moody, with an icy stare that seems to penetrate your soul, King Aksel may have hired me to take care of his daughters but he wants as little to do with me as possible.

Yet the longer I share these palace walls with this man, the more that I'm drawn to him. His chiseled face and sexual swagger are only part of the package. It's in the long, intense glances at the dinner table, the way we'll brush up against each other in the halls, the rare glimpses of the man deep inside, like the sun passing through clouds.

But no matter how I feel about him, we can never be together.

You think it's bad enough being in love with your boss?

Try falling in love with a king.

—> PS REVIEWS OF THE WILD HEIR AND OTHERS ARE much appreciated! They really help the book world go round and help author's out in so many ways. If you leave a review of THE WILD HEIR, you'd make my day <3

If you're wanting to check out any of my other romances, I have TOO MANY to list, but here are some of my favourites (and all are available on Kindle Unlimited):

- THE SWEDISH PRINCE (Prince Viktor's story)

- BAD AT LOVE (a quirky friends-to-lovers romance)

- BEFORE I EVER MET YOU (young single mom falls for her father's best friend)

- LOVE IN ENGLISH (the ultimate forbidden romance with the sexiest Spanish soccer star ever)

- THE PACT (two best friends agree to marry each other by the time they're thirty)

- THE NORTH RIDGE SERIES (A trilogy about three rugged mountain men from Canada with very dangerous and thrilling jobs and the women who love them)

-> If you want to connect with me, you can always find

me on Instagram (where I post travel photos, fashion, teasers, etc)

-> or in my Facebook Group (we're a fun bunch and would love to have you join)

-> Otherwise, feel free to signup for my mailing list (it comes once a month) and Bookbub alerts!

AFTERWORD

Every book is a completely new experience.

With the character of Magnus, I had an idea of where I wanted him and the book to go.

I had no idea where he would take ME.

You see, after his appearance as the fun-loving, cocky thrill-seeker in The Swedish Prince, I knew he was a man who was both a playboy and an "adrenaline junkie."

When I started to write The Wild Heir and uncover his character (I don't build their character, rather I always see my characters as already existing and slowly revealing themselves to me - I liken myself to a palaeontologist, digging up the bones of the story, but I digress), I had to figure out WHY Magnus was attracted to things like BASE jumping (because seriously...Google that stuff at Kjerag, it's insane).

After exploring different personalities and the roots and causes of those, I found out that people with ADHD were more likely to seek out adrenaline-based situations.

So I said to myself, great. He'll have ADHD and probably not even know it. As someone who comes from a family of mental disorders, and having anxiety myself, I knew that a hero with this quality should be celebrated more.

LITTLE DID I KNOW that while researching the hell out of ADHD, I discovered that I actually have it. After scoring nearly 100% on test after test, I decided I had to look into it and I was eventually diagnosed with it.

Like Magnus, I had no idea I had it but once I learned that I have this "disorder" everything made perfect sense.

It was eye-opening.

It was a relief to be able to finally put a name to why I am the way I am, why I act and think the way I do.

The condition is not at all what I thought it was, which is why it never occurred to me that I might have it (for example, I am not hyperactive in the least...but I am hypersensitive and I have an overactive brain), but now that I know... honestly, I have never been happier.

Yes there are many different routes for treatment but as it is for me right now, I don't necessarily *need* to change. I just need to learn how to handle myself and certain situations (and, like Magnus, cut myself some slack).

I thought twice about admitting this publicly and in this book but I wanted readers to know that I'm not some author making shit up on the fly, I'm not someone using this for gains - Magnus's experiences are MY experiences, his brain is my brain (and while you'll never catch me skydiving, I DO write everything under deadline panic and listening to heart-thumping Hans Zimmer soundtracks because the adrenaline helps me focus).

Mainly I'm admitting this because this book releases in May and May is Mental Health Month and I just want to point out that ADHD or anxiety or depression or any mental issues are NOTHING to be ashamed of and you can live a healthy and productive life with it.

I mean, who knew that someone who can't even remember to pay taxes or mail books, or failed math class repeatedly, could also write over 45 books in seven years and hold down a somewhat successful career as an author?

My point is, don't let the stigma of mental illness scare you from being open about it because the more we have dialogue, the less alone we feel.

AND don't let the preconceived notions about mental illness cause you to make snap judgements about people who are affected by it. Be open-minded and compassionate when it comes to this...when it comes to everything, really.

BE BOLD, BE FIERCE. LOVE WITH A VIKING HEART!

ACKNOWLEDGMENTS

I'll keep this short because lord knows I've babbled on enough at this point.

Thank to my beta readers, Sarah Sentz, Sarah Symonds, Nina Decker, Pavlina Michou, Heather Pollock, Renery Gatpayat. You guys rock!!!

Elsi Gabrielsen for being my Norwegian eyes...let it go and tusen takk!

Always love to Sandra Cortez, Ali Hymer, Tarryn Fisher.

Hang Le, you're the (does that make sense?) Without you my books are only half as good - thank you for your tireless work (with me) and on the covers!

Nina Grinstead and Chanpreet Singh, you make my world go round.

Kara Malinczak for your enthusiasm and support.

Roxane Leblanc for going above and beyond.

Of course, I have to thank all my family in Norway because without you I wouldn't have my own Viking heart. To my father Sven Halle, this is especially for you!

Last but never last (or least) in reality, my husband Scott

for putting up with me all these years. And our dog, Bruce too, but he's the same brand of crazy as I am.

And if I'm missing anyone else, I'll just blame my ADD :D

TUSEN TAKK!!!!!!

A SNEAK PEAK OF "SHOW ME THE WAY" BY AL JACKSON

Rex

My eyes went round, and I came to an abrupt stop in her doorway.

"Are you sure that's what you want to wear?" Sweeping a hand through the long pieces of my damp hair, I gave it my all to keep the panic out of my voice.

Honestly wasn't sure if I wanted to bust out laughing or drop to my knees and cry.

Such was my life.

We were already ten minutes late, and there she was on her bedroom floor, wearing a hot pink tutu over a bathing suit.

"Uh-huh. We gots to look so pretty for dance. Annie said all the best dancers wear leg warmies, and her mama bought her all the pretty colors. Like a rainbow," she rambled as she tugged on the black high-top Converse she'd talked me into at the mall last weekend.

Right over a pair of old tube socks she must have found in one of my drawers.

The hideous kind with the two blue stripes at the top that should have been burned years ago.

"So I gots these." She rocked her heels on the ground as she sat back and admired her handiwork.

She suddenly looked over at me with that smile that melted a crater right through the stone that was my heart. Her single tooth missing on the bottom row and her attempt at a bun that looked like she'd just walked out of a windstorm were about the damned cutest things I'd ever seen.

"I'm the best dancer, right, Daddy?"

"You're the best, prettiest dancer in the whole world, Frankie Leigh."

I just was betting that uptight bitch, Ms. Jezlyn, wouldn't agree. I'd already gotten one bullshit letter about "appropriate ballet attire," which was strictly a black leotard with *salmon* tights (what the fuck?) without any runs in them. Apparently, Frankie wasn't living up to those standards.

That was what I got for picking Frankie up late from Mom's and then coming home and telling her to get ready while I grabbed a quick shower. I'd been at the work site the entire day, had been drenched in sweat and grease and grime, and was trying to put my best foot forward.

Problem was, I was having a hard time figuring out how my best could ever be enough.

I pressed my palms together in some kind of twisted prayer. Then I dropped them and blew out a resigned breath. "All right, then. We need to get out of here before I get you in any more trouble."

Frankie hopped onto her feet and threw her hands in the air. "Ready!"

I chuckled beneath my breath, grabbed her dance bag

from the pink bench right inside her room, slung it over my shoulder, and extended my hand. "Let's go, Tiny Dancer."

Giggling, she pranced over to me and let me take her miniature hand, so small and vulnerable in the massiveness of mine.

Following me out the door and down the hall, she skipped along at my side.

Innocently.

Joy lit up my insides. I swore all her sweetness held the power to blow back the thousand pounds of blackened bitterness built up around my heart. Like when this kid was around, it weighed nothing at all.

The day she was born, I'd sworn an oath to myself. I'd never allow her to be torn up by this vicious, cruel world. Refused to let it tarnish her the way it had me.

My entire life was protecting her from it.

I snagged my keys from the entryway table when I heard the sound of a door slamming somewhere outside. Frowning, I leaned back so I could get a glimpse out the window and across the street.

An older white Jeep Grand Cherokee was parked in the driveway of Mrs. Dayne's old house.

Guessed they had to finally be putting the place up for sale. Mrs. Dayne had lived there forever, long before we'd moved in across the street from her five years ago, but the place had been sitting empty for the last two months.

A fist tightened in my gut, grief I really shouldn't be allowing myself to feel. She'd just been so good to Frankie that it'd been impossible to keep her shut out. Hell, she'd barged right into our lives like she was supposed to be there, constantly bringing over dinner and those delicious pies from the diner-style restaurant she'd owned downtown.

Frankie rushed out the front door and onto the deck at the side of our house.

It was the way all the homes were situated in our neighborhood. The houses were elevated from the ground with the main doors located on the side rather than out front. Each had an open deck that extended out from the side of the house, giving a view of the street and neighbors' houses. The porch steps angled that direction and led down to the driveways that came up to the far side of the houses.

It probably would have looked strange if not for the big, leafy trees that outlined each of the lots.

They made everything feel cozy and secluded.

Just the way I liked it.

It was one of the main reasons I'd insisted on this place when I'd been looking for a fixer-upper to renovate.

Frankie released my hand and pointed across the street. "Hey, Daddy, look it. Someone's at Mrs. Dayne's house!"

Stepping out behind her, I closed the door before I attempted to tame a few pieces of hair that'd fallen from her bun and were now flying around her face in the hot breeze. I dropped a kiss to her forehead. "It's probably a realtor putting it up for sale, Frankie Leigh. Remember how we talked about that?"

With her head tipped back, she peered at me with confused but hopeful brown eyes. "She wents to heaven?"

"Yeah," I murmured softly.

The screen door at the side of Mrs. Dayne's house slammed, and I jerked my head up to find a woman crossing the small deck and jogging down the steps back toward the SUV.

Goddamn.

Maybe I was just caught off guard.

But just looking at her knocked the air from my lungs.

Let's just say I was unprepared for a woman that looked like that. Guess I'd been expecting someone dressed up. Older. And there was this girl, disheveled in a sexy, careless way. A massive mound of hair that was wilder than Frankie's was piled haphazardly on her head, wavy pieces falling out all around her. She wore a super tight white tank that disappeared beneath high-waisted jeans.

Those jeans should have made her look frumpy and unkempt, but instead, the whole package sent a skitter of lust racing through my veins and prodding at my dick.

She was the kind of woman who could make a grown man stumble on his feet.

Stunning.

Gorgeous.

Too sexy for her own damned good.

Or maybe mine.

I could call it a complication of abstaining for too long, but I was sure no woman had ever incited a reaction like this in me with just a glance.

She raked her arm over her sweat-drenched forehead as she headed straight for the cargo area of the SUV, which was crammed full of moving boxes. I wouldn't mind all that much if she were hauling stuff out of that house directly across the street, but it sure as shit looked like she was moving her things in.

Tell me this girl is not moving in next door.

I clenched my jaw and grabbed Frankie's hand, needing to get the hell out of there.

"Come on, Frankie Leigh, we've got to get a move on. You're already late."

But Frankie was already moving, bouncing down the stairs and along the walkway, waving her free hand in the air. The kid just adding to the stark sunshine that burned bright in the waning day. "Hi, hi, hi! I'm Frankie. Whose are you?" she shouted across the street.

Startled, the women's gaze darted our direction, and the determination in her step slowed when she caught sight of my daughter.

An amused smile grew on the rosy bud of her mouth when her gaze swept the ridiculous outfit Frankie was wearing. She seemed to hesitate for a second, eyes glancing around her like she was looking for something before she changed direction, heading our way. "Hey there, Frankie, I'm Corinne Dayne, but everyone calls me Rynna."

Rynna Dayne.

What the ever-lovin' hell?

Could damn near feel the bewildered excitement roll through my daughter while I stood there cursing the world that just fucking loved to curse me. "Your name's C'Rinne, too? That's Mrs. Dayne's name. She worked at the restaurant called Pepper's Pies and cooked all the pies, and my daddy ate them all, all, all the way gone. Sometimes we wents to go eat there, but mostly we ate at my house right here, but now she wents to heaven."

A bolt of sadness streaked through her expression, and fuck, if it didn't hit me, too. Still, the smile she wore only grew. "She made the best pies in the whole world, didn't she?"

Frankie's excitement only amplified. "Yes! You know Mrs. Dayne, too?"

She started to cross the narrow street, all chestnut hair and java eyes and a body that was built for temptation.

Awareness ridged my spine like a steely stake of lightning, and I stepped back, my jaw tightening at the same time I protectively took hold of my daughter's hand.

That was all that women were.

Temptation.

Trouble.

Forbidden fucking fruit.

Because all they did was condemn you in the end. So, I stayed away. Kept my distance. If I didn't step into the fire, then I wouldn't get burned.

Kneeling in front of my daughter, she stuck out her hand. "It's so nice to meet you, Frankie. It sounds like you were a good friend of my grandma's."

So yeah.

I'd already figured it out.

It didn't stop me from flinching.

Frankie had stars in her eyes as she enthusiastically shook her hand. She might as well have been meeting Taylor Swift. "She told me I was her favorite, favorite friend, and sometimes she even let me go to her house and make some pies."

"Is that so?" Rynna said with a tease in her voice.

"Yep."

Rynna leaned in, and I caught a whiff of something sweet. "Want to know a secret?" she whispered.

Frankie bounced on her toes. "Oh, yes, yes please, I love secrets. I won't tell nobody."

Soft laughter floated out from Rynna's mouth, a mouth that was getting harder and harder not to stare at, all plush and pink and perfectly pouty. "Well, this is a secret I hope you tell everyone, because guess what? I have some of the recipes for those pies."

Frankie's mouth dropped open, and damn it if my stomach didn't fucking growl.

"You gonna make me some?" she gushed.

"Definitely," Rynna said, taking that moment to look at me with the threat of a smile on her pretty face, the angle of her jaw sharp while everything else about her was soft.

That sweet scent was back. Billowing in the breeze. This warmth surrounding her. Hot cherry pie.

My teeth ground together, and the smile slid from her face when she saw what must have been my irritated expression, and I swore I heard the slight catch of her breath when she met my glare. Could see a slight quiver in her throat when she straightened and took a step back.

Still, she stood her ground.

There was something unwavering about her. Like she had something to prove. To herself or me, I wasn't sure.

"Hi. I'm Rynna Dayne. Was named after my grandmother," she managed, though the words were rough as she stuck her hand out toward me like she'd done to my daughter.

I just stood there staring at it like it held the venom of a viper bite. Finally, I lifted my chin at her and gathered all the pleasantness I could summon. It wasn't much. "Rex Gunner. I'm sorry about your grandmother. And we're late . . . so if you could excuse us."

I gave Frankie a gentle tug of her hand. "Come on, Frankie Leigh. We've got to get you to dance."

Frankie trotted along at my side, looking back over her shoulder with what I knew had to be one of those adorable grins.

"What a jerk," I heard Rynna mumble behind my back when I turned and led my daughter to the passenger side of my truck.

Bitterness burned.

Yeah.

I was a jerk.

An asshole.

Whatever.

Better to burn bridges before anyone had a chance to cross them.

Shaking it off, I hoisted Frankie into the high cabin, making her squeal and pretend like she was flying. I strapped her in her car seat and jogged around to the front. I hopped into the driver's seat, wondering if it were possible for the roar of the engine to cover the hurt that sagged Rynna's shoulders as I took to the street.

Wondering why I felt like a complete piece of shit when I caught a glimpse of her in the rearview mirror. She just stood there in the twilight like she was caught in a dream.

Watching us go with disappointment on her face.

Befriending a sweet old lady was one thing.

Allowing a girl like Rynna Dayne into our lives—a girl that made my body react the way it did? Now that was pure stupidity.

Want to read the rest of SHOW ME THE WAY? Download Here (add hyperlink **http:// smarturl.it/SMTHAmzn2)**
Read FREE on Kindle Unlimited

ABOUT THE AUTHOR

Karina Halle is a former travel writer and music journalist and The New York Times, Wall Street Journal and USA Today Bestselling author of The Pact, Bad at Love, The Swedish Prince, Sins & Needles, and over 45 other wild and romantic reads. She lives on an island off the coast of British Columbia with her husband and her rescue pup, where she drinks a lot of wine, hikes a lot of trails and devours a lot of books.

Halle is represented by Root Literary and is both self-published and published by Simon & Schuster and Hachette in North America and in the UK.

Hit her up on Instagram at @authorHalle, on Twitter at @MetalBlonde and on Facebook (join her reader group "Karina Halle's Anti-Heroes" for extra fun and connect with her!). You can also visit www.authorkarinahalle.com and sign up for the newsletter for news, excerpts, previews, private book signing sales and more.

ALSO BY KARINA HALLE

A Nordic King

The Devil's Duology

Donners of the Dead

Veiled

CPSIA information can be obtained
at www.ICGtesting.com
Printed in the USA
LVHW040011030623
748651LV00006B/533